THE HENDERSON MEMORIES

A Novel

Doug Ingold

Wolfenden

THE HENDERSON MEMORIES

Copyright ©: 2010 by Douglas A. Ingold

Publisher's Cataloging-in -Publication
(Provided by Quality Books, Inc.)

Ingold, Doug.
    The Henderson memories/Doug Ingold.
    p. em.
    LCCN 2009939091
    ISBN-13: 978-0-978695149
    ISBN-10: 0-978695143

1. Volunteer workers in community development–Brazil–Fiction. 2. Peace Corps (US)–Brazil–Fiction. 3. Daughters–United States–Fiction. 4. College teachers–British Columbia–Fiction. 5. Family secrets–Fiction. 6. Brazil–Fiction. 7. Detective and mystery stories. I. Title.

PS3559N42H46 2010   813'.54
                     QB109-600194

Published by

Wolfenden

WOLFENDEN
780-A Redwood Drive
Garberville, CA 95542
wolfendenpublishing.com
Phone/facsimile (707) 923-2455

Cover Design:
Robert Stedman Pte Ltd
Book design and layout by
Robert Stedman Pte Ltd, Singapore

Printed in the USA

DEDICATION AND DISCLAIMER

The characters in this story are fictitious, products of the author's imagination. In creating characters, an author creates himself. I am Jolene Henderson and Kyle, as much Connie Scheel as Clint Estergard, as surely Nascimento as Oscar. The technique, though, has its own brutality. Lives of real people are seized upon and dismembered, large parts discarded, others stretched and twisted and stitched onto bits and pieces of still other lives remembered or forgotten, real or imagined. To each of you who recognizes some sliver of yourself in these pages, this book is dedicated. And to all those who have answered, or will, the call to Peace.

With special thanks to Betty Cleeland, Jim Quast, João Palomo, Rhonda O'Kane and my dear Nina.

The religion known as *Condomblé* has several names and many gods. The gods, too, are known by various names. One of the names of one of the gods is Oxossi, the hunter.

CONTENTS

Chapter	1	Origin	1
Chapter	2	The Prayer	11
Chapter	3	Emily's Heart	15
Chapter	4	An Unfortunate Dress	21
Chapter	5	The Key	33
Chapter	6	Ilhéus	49
Chapter	7	Nova Santana	69
Chapter	8	Jacarandá	83
Chapter	9	Alone	91
Chapter	10	Green Oranges	113
Chapter	11	Siblings	135
Chapter	12	The Black Sheep	145
Chapter	13	Nascimento	159
Chapter	14	Humdinger	175
Chapter	15	The Rain In Nova Santana	195
Chapter	16	Master Detective	211
Chapter	17	Making A Difference	223
Chapter	18	Along The Fraser	235
Chapter	19	Mistakes	251
Chapter	20	Daiquiris And Drums	261
Chapter	21	Rumor Of Sorcery	281
Chapter	22	The Rain In Jacarandá	297
Chapter	23	Walls	299
Chapter	24	A Conversation With Kyle Henderson	311
Chapter	25	The Phone Call	323
Chapter	26	Shrine	335
Chapter	27	The Hunter	345
Chapter	28	The Violin Lesson	361
Chapter	29	High Tea	369

Chapter One
ORIGIN

Connie Scheel likes to eat her lunch alone in her office at Henderson Developments. With the two boys at home and most of the day either on the phone or in meetings, lunch offers a rare chance for some solitude. Usually she has a Greek salad that she gets from a shop two doors away and a diet soda from the machine in the staff lounge, and she closes the door and sits down at her desk and eats by herself. She has a fondness for olives and the salty taste of feta cheese. The salads are fresh and come with two round multi-grain crackers in a separate little bag with a paper napkin and a plastic fork. If she calls ahead a fellow named Peter who has tattooed chains circling his wrists and wears a white apron and a sort of stocking cap on his head has everything ready when she arrives.

The office is located in a strip-mall southwest of Chicago. Kyle Henderson, developed the mall and her office had been his office. It's the place her mother used to jokingly call 'the Blonde' because of the time Kyle spent there and the shade of the maple wood flooring and the trim that he had personally cut and sanded and installed around the doors and windows, each finishing nail carefully countersunk and not a hammer crescent to be seen.

Kyle Henderson had been Connie's dad. He had raised her and on her birth certificate he is named as her father. So, legally, she assumes, he was her father. That should be the end of it, she tells herself, but it isn't.

Connie eats half of her Greek salad and turns to her laptop. She enters two words into a search engine, a first name and a last. She pauses, feeling somewhat apprehensive. She closes her

eyes for a moment and asks for guidance. Then she opens her
eyes and presses her finger against the mouse. The screen blos-
soms into a bouquet of leads. Connie picks up her salad, takes
a bite and smiles.

Clinton W. Estergard, Ph.D. sits alone waiting. He is on the
deck outside his condominium, sitting in his chair with a pair
of field glasses in his right hand. It's getting close to dusk and a
breeze is coming up off the Fraser River. The air has a pleasant
damp smell but it's cool. He has on a jacket. A blanket is spread
across his legs and he wears a beret on his head. He is known
for wearing berets and people tend to give them to him. This
one he got many years ago, it's well-worn and gray and made
of wool. He wears it forward and to the right side of his head
above his glasses and his large hooked nose.

The view is pleasant from the deck with the river in the distance but he is not looking at the view. His attention is on a red
brick chimney that rises above the steep roof of a blue house
half a block away. Now and then he removes his bifocals, sets
them in his lap and places the field glasses against his eyes. He
finds the chimney and studies the air above it. Then he lowers
the field glasses, puts his bifocals back on and sits waiting.

Finally, he spots them. He removes the bifocals, places the
field glasses to his eyes, locates the chimney and raises the glasses
slowly until his vision is filled with birds. Swifts, Vaux's Swifts.
Maybe a hundred dark shapes swirling against the dusky sky
in what seems agitated chaos, gathering and dispersing, rising
and falling, until they sweep upward en mass, turn and forming
themselves into a long plume of bird hurl themselves down and
into the chimney. He tries to imagine the activity in that dark and
crowded chamber. Are they pushing and stepping on each other,
desperate to halt their plunging descent and obtain purchase on
the vertical surface? Or has some elegant coordination evolved,
perhaps some form of cooperation? He continues to watch the

sky. The birds have all disappeared. The sky will remain empty until dawn. He lowers the glasses, puts on his bifocals, turns and enters the condominium.

Clint's second wife got the house, and he purchased the one bedroom condo in a new building a few kilometers from the university. The house, which he had owned before their marriage, was the price he paid to loosen her grip on his retirement funds. Everything else was split down the middle. No kids, no alimony, no child support, so it had been less costly than the first time around, but it did hurt to give up the house.

What attracted him to the condo was the well-designed kitchen and the ease of maintenance. He pays a monthly strata fee and everything around him, the lawn, the walks, the parking garage, even the exteriors of his windows, are kept neat and orderly. The refrigerator, though new at the time, is absurdly loud, something he discovered the first night he slept over, but soon he adapted and by now, five years on, he rarely hears it.

He has furnished his new space carefully and sparely. Clutter was a frequent topic in Clint Estergard's casual conversations those first weeks after the separation from Michelle. The evils of clutter. Like sediment in a slow moving river, he was fond of saying, clogging the channels of activity. Since Michelle insisted on the house, he told himself, (this was not something he would express to her or to a colleague) she could have everything in it from the closets to the over-stuffed garage. Among its other benefits, he decided, divorce provided a free dredging.

His talk of clutter in those days, like most everything else he discussed, was generic, phrased in the abstract, applicable to any-one at any time and place. The personal pain, the grief of losing Michelle after fifteen years, was something he kept to himself. But he was adamant about the clutter. Do you want any of this stuff, she would call and ask. Stuff from his first marriage, stuff that had belonged to his sons. Get rid of it, he would say. If you want it, keep it. If the boys want it, they can have it. Otherwise, get rid of it. He was on a new tack.

There were exceptions, of course. His cast iron skillet, his copper-bottomed pan set, both predated the marriage. A couple cases of books. His music collection including the boxes of vinyl albums that he had salvaged from his parents' house after his mother, graceful to the end, had turned herself in to a skilled nursing facility and died in what they told him was her sleep thirty-six hours later. Died in the middle of the night, safe from those who would grab her up and resuscitate her. For some reason he cannot quite explain to himself, he hopes she had not been asleep but awake at the end, alone but not lonely. Which is the way he likes to think of himself these days, alone but not lonely.

In talking with Michelle, following the breakup, he would keep the conversation, whatever the subject, sharp and clear. Not hostile, not angry, but well back from the edge of sentiment. His mother's death, her father's senility, his cycling accident. All of that happened after the divorce but they still spoke regularly and her thoughts gravitated toward the unfortunate incidents in life. Once there, she veered toward pity. It was enough she had wanted out of the marriage, he was not about to let her pity him for the breakup, or anything else for that matter. Michelle, he would say, get a grip.

But with friends and colleagues he would talk with enthusiasm about the condo and the way he was furnishing it. The bedroom closet, for example, was far larger than what he needed so it housed not only his hanging clothes but also his chest of drawers and still he had room to turn around. This left more than enough space on the bedroom floor for a bench press and a mat where he could do his exercises. The dining table (there was only one table) and matching chairs were dark-stained, almost Shaker-plain, and could comfortably accommodate no more than four diners. A tweed-covered futon faced the gas fireplace, a couple of simple though graceful end tables. Chairs could be moved from the table to the sitting area if needed. Before the fire he can accommodate the seven men in his book group or the members of his string quartet with their cases and music stands when his turn comes to host. But that is pretty much the limit. He keeps it simple. He wants space to move around, emptiness of wall, the hardwood floor exposed and gleaming.

Of course he established a work space in the den off the sitting area, a large desk with his computer and all the usual attachments, a file cabinet within reach. Room on the desk for a phone, dictionaries, both English and Portuguese, a thesaurus. He has a long-term project, a book on evolution and cooperation he has been working on without contract for more than a year.

The space beneath the window that offers a view out across the deck toward the river is a natural spot for the desk, but he prefers the opposite end of the room, where the incoming light is behind him and the wall with a calendar and several schedules in front. When he works, he works, he tells himself. If he wants to enjoy the view, he can turn around.

At first people brought him plants. Most suffered a short life and a slow and desultory death. The philodendron, however, that Karl and Yvonne Munch had given him refused to die however shoddily he cared for it. It stands now beside his desk, spindly, root-bound and asymmetrical, reaching for the light, scarring his walls with air roots, recipient of his reluctant admiration.

Clint places the field glasses on the window sill and pulls a piece of paper from his shirt pocket. Earlier in the day, he had been Googled. He knows about the search because the Googler had followed with a phone call to the Zoology Department at the University of British Columbia where he has served on the faculty for years, and where, the month previous in a modest ceremony, he had gone from Professor Estergard to Professor Emeritus. The new status has placed him on retirement pension but allows him to retain an office and keep a finger in the stew: proctoring two graduate students and continuing to teach his favorite seminar, a survey course on the writings of Charles Darwin.

The phone call was taken by the assistant to the dean, or actually by the assistant's assistant, Emily, an undergraduate, who wrote it down on a yellow Post-it in a bold flowing hand and attached it to the side of his inbox. When he found the note later that afternoon, he read it quickly, folded the glue back on itself and stuffed it into his shirt pocket. Now he looks at the note again. In her signature at the bottom of the message Emily drew a small heart to replace the dot above the 'i'. Clint finds himself musing about that heart. It was not intended specifically for him, of course. He's old enough to be Emily's grandfather and a man she hardly knows. The heart is part of her signature. It's a message she sends into the world every time she signs her name. But why?

Clint picks up the phone. He has been putting off returning the call and it has gotten late there. There are two numbers, both with a Chicago-suburb area code. 'Work' Emily had written after one. 'Home' after the other. It would be well after ten in Illinois.

When the call comes Connie Scheel is online reading about 1031 property exchanges. She is in her study, what had been Kyle's study, in her home outside Chicago, the house that had been her parents' home. It's a spring night with the boys asleep in their rooms and crickets outside the window.

A week or so before Kyle's sudden death, he had tentatively agreed to sell the Spruce Street project to Juan Hernandez. Juan owns an auto parts business and rents the largest unit in the seven-unit development. Nothing binding, just an oral promise by Kyle to consider it. But Juan mentioned the conversation to her at the memorial service and later Connie found reference to it in the business narrative Kyle maintained on his computer. Connie likes Juan, who had approached her so gently and sensitively at the service, and she knows she will find satisfaction and healing if she can carry out one of Kyle's last wishes. Juan is offering a fair price and is a natural fit for the project since the area is rapidly turning Hispanic.

The problem is that Spruce Street had been one of Kyle Henderson's earliest projects. His company built it more than thirty years before and even though it had taken all her parents' reserves and everything they could borrow at the time, it has been debt-free for a decade or more and is now worth multiple times what it had been new. The tax on the capital gains is enough to ruin the deal. Thus she is trying to educate herself on a process that would allow her to defer the taxes by transferring the Spruce Street tax basis to a newly acquired property. The process is tricky for a novice and she wants to know as much as she can before she meets with the company's tax advisor in the morning. Learning is what she is doing these days, learning as much as she can as fast as she can. So the ringing phone irritates her until she realizes that Clint Estergard is on the other end. He apologizes for calling so late. He has a strong clear voice and he speaks slowly.

Oh no, Doctor. I'm so happy you called! Give me your number and I'll call you back. This should be on our dime.

That won't be necessary, he says. There is a moment of dead air. As to the question that I understand prompted your call....

Yes?

You are quite correct, I am the Clint Estergard who knew Kyle and Jolene Henderson in Bahia those very many years ago.

Oh, that's wonderful! I am so happy. All of this has come as a complete surprise to us!

I don't understand, Clint says.

That they were in the Peace Corps! They never mentioned... not a word to either of us in all these years.

I see. And you are?

Oh, I'm sorry. Their daughter, Connie, Connie Scheel. Scheel is my married name. Or was my married name. I mean, it is my name. I'm just not married. Not to Mr. Scheel. Well, not to anyone. I mean, Connie Henderson growing up. Why was she going on like this? she asks herself. She is sounding like an idiot.

After a pause, Clint says, You mentioned 'us.' A surprise to 'us.' Oh, I'm sorry, she says, realizing that she is saying that word again. My brother Phil. Phil Henderson. My younger brother, three years younger. My only brother, actually. But still, not a word to him either. Isn't that amazing?

So your parents, Kyle and Jolene, are they...?

Oh, I am so sorry. Yes, gone, both gone. I mean deceased, she finds herself adding, as if he might have inferred they were at the movies. We lost Dad last month, very sudden. He had a debilitating illness but we assumed he had several good years left. Then a massive heart attack. And Mom, Mom died almost seven years ago now. Cancer.

The voice at the other end of the line softens. I am very sorry to hear it. Please accept my condolences. They were so young when.... His voice trails off.

Yes, Dad was only sixty-seven. Mom fifty-seven when she died. And now this.... We're both astounded, Doctor. It seems so unlike them. I mean, the Peace Corps! Some little town in Brazil!

Yes, Nova Santana, Clint says. That was their town. It's in the state of Bahia.

Phil and I are flabbergasted! It seems impossible. You have to understand, Doctor, the farthest we ever traveled as kids was up to Wisconsin. Lake Otowan. The same lake Mom went to when she was a kid, would you believe! And later we couldn't get them to go anywhere. Not even Hawaii. On their thirtieth anniversary we offered to fly them to Hawaii. Free! All expenses paid. They'd have none of it. 'No thank you, Dad and I are happy where we are.' Stay at home stick-in-the-muds, that's what they were. Phil and I used to tease them about it. Connie starts to giggle. She's giggling uncontrollably. She hears her giggle turn into a cackle. She's sounding like a flock of crazed chickens.

I see, Clint says when she finally stops. So, how did you find out?

Connie takes a deep breath. The boys and I were cleaning

out the attic last weekend. Andre found a large leather pouch down inside a trunk. And inside the pouch was a journal and....
   A notebook of some sort?
   Yes, a spiral....
   I have some memory of that notebook, Clint says. I mailed it to Kyle and Jolene along with some other things. Your parents left Brazil rather suddenly. I promised to clear out their house. I gave away most everything, but that notebook, a few other papers, some jewelry, I packaged up and mailed off to them.
   Yes the jewelry! They were in the pouch too. Some beautiful things, earrings, a necklace. Mother never wore them so far as I know.
   She wore them in Bahia, Clint says quietly. So you found my name in the journal?
   Just your first name. That was frustrating, but then I found a letter you had written to Mom and Dad after they returned. Opened but still in its envelope. The return address had your full name.
   Funny they should have kept those letters. I sent two or three. We only found one.
   It was mostly about Eduardo, I suppose.
   That was so sad to read.
   Yes. That was a loss. Your mother was close to Eduardo, we both were.
   The two of them fall silent. Finally Connie speaks. Doctor, I'm going to ask something and, please, I will understand completely if you refuse. I'm sure you're very busy and I've no right to take you away from your family, but I'm going to ask anyway. I'd like to free up my schedule in the next month or so. I'd fly out to Vancouver, get a hotel room somewhere, and meet with you. I'll try not to take too much of your time, but I really want to sit down face to face. My parents have become strangers to me. I read this journal and I ask myself, who were these people? What were they up to? Dad seems so...

Dedicated?

Obsessed if the journal is any reflection. And of course I don't get Mom's perspective at all. Her handwriting appears on a couple of pages, just names of families and the number of children, that sort of thing. You don't know me from Adam, Doctor, so I will understand. Really.

Clint hesitates for a moment, but when he does speak, the words surprise him: Actually, I don't have a family.

Pardon?

So you can't take me away from that. Well, a sister in upstate New York whose husband gives me the creeps. A couple of ex-wives, one of whom I have no contact with, and two sons from my first marriage. Michael married a Filipina and now lives in Singapore. Devon works the salmon fishery out of Alaska when he needs money. The rest of the time he follows the waves.

Follows...?

Yes, all over the world. Last card I got he was surfing a bizarre river current in Munich of all places. I'm still connected to the university, as you know. And of course I have my routines, a book project I'm working on. But what are you thinking of, an afternoon, maybe two? It was a very long time ago, Ms. Scheel. I'm afraid you'll have drained my memory in a couple of hours.

Oh, Doctor, just that much would be wonderful! I feel so blessed that you have called.

Yes, Clint says slowly. I regret that I can't offer accommodations. My digs are modest, but I might make a recommendation or two. Will your brother be accompanying you?

Phil? No, he'll be satisfied to get my report. And like you, I have two sons, but they can stay with their father.

They exchange email addresses and agree to work out the details. Clint hangs up thinking it may have been a mistake.

Chapter Two
THE PRAYER

Ironically, the first words Connie read in Kyle Henderson's journal were the last words he wrote. When she first opened the notebook and recognized his handwriting, she quickly flipped through the pages to get some idea of the length. Reaching the blank pages at the back she reversed herself until she came upon the final entry. Many passages in the journal disturbed her, but none troubled her more than this one.

September 30, 1965
Even the things I turn to for solace, I now find troublesome. Two words in and already we've entered ambiguous territory. Why "Father?" Yes, it implies an intimacy. But why not "Mother," or "Brother," or "Friend?" The relationship of father to son is always complex and inherent with conflict. Even if we question the fullness of Freud's analysis, though homage must be paid to it, still some things are certain: the father is older, larger, stronger, whether present, absent, dead or alive. (An inherent design flaw with the game we call human life is that you must begin small and helpless. Thus we absorb ideas and beliefs from a dependant, vulnerable position and they cling to us as we age and strengthen.) Typically the father sets the rules and enforces them. He is the chosen of the mother. He stands between us and she who has given us life and nurtures us. He represents the static, the past, the shelter we need and must learn to live without, the summit we set ourselves to rise above. To mature is to learn his defects, his weaknesses, his deceits, to watch him age and weaken. He can be frightening, and of the several things the prayer says, one

of them is fear of the Father.

So, being fearful, the Son flatters. "Hallowed be thy name," He mutters. "Thy kingdom come, Thy will be done, on earth as it is in heaven."

Flattering and odd. The song of a cheerleader. Hearing it, we recognize that the Son is immersed in struggle. The Father's writ is limited to one place and the Son wants it extended to another. The Father, we understand, wishes that as well. The Father is thus not all powerful. Even together there are forces outside of them over which they lack control. The outcome is uncertain. Drama surrounds us.

Still the Father can provide. For Himself and for us the Son asks very little. "Our daily bread."

And can forgive. As the Son asks little for us, so He demands much of us. He and we should be forgiven only if we too forgive. But what is this forgiveness thing? Forgive what? And why shouldn't He forgive us? And what is there to forgive: debts, trespasses, transgressions, sins? Who signed on for any of this? Obviously we have fallen back into the small child in the face of the large and arbitrary rule maker, the enforcer.

And from that there follows the five oddest words in all Christendom: "Lead us not into temptation."

So we learn that the Son accepts and does not bother to hide from the Father, the possibility that the Father is malevolent. That He would toy with us. That He would deliberately lead us astray and then punish us for having strayed. This is the same guy who put the apple tree in the garden. Who sent Abraham out to butcher his own son. You gotta watch the Father. The Son is begging here. He sees that we have no bargaining power. The Father is bigger and more powerful and can't be trusted. The family, in short, is dysfunctional.

"But deliver us from evil," He adds. And we have to ask: From whence comes this thing called evil? If the Father has the power to deliver us from it, why does it exist at all? He can but

He doesn't have to. He may, but then again He might not either. Comfort eludes us because nothing is certain.

And so we have the last hurrah. In the face of overwhelming untrustworthy power the Son flatters, flatters, flatters. "For thine is the kingdom," he cries, "and the power and the glory forever." Not much else one could do, given the circumstances.

So what are we left with? Why should any of this be remembered or remarked upon? This man praying is just like me. Just another lonely, unstable, desperate man praying to his distant, untrustworthy god.

I search these words for comfort and all I find to give me hope is the first word. The Son has not forgotten us, desperate and lonely though he is. He seeks no personal advantage. There is nothing "only begotten" about this prayer. It is "Our Father," "our bread," "our trespasses." Whatever He can do, whatever authority He has to speak, to intercede, He does not for himself alone but for all of us. He pulls us along with him. The weight is enormous. And that is the example, the message, that rings down through the ages. The favored one, in his torment, has not forgotten us. And this being so, we who are also favored, are called upon to not forget each other, not even the most lonely, the ignorant, the enslaved, the most lost among us. This is all I have to cling to. Amen.

Chapter Three
EMILY'S HEART

The next afternoon when Clint Estergard sees Yvonne Munch, the dean's assistant, he pulls the Post-it out of his wallet and shows her Emily's signature.

What a marvelous thing, he says, this curious insistence by Emily to insert a tiny heart into her name. It represents the urge to adorn, I suspect. The persistent desire we possess to make beauty at the expense of efficiency. It has persisted for millennia and now we see it in Emily.

Mrs. Munch takes a cooler, more practical perspective. At least Emily is not into piercing, she says. Nothing hanging off her eyebrows or lips. Mrs. Munch is not sure she could handle that in the office day after day. She relates a story she read in the newspaper recently about an incident that happened in the States. A woman complained that an airport security guard had insisted she remove a ring from the nipple of her breast before she boarded the plane.

Yes, well, Clint says. Must have set off the alarm bells, though I hardly see the threat to national security.

The guard apparently gave her a pliers and set her the task of getting it off if she was going to make her flight.

The place of my birth has become a frightened country, Yvonne. And of course tattoos are back with a vengeance down there. Females, I would say, even more than males. I saw them popping out from all kinds of places on my last visit. A waitress bends and there's a tattoo. When I was a kid it was a male thing associated with sailors. Men home from the war. You saw them on carneys and among the workers at amusement parks.

Then later it was those huge men on Harleys with their massive arms and guts. Now it's the smiling gal making your latte. Hard to imagine them in their sixties walking around covered with somebody else's faded art.

It's not something either of us will have to witness, Doctor, Yvonne Munch says with a brief smile.

He admits this is true. It also occurs to him that Yvonne Munch, though ever discreet, is trying to make out the contents of the note that he still holds absently in his hand. He moves it up before her eyes, sliding his thumb away from the text. Take a look at this, he says, as if she hasn't been.

Well, she says after reading the note, has she got her man?

English is not Yvonne Munch's first language. You know that only because she speaks more precisely, more correctly than most native speakers. But now and then a phrase like, 'Got her man?' pops out as a wild deviation, reflecting, he expects, her and her husband's late-night affection for old black and white movies and television reruns. Is this Lord Peter Wimsey speaking? Or perhaps Sergeant Joe Friday?

Yes, I'm her man all right, he answers. It came as quite a shock I have to tell you. Not a word in forty-plus years. The caller was their daughter.

I didn't know.

That I served in the American Peace Corps? It's probably on my resumé somewhere, written on a manual typewriter and filed away in one of those cabinets of yours. But yes, a long time ago. Let's see. This August I will have been home from Brazil for forty-three years. So it was forty-five years ago when I arrived down there and first met the parents, or the would-be parents, of this woman. A long time ago, Yvonne. They're gone now, both of them.

I see. Yvonne Munch begins straightening the papers on her desk.

The daughter intends to come visit me this summer, Clint

continues. She wants to know all about it. It seems her parents never said a word. That's kind of odd, don't you think? That she'd be all that interested? I mean something that long ago and they're both dead. It will cost a bundle with the airfare, hotel room. I told her I could not put her up but that didn't slow her down for a second. She might be a religious nut as well. Said she felt 'blessed' that I called. There must be money in the family to spend it on something like this.

Yvonne Munch turns off her computer, removes a covering from a desk drawer and slides it over the monitor and keyboard. He doesn't have a cover for his computer. Like most computers in the building his is never covered and only rarely turned off.

Maybe there's something else, Yvonne pauses, wondering. Some deep family secret.

Lord Wimsey is back, Clint thinks, shaking his head. Sorry, Yvonne. No windblown heath in this story, no gothic towers. Just a couple of midwestern kids who had a hard time. No, I suspect this daughter is a princess, maybe a religious kook, and she's miffed that Mommy and Daddy held out on her. Now she's determined to spend some of their hard-earned money to find out why. Though it does surprise me they would have money. More saint than sinner, both of them. And we both know it's the sinners who end up with the loot.

Yes, Yvonne says absently.

But back to Emily's signature. Now that's something interesting and it got me started. This morning I found a BBC article online about early jewelry, adornment really. It said that a Norwegian crew, your countrymen, recently found clusters of small mollusk shells in a cave in South Africa. The shells were seventy-five thousand years old, Yvonne. They all seem to have been perforated in the same way and the perforations show patterns of wear resulting from the cord or strip of leather the Norwegians assume was used to string them together. In addition the shells seem to have been shaped from having been rubbed together as they were worn and there is evidence they had been colored with red ochre. It seems reasonable to conclude, as the Norwegians did, that the shells were worn as part of a bracelet or a necklace. Seventy-five thousand years ago, Yvonne. That predates what we refer to as the 'great leap' forward, which is thought to have occurred around fifty thousand years ago. Clothing sewn from hides, ritualistic burial, sophisticated hunting techniques, that sort of thing. So, already, twenty-five thousand years earlier, we are decorating ourselves. And now we have Emily and her heart.

Clint feels a little foolish. He has gone on too long about the adornment thing. He is sounding sentimental. He watches as Yvonne Munch gets up from her chair. It often surprises him when she stands, how tall she is. Five-ten, maybe more. She has grown a little thicker over the years but she carries it well, though of late a little stiffly. Still, a handsome woman, he thinks, though in the last couple of years, following the death of her father back home, the look in her eyes has changed subtly. What had been irony seems now more haunted. He believes she is truly interested in what he is saying. But she is anxious to be off. Hubby is waiting. Some married people seem bound in such rigid schedules. Had he been? It hadn't seemed that way at the time.

Genes at work, he goes on, as she takes up her purse and sweater. That would be Karl's explanation, we can assume. Emily is acting as handmaiden for her genes. She draws the heart because the adornment makes it more likely she will find a mate and produce offspring. And as Karl would point out, it is a heart she's drawing, not some neutral symbol, if such an animal as a neutral symbol exists. But still, that argument seems simplistic to me. Adornment takes time. It doesn't give us more food, or in Emily's case, more money. That's what I mean by 'at the expense of efficiency.' It seems we want to create beauty for its own sake, even though it takes time and energy to do it.

Yvonne Munch is standing beside the door, keys in hand. He passes out into the corridor so she can close it.

Well, Doctor, I see you have something to ponder this weekend. Why don't you come over on Saturday afternoon? We're having a small gathering. I'm sure Karl would love to see you. Show him the heart, he would certainly enjoy arguing about it.

Yes, Clint thinks, Karl would delight in battering him with Emily's heart. Tell me, Yvonne, does it seem to you that Karl and I always argue?

Doctor, Karl doesn't think he's in a conversation unless it contains an argument. You are one of the few willing to go head to head with him. He treasures you for it.

Well, I would enjoy it as well, I'm sure. But I have a memorial service to attend, I'm sorry to say. The wife of one of the men I used to cycle with. Only sixty and very sudden. A wonderful couple.

I'm sorry to hear that.

He nods. Memorial services. They're going to become more common for us, Yvonne. Attending memorial services will become a sort of avocation as we age.

Mrs. Munch closes the metal door and locks it.

At least at the last one, we get to be the star, she says with that brief smile.

She makes him laugh, as she often does. Give my regards to Karl, he says.

Chapter Four
AN UNFORTUNATE DRESS

Clint Estergard meets Connie Scheel on a Tuesday morning in July. A front had passed over the southern coast of British Columbia the evening before and this is a day of scattered showers and scudding clouds, the temperature hovering around fifteen for him and sixty for her. Since she would be flying in and he lives in nearby Richmond, he had recommended three hotels near Vancouver's international airport. The options ranged from modest to luxurious. She had chosen the one in the middle and in addition to a room for herself had reserved a conference room where they would have a table and a private space to talk. It is to this room that he is directed when he arrives at the front desk.

As he wheels himself into the room Clint sees an expression of disappointment cross the face of the tall Caucasian female who stands waiting for him. He has grown accustomed to that look. To recognize vulnerabilities is an ancient habit, he tells himself, common to both predator and prey, and he tries to not take it personally.

She is of early middle age, perhaps forty, plump, her skin smooth and clear. She has dark hair and eyes, the hair just beginning to gray at the temples. Unlike Emily, the assistant in the Zoology Department, who being not more than twenty, prefers low-waisted jeans and scanty tops that expose an enhanced cleavage above and a more than ample midriff below, Connie Scheel is dressed elegantly and expensively but in a manner that does not emphasize her sexuality: a gray skirt reaching to mid-calf, a black well-cut vest over a gray blouse. Small gold earrings. A collection of loose thin bracelets dangle on her left wrist, rings grace three of her fingers including her left thumb, but none signify marriage. The eyes are surprisingly dark and alert.

She makes a pleasant appearance, he decides, though he, too, feels a certain disappointment. Unconsciously, he now realizes, he had hoped to see Jolene Henderson, or at least a daughter who closely resembled her. But then he reminds himself that this daughter is twice the age the Hendersons were when he knew them.

If the disappointment registers on Clint's face, Connie does not see it. What she does notice is a passing sense of amusement. And since she is acutely aware that this man is of her parents' generation and a college professor and since her own brief semester at a university was an unqualified disaster, she fears that the expression passing across Clint's face reveals a sense of superiority, perhaps contempt.

But what amuses Clint is not Connie but his own quirky mind. The mental images he has of Kyle and Jolene Henderson, he realizes, have never aged. In his brain the Hendersons have enjoyed forty years without ever leaving their early twenties. That thought leads to those age-enhanced photographs that newspapers print of long-missing people. Newspapers produce such images but the brain does not. On the other hand the brain invents the computer programs that allow the newspapers to produce the photographs. So the brain created a process that it itself does not perform. The smile, what Connie fears is a smirk, follows.

Undaunted, Connie Scheel is extending her hand. Clint Estergard pulls off his beret, curls it up and stuffs it into the pocket of his jacket. He reaches for her hand.

Doctor, I'm so very pleased to meet you.

Ms. Scheel.

Please, call me Connie.

Agreed, he says, but only if you call me Clint.

They shake hands again and she thanks him for coming. On the table he notices a digital recorder feeding directly into a laptop that is up and humming. She has also arranged to have a pot of coffee, a pitcher of water, some fruit and juice delivered to the room. Beside the recorder is a thick photo album and what he takes to be the journal she had spoken about. The notebook with its stained and discolored green cover, its rusty spiral, looks soiled and out of place, but in an odd way more real than the objects around it.

A pleasant room, he says, glancing around.

I chose the hotel because of this room, Connie says. The internet is such a blessing. I was able to take a virtual tour of the places you recommended. I liked this meeting room the best. Comfortable but not large or pretentious. It was this floor-to-ceiling window, though, that closed the deal for me. In the photograph, I could see part of the window, but not the view. I had to reserve the room just to get a peek out the window.

The words tumble out of her with a giddy intensity that he attributes to the large nearly-empty cup of coffee beside the computer. He peers out the window. The conference room being on the first floor, the view offers nothing more than a corner of the hotel parking lot.

Probably not what you were hoping for, he says, motioning toward the view.

I'm not disappointed. The space is very pleasant. And from my room I have a water view. Besides, I'm here to learn from you, not look out a window.

A polite lie, he thinks. She is disappointed, anyone would be.

Yes, well, I hope you have an opportunity to do some sight-seeing while you're with us. You'll be charmed, I assure you. I am fortunate to have lived most of my life in a beautiful spot on this earth.

They exchange small talk, her flight out, his recent retirement from the university. When she asks how a Canadian ended up in the American Peace Corps he responds with a curt statement:

You've asked the wrong question, Connie.

His voice has a heavy thick quality and the words come out with a studied authoritarian slowness. She can't think of how to respond but it's clear he isn't expecting a response. He's more than willing to launch into a description of Pamela, his first wife, the mother of his two sons, a Canadian student at Berkeley when he met her there in the late sixties and the daughter of a Royal Canadian Mounted Policeman. A man who was, Clint adds, no Sergeant Preston, I can assure you.

Connie doesn't know who Sergeant Preston was but Clint seems to assume she should.

No, I did not come to Canada to avoid the draft, he continues, though I did avoid it. The Peace Corps and educational deferments accomplished that goal. But I have never regretted my decision and I remained in Canada after the marriage broke up.

As they're talking Connie clears a space for him at the head of the table. She asks if he would like some coffee. He demurs. Some fruit or a glass of juice? Perhaps later, he suggests.

Connie pours herself more coffee. She takes the chair in front of the computer and sits facing him.

Well then, I suppose we should begin. I've put together a list of questions. She turns toward the keyboard and begins scrolling down the page. I have a lot of questions, as you can see.

When Clint doesn't respond, Connie hesitates, feeling somewhat uncomfortable. But then she speaks again asking his permission to record their conversation. She wants a record for her brother as well as for herself.

Again, Clint says nothing. He appears to be staring at the items arrayed on the table. For a moment she fears he may be experiencing a stroke or some other physical problem. Years spent caring for her parents, time in the company of disease and death, have made her alert to calamity.

But the man across from her sits poised and straight and in no distress. He is a large man with a long face, a strong if stringy neck, heavy arms and shoulders. There is something vigorous if disheveled about him. He looks older than Dad, she decides, though she assumes they were of the same or similar age. Kyle's fine hair never lost its color, and his expression always struck her as somehow youthful and innocent. By contrast age has marked the skin on Clint's face and the backs of his hands. It has stolen the color from his hair though not the hair itself which he keeps short, perhaps, it seems to her, cutting it himself. Brownish shoots sprout from his ears and his eyebrows are unruly and in need of a trim. His nose is pronounced and has a bluish tint; perched on its bridge, slightly askew, are a pair of glasses in black plastic rims. He is clean shaven but she knows his beard is white because shaving this morning he missed a thin line in front of his left ear. She feels almost tender toward him at this moment, grateful that he has come. All that changes when he speaks.

I didn't come here to be interviewed, Connie, he says carefully.

Pardon?

You have come to me to learn about your parents. Thus, I will choose the format, the manner in which it is presented.

She blushes. But...

As to the recording, that I don't mind, but there is something more I need to say.

Yes. She removes her hand from the recorder.

Turn the recorder on, he instructs her. This should be part of the record.

The record, Connie thinks. She reaches out, activates the recorder and sits back in her chair.

In the days since we first talked, he says, I have had some misgivings.

She waits, watching him.

Kyle and Jolene Henderson were friends of mine. Although more than forty years have passed, and although we were together less than a year, the three of us shared experiences that shaped our lives. I cared about them both and even now I feel a sense of loyalty toward them.

Connie waits.

So the dilemma presents itself. If your parents chose to not reveal their Peace Corps experiences to you and your brother, why should I? Am I not betraying them by talking to you?

I see, she says, and it seems to him that she has slumped slightly in her chair.

I don't know why they kept the information from you. Certainly it was their right, and just as certainly, it required a sustained effort over decades. Obviously, they never changed their minds. If they slipped now and then, neither you nor your brother picked up on it. It's rather astonishing when you think about it.

She waits, biting her lower lip.

I've decided, however, to go ahead under certain conditions that I will explain to you. I've agreed because I think they were being unfair. No, not unfair to you or your brother. To themselves. I speculate, I don't know, but I speculate that they felt shame. If so, they misjudged their experience, and now that you know they were in Brazil, that they came home before the scheduled end of their tour and never spoke of their experiences, it is reasonable for you, and your brother, to imagine the worst. Thus the responsibility falls on me to tell you what happened as best I can remember it.

Connie releases a deep breath. Thank you, Doctor, thank you very much.

I believe we agreed on Clint and Connie, he says, smiling for the first time.

Oh yes, I'm sorry. Clint then. You mentioned conditions, Clint.

Yes, they are simple enough. I will tell you everything I know as honestly as I can. I hope in time, to answer every question you have. But I will tell the story my way, in the manner I choose. You may ask questions as they come to you but I am free to refuse to answer them until they are appropriate to the narrative. If these terms are acceptable, I am prepared to proceed.

For a long moment Connie studies the computer screen. Her precious questions. Formulated, revised, organized and rehearsed. She had prepared them as a lawyer would before a crucial cross-examination. Designed to lead him down paths she thought he might not take alone. She feels suddenly powerless and it strikes her that information is a unique commodity. A weightless thing without physical characteristics and in this case without value to anyone but her. But precious to her, unavailable on the open market and possessed perhaps in the whole world by this man alone. These thoughts make her aware suddenly of realities she would prefer to ignore: of men grabbed off streets, thrown onto planes and flown to dank horrific chambers. For information.

Yes, she says, that is acceptable.

Then we have an understanding?

We do.

Good. Now, I must also tell you a second thing. From the moment I learned of your call, images, smells and memories have been popping into my head at odd and random times. Some quite vivid. They did not present themselves in any organized fashion but as I jotted them down they served as guide posts for a more rational reconstruction of that time in my life. As a result I have made myself some notes, an outline of my memories, if you will. Clint removes several sheets of paper from an interior pocket of his sports jacket. He unfolds and shuffles through them. And I should warn you, he adds, looking pleased with himself, as a lecturer I have a reputation for not stopping when the bell rings. In other words, I like the sound of my own voice and I am quite enchanted by my own thoughts, a habit much deplored by students over the years. You'll understand if you get to visit the U.B.C. campus and observe how huge and spread out it is. What I am trying to explain is that if your parents' story, and my own, is to be told well, it will take more than the couple of hours I originally anticipated.

Connie tells him that she has arranged to have a week in British Columbia. My first real vacation since I was a kid, she says. I'm very excited.

Well, I'll try to not use it all up.

She blushes. Oh, no, I didn't mean it that way. Use as much as you wish. I am indeed grateful you have come at all.

Very well. He studies his notes for a moment. Okay. Well, I will begin by saying there was a girl.

Mom?

Clint frowns. It isn't just the interruption that bothers him. It's the intensity. The word exploded from her mouth, an outburst more than a question. After a long pause, he says, No, Connie, not your mother. I think we will proceed at a better pace if you resist that kind of instant response.

Yes, I'm sorry.

I said 'girl,' but these days we would say a woman, a young woman, in her early twenties. We were all in our early twenties. This young woman had a very unusual first name, Smookie. A nickname I'm sure, but if I ever heard her real name I have forgotten it. Smookie Collins. Smookie was a nurse, a downhill skier from Boulder, Colorado, a delightful girl who had grown up with four brothers. At the time I had a crush on Smookie Collins and it was she who introduced us to your parents.

I'm sorry, you said 'us?'

Yes, Vern Cuthert and myself. Vern was from Tennessee. He, Smookie and I had trained together in Arizona. Vern, incidently, ended up marrying Smookie, but that's another story entirely. Your parents didn't train in Arizona.

In Madison, Connie says. My parents trained in Madison, Wisconsin. That's in the journal. Another bizarre thing? I have been to Madison with my parents. They never mentioned having been there before or wanting to visit the campus. So, bizarre.

I see. Did Kyle write about the training?

Very little.

Then perhaps I should explain a bit. State-side training took three months. Even though we were in different parts of the country, we trained for the same project and our experiences would have been similar. You began by applying to serve in the Peace Corps. If deemed worthy, you were sent an invitation to train for a specific project and country. Our country, of course, was Brazil and our project was described as 'Public Health/Community Development.' The details probably varied somewhat from place to place. In Arizona we spent time on the Pima and Maricopa Indian reservations, for example. And being in the desert we learned something about irrigation. In Wisconsin, those details would have been different.

Yes, Connie says.

Six hours of Portuguese a day, all oral. No textbooks allowed. Brazilian and Latin American history, world affairs, and, though it seems ludicrous now, a lecture on communism. The hands-on stuff was the most interesting. We gave injections, drew blood, built sanitation systems, watched mothers giving birth. We learned and practiced first aid. We were introduced to tropical diseases. We raised and killed rabbits, planted gardens. We boys spent a day wiring a house.

Pardon, but what does wiring a house have to do with public health?

Anything practical would have served, Connie. The instructors were training a group of young mostly inexperienced college graduates. They needed to flush out the textbook attitude and instill some real world confidence. We'd be confronting real problems in a foreign country and we needed to deal with them not academically but practically.

I see.

So, I met Kyle and Jolene Henderson in Rio de Janeiro some time early in December, 1964. I met them at a reception for newly arrived Volunteers. To set the stage, President Kennedy had been dead for a year. I realize this is ancient history to you, but John Kennedy was a big part of why we were there. And his brother-in-law, a man named Sargent Shriver was the first director of the program. So, do you want some first impressions?

Of my parents? Oh, yes! Of course, anything.

Our group had arrived in Brazil only one or two days before the reception. We were all running around Rio trying to absorb as much of that beautiful city as we could in the short time we would have there. In the course of her explorations, Smookie had met the Hendersons. When she saw them at the reception, she wanted to introduce us because like Vern and me they were going to be stationed in Bahia.

This Smookie wasn't going to Bahia?

No, and that was a major concern of mine. We had learned earlier in the day that Smookie would be stationed in Mato Grosso, a huge state in the vast interior of Brazil. West from Rio, thousands of miles from Bahia. And we, that is the Bahia contingent, were leaving the following morning. I was concerned, quite rightly, that I might never see Smookie Collins again. I want to tell you about this evening not only because that was when I met Kyle and Jolene Henderson but also because they played a role in what happened that night. But at the time, you should understand, from my perspective, your parents were minor characters.

I understand.

I remember that when Smookie pointed them out they were seated at a table by themselves across the room, maybe thirty, forty feet away. They sat beside each other but they weren't engaged with each other. They weren't looking at each other, they weren't talking to each other or to anyone else. I thought at the time it was your mother's dress.

Her dress?

Yes. I thought she was embarrassed about her dress.

Clint sees Connie's cheeks redden, as if the dress represented a family disgrace, as if none of them had ever been able to dress properly.

Don't get me wrong, Connie, he says, smiling in a manner that seems to her smug. The dress was beautiful. Teal colored, if I remember right. Low cut with straps on each side coming from front and back and tied into knots, the knots resting not against her shoulders but her arms at the deltoid muscles. A beautiful somewhat daring dress. We found out later that she had made it herself.

That's my mom, Connie says, grinning. She made all her own clothes and she was so disappointed that I never got into patterns, dress making. She tried her best to encourage me, but I hated it. I didn't want to make my clothes and I didn't want her to make them. I wanted clothing off the rack. I wanted the label. I feel bad about that now.

Clint shrugs. You're right, of course. You mother was very adept at that kind of thing, as I was to find out later. But at the time, I thought it was too much dress, or too little, for the occasion. Or that she thought so. We boys were in suits, white button-down shirts, the thin ties we all wore then. The women for the most part had chosen dresses or skirts and blouses that were less formal, less 'promish' than your mother's. Anyway, that was my first impression, this attractive woman sitting beside her husband somewhat frozen in place by embarrassment.

Connie leans forward slightly looking at him. Did you find my mother attractive?

The question brings another frown to Clint's face. I think most people would have judged your mother attractive. At the age I knew her.

They're silent for a moment and then she asks, And my dad? Do you have a first impression of him?

Ah, your father. My first impressions of Kyle Henderson were of his hands.

His hands?

Kyle Henderson loved shaking hands. He must have shaken

my hand three or four times that night.

Connie laughs, nodding her head. I'm sorry, but did he give you the homily?

The homily? Clint asks, thinking that he needs to find a way to discourage these interruptions.

His theory about the evolution of the handshake?

Well, let's hear it.

First there's the little speech about table manners. I must have heard this a hundred times. Table manners, he liked to say, developed to convey a message. A simple message that says, although we sit side by side devouring flesh with weapons in hand, I do not intend to kill and eat you.

He was serious, I suppose.

The comment strikes Connie as so condescending that for a moment she feels a rush of anger.

Dad was always serious, she says, calming herself. Then he always told the story about the Alhambra. Supposedly, when a horseman approached the great gate of the Alhambra he had to hold out his right hand to show it was empty.

Okay.

So, the handshake, Dad would explain, developed as an extension of these concepts. The handshake tells you that I wish you no harm. But it also says I trust that you do not intend to harm me either. Connie Scheel extends her right hand across the table to Clint Estergard. See, my sword hand is empty. I offer it open to you, that you may grasp and imprison it for a moment. Clint takes her hand in his. And then my dad would say, 'The handshake may commemorate one of the great milestones in human development: the possibility of trust among strangers.'

As Clint releases Connie's hand, he sees that tears have formed in her eyes. But she has prepared for this eventuality as well. In addition to the laptop, the recorder and the other items, Connie has thought to place a packet of facial tissues on the table. She excuses herself, reaches for one and dabs her eyes.

Midwestern stock, he thinks watching her. Like people he has known from the interior, in Canada as well the U.S. Brought up to think ahead, inculcated with a sense of reserve and propriety. Qualities that would get you through, maybe a little predictably, maybe a little boringly, but would get you through.

Seeking to ease her discomfort, he motions toward the album. Does that contain what I hope it does? While you are blind to a few months of your parents' lives before you were born, I am blind to everything that happened after they left Brazil.

She's embarrassed. Oh my, I brought this to share with you. I hoped it would serve as an icebreaker and then I forgot all about it.

So, they go through the photos and Clint watches the aging of Kyle and Jolene Henderson, his interviewer and her brother, page by page, birthday by anniversary by holiday. He is surprised when a handsome African-American man appears beside Connie and then two sons, and then the man disappears and the boys grow until they sat side by side on a sofa, ten and twelve, the older looking heavy and removed, the younger defined by a clear-eyed grin that he has been perfecting since the nursery. When she finally closes the album she dabs her eyes again.

She has a fondness for darkening the skin around her eyes

with liner and shadow. He noticed the tendency in the photos and it is true now as well. The practice doesn't particularly work for him, but the eyes themselves are striking. Darker than her mother's. He can not remember her father's eyes.

Your brother. Philip is it?

Phil, yes.

In some of the photos he strongly resembles your father at the time I knew him.

Everyone says Phil's a spitting image of Dad, physically that is. In other respects they're very different.

Clint decides to not explore that. There was another thing about your father's hands, he says.

I loved his hands, Connie says, interrupting him. I was their caretaker. First Mom and then Dad. Sometimes at the dinner table after Mom had died, or when we were watching TV, he'd reach over and take my hand in his. He wouldn't say anything. He'd just hold my hand for a while. That's what I remember about his hands.

She is heavier than her mother. The photographs showed that Jolene had remained trim for the remainder of her days. There had been one snapshot taken at a birthday party. It wasn't intended as a portrait of Jolene but he recognized the thin woman at the edge of the frame. She was sitting in a stuffed chair beside a tray cluttered with pill jars. She wore a yellow terry-cloth robe. Her head was wrapped in a scarf, a tube in her nostrils, a warm smile on her face. He found the photograph painful to look at.

Near the end? he had asked, to which Connie had nodded.

Kyle Henderson had very thin hands, he says now, that's what I remember. Long thin fingers, the knuckles standing up like abrupt little mountains. I used to think they were hands you might see in a medieval painting, a saint at prayer, though my perception may have been tainted. I knew he had gone to a Catholic boarding school with the intent of becoming a priest.

Connie grins, dimples appearing on her cheeks. Except Mom

smuggled him away, thank goodness.

My point is that in spite of their shape, Kyle's hands were not just those of an ascetic. He had a strong physical side as well. He liked to talk about the physical work he had done on the farms near the town where they had grown up.

Stanton Grove, Connie says. Not far from Bloomington. It's a farming community on the prairie. We often visited there when I was young.

He claimed to have put up hay, built housing for pigs. Then later at Nova, there was the garden project. His hands showed that. They were callused, the nails chipped, bits of grit. He took pride, I think, in having the hands of a workingman, though at first glance they seemed anything but. Later, I would see it more clearly, but even at the beginning I thought the contrast between the thin, delicate look of his hands and the hard use he put them to represented a conflict at the center of his being. Kyle Henderson was in conflict when I knew him.

Clint pauses, waiting to see how she will react to his assessment. She responds in a way that surprises him.

I'm sorry, but I don't understand. Are you saying there's a conflict between spirituality and physical labor? Or that thin hands make you somehow holy? Our Savior was a carpenter, after all. Yes, Dad was thin, but all his life he built things. He had a shop in the basement full of woodworking tools. He loved wood. He put in a hot tub for Mom. A pond in the backyard with a waterfall and several huge koi. There's still a cement mixer rusting out back of the garage, a large garden, neatly fenced. Manual labor was a kind of recreation for him after hours of office work. He hated to sit around. Later when he began to show symptoms of the disease he lost the ability to do physical work. That was very difficult for him.

'Our Savior?' Clint thinks, stifling a grin. He's tempted to ask if she is referring to Darwin, a man of many talents, though carpentry is not among those usually mentioned. But like the grin, he represses the jab, saying instead, I would never have guessed Kyle would end up a realtor.

Connie purses her lips. I might have said realtor but he was much more than a realtor. He was a developer. He saw that population growth and social tensions were forcing people out of the city and the near suburbs. He bought up land, most of it on credit. He developed housing tracts, commercial strips, a mall. He was very good at what he did and he made a lot of money, most of which he gave away.

That comes as a total surprise to me, Clint admits, though not the giving away part. I thought of him as verging on sainthood and he ends up a real estate magnate.

What?

It's so, typically 'American,' if you know what I mean. Not that there's anything wrong with being a real estate developer, but it's far from what I would have imagined. I suspect the Kyle Henderson I knew was very different from the father you grew up with.

Connie waits a beat. That's why I'm here, she says simply.

Of course I knew them for less than a year, a tiny fraction of their lives.

That's true, she agrees, feeling some satisfaction. He and Mom grew up in the same town, did you know that? Mom was best friends with Aunt Connie, that's my dad's sister, and that's where I got my name. Dad had six brothers and sisters. Mom had a brother and three sisters. So, both families were pretty large by today's standards.

They talked about all of that. He Catholic, she Protestant. They were proud, as I recall, of their cross-denominational marriage. They thought it daring, at least in that town, at that time.

I'm sure it was, Connie says. Stanton Grove is still lily white and surrounded by farm land. A town square with stores selling things like horehound candy in fake barrels. My husband said he felt more nervous going to Stanton Grove than he did to

Mississippi, which is where his family came from.

All those aunts and uncles and no one spilled the beans? Connie shakes her head. Not a word until I found the journal. It's enough to make you believe in mass conspiracies. She smiles, but the smile seems to him more wistful than happy. Aunt Connie and Uncle Darrell are my godparents. She was like a second mom to me growing up, even though she lived almost a hundred miles away. I spent a week at their house every summer. Their kids are my closest cousins. I felt betrayed, to tell you the truth. By Mom, by Dad and by Aunt Connie.

I see.

Aunt Connie sounded really nervous when I called. She had a higher obligation, she told me, a promise she made to them before I was born. Beyond that she wouldn't say much. They had gone to Brazil with the Peace Corps but it hadn't worked out and they came home early. 'Look what he accomplished later,' she told me, which made me wonder even more about what happened. But it's hard to say, the whole thing is murky. My grandfather, that is my dad's father, he had a problem with the marriage. It wasn't, you know, Hatfields and McCoys. He was cordial. We were welcomed in the family. But Mom told me Grandad had opposed the marriage. He thought if it hadn't been for Mom his oldest son would have become a priest, and that's what he wanted. Maybe that has something to do with it, I don't know. That's why I'm here. I want to know what happened. It's important to me personally.

Yes, of course. I assume you realize they were already married when I met them.

Newlyweds, Connie says. They got married in July of 1964 and entered the Peace Corps a few weeks later.

They had a mid-western, small-town innocence about them, Clint says. The director of the program in Bahia was a guy named Charlie Pell. I called him Charlie, most of us did, but Kyle and Jolene always referred to him as Mr. Pell. Not only to his face but in conversations we had when Charlie wasn't around. Clint chuckles. Of course, Charlie was an old man to us, in his late thirties, only thirty years younger than I am now.

Younger than I am then, Connie says.

Clint has not asked her age, but she is older than he thought she would be. Forty maybe. Five or six years older than Michael, his oldest son. She must have been born within two or three years after they returned from Brazil.

So, is that all you can tell me about that night in Rio?

Oh no. I could go on and on, I assure you, but mostly about Smookie Collins. That's where my focus was. But it's true, I spent most of the evening with your parents and they gave me a gift that night I appreciated.

Mom and Dad?

He nods. The reception lasted a couple of hours, I suppose, and then we went to dinner. Smookie and I, your mom and dad and Vern.

The guy who ended up marrying Smookie?

That's right, the five of us. We walked to a restaurant that Smookie had heard about. A balmy, fragrant December evening. The seasons down there are reversed as I'm sure you realize. So it was late spring, almost summer. We were in the center of the city. The reception had been at a private club off the Avenida Rio Branco, not far from the American Embassy. We had been to the embassy the day before. They had taken us there in chartered busses from the airport and had issued us our first allotment of cruzeiros, the Brazilian currency at the time. We each got a thick wad of it. Brazilians were enduring manic inflation. The largest denomination was a five thousand cruzeiro note and it was worth less than three American dollars. Printing the stuff must have been a major source of employment.

I was disappointed about the dinner plans. I had been hoping for a quiet romantic dinner alone with Smookie. During the three months of training she and I had enjoyed what I would call a playful though cautious flirtation. It had to be cautious because we knew ourselves to be under constant surveillance.

Surveillance?

Yes, that might sound a little odd. You went into the Peace Corps as a trainee, not a Volunteer. Only those who successfully completed the program became Volunteers. In your parents' case, both went or neither. So, we felt ourselves being watched, evaluated. A sense of vulnerability pervaded the lot of us. You wanted to appear enthusiastic, upbeat, flexible, full of the 'can do' spirit of the New Frontier.

The New Frontier?

Kennedy administration. The New Frontier had been murdered in Dallas the year before but it lived on in our imaginations, if nowhere else. My point is that a romantic entanglement between two trainees would suggest indulgence and a lack of resolve. They meant it too. A dozen of our number had been removed at the midpoint, another seven or eight at the end. Others left of their own accord. Of the eighty or so who started in Arizona, only forty-eight of us met in New York for the flight to Rio de Janeiro.

Did my parents fly with you?

If they did, I don't remember it. It was a regular overnight Pan Am flight with a stop to refuel in Port of Spain, Trinidad. In those days air travel had a certain glamor. They gave us little booties for our feet, fed us a decent meal. For most of us, it was one of the first flights we had ever taken. I doubt that more than one or two of us had been outside the country before. Vern had been to Germany. He was a couple of years older and had served in the army. But I was entering a new world, and I'm sure that was true for your parents as well.

Smookie and I sat together near the back of the plane, where, if you don't mind my saying so, we had a little make-out party. We saw ourselves as Volunteers now, not trainees. As adults, not children. Later we snoozed on each others' shoulders. I remember waking around dawn and looking out the window. We seemed to be flying over an endless expanse of green. I wanted to lean closer to the window, hoping to catch sight of the Amazon, but Smookie, the poor kid, had fallen asleep with her head against the crook of my arm. It was quite uncomfortable but I knew she was exhausted and I determined not to move for fear I would wake her. I never did see the Amazon on that trip. I fell back asleep and when I woke we were descending into Rio.

It must have been very exciting, Connie says.

Exhausting is what I remember, and a bit unnerving. After a couple days in Rio we would be shipping out to our projects. But we had no idea where. The rumors changed from hour to hour. First we were all headed to a state then called Guanabara located across the bay from Rio. That sounded ideal. Then we heard that only a few of us were going to Guanabara. Most were headed into the vast Northeast, the poorest and most arid region of the country. The remainder would be scattered among ongoing projects in different parts of the country, though who was going where was still a mystery. That afternoon, just before the reception, the final word came down. From the Arizona program just five of us, Vern and I, a nurse named Jean and the Lehmans, a couple from Texas I didn't know very well, were going to Bahia. Your parents, of course, were also slated for Bahia, but at that point I hadn't met them. Smookie and several others were on their way to Mato Grosso.

I see.

I should explain that communication in Brazil at that time was not easy. The internet didn't exist, of course, but neither did phone service, at least not in the rural areas and not over long distances. Mail delivery could take weeks and the letters arrived in bunches. So that night was, I suppose you could say, an emotionally charged one for all of us.

Connie cocks her head, conducts a small internal debate and then, too curious to resist, plunges ahead: I hope you don't mind my asking a personal question, Clint, but were you in love with this Smookie?

She watches as he brings his hands up to the level of his chest and slowly rubs them together. His own hands are large, she thinks, noticing them for the first time, his fingers thick. Now and then in a meeting or when she is having a disagreement with one of her sons, she is embarrassed to find her hands flying wildly about as she talks. This would not happen to Clint, she realizes. He gives the appearance of deliberation, and when he speaks his hands rest quietly in his lap.

Well, you're right, he says at last. That is a personal question.

She blushes. I'm sorry. I didn't mean....

He pauses again, seeming to enjoy her embarrassment. Love, he says, pronouncing the word with a professorial formality, is not a word I use. It's a term without structure. You can stretch it to describe most anything. Feelings for your mother, your lover, your child, but also your favorite hockey team, the sushi bar down the street. Let's just say that on that evening, Miss Smookie Collins and I had the hots for each other. You'll agree, I hope, that having the 'hots' is different than what you call 'love?'

Yes, I...

And that the word 'hots' communicates something meaningful?

Yes.

Good. Then we understand each other. On that point at least.

They are silent for a moment, and then Connie says, So, you had dinner at the restaurant?

Good restaurant. I can't remember the name anymore, but it specialized in seafood: lobster in butter, prawns in coconut milk, different kinds of fish, various stews, that sort of thing. Quite pleasant, really. Decent wine, good conversation. Vern was excellent company. Droll. He didn't take life too seriously. At one point he told us about his brother, who when he was eighteen or nineteen, drove off a bridge and drowned in the Tennessee River.

That's terrible, Connie says

Well, certainly fatal, Clint adds, dryly. Everyone was shocked, of course, and Kyle started talking about how difficult it must have been for Vern to lose his brother and how hard for the family, particularly Vern's mother. He went on like that for a while. Finally Vern said, with a perfectly straight face, mind you, that yes, it had been particularly hard on his mother because she had been in the passenger seat.

Oh no!

Oh, yes. Clint lowers his chin and peers at her over his glasses, a shine in his eyes. It amuses him that she is making the same mistake her father made forty years before.

Soon as Vern said this, he looked down at this lap and his body started shaking. We thought he was crying. But no, just the opposite; he was trying not to laugh. His mother had not been in the car it turned out. To this day I can't swear his brother drowned either though he always maintained that part of the story was true. Vern Cuthert was drawn to the sauce. He would get lit up and tell whoppers. What set him off this time was Kyle's sincerity. A very earnest young man when I knew him, Kyle Henderson. He rarely touched a drop and was not known for...

His sense of humor?

Precisely.

Connie rolls her eyes. Mom and I liked pranks. You know, April fool jokes, that kind of thing. Nothing cruel, but funny. She used to say that it was useless to pull an April fool's joke on Dad first of all because he was so gullible there was no challenge. And then you had to spend so much time explaining that it had been a joke and why you did it and all the time he would be looking at you like you were from a different planet.

I see. Well, Kyle made a speech that night at the restaurant that gave me the first inkling about who he was and what he believed in. He told us he had come to Brazil to immerse himself in the culture. He wanted to live the way the 'real' people lived, eat what they ate, work side by side with them, be a part of their world. He claimed the trip to the American Embassy had been distasteful to him. He didn't want to be identified with American power and influence. He also told us he felt 'immoral' sitting in a fancy Rio restaurant drinking wine and eating lobster. He talked about the people he had seen along the road when he rode the bus in from the airport. Children in tattered clothing playing around little wooden shacks. Women hanging out their laundry. Workmen smoking on loading docks. Those were the people, he said, that he had come to be with. And he would be happy when he finally got out of Rio and up to Bahia.

We had all seen those people, of course. We had been told in training what to expect, but still, it was a bit of a shock. And all of us were idealistic in our way. We wouldn't have been there otherwise. Even Vern had his idealistic side. He kept it well hidden, but he did good work as a Volunteer. So, it wasn't pleasant to be told by Kyle that there was something 'immoral' about enjoying a final night together in a decent restaurant.

Connie grimaces.

So, my first impressions of Kyle were not positive. And Vern. Well, Vern was ready to paste him with an empty bottle. For me it was a passing thing. My attention was elsewhere. And the more I drank and the more I looked across the table, the more attentive I became. Smookie was looking great, smiling and winking. Clint laughs, shaking his head. That young lady had me in a lather, I tell you. Then, after the meal, when we were out on the street, I thought my chance had come.

And Mom? Connie inserts. You've said almost nothing about her except the dress.

Clint pauses, his train of thought broken. The woman looks piqued. Somewhere in her fertile imagination he has slighted her mother.

Yes, the unfortunate dress. However, I believe when you listen back on your recording, you will find that I made clear from the outset that my real interest on the evening we're discussing was Smookie Collins.

Who would later be Vern's wife.

That's true, he says slowly, but hardly to the point.

Connie blushes. You're right, of course. I'm sorry.

I believe I have also intimated, that your mom did have a role to play before the night was out.

Oh yes, of course. An embarrassed laugh. I just have to be patient.

Indulgent is probably more accurate, Clint admits. Anyway, now that I am reminded of the dress, there was something else that happened at the dinner table. Your mom showed off her keloids.

Connie blushes again. She told you the waterskiing story?

He nods, watching her.

Oh, my. Well it was her favorite morality story. I must have been about ten the first time I heard it.

Apparently, the experience almost took her life. And she probably learned...

...to never go waterskiing with older boys who have been drinking, or to have anything to do with such people. That's what she learned. She actually showed you those ugly scars?

Well, her shoulders were bare anyway, he says. They are quiet for a moment, and then changing the subject, he asks if she has ever been to Rio de Janeiro.

She hasn't.

Something to look forward to, Connie. A remarkable physical setting, as you may know. Tropical, of course. A large bay. Beaches like Copacabana and Ipanema. Surrounding hills including the dramatic Pão de Açúcar standing at the head of the bay and the Corcovado, the hunchback. That's probably Rio's most famous mountain because at the top is a giant statue of Jesus, tall as a football field is long, standing with arms outstretched over the city.

I've seen pictures of that.

It might interest you to know that for a couple of months in 1832, Charles Darwin lived in a cabin on Botofogo Bay at the base of the Corcovado. That would have been a century before the statue was erected.

Connie frowns. What was he doing there?

Making observations, of course, collecting specimens. You should familiarize yourself with Darwin, Clint adds, enjoying himself. A great naturalist. At that time, incidently, he was the same age your parents and I were when we arrived in Rio. Among other things Darwin commented on the unusual rock formations. He was a wonderfully observant man and meticulous, a fine writer. I bring the subject up because after we left the restaurant that night, Vern suggested we find a cab to take us to the viewing stand at the base of the statue.

The two of you?

No, all five of us. The idea excited me. Not because I wanted to go, but because I didn't.

I don't understand.

Clint offers a rather smug smile. I saw this as my big chance, you see. Vern and I were rooming together at the hotel. If he and your parents went up to Corcovado, that meant the room would be free for an hour or more. Free for Smookie and me.

Of course, Connie says. I get it.

It didn't work. Smookie wanted to see the statue too and I couldn't talk her out of it. So we all went. The cabbie drove like a mad man, one foot on the throttle, one hand on the horn, the way they do in Rio. We were all quite reasonably frightened. But I had had my share of wine and somewhere along the way, I said to the driver in crude but very understandable Portuguese, 'We're in a hurry. A little faster, please.'

Clint laughs at his forty-year old story until tears come to his eyes. You should've seen the look on that cabbie's face, he adds, pulling off his glasses and reaching for a tissue.

Yes, it must have been very funny, Connie says, feeling bored. You have to understand, we were very young. Not just in years, but young people in a young age.

Another time, I guess.

Another time all right. I suppose, even then there were men at the center of American power, men who saw us Peace Corps Volunteers as insignificant units in a vast program. A program to market the brand called America to the larger world. In that sense we were no different from Coke or John Wayne, the Blue Angels or Gillette Blue Blades. We knew nothing of those men, of course, and had we known, it would not have mattered. We believed in what we were doing. We thought the world could be made a better place. We thought mistakes were being made that could be fixed, that people drinking bad water could drink good water, that people who were hungry could be fed, that people without shelter could be housed, the ill receive treatment. We believed the world was being held back by ignorance and that the antidote was education. We believed that if people understood they would change and with them the world would change. And for all our youth, for all our personal self-doubts and insecurities, we believed we had something to give. We saw ourselves, you see, marching with humanity along a road called progress. A one-way road called progress.

My parents believed that all their lives! Connie exclaims, hopping in her chair and flailing her arms. A dark curl falls onto her forehead and she brushes it back. That's why Mom was a teacher. A teacher has to believe that. That's the only thing that gets you through the day if you're a teacher. And that's why Dad gave so much to the organizations he believed in. She sounds a little out of breath.

Good for them, Clint says.

His tone brings her to a halt. Pardon?

I'm sorry. I didn't mean to sound sarcastic.

You don't, I take it.

I'm a teacher, too, remember.

Oh, yes. I'm sorry.

And I certainly believe there are better and worse ways to organize societies. But a one-way road called progress? Human culture, I would propose, and human motivation, are more complex than we thought at the time. But we're not here to talk about me. It's your parents we're talking about and the day I met them.

Agreed. And you were in a taxi, I believe, going too fast.

We're out of the taxi now, Clint says. We're standing on the viewing platform below the massive, light-flooded, bug-encrusted Christ the Redeemer. That's what the sculpture is meant to represent.

Yes. Our Savior. I would love to see it.

Yes, he says, pausing. I know your parents were with us, but I don't remember them in that setting. What I do remember is Smookie, Vern and me standing with our arms around each other. The warm and buggy air, the black night, the enormous silent figure above us, a million city lights, the strange perspective that gave the sense we were floating untethered out over it all, the alcohol, the lingering jet lag, the odd new world in which we found ourselves, the longing I felt for Smookie, the way our group was being broken open like a tangerine and pulled apart segment by segment, the unknown into which come morning I would be flying. Brazilians have a word. *Saudade,* It's unusual to listen to a Brazilian song and not hear that word somewhere in the lyrics.

What does it mean?

Longing. A sweet longing you might say. A sense of separation that you wish did not exist but you still enjoy in some way. My urgent desire for Smookie had dissipated in the warm night air and all that remained was *saudade*, a sweet sad sense of what might have been.

I see.

Clint feels embarrassed. I'm giving you more detail than the moment deserves, he admits. It sounds sentimental, I know. My only justification is that I cannot report what your parents were thinking at that moment. I give you my own thoughts on the shaky assumption that theirs were similar. Anyway, when we got back to the hotel, Vern went straight to our room and closed the door behind him. He knew what was about to happen even if I didn't. He was already falling for Smookie, and I had no idea about that either.

So, the four of us were in the lobby, your parents, Smookie and me. We all embraced each other and then, as I was turning to go to my room, Jolene said something. At first I didn't think she was talking to me, but she spoke my name and I looked back. 'We have a present for you, silly,' she said. 'For the two of you.' She nudged Kyle who dug into his pocket and held out his hand. In the thin open palm was a key to your parents' room. He would sleep in my bed and Jolene would sleep in Smookie's. So there it was, a gracious act that I still appreciate. A fine gift, a brave gift, given the time and the role we saw ourselves playing, that of ambassadors for our country. And of course the two girls, women, I mean, had been plotting it all evening though I, and probably Kyle, knew nothing about it until the last minute. Kyle was a good sport. He didn't look too happy but he went along.

Connie is nodding her head and grinning. So, you're the one, she says, placing her hand on the journal.

Connie Scheel pushes her computer back from the edge of the table. She opens the spiral notebook and sets it down in front of her. She smooths the pages carefully with her hands in a manner that reminds Clint of the way her mother touched and smoothed fabric.

Dad didn't write about Rio, Connie says, but he wrote a whole section he called Ilhéus.

Clint repeats the name, correcting her pronunciation. It's a small city on the coast of Bahia, he tells her. We did our in-country training there. I would like to hear what he has to say about that.

Most of the entries he dated, she says, but not all of them.

All right.

Connie begins to read:

Thursday December 10, 1964

It's almost ten-thirty and I'm lying in bed with Jo beneath a mosquito net in a cheap hotel in Itabuna, Bahia. We have chased the roaches from the mattress, washed the closets with Lysol (which Jo was so smart to bring along, for her comfort if nothing else) and have built a semi-protective shield around us for sleeping. It has been a long day and we have come far.

It began in Rio around six thirty when I woke up to recognize a problem. The night before, we had given our room to a couple of unmarried Volunteers for a tryst.

Connie looks up, smiling.

I've been immortalized, Clint says.

I'm not going to go into the whys and wherefores, or the moral implications of our decision. On the bright side my dear Jo's kind heart showed itself once again. Unfortunately we made no arrangements for this morning when Jo and I had a plane to catch. I slept in the boy's room and Jo slept in the girl's room while the stuff we needed to pack was in our room along with the couple.

What to do? I couldn't just bust in not knowing what they might be up to and I didn't even know which room Jo was in. Anyway, it all worked out. Jo had taken the alarm clock and she was in the lobby having breakfast when I got there. Seven-thirty came with no sign of the couple so we went to the door and knocked. They were embarrassed, of course, and quickly got themselves together and cleared out.

Our packing was difficult. When we left the States our suitcases were already over the weight limit and so stuffed one of them popped open on the baggage carousel in New York. And now we had additional items we purchased or had issued to us in Rio including two medical kits in heavy metal cases and a *visitadora* bag with a shoulder strap that Jo is supposed to use in her work. We headed for the airport with two suitcases, three wrapped packages, two umbrellas, the two medical kits, my typewriter, my trench-coat and the fully-loaded *visitadora* bag. We were well over the weight limitations.

For two hours, we and the other fifteen Bahia Volunteers stood around the airport amid mounds of luggage while Willie made arrangements and negotiated prices. Willie is a Volunteer who has completed his tour and is helping get the Bahia project up and running. I'm glad Willie was there. The terminal was loud, crowded and confusing. The flight itself was pleasant, though the plane, a DC 3, felt small and shaky. We made one stop in Vitoria in the state of Espirito Santo, where we bought some of their famous chocolate, thus adding yet another package to our load.

It was early afternoon when we landed in the coastal city of Ilhéus, Bahia. Awaiting us was a new world, as different from Rio in some ways as Rio had been from the States. We are the first contingent of Volunteers to work in Bahia and our arrival caused a sensation. People gathered at the airport to stare at us. As we trooped down a narrow street with all our belongings, crowds of children ran beside us. Adults stopped their activities to look us over. I was enthralled by the intensity of light, the dense vibrant green foliage, the pretty little houses. For the first time I felt not with exactly but at least near the people we had come to serve.

The road led to a dock where we piled our baggage into one small boat and ourselves into two others. Soon we were motoring across a choppy bay. The boat was crowded and rocked around causing water to splash over the sides and onto our laps. A young boy stood at the front assisting with a pole while an old black man with a white beard ran the engine and navigated our route with the rudder bar jammed between the two largest toes of his left foot. The outlet to the sea is very small and the bay is surrounded by hills, some all green, others covered with what seemed to be precariously stacked houses. As seen from the bay the surrounding country looks lush and picturesque, though I was reminded of a quote I read once: what the tourist calls picturesque is really somebody else's squalor. Hopefully we are going to be something other than tourists.

Our boat landed in the center of town. Again crowds of people clustered around us. Old men, some with burros. Young boys in ragged shirts and bare feet. They talked to each other and laughed at the strange new arrivals. Half of our group stayed in Ilhéus to train for a month. The rest of us had a wild bus ride to this hotel in Itabuna where we start training at the local health post tomorrow.

We have seen a lot of Brazil today, her landscapes, her people and her modes of transportation. It was exciting and at times frustrating. Jo felt both very deeply and I realize we will need to stay close during the first difficult months of service. Training begins at 7:30 tomorrow.

Connie looks up. That's the end of the entry. He didn't write every day, a couple of times a week at this point. Later he wrote less and less. Do you want me to go on?

I'm surprised to hear they were in Itabuna, Clint says. I didn't remember it that way. Yes, please read the whole section on our in-country training.

The next entry is for Saturday December 12, 1964.

We spent yesterday morning touring the modern health clinic in Itabuna. The doctor who led the tour explained their programs and what our training would consist of. Since he spoke in Portuguese there was a lot I could not understand. Some of the other Volunteers, especially the girls, and those who have had several years of Spanish or French, understand more than I do. I find this extremely frustrating. It is like walking through a landscape that has large black holes in it.

At the end of the day, the doctor decided that all the boys should train in Ilhéus. Since we are married, Jo returned with me and one of the girl Volunteers in Ilhéus went to Itabuna. So we had to pack everything up again. The move was frustrating because Jo had worked hard to fix up our quarters, cleaning the room, organizing the chest of drawers, emptying the suitcases and hanging our clothing in the closet. But we are glad to be back in Ilhéus. The hotel is better, though a little more expensive, and we are on the coast.

Okay, Clint says. I thought we trained together in Ilhéus. Connie continues.

I'm turned around in this town. What seems east is west and what seems north is south. I assumed the ocean lay on the other side of the bay beyond the airstrip. But last night we walked in the opposite direction to take a closer look at a large church we could see in the distance. As we neared the plaza the wind picked up and the air became noticeably cooler. I thought we were about to get soaked. Then looking left from the church, we saw the Atlantic in all its nightly glory with long lines of surf fluttering like white petticoats against the shore. The surprising discovery did nothing to change my sense of direction. I felt like I was looking at the Pacific, not the Atlantic.

But what a thrill this was for us! Except for a short walk on the beach at Copacabana, neither of us has seen the ocean before. At Copacabana there were thousands of people; here we had the place almost to ourselves. The beach seems to extend indefinitely in both directions bordered by a walkway made of small black and white tiles set in a wave pattern. The breeze coming on shore was wonderfully cool. It pushed back the smells of the town just as the sound of the surf muffled all other noises. We walked along the path, watching the waves break and talking about our lives. The biggest problem for Jo is the uncertainty of our situation. The hotel in Itabuna was not great but at least we thought we would be there for a month. Then the trek back to Ilhéus. Jo longs for the day when we can finally be in our own house in the town where we will be stationed. We still don't know what town that will be. Apparently, Mr. Pell, the project director, and one or two veteran Volunteers are searching the state for suitable sites. Everything is going on outside our knowledge and control. I don't have a serious problem with that–I have to believe it will all work out–but it bothers Jo.

After a while we came upon a marble bench. Sitting there alone was one of the Volunteers we had met in Rio, the one, in fact, we had loaned our room to the night before we left. This boy is fairly miserable at the moment. The girl half of the tryst has been stationed far from Bahia and he can't seem to get her out of his mind. He welcomed our company and we sat with him. He had a bottle of wine between his legs. He offered us a swig but I refused. After a while I went back to the hotel to study Portuguese. The most important thing for me is to understand these people and make them understand me. Drinking wine and talking in English about lost love will not help with that goal so far as I can see.

When Jo came in an hour later she was worried about him. I'm worried too. I just don't see where we can help. He just has to get over it.

Connie looks up.

That's probably accurate, Clint says, somewhat sternly. So far as it goes. Please continue.

Jo and I had a bit of an argument this morning about money. After I had calmed down, I realized she was right, and I apologized. The thing is, I have never been very good with money. I never bicker over prices or look for bargains. Jo, on the other hand, is a very practical shopper. This morning as we were leaving the market she accused me of being weak because I refused to bargain. The fact is, I don't see the trip to the market as a shopping trip so much as an opportunity to engage with the people, to speak, to listen, to communicate. Since Jo speaks better than I, and is a more practical shopper, the tendency is for her to shop while I follow along with our market bag. As a result, her language skills improve while all I get is exercise for my arms.

Today, I insisted on doing some of the shopping. She gave me a list and off I went. When we met again, she examined everything and wanted to know how much I had spent for each item. She decided I had gotten screwed all around. The biggest mistake was the bananas. At home, bananas are bananas. Here there are yellow bananas, red bananas, bananas the size of your thumb, others as thick as your wrist. Well, bigger is better I thought so I bought a large bunch of what I now know are plantain bananas. Plantains, it turns out, are basically inedible unless you cook them in some way and since we're in a hotel room, we have no way of cooking them. Also I paid a premium price, not only for the bananas, but for everything else.

I do have a hard time bargaining with these people, though it's not because of weakness. When I look at their tattered clothing, their bare feet, their meager possessions, their naked children running around, it feels positively cruel to argue over what amounts to a few pennies. Jo correctly suspects that the merchants think all Americans are rich so they jack up the prices when they see us coming. And as Jo says we are not rich. We each get about 75,000 cruzeiros a month which comes to around $45.00 each. Not much since we have to pay for the hotel and eat our main meal everyday in a restaurant. On the other hand, compared to the people in the market, we are rich. Still I did apologize for getting angry and I agreed that I don't want to be taken for an idiot.

All in all, though, I really did enjoy the little shopping trip. I'm getting better at this. I'm more willing to make mistakes, to make a fool of myself, to do whatever it takes to engage with the people I have come to live with and serve.

Speaking of serving, it seems to me, there are three possible levels for a Volunteer in the field. The first and lowest is simply survival. That means staying as healthy as possible, not going home and trying to maintain some semblance of a self-respecting life. At this level one is being totally selfish and cares not a cruzeiro for the Brazilian people. I don't mean to be critical but there are one or two boys in our program, who I suspect may not be interested in going much beyond this level. I'm not talking about ability but about dedication.

Connie pauses again, looking at Clint expectantly.

Yes, you're right, he's probably referring to Vern and me. Your dad had his prudish side, in my opinion. At the time Vern and I were making what we jokingly referred to as a sociological study of the Ilhéus night life. Vern had concocted the theory that he spoke better Portuguese when he was drunk than sober and my job was to follow him everywhere and document his communication skills as the night got later and his sobriety lessened.

Was he right? Connie asks, deciding to not comment on the 'prudish' accusation.

The question seems to enliven the scientist in Clint, and he answers it seriously. You'll never speak a foreign language unless you're willing to make mistakes, as Kyle mentioned, and a bit of alcohol as we all know relaxes our inhibitions. So, it's probably true that a glass or two improves our ability to communicate in a foreign language. On the other hand, a drunk is a drunk, and a drunk doesn't communicate that well in his native language. Not that Vern was a blathering drunk. He wasn't. What we were really doing, of course, was being young single men. And missing Smookie, he as much as I, though he never revealed that to me and I was unaware of it at the time. Go on please, Kyle's standards for the noble Volunteer.

At the second level the Volunteer seeks to live on a par with the Brazilian people. He tries to gain their respect and live with courage and dignity. He must be able to communicate freely and feel comfortable living and working in Brazil while not surrounded by other Americans.

At the third level one has accomplished survival and assimilation. But now the Volunteer is also able to so immerse himself into the culture that he can consciously and purposely influence the people around him. He works with Brazilians in such a way that when he leaves, the activities he has set in motion will continue on without him. When one thinks about it, that would be quite an accomplishment and it is the standard by which I will judge our stay here.

What Kyle was describing, Clint says, is what we called community development. It was the burr beneath his saddle as it turned out.

Connie shakes her head. I don't understand.

I mentioned that our project was characterized as Public Health/Community Development. I've described the public health training but in a sense community development was even more important. This idea that you could set up programs that would have their own internal energy and thus sustain themselves after you left. That was the heart of community development.

What does it mean? Community development?

In some sense it meant that we were being trained for a subversive activity. No, not James Bond subversive, Clint adds, smiling. Subversive in the sense that when Peace Corps administrators interfaced with the Brazilian establishment, they emphasized public health, and when they talked with us they emphasized community development. We were trained in public health as I explained, and within the narrow confines of our responsibilities, we were capable of the work to which we would be assigned. A few of us had more formal training. Smookie, for example, and several of the other women were nurses. Another guy I knew was a pharmacist. Vern's army experience in Germany had been as a medical corpsman. But behind the assigned work was a higher purpose. And that was community development. I'll have more to say later about community development and how it affected your father. Please, go on.

Connie hesitates and it occurs to Clint that she is annoyed by his refusal to elaborate on the subject. But then she lowers her eyes and starts again to read.

Wednesday December 16, 1964

On Monday we began our training at the clinic here in Ilhéus. In the morning the boys received a lecture on the work of an *Auxiliare do Sanitário*, which is the job title we will be assigned at our duty station. Our instructor has developed a cement privy the parts of which are manufactured at the clinic. They can be transported to a home and installed in a hour or so. That afternoon we visited a number of sites where the clinic has installed central, sanitary water systems for communities. Meanwhile, Jo and the other girls were working at the clinic. They visited different departments such as pediatrics, injections, etc. Jo saw children with some of the diseases she had learned about back in Wisconsin and others she had never heard of.

On Tuesday and again today we divided into smaller groups. I was assigned with two other Volunteers to work with Aldo, an *auxiliare*. Aldo has been taking us on tours of his *zona*, or the area of the *favelas* that are his responsibility. We're lucky to be assigned to Aldo. He knows his job. He enjoys talking with people and seems honestly concerned about their welfare. He's also a bit of a philosopher and discusses many things with us in clear and simple Portuguese.

The *favelas* are stacks of humanity piled on the hills around this city. Most of the people live in shacks with mud floors. Most do not have privies or shower facilities. These are the improvements that Aldo, as an *auxiliare*, is trying to convince them to acquire. These hills are the land of the distended stomach. They're crawling with little kids, most of whom have a belly full of worms and are suffering from malnutrition. We rarely see the men. They're working on construction, or in the market or on the docks or out on the *fazendas*. The women are always home, washing or making clothes, cooking or cleaning the house.

We arrive at a typical house by passing down a steep trail of red dirt, the ever-present chickens scattering in front of us. The woman knows Aldo. She asks us in and hurriedly finds enough chairs for all of us. On the walls hang a crucifix, a picture of the Virgin Mary wearing blue and white, another of Jesus, back lit, with his long auburn hair washed and combed. There are a number of handmade cages containing small birds. Several kids fill the room. The smallest are completely naked. Older ones, five or six years of age, still have pacifiers in their mouths or hanging around their necks. One little boy, his brown body naked from his feet to the top of his head, his eyes strangely bright, stands beside my chair. He can't be more than two years old. He stares at me. He reaches up and begins to rub his hand slowly up and down my arm. He does this for several minutes. Perhaps he has never seen skin so pale as mine before.

The woman is pretty. She's probably in her mid-twenties but looks older, tired. Still, she is pretty with soft brown eyes, smooth skin and a gentle smile. Aldo talks to her about a privy. She doesn't install a privy, she says, because she has no money. Yes, she knows about germs, and yes, she knows that people with privies and showers have less disease. She knows all this but she has no money. And while the clinic will provide the materials, she must pay to have the hole dug and she has no money. It is the same reason she does not take her little boy to the doctor even though he is sick.

Later we visit a home where the family has installed a privy. Maybe, Aldo says to the woman, you are ready now to build a shower. He explains that if she builds the hut, the clinic will provide the tank and tubing. She says she will talk to her husband.

The process is slow. Aldo has to visit each house several times but he believes change is happening. Today, 50% of the houses have privies. When the clinic first opened, the infant mortality rate was 420 per 100,000, now it's 88. Aldo is proud of the progress and as he talks I remember how in training we were told about the Brazilians' inability to get anything done. It's refreshing to find a clinic like this one in Ilhéus and a man like Aldo. We have been told, though, even by the Brazilians, that this clinic and the one in Itabuna are exceptionally good.

We get off at five, and as we have the previous days, we go for a dip in the ocean. Most of the Volunteers are there. The sun is setting and the waves are pounding in with a vengeance. The water is amazingly warm. Jo was reluctant to enter the water at first but now it's becoming a part of her life. She's a better swimmer than I, all those years at the town pool and at the lake in Wisconsin, and she enjoys the water more than I do. Still it is very refreshing even for me after a hot day climbing around in the hills.

After a dip I stretch out on the warm sand and start to think about the program with the privies and the showers. Why do people have to pay? Why must they build the hut or dig the hole? I know the answer, of course. We want them to invest in the idea. If you just give a person something, the thinking goes, they won't appreciate it. But a toilet? A shower? Must one actually have an emotional investment in his toilet and his shower? I would like to discuss this with Aldo, but as I contemplate how I might phrase my argument, I immediately run up against the language barrier. It's one thing to ask a simple question, or request an item in a store or talk in general terms about the weather. It's something else to discus complex issues that might be sensitive to myself or the other person. Communication at this level is subtle and treacherous with nuance. Thus while I can speak some Portuguese and understand more, whole areas of thought and discussion are denied me. I am quite literally a simpleton in Portuguese. When I was a boy, maybe six or seven, a child came to our town as a refugee from the war in Germany. His name was John and he was staying with a family in the parish. I assume now, though I did not think much about it at the time, that John's parents had probably been killed in the bombing and he was an orphan. We kids were encouraged to be friends with John, to help him feel at home in his new country. But John could speak only a few words of English and those he spoke with a harsh and ugly accent. Whatever our intentions at the beginning, we came to think of John as an idiot. Rather than making him our friend, we chased him around mocking his speech and calling him a Nazi. That's why I want to practice, practice, practice my language skills.

As I watched the other Volunteers playing in the water, my

mind kept going back to that little boy who so intently and patiently rubbed my arm. I can still feel, even as I write these words, the touch of his fingers on my skin. What, I ask myself, is the future for that little boy whose family shits in a banana patch? Why does his pretty mother find herself with a mud floor and a house full of kids and caged birds? How is it that her husband works all day at some hard job and yet they cannot afford to take their sick child to the doctor while other families down here in town live lives that seem comfortable even by our standards at home? What explains this injustice? How did it come about? Why does it persist?

When I pose these questions the other Volunteers come up with the usual explanations: a class system, a hidden racism, a lack of good schools, a lack of unions, a failed legal system that does not provide or enforce a minimal living wage, a culture of learned bad habits, grossly unequal distribution of wealth. But ultimately my questions are different than that. I don't care so much how it came about or even what prevents it from changing. My real question is why do we accept it? How can we live with it? Why aren't thousands of people rushing up into those hills to build houses and water systems and schools? How can a man like Aldo—a fine man—see what he sees every day and then go home at night to his wife and family? Why aren't people screaming in the streets? Why am I not screaming in the streets?

That's true to my memory of Kyle, Clint says when Connie pauses. Kyle was always asking those kinds of questions. Please, go on.

Friday December 18, 1964
Yesterday I woke up sick at 4:30 in the morning. I had chills and cramps and a loose bowel movement. I stayed home all day feeling weak and generally lousy. All I ate were two bowls of soup. This morning I felt better and went to work. I hate to stay

home. I live for the time when I can truly communicate with these people and I need all the practice I can get. But climbing hills in the hot sun on an empty stomach with frequent cramps made for a miserable day. Jo also had a tough time. She is suffering from the same thing. We're having trouble with the food. Right now it all tastes the same. It's the oil it's cooked in, I think. The oil is all I can taste, and even the smell of cooking goes against me. Neither of us is eating much and we feel very weak. It's something to be expected. And I am convinced it is a passing thing.

Nine o'clock and fully dark outside. Night comes early and very fast here, around six. By now most of the racket that begins before five in the morning has subsided. The mules and burros have stopped passing on the street below, the boys with their wooden hand carts have stopped rattling past on the cobblestones, people have stopped yelling at each other and the boys who live in the doorway below our window have ended their nightly singing. That they sing at all astounds me. Their laughter and songs are miraculous testaments to the human spirit. That they who live in a doorway should sing while I lie on my comfortable bed complaining about the smell of the food and a few stomach cramps, shows just how far I need to travel if I am to become worthy of their respect. I who have come to help them!

I remember those boys. They beat on metal cans and sang. And Kyle was right. They lived in the side doorways of the hotel.

Sunday December 20, 1964
My wife now takes herself and pulls me to the ocean every chance she gets. She's in love with the beach, with its endless white sand, the palms, the rolling surf. For her, the seashore is a treasure. She can't believe that the people of Ilhéus almost never leave their houses and walk the few blocks to the water. She would spend hours every day walking along the hard wet sand, picking at shells, feeling the wind in her hair. The ocean

awakens something in her that is new to me, something that maybe even she never fully recognized before. Perhaps the ocean simply reminds her of the lake in Wisconsin where she vacationed every summer with her family. I'm happy she has this comfort for a few weeks. The transition from home to here has been very difficult for her. I don't know how she would have handled it were it not for the ocean.

This afternoon we stood at the edge of the surf, our arms around each other, the water foaming at our feet, and watched a cargo ship, the *Anne*, head out to sea. We had seen the ship earlier docked near the hotel and now as it slowly moved away we noticed something in the water clinging to its side. At first we could not identify what it was. The *Anne* stopped for a few minutes, disconnected itself from the little object, and then moved off again, this time at greater speed. Left behind was a small sailboat. After a few minutes the crew set up the mast and rigged the sail. Soon they were headed back toward shore. When Jo recognized what was happening, she gasped and I felt a shudder pass through her body. "Oh, wouldn't that be wonderful," she said, "if we could do that? If we had a boat and we could bum a ride out and then sail back. But we wouldn't sail back would we? I would want us to sail out. I would want us to sail away."

Connie stops. She places her finger to mark the spot. I have to work to imagine them as young, she says. Much younger than I am now. They were almost newlyweds, married less than a year. My mom had just turned twenty-one.

I don't remember her speaking with any particular fondness for the ocean, Clint says. Of course our duty stations were several hours inland so it would not have come up automatically.

She lived her life in the middle of the country, Connie continues rather sadly. Not like here in Vancouver where glimpses of water seem to be everywhere.

Yes, I have been fortunate in that respect.

Thursday December 31, 1964

Afternoon and Jo and I are back on the beach. We've had a brief swim and are enjoying the cool breeze. The clinic is closed this last afternoon of the year, though we did work this morning. Four of us boys completed construction of a brick-lined privy hole which we have been working on for three days.

Last Thursday, the day before Christmas, I had a temperature of 103 with hourly trips down the hall to the john. A doctor from the clinic came to the hotel and injected me with a shot of antibiotics that had me feeling well enough the next day to attend a Christmas party given by another doctor, this one in Itabuna. These parties are sumptuous affairs held in beautiful houses with platters of delicious Brazilian hors 'd oeuvres and lots of whiskey for those who want it. But now it's a week later and things are a little sad around here. Most of our contingent left a couple of hours ago for Salvador where next week they will be scattered out to their duty stations. Included were the girls Jo felt closest to. On Monday most of those remaining, including the last of the girls, will have left. Only Jo and I, along with Clint will still be here. We leave on Tuesday.

We have finally learned the name of our town. Nova Santana is located north and inland from here. So we will not be near the ocean, as I'm sure Jo has been secretly hoping. Other than that, we know nothing about it. We began our training in Wisconsin exactly four months ago today and by this time next week we will, I hope, finally be settled in Nova, as I understand it is called. Settled and ready to begin our twenty months of service. Clint will be our closest Peace Corps neighbor. He'll be stationed in a larger town a couple of hours beyond Nova.

This holiday weekend I hope to put together our first article for the local paper back home. I want to describe the experiences we have had in Ilhéus, including the excellent training, the natural beautify we have found here, the generosity of the people we have met. But I also want to touch upon the poverty we have witnessed, the extremes of economic disparity. Jo is worried that I might scare our readers if I come on too strong. Of course that would be counter productive, but I'm not writing just a travel log.

Have you tried to look up the newspaper articles?
No luck so far. The newspaper went out of business years ago. Aunt Connie said there were three or four articles. She is going to check at the library and ask around in the family to see if anyone saved them.

Saturday January 2, 1965
Sometimes it's hard. I'm beginning to fully realize just how much I have asked Jo to do, just how much I have asked her to sacrifice, just how great an adjustment she has to make.

In the first place she would not be here on her own. She would still be in school. Thinking back I can remember how excited I was after my second year, how much I wanted to continue. It's the same for her. While I completed a wonderful experience, hers was interrupted.

Secondly, I have asked her to leave her family. She is very close to her family and she needs their affection. It is up to me to supply this missing affection, attention and understanding. When I fail, it's bad, and I fail frequently.

Thirdly, I have torn her away from most of the activities that she finds comforting and meaningful. She misses those few weeks we had last summer when our marriage was relatively normal, when we had an apartment and jobs, and she could cook and sew and have a home to maintain and be proud of.

Removed from all that is familiar, she has been somewhat pushed into a foreign culture with a foreign language and provided no security. Take this move to Nova Santana. We leave Tuesday, when Willie gets back with the Jeep after taking three other Volunteers to their stations. We thought it was just going to be Willie, Clint, Jo and I, but now another Volunteer is going to be stuffed in with us as well.

At last report we have no place to live in Nova Santana, no house, no hotel, nothing. Also, we're not sure what we will be doing there. We heard they needed *visitadoras* but we also heard that they already have two, and given the size of the town that should be plenty.

We have little money. We were supposed to earn per diem rates while in Ilhéus but the money has not come through. We are already spending our salaries for January and February which are not much as I have written and with inflation are worth less every day. We know we'll have a lot of expenses when we get to Nova.

Now these things have a way of working themselves out. I try to convince my dear Jo that we are going through a difficult patch, that we will soon be settled in Nova with a home of our own, regular jobs and a chance to make a contribution. She wants to believe me. She wants it to work out just as I do. The thing is, deep down privately and personally, I know that I am in the very spot on this earth where I am supposed to be. I am ripe for this. On the other hand, I meant for these two years to be rewarding. I wanted them to forge a bond that would solidify our marriage. But if they are not rewarding, if the forces work to separate rather than join us, then it's our marriage and our health, both physical and mental, that are most important. And if I must choose between our duties here and our marriage, I must be prepared to choose our marriage. Just writing these words, though, scares me.

Connie stops reading but continues to stare at the page. I find that very moving, she says after a moment.

I understand.

My relationship with my parents was not always smooth.

I see.

So reading those words I saw them, Dad in particular, in a

new way. In my struggle as a child to grow up and become free, I developed defenses.

Yes, we all do, Clint says.

Then one day my parents were gone and I didn't need the defenses anymore. I wished that I had never needed them. Or at least that I had given them up more fully before it was too late.

Yes.

Then you come across something like this.

Yes, Clint says again.

Connie sighs. There are just a couple more about Ilhéus. Please, if you don't mind.

Monday January 4, 1965

The vacation is over. Monday, a new week, a new year and time to get to work. Today we are wrapping up our stay here in Ilhéus. We mailed off our first article for the newspaper at home along with letters we have written over the last few days. We took back the bottles which have deposits along with all the little receipts we could find so we could get our deposits back. We have clothes washing and Jo is ironing. We still have packing to do and we need to settle our bill with the hotel.

Tomorrow we leave for Nova Santana and our new life. Tomorrow will be one of the most important days in our P.C. experience. At long last our training is complete and we go to Nova Santana where we will set up a home and make a life for ourselves, and where, if we are successful, we will make a positive contribution.

Wednesday January 6, 1965

Tuesday we got up early. We finished packing, had a good breakfast and waited for Willie. He was supposed to arrive at 7:30 with the Jeep. At 7:30 there was no Willie. When he had still not arrived at 8:30, I went down the hall to Clint and Vern's room. They were still asleep. Apparently they had enjoyed a little celebration the night before. Anyway, they had not heard anything from Willie either. Back in our room, we sat on the bed surrounded by mounds of luggage, not only our own, but also several suitcases belonging to Volunteers who had flown to Salvador earlier. Suitcases that Willie was supposed to deliver to Salvador after he had dropped us off.

Around eleven Willie opened the door to our room and pronounced that most familiar of P.C. slogans: "Stay flexible." The night before, Willie had wrecked the Jeep.

We would have to take the bus, and the next bus would not leave until 4:30 this morning. I could feel Jo slump back on the bed. I knew what she was thinking, another meal in the same hotel restaurant, another day and another night in the same dreary room in the same dreary hotel. She was ready to cry.

Willie and I walked to the clinic where we made arrangements to store the other Volunteers' luggage. Then the group of us carried the suitcases over and stored them in a spare room.

The dreary night ended at 3:15 when the alarm went off. We had to be at the bus station with all of our stuff in time for the 4:30 departure. We found ourselves staggering along dark and lonely streets loaded down with our possessions. We caught the bus and it took us to Itabuna. A short way beyond Itabuna, we turned onto a gravel road. The morning was foggy and very gray in the predawn. We passed through hilly country, the tops of the hills disappearing in the clouds. The land was forested with *cacao* and other trees, some with moss hanging from them. With the fog, the dense and mossy forest, the scene felt appropriate for travelers leaving one world and entering another. Bouncing along on that road, holding Jo's hand, I suddenly felt quite alone. The P.C. had broken us away from the group slowly but firmly. Now there were just four of us, and soon there would be only Jo and I.

Eventually the sun came out and after three hours of bouncing and weaving we finally pulled into Nova Santana. We have arrived in our new home.

Chapter Seven

NOVA SANTANA

The restaurant where Connie Scheel and Clint Estergard have lunch is located across the lobby from the conference room. It's a spacious interior with a high ceiling and has a vaguely Asian feel with statues of elephants and a Buddha or two peering out from the plant life. On two sides of the room a raised level is separated from the main floor by a bannister. A wall of windows looks out on the street corner.

The management had explained to Connie that she could leave her things in the conference room during lunch. The doors would be locked and the room secure. But Connie decides to take the computer, the recorder and her father's journal with her, stowing them in a large black leather shoulder bag that she steadies on her hip. They choose a table on the main level and Connie places the bag on the floor between her feet.

The restaurant has a reputation for seafood and Clint orders a dozen grilled oysters served on the half shell topped with a smear of wasabi. Connie chooses a salad. He drinks a glass of Sauvignon blanc. She has a diet soda.

My ex-husband likes oysters, Connie says. He always wanted me to eat them but I never could. Too slimy for my taste.

I find oysters comforting, Clint says.

Comforting?

According to the fossil record they've been around for 300 million years, virtually unchanged so far as we know. Very successful, very stable. Also delicious. That's a comfort, isn't it?

Do you really believe the world is that old?

The world? Older, much older. Around four and a half billion years, is the accepted age. Of course life as we think of it came later.

How do you know that?

What? That life came later?

No, the age of the earth.

Rocks. Radio-metric dating. We've found rocks of that age here on earth and it's consistent with what we know from lunar samples and meteors. So, in that sense the oyster is a relative newcomer, though not when compared to us.

She doesn't respond, preferring to focus on cutting the asparagus stalks that lie across her salad. Yes, one of those, he thinks, and the daughter of a teacher no less.

I remember the day Kyle and Jolene arrived in Nova Santana.

Connie holds up her hand, stopping him. Her choice of food might be timid, he tells himself, but she can be assertive when needed. She reaches into the leather bag, removes the recorder and sets it on the table. I don't need the computer, she says. There's a memory card.

Clint shakes his head. I shouldn't have brought it up. Let's wait until we finish the meal. Tell me something about yourself.

You don't want to hear about me. I'm completely uninteresting.

I'm sure you're wrong about that. Please. Did you go to school?

Two years at a J.C.

I see.

I was thinking of becoming a nurse. Then one day driving home I came upon an accident. An old man tried to drive his car across a train track at absolutely the wrong time. I was one of the first people there. That ended my nursing career. Then a semester at the U. of I.

Indiana?

Illinois. Dad's alma mater but it didn't work for me. I took some accounting classes, which was about as far from blood as

I could get. I'm pretty good with numbers actually, but at the time I wasn't ready for it. Too much fun being away from home for the first time. I hung around campus for a while. Got into some stuff I should have stayed away from. Met a guy who had a motorcycle and ended up in Davenport, Iowa selling soft ice cream in a mall. Another thing I need to stay away from is ice cream. A third thing is that. She points to his wine glass.

I see.

Had enough? she wants to know.

Not at all. I look at you now and want to know how you got from there to here.

Well, it wasn't by motorcycle. That guy was long gone. Four or five years in there are best forgotten. You know, ups and downs, fresh starts and crashes to the floor. But even at that time I could stagger along in the franchise game. Not ice cream, not bartending, though I tried that as well. Clothing. Like I said, no home-mades for me. Retail clothing at a chain store in a mall, that I knew. The bar is pretty low in those places. Show up every day more or less on time. Be straight enough the customers don't know you're stoned. Don't steal too much. That's about it. Before you know it, you're in charge. Then life get's really complicated.

Complicated?

You bet. The pay's still miserable, the hours are worse and now you have to supervise. You have to hire and fire people who care even less about the place than you do. People whose grip on reality is as precarious or more precarious than your own.

And your parents? How were you getting along with them at this time?

Thanksgiving and Christmas, Connie says. Once or twice during the summer. Now and then a phone call. We talked about the weather. About people we knew. I used to imagine sighs of relief coming out of their house when I drove away.

It's complicated, Clint says, thinking of his own sons.

Eventually I met a woman named Francine Lauffer. Francine

was a single woman raising a child who had been through a lot of what I was going through. But Francine had come out the other side. She was a pastor at a small church in Rock Island, Illinois, across the river from Davenport. And on Sunday mornings her church was filled with people just like me. I had lost my Catholic faith. But Francine took me in. She took my hand and she led me to Jesus.

I see.

Wasn't long after that I met Gilbert. He was pitching in the Midwest League and headed for the majors, or so he thought. Didn't work out that way. And we didn't work out either, after a while. He's a policeman now, a good man and a good father to the boys.

Is that it? Are you still selling clothing? You dress very nicely by the way.

Thank you. No, not clothing and not retail. We're just at the beginning, I'm afraid, and you've already finished most of your oysters.

You've got a point, Clint says. I'll sip my wine and give you time to eat your salad.

Back in the conference room, Connie sets up her apparatus and arranges her things and asks him to tell her about Nova Santana.

Clint removes the notes from his jacket and sets them on the table.

Nova Santana. It was mid-morning when we arrived. I had slept for most of the ride from Itabuna so I don't remember much about the country your dad described. The bus stop in Nova, at that time anyway, was located in front of the *farmacia* just off the plaza. Nova had one main plaza and this pharmacy was about half a block away. It was already hot when we got there. The windows of the bus were open, flies buzzing in and out. Some of my strongest memories of Bahia are the smells. The air on that morning probably smelled of roasting coffee, wood smoke, donkey and mule manure, the sweat of the crowded unwashed passengers who were making their way down the narrow aisle toward the door. A large percentage of the people in Bahia are of African descent so what you saw were dark glistening bodies.

Like my children.

Yes.

My parents never objected to my marrying Gilbert. I want you to know that.

Good.

It wasn't because of race we broke up either.

All right.

I just felt I needed to tell you that.

Okay.

Are most Brazilians of African descent?

Oh no. Brazil is a racially mixed society and there has been a lot of inter-breeding among the races and nationalities. Portuguese, of course, the native peoples, Blacks. The 19th century Emperor, Dom Pedro II, encouraged German immigration and in the south you see blond blue-eyed people whose ancestors came from northern Europe a century or more ago. Even some Asians, Japanese in particular. But Bahia....

I know where the State of Bahia is located, Connie says interrupting him. Along the coast, north of Rio, though south of the Amazon. I ran to an atlas after I found the journal. I couldn't have told you anything before. Anyway, you were speaking about that day in Nova Santana.

Actually, about the racial mix of Bahians, I believe. If it's of interest to you. It is significant in a way, given what happened.

What happened?

To your parents.

Then yes, please.

Well, at least traditionally, Bahia had more people of African descent then the other areas of Brazil. They are descendants of slaves, brought first by the Dutch to work the sugar cane fields. And they arrived in numbers large enough that they have retained elements of their African roots. Food, dance, religion, that kind of thing. The food of Bahia, for example, which is often considered the most interesting of Brazilian foods, has significant African influence.

Okay, Connie says. So, you arrived in this town and I'm sure Dad and Mom were happy to get there.

Kyle, at least, was very happy. I suppose Jolene was as well. But I remember Kyle. 'Just look at the people,' he said to Vern and me. He was referring to the people getting off the bus and those walking along the crowded sidewalk outside the window. 'Here are the people of the earth. The everyday people who live and work and raise their young and every day die on this earth. These are the people we have come for, the real people.'

You've mentioned those words before. Did he really use those words?

Most definitely. Vern would joke about it. 'Does that mean we're not,' he would say to me. Meaning 'not real.'

I get it, Connie says.

Vern had a hard time with Kyle, as I said. On the other hand, I had become quite fond of him and Jolene during our month in Ilhéus. Jolene had given me a chance to talk my way through the Smookie thing without judgment or pity. And I was often with Kyle during the day. He was very observant and inquiring and eager to do his share. He pushed himself in physical work, digging in the sun, lugging bricks up a hill. He was determined. I had the feeling he was not naturally gregarious but he forced himself to engage people, to ask questions and to speak. 'What was that word?' he was asking all the time. 'What did he mean by that?' He had a quote from somewhere he liked to use. Small minds discuss people, he would say, average minds discuss events, but great minds discuss ideas.

Thomas Jefferson, I believe. I heard him say it many times.

Jefferson was it? Anyway, he tried to keep our discussions at a higher plane. We all looked up to him. We thought he would to do wonderful things in Brazil. Vern's main complaint was that Kyle lacked a sense of humor, which you and I have also noted. 'Watch him,' Vern told me once. 'He might laugh at a joke, but soon as the laughter dies down, he'll steer the conversation back to something serious.' This turned out to be an accurate observation. In my presence Kyle rarely showed any sign of humor on his own, but I never saw that as a defect. He was serious, committed. As he reported in the journal, he was concerned about the deficiency of his language skills and his ignorance of the inner workings of the culture. These were deficits we all shared, but he felt them more intensely. Vern also complained that Kyle never drank, or would at most nurse a single beer or glass of wine. Vern was suspicious of anyone who didn't drink.

That's silly. No, Dad never did drink. Maybe a few swallows of champagne at a wedding or something. But it's bizarre that your friend should consider this a character flaw. Surely he was aware of the lives ruined by alcohol.

Her intensity makes Clint smile. Actually Vern had considerable personal experience with the deleterious effects of alcohol. I've heard him tease nurses by bragging that he knew more about their profession than they did since he had personally nursed so many hangovers.

Connie frowns, shaking her head. I don't think I would have liked your friend Vern. I'm sorry he ended up with Smookie.

You might have liked him. He was an interesting person to be around. Stunningly handsome, well-proportioned with wavy sandy hair, low flat eyebrows, a strong jaw, deep blue eyes. Its hard to overestimate the power of physical beauty. It trumps a lot of other qualities. Beyond that he was unflappable, full of good stories, never morose.

You haven't persuaded me, Connie says. What did Mom think of him?

The question makes Clint pause. He looks away for a moment, his right hand reaching up to scratch his head. That's an interesting question and I'm drawing a blank. They weren't together often so far as I know. In Ilhéus she had Kyle and she was close to Polly Lehman, the other married woman Volunteer. After that, except for a conference and one or two other occasions, I doubt they ever saw each other.

So, if Mom wasn't swept up by his supposedly endless charms, I doubt I'd have been. Connie smiles broadly, thinking she has scored an important point.

You may be right. I can tell you though what Vern said about Jolene.

Really?

Vern saw Jolene as one of those unapproachable women who men gaze at longingly from afar. She's the kind, he would say, who when they pass your table in a bar late at night they make you realize just how lonely you really are.

Hah! Connie says. I like that. She's beaming. And it figures, doesn't it, that he would use a bar analogy?

Yes, I suppose so. It came up because I was defending Kyle one day by saying he was a good husband, kind and solicitous toward his wife. Vern didn't think of that as a great accomplishment given what a catch your mother was.

Connie hops out of her chair and begins to pace beside the table. What's with this guy anyway? He pounds on what he thinks are Dad's bad qualities and dismisses what he admits are his good ones.

I may be over simplifying, Clint says, grinning. It was a long time ago. But you requested, I believe, a picture of your parents at this stage in their lives, and that's what I'm trying to give you, as best I can. You've come to a scientist for a report. So, for better or worse, you're going to get an objective one.

I'm sorry, she says, stopping. You're right.

Vern had a theory about Kyle and I think it's important that you hear it. You might not agree with it, but you need to know it. All right.

Vern saw those two qualities I described, that is Kyle's strict sobriety and his lack of a sense of humor, as intertwined. He thought Kyle didn't drink because he was afraid to.

That's ridiculous, Connie says, starting to walk again.

Simplistic, perhaps, but not ridiculous. Remember, I was on Kyle's side. I was defending him. And while I didn't fully accept Vern's characterization, I did see his point. Kyle was very serious, very controlled. It was not unreasonable to assume that he was afraid of what might happen if he let himself go.

I think this Vern guy was rationalizing. He's a boozer so he makes out that anyone who doesn't get drunk has some kind of problem. Believe me, I know the type. I've met a few of them myself.

Connie realizes she is waving her arms in the air as she walks and she deliberately lowers them to her sides.

I just wanted you to hear it, Clint says slowly.

I understand. Connie returns to her chair and sits down.

Anyway, Nova Santana. Our layover could not have lasted more than twenty minutes. When the bus pulled out with Vern, Willie and me on board your parents were left to their own devices. It was a difficult time for them. Having heard what Kyle wrote concerning the struggle Jolene was having, I am more aware now than I was then of how difficult those first few days in Nova were.

What happened?

It's what didn't happen that's most significant. Willie, the veteran Volunteer who had scouted out the sites where we would be stationed, and the guy who was taking us there...

Yes.

I don't want to underestimate the challenge Willie was facing. You go into a town, you meet a few notables, ask a few questions. You might spend a day, two at most, and then you have to decide if this is a good place to station a Volunteer, or in your parents' case, a pair of Volunteers. Having said that, Willie was a bit of a cowboy, macho, abrupt. He bragged that he had served in the Amazon, somewhere upriver from Belem. When he described his tour he sounded more like a 19th century explorer than a Peace Corps Volunteer. He claimed, for example, to have shot a jaguar. He said he had the skin in his luggage though I never saw it. And as your dad wrote, he had just wrecked the Jeep.

Yes, I remember.

Which is why we were on the bus. Had we been in the Jeep we might have stayed and done a better job of getting your parents situated. Anyway, Willie had made arrangements for Kyle and Jolene to work at a community health clinic in Nova And the doctor, the head of the clinic, was supposed to have met your parents at the bus stop. Only he wasn't there.

Wait a minute, Connie says, raising her hand.

Pardon?

You've talked about how bad communication was in Brazil at that time, right?

Yes.

And Dad wrote in the journal about how the three of you were going to be taken to your towns on Tuesday by this cowboy guy...

Willie...

...yes, in a Jeep.

Yes.

...and because Willie wrecked the...

Yes.

...you had to wait another day and go by bus.

Correct.

So, how would the doctor know you were coming on Wednesday by bus and not on Tuesday by Jeep?

Clint leans back in his chair. His eyes brighten and a smile crosses his face.

Very good, he says, after a moment. That's very good.

Connie blushes. Well, I....

No, really. That's an excellent observation. You're obviously paying close attention.

Thank you, I....

The answer is a ham, Clint says chuckling.

A what?

A doctor at the clinic in Ilhéus where we stored the luggage was a short-wave radio buff. He had contacts in Nova Santana and in Jacarandá, the town where I was stationed.

I see.

Anyway, no one was there to meet them. I don't know what happened. I don't know if Willie misunderstood, or if the message didn't get through or the doctor just didn't bother to show up. The day we arrived was a holiday, Three Kings Day, the day the three kings supposedly arrived at the manger with their incense, frankincense and myrrh. Everyone, by that I mean everyone with money, the doctors, the mayor, the professional people, were out on their *fazendas* enjoying the holiday.

Fazendas? Dad uses that word too.

Farms, ranches. This part of Bahia from Ilhéus inland to Nova Santana and on to Jacarandá, was *cacao* country.

Chocolate? She looks suddenly lascivious.

Yes, Connie, the substance that chocolate is made from. *Cacao* and cattle, those were the agricultural products in the area. Later, decades after your parents and I left, all that changed. A fungus came through that wiped out the *cacao* trees. But that was later. At the time we were there, *cacao* was king.

I see.

Anyway, everybody who was anybody had his ranch outside of town. Willie tried to get the bus driver to stay longer but he refused. While Vern and I guarded the luggage, Willie ran Kyle and Jolene down the street to the only decent hotel in town. The hotel had no rooms available, so they ended up in a seedy place across the street from the bus stop. They were standing on the sidewalk beside their piles of luggage when we left.

Clint pauses for a moment, visualizing the scene. Kyle described the sensation we caused when we arrived in Ilhéus, so you can imagine how out of place they looked in this much smaller town. A cluster of young boys stood behind them jostling each other, grinning and staring at the two Americans as if they had just dropped out of a space ship.

And you left them there, the three of you.

We did. They waved and smiled bravely. You know, the 'can do' thing, but they looked forlorn, I have to tell you. It would be several weeks before I saw them again.

So you and Vern went on to your duty stations?

That's right, the next major stop was Jacarandá, about two hours down the road. Vern was in Conquista another few hours past that and back toward the south.

It makes me sad, Connie says, to imagine them there, so young and vulnerable.

No, pity would be a mistake. This was their great adventure, perhaps the greatest adventure of their lives. And they had finally arrived at their station after all the training and preparation. No, don't pity them. This is what they had come to do. They had completed their training, and as your father said, he was ripe for it. Of that I have no doubt. There is one other thing I should tell you, though. The doctor who, at least according to Willie, was supposed to have met them?

Yes?

His name was Nascimento. Doctor Nascimento.

That name is in the journal.

He was the man in charge of the clinic where Kyle and Jolene were supposed to work. Kyle grew to hate that man.

No, Connie says, shaking her head. That's wrong about Dad. Not hate. I've known him all my life and I have never known him to hate anyone or anything. It was one of the themes of his life:

the self-destructiveness of hate. He would point to the Middle East and Northern Ireland and talk about the futility of revenge and the need for forgiveness. The hater, he would say, might or might not damage the person he hates, but he always damages himself. No, I'm sorry, I can't accept that Dad hated this man.

Clint ponders her words for a long time before he begins to speak. I'm sure what you say is true, Connie. But I don't think hate is too strong a word in this instance. Maybe it was in Bahia that Kyle Henderson learned the lessons that later he would teach to you.

At that moment a sound emerges from Connie's computer. It's the third time this has happened. Clint wants to know what it is.

I've just gotten an email, Connie says. This room is live. See. She clicks the mouse and turns the laptop so he can also see the screen where a message has appeared:

Mom. Dad says Andre can go to football camp but I have to go to soccer camp. Thats not fare! Soccer sucks! Tell Dad I can go to football camp. Marcus

Clint chuckles. You better answer that one immediately. It sounds urgent.

Connie smiles but shakes her head. No, that one has to be answered carefully. That one I'll answer later. She clicks again and another message appears:

You sure you want me to check out that Deerfield property? Those are residential units.

I need to respond to this one. Do you mind?

Of course not.

I know they are residential units, Mel. We need at least three properties to choose from, and we need to get on it. Mr. Hernandez has been very patient. The price is in the right range, the location is good for us. Yes, I want you to gather all relevant information. Have it ready when I get back.

Connie apologizes. She's frowning. Please, tell me more about Dr. Nascimento.

You'll come to know the doctor, Clint says. But first I want to describe my situation in Jacarandá. You may have to indulge me a bit here because this tangent is about me, not your parents, at least not directly. It's relevant because the welcome I received in Jacarandá differed markedly from what your parents experienced in Nova. Had our stations been reversed things might have turned out differently for them, and for me. Also Jacarandá became an important place for Jolene.

Not Dad?

There is a pause. After which, Clint says, I chose those words carefully, Connie.

All right. She looks away momentarily. The bracelets on her left wrist tinkle as she slides her bottom further back in the chair. Her mind is on Mel. He's ten years her senior and was her dad's assistant for two decades. She has never spoken to him that way before. Maybe she should have kept that email for later as well. The exchange with Mel has left her feeling both apprehensive and exhilarated.

Clint thinks it's about him. She wants to control the agenda and he won't let her. Well, he's not a sales clerk in a mall. He's accustomed to being in charge as well. And in this instance he actually is. They have finally reached a place in the narrative that he remembers vividly. The story may be about her parents, but she'll just have to get used to the fact that it is his story as well.

The city of Jacarandá, he tells her, is located on the Rio de Contas, the same river that flows past Nova Santana. Back in the mid-sixties at least, it was three or four times as large as Nova Santana. Jacarandá boasted of a commercial air strip and a two-story hospital. The hospital became my home for twenty months. I had a room on the first floor and I ate in the hospital dining room.

The building was old and square with a tiled roof and a courtyard in the center. Its color was a faded brownish yellow, a color that struck me, the first time I saw it, as a failure of color. Its walls were thick, its windows unprotected with either glass or screening, though the window in my room since it was on the first floor had heavy metal grating and could be shuttered. You could take an elevator between floors. I remember that old elevator fondly. It was a large open cage that shuddered and squeaked as it moved. Only the floor was solid and so as you rose or descended you saw the cables and the flat charcoal inner workings of the building. I used to imagine that in exchange for risking a ride in the old contraption you were given a view of something forbidden.

The hospital had its own life, its own sense of community. The emergency room possessed an erratic pulse of boredom punctuated with panic—vehicle accidents, stab and gunshot wounds, machete gashes, bones fractured and jutting through the skin, dehydrated infants with distended bellies and loose skin. We had a surgery, a ward filled with mothers and the newly born, another for the aged and infirm, a third for the insane, a fourth for the acutely ill, an X-ray unit...let's see, an outpatient clinic, an administrative wing that included a public health department to which I was marginally attached. Crosses hung on walls, Madonnas looked out from little alcoves. People came to work and left to go home. Others entered to die or to heal, but I alone lived there. On sleepless nights when I walked through the floors it was as though I were pacing along my own arteries.

It sounds as though you loved it, Connie says, consciously trying to focus her attention back on Clint.

It was a special time for me all right. In large part because of Oscar. The director of the hospital was a man named Oscar. He was a medical doctor and a generous, kind man. His Portuguese was lyrical and clean and eminently understandable. He had spent a year in London many years before and he spoke decent English but except in emergencies he never wasted it on me. He smoked three packs of cigarettes a day and coughed incessantly. He was married to a beautiful woman and the father of three children. As director he had little time for an active medical practice though he did look after the health concerns of his family and close friends, including myself and the three women who resided at his favorite brothel. Oscar was and remains, though he has now been dead for years, one of the most important persons in my life. His curiosity, his careful observation, his passion for truth, strengthened my desire to become a scientist.

Did this man meet you at the bus?

No, he sent two young men to meet me. Two brothers, Eduardo and Walter. It was still the same day, remember, Three Kings Day, and Oscar was out at his *fazenda*.

The Eduardo? Connie asks. The one you wrote about in the letter?

Yes, it was that Eduardo, and here I can introduce him to you. He and Walter were both clean shaven, their black hair slicked back, their eyes bright, their smiles wide and welcoming. In other respects they differed dramatically. Walter was older by a couple of years. He was chunky, strong, practical. An agronomist, married and the father of two young children. Eduardo was thin and flamboyant. He liked to wear necklaces and expensive pastel shirts and slacks. He had studied engineering, but only a few months before I arrived, Eduardo had stunned his family by announcing that he was opening a restaurant.

Eduardo's.

Restaurante Eduardo was the official name. The name was in the letter, I take it.

You wrote that it had been closed and you thought it would never open again.

I was right about that, I'm sorry to say. Clint takes a moment to look through his notes. I want now to introduce you to Don Alfonso and Dona Neyde. Eduardo and Walter were their sons. They also had three daughters, one of whom, Flora, got married while I was there. Dona Neyde possessed hips so enormous that to pass through doorways she swung them to the side and entered at an angle the way you would to deliver a couch.

Connie giggles.

I'm not exaggerating. She was reputed to be the finest cook in Jacarandá, which was probably true with the exception of her son, Eduardo. Don Alfonso was known to be the richest man. He was a lawyer by training but his wealth came from a huge *fazenda*. Three hundred people lived on that ranch. Don Alfonso had been elected or appointed to a number of state and national offices over the years.

Were they of African descent, this family?

No. Like most of the well-to-do, Eduardo's family was Caucasian. The father, Don Alfonso, was proud to have descended from early Portugese settlers. It may be that Dona Neyde had some Arabian in her past. My memory is faulty on the details. She had a fiery personality, I remember that.

And those huge hips, Connie says.

Indeed. So, I arrived and Walter and Eduardo were at the station to pick me up. Vern and Willie went on to Conquista. We dropped my luggage at the hospital and Eduardo and Walter invited me to their parents' town house for dinner. I had no idea, of course, who these people were, or what to expect. The dining room was located at the front of the house and dominated by a long table. Fourteen people could sit at that table and on that day nearly every chair was taken. Eduardo and Walter approached their father, Don Alfonso, who, of course, sat at the head of the table. They each took his hand and kissed it. Then they turned and introduced me.

Clint chuckles. He's enjoying himself. He feels the way he sometimes feels in the middle of a good lecture when he knows he has everyone's attention and his pacing is right and he doesn't care if the bell ever rings. He's going to miss those moments, and he knows it.

I didn't know what to do, Connie. Was I supposed to kiss this old boy's hand or what?

So, did you? she asks, grinning.

I got saved at the last minute. Or to be more precise, I jumped out of the pot and landed in the fire. Don Alfonso said in harsh English, 'Oh, American, we shake.' He took my hand and damn near crushed it. Then he pointed me to a chair and ordered the boys to bring me whiskey. Walter took a water glass and poured in some Scotch. 'More,' his father commanded in Portuguese. 'He's an American. Americans drink whiskey.'

I started stammering, waving my hands to make him stop. The Peace Corps had given me no training for moments like this. But it made no difference. Whatever resistence I could muster would have been interpreted as a fumbling attempt to be polite.

So you got some whiskey.

A glass full. Scotch. No water, no ice, just Scotch. Then Dona Neyde started bringing out food. Serving tray after serving tray of food. She hovered like a giant machine over the huge table and her many guests. If she thought I took too small a helping, she would grab the spoon and shovel more onto my plate. 'Eat more,' she commanded. '*Magro*,' she kept saying. '*Magro*.' Meaning that I was skinny. What I am trying to illustrate is the contrast between my welcome and that of your parents.

I understand.

They could not have been more different. From the day I arrived, I had a place to stay and I was on my way to becoming part of a family. At the same time, I was scrambling on every front. The conversation, for example, was lively. Sometimes it was one conversation, other times it broke into fragments. I could understand virtually none of it. It went by too fast. It was too rich in idioms, in local history and gossip. Only when someone slowly and clearly addressed a question or comment directly to me, only then did the blur of voices and laughter come into a focus that I could more or less comprehend.

The whiskey was a factor, I suppose.

Perhaps, Clint admits, Vern's theory to the contrary. At the center of everything was Don Alfonso, the family patriarch. Alfonso was probably in his late fifties at that time. He was partially bald but what hair remained had some wave in it and retained much of its color. He was a short man and thin, but his arms were muscled and strong. He was a horseman, an outdoors man. I always felt there was something vaguely reptilian about Alfonso. I don't mean to suggest a sly or evasive nature. The opposite was true, he was direct and firm. The impression had to do with the thick, outdoor quality of his skin and the dark penetrating stare with which he studied you through his tinted glasses. His steady gaze gave the impression he was boring in on you, though, in fact, he heard nothing you said.

Was he deaf?

Not at all. It was a listening, not a hearing problem. An example. Somewhere in the course of the evening Don Alfonso announced that Americans wore red when mourning.

Red?

I, of course, protested, but he overruled me. He knew for a fact it was true. He had seen a photograph of a famous American actress who had arrived in Rio a few days after her husband's death wearing a red dress. End of discussion. And that was typical of Don Alfonso. No one ever contradicted or overruled him.

Clint stops talking. He picks an apple from the basket on the table, polishes it on his slacks and takes a bite. There's a legend here in Canada, Connie, that in the State of Washington apples are divided into two categories. The best ones are shipped up here to us while the inferior ones are distributed to you in the States. It's unlikely to be true, of course. But it does show something about how we Canadians think of our neighbor to the south. Do you know that we live longer, are healthier and wealthier, primarily because we are burdened by much less debt? We are sexier, we travel more, work less, spend more time with our families. I've read all this in the popular press. We are somewhat obsessed by our neighbor to the south, actually. We are very proud of any Canadian who succeeds in the States, who wins a Grammy, for example, or is nominated for an Oscar. Your hockey teams are filled with our boys, as we are forever reminding ourselves. I guess it's inevitable, given the difference in size. Yes, we're a big country physically, but in terms of population, about as many people live in California as all of Canada. Your economy belches and we get the gas.

I keep thinking of my parents, standing back at the bus stop, Connie says, returning Clint to the subject at hand.

He smiles, chewing the apple. Forgive my little diversion. If you've seen the contrast between my situation and that of your parents, then I have achieved my purpose.

Can we get back to them?

Of course. But I did want to introduce you to Jacarandá, to my life there, and to Eduardo and his family. They will all figure in the story as we go along.

Chapter Nine
ALONE

Connie Scheel recognizes that something inside her, something clenched, has begun to ease. I would like to talk about the journal for a moment, she says. Would you mind?

He doesn't mind. It's the narrative he wants to control, the timed release of information, the shape of the story. And he's interested in the journal. He has imagined its discovery. The very idea of an attic appeals to him. In his grandparents' house back in Ohio you reached the attic by a set of stairs covered with a rubber, reddish-brown runner. The attic was a room in which an adult could stand erect beneath its center beam. Maybe in the 19th century when families were larger, children slept there. During his own youth, in the forties and fifties, the door at the top was always closed, but the inside was magical to a boy. The room was remarkably hotter or colder than the rest of the house with rough-cut floorboards, and suspended particles of dust seen in the yellow light entering from a small window. The air long undisturbed had become saturated with smells absorbed from the crates and boxes and racks of old clothing. His grandparents' attic, like the particles of dust, existed in timeless suspension, isolated from the sounds and events beyond the window and below the floor. A place secret and vaguely forbidden for a child. That was his idea of an attic. So when he pictured Connie Scheel first looking into the journal, it was not in Kyle and Jolene Henderson's attic, but in the attic of his grandparents. He thought of her crouching down, her knees resting on the curl of an old rug, the heals of her shoes sinking into her substantial hips. That rogue strand of curling black hair repeating its little ritual of falling down on her forehead and being absently swept back and away. The journal resting open on the leather pouch, her feet and ankles aching. Imagining Connie kneeling in his grandparents' attic makes her, in Clint's mind, a sort of contemporary.

Much of what Dad wrote was day-to-day stuff, Connie says. Purchases they made, how much they paid, lists of things to do. But there's a long section, the first substantial entry he wrote after they got to Nova Santana that was written in early March of that year.

That would be 1965.

Right. Earlier that day, the day he wrote the entry, you had driven over to visit them.

Driven? Clint says. Something's amiss. I didn't have a car in Brazil.

Well, according to Dad you delivered some of their things. It was right after Carnival. Perhaps reading it will jog your memory.

Fine, let's give it a go.

Would you be willing to do the reading? Connie asks.

The suggestion amuses him. Now, why's that? he asks. You spoiled me by reading the earlier part. I hadn't been read to in some time. I rather enjoyed it.

Connie has been feeling somewhat bullied by Clint's presence and she needs to have him do something she wants him to do.

I found parts of this entry difficult. So, if you don't mind. She stands up holding the notebook, finds the right page and sets it on the table before him. Then rather than sitting down, she begins to pace back and forth beside the long table.

Well, all right. It's dated Thursday night, March 4,1965. That would be almost two months after we left them off at the bus station in Nova.

Okay, she says.

For the first time since our marriage last July, I have a night alone. Jo got a ride to Jacarandá to buy some things for the house...

She rode with you. He's quite clear about that. You'll see. All right.

Jo got a ride to Jacarandá to buy some things for the house, some towels and linens, a couple of pillows, the kinds of things you take for granted until you find yourself in possession of an empty house. And all those wedding gifts, useless to us now, stored back home in our parents' houses! We received no less than six blankets as gifts and I had to take some good natured ribbing at the reception about how everyone must be assuming I would be unable to keep Jo warm.

No problem about that here, though even in Nova you want a covering most nights. That's in addition to the mosquito netting which of itself holds in some of the body's heat. So far we have been using my trench coat as a blanket. A name with grim associations, when you think about it. It must have come from the trenches of World War One. Many's the man, I suppose, who lay through cold and bitter nights wrapped in such a coat in that miserable outpost of hell. Those soldiers must have imagined they were witnessing the worst that man could devise, and then three decades later came the Holocaust, Stalingrad, the bombings of Dresden, Hiroshima and Nagasaki. And now we've had Kennedy and Khrushchev standing eye to eye, each threatening to blow the whole world to smithereens rather than back down. What can you do in the face of that but start at the beginning to remake the world from the inside out. As Dorothy Day said, "The greatest challenge of the day is: how to bring about a revolution of the heart, a revolution which has to start with each one of us."

I found those words touching, Connie said, stopping him. Dad never wavered in his affection and loyalty for Dorothy Day and the Catholic Workers movement. He gave them a lot of money over the years.

So, he remained with the church?

Oh yes, to the end. Faithful to it as an institution and also to its fringes, at least those he believed in.

Should I continue?

Yes, please.

I want to assess where we are, what we have done so far and where we need to go from here, so we can make as strong an impact on this community as possible.

At long last we have our own house. I'm at the table in the kitchen/dining room, sitting beneath a bare hanging bulb that is one of three lights we have. Other than the hotplate and water filter, this table and its four chairs are the only pieces of furniture we have bought so far. It's a handsome table, though I'm not too sure of its long-term stability. More style than strength I fear. The table and chairs were made by a local man from wood grown near here. The surface is blond, while the trim and the legs are dark brown. The same pattern is repeated in the chairs. The man's shop is not far from our house on the road just below the *favela*. He and his workmen probably live in houses near our own. I feel good about supporting him.

So, Mom and Dad were living in a slum? Connie asks The journal is somewhat confusing on this point.

Their house was pleasant and beautifully situated on a hill, but it was surrounded by poorer homes and you had to pass through a poor area to get to it. I can describe that for you if you'd like. There was some tension between your parents about the house.

Let's read the entry first, if you don't mind. Then you can add your impressions.

Fair enough, he says.

Other things in the house we've made ourselves. The mayor showed us where to buy some wood. His assistant loaned us a handsaw and a hammer. (I went to what passes as a hardware store here in Nova to get some nails. The word for nail is *prego* but I asked for *pragos* which apparently is the name of an insect that attacks the *cacau* plants. The store owner thought my mistake was very funny. He said he had millions of *pragos* he could give me for nothing.)

See, Connie says, stopping him. He did have a sense of humor.
Yes, Clint agrees, a nascent one at least.

With these tools we built a bookcase-like structure we're using to store dishes and cooking utensils, and a simple frame for our bed. We bought two single grass-filled mattresses and set them side by side for a double bed. Jo is happy, I think, to finally have an opportunity to make this house into our home.

It's a beautiful night. There's no moon and very dark. I have doors and windows open. I can smell the fresh evening and hear the sounds of the neighborhood: some distant music, kids playing under the one streetlight, an occasional donkey sounding off. The night is cool with a strong breeze. Surprisingly, the evenings are often cooler than summer evenings in Illinois. Whenever possible we open the doors and windows in the late afternoon and shut them during the hot part of the day. I enjoy the flow of air. Unfortunately hundreds of flies and other insects also find their way in. We kill them as best we can but the supply is endless. In the late afternoon I like to sit in the doorway at the front of the house and look out at the view while I study my language book. The property is fenced in part but not enough to keep out the occasional chicken or the dozen or so turkeys that wander through making soft clucking noises as they pass among the trees.

Lately some of the neighborhood children have begun to enter through the gate and approach the house. They stand in shy little clusters, eyes gleaming. The brave ones ask for coconuts and oranges off the trees. It's like trick or treat without the masks or the implicit threat. I try to get them to talk to me. That is the price I want for the fruit, but they're reluctant to speak beyond their well-rehearsed request. They seem more comfortable with Jo than me. She's lighter, gayer than I. I must seem old and stern and very foreign to them in spite of my efforts. I will struggle to change their perception. I will know I have succeeded when they can giggle and smile with me in the same way they sometimes do with her. I still have a long way to go.

We have now been in Brazil almost three months and we have accomplished very little of benefit to the Brazilian people. Our English classes continue but the young men and women students hold middle class positions, most with the local branch of the Banco do Brasil. That to my mind has nothing much to do with our real mission here. Last Thursday and Friday we assisted in a vaccination campaign. We vaccinated for small pox and gave Sabin for polio. Jolene gave the Sabin, which is given orally. A couple of other women administered the vaccinations. All I found to do was hold the occasional little one who was not appreciating what was happening to him. It wasn't much of a contribution. Others could have done it. At least we know that four hundred or so of these kids won't get polio or small pox. But that's like scratching two items off a list of hundreds that deny them a full and happy life. Except for the vaccination program, our contribution at the clinic continues to be useless. We are not touching the core of the problem. No one else seems to notice the problem even exists.

We are often sick. Not as sick as in Ilhéus, but not well either. Vague gastrointestinal cramps and pains, low energy. Jo had a serious sore throat for several days and did little more than sleep. We're both dispirited, Jo, more than I. She is often quiet and I have to encourage her to talk.

I had hoped that once we got out of the hotel and into a house everything would change. I hadn't figured on the amount of cumbersome labor it takes to establish a home or get anything done here. The house was truly empty. I do feel good about building our own furniture. I think it sets a good example. There is an unfortunate tradition in this country that educated people, people from the upper classes, don't do manual labor, which is thought to be below them. I mean to counter that tradition. As foreigners we have a certain status above what our age and resources would deserve were we natives. By hauling wood and carrying our supplies through the neighborhood, by sawing and pounding out our simple furnishings, I hope to demonstrate that manual labor is noble and good.

Of course, we walk wherever we go since we have no car or mule, the mule or donkey being the rich poor man's car in this town. I say rich poor man because many families are too poor to have a mule or donkey. So, like the lower classes we walk. We have purchased a large woven basket to carry our purchases home from the market. A neighbor boy, he's probably ten or so, runs a sort of trucking service with the family donkey. The mother suggested to Jo that he could haul supplies for us. We were torn about it. Jo liked the idea because the money would help the family. They have about seven children and except for the donkey and a flock of chickens are very poor. But I thought it more important to demonstrate the value of labor and personal sacrifice so I have continued to carry the basket and other supplies myself.

When the women downtown shop at the market, they have a maid walking behind them carrying the basket. The dona selects the produce and does the visiting and when she has purchased something she turns and puts it in the basket. Personally, I find this reprehensible. It reminds me of the ante-bellum South. The image is more than coincidental, the maid carrying the basket is invariably darker than the dona of the house. Of course Jo doesn't want to go that far. She's just talking about hiring Alipio and his donkey to haul our basket home. But to me, the principal is the same.

We do help the neighboring family in other ways. The grandmother, who smokes a corncob pipe, wanted to cook for us, but of course we turned that down. Having a servant in the house would be totally unacceptable and contrary to our purpose. Also Jo loves to cook and keep house. It's one of the few familiar things she has in her life. I think it's a comfort to her although the conditions she is working under are much more difficult than at home.

I did agree to hire the mother to do our laundry. She washes our clothing in the river along with the clothing from a couple of other families. What a shock the first time I saw my underwear stretched out on a rock to dry. Jo asked why if we allow the mother to do the laundry we don't hire the son to haul the groceries. I don't see a contradiction. I believe in the division of labor so long as all labor is respected and adequately compensated. I don't think I should stay home making my own shoes, for example, when I can be out meeting people and encouraging them to improve their sanitary conditions. But if I believe in the nobility of manual labor I would be a phony if I practiced the opposite by refusing to carry my own food home from the market. Jo said *that* was phony. She said we are rich relative to them and it would cost very little to hire Alipio to haul our groceries. She accused me of showing off, of performing. She said it was phony of me to carry the groceries, because by doing so I was acting like I wasn't rich, when in fact I was. I agreed that carrying the basket home from the market was a kind of performance but I denied I was showing off or being phony. I am demonstrating my beliefs, which is the opposite of being phony.

Another thing we do to help the family is buy eggs from them. Twice we have also bought chickens. All of these negotiations are carried out between Jo and the mother. The father is a mysterious distant fellow. He carries a machete on his belt and is here often enough to keep his wife pregnant, but I know little about him. Sometimes when he is gone the donkey is also gone, other times when the donkey is here I don't see the father around.

I know the man well enough to say hello but that's about it. He's a slight fellow with a shy smile, very bad teeth and downcast eyes. I don't think he understands a word I say and were he to say something more than hello to me, I might not understand him either. I'm surprised to learn that no two people speak a language the same way. Some mumble, others don't. Some slur their words, or talk very fast, or very soft. Many have few if any teeth, some appear reluctant to open their mouths. A few are so shocked by my accent they burst into giggles. I'm beginning to think it's astounding that we humans can understand each other even in our native languages.

The mother does not talk to me either, other than to ask if Dona Jolene is home. She is surprisingly young to have such a large family, probably only a few years older than I am. She too avoids direct eye contact but her cheeks are rosy and her belly round and growing. When we order a chicken she goes out and catches one. She cuts the throat, drains the blood, removes the feathers and guts and delivers the bird to our door in a matter of minutes. The scaly yellow feet still attached, the nails sharp from digging in the dirt. The first time we thought it was an accident that the last segment of each wing was missing. But the same was true the second time. Jo was a little upset. We pay a good price for the chicken and we deserve the full chicken, though we were happy to let her keep the blood which she uses to make some kind of sauce. So we wondered about it. Should we confront her about the wings. Is this a common practice? Does the mother think we don't know the anatomy of a chicken? But then when we sat down to our chicken dinner, we talked about that family eating their dinner and the role played by the ends of two chicken wings.

On the surface, the gap between this family and us is

enormous. When I reach out to them they shy away. To them it must seem as if we have dropped down from the sky. One day two shining white people arrive grinning and speaking strangely and take up residence in the house next door. Who are these folks, they must wonder. Why are they here? Maybe they are even asking themselves how to profit from this. I can't blame them for thinking such thoughts. What they don't understand, and what frustrates me because I can't communicate it, is the great admiration and respect I feel for them. How resourceful they are to raise a large family under these conditions! The husband probably works on a distant *fazenda* which would explain his comings and goings. The wife, in addition to raising the family with the help of the grandmother, and taking in laundry, also makes small manioc cakes that she sells in the market for pennies. Alipio hires out the services of the donkey when it is available. They have their flock of unruly chickens and their swarm of children, several of whom I cannot tell apart.

What is true of our relationship with this one family is true of our relationship to this town as a whole. On the surface the gap between us is huge, though of course with those who are better educated and more traveled, the differences are less dramatic. But I refuse to accept the possibility that the gap is fundamental, or in the true sense, real at all. Yes, we come from different hemispheres and cultures. Yes, our languages are only distantly related though I am working hard to learn theirs. The parents next door have probably spent less weeks in schools than I have spent years. But we all belong to the Family of Man and in that sense we are one. So my initial goal is to bridge this gap and make it disappear. Jo is already making progress with the mother. They chatter about the children and food, though the mother is always careful to defer to Jo, referring to her as *a Senhora* or *Dona* when we would prefer they think of us as neighbors or even friends.

I sometimes have the sense as I walk through the town that

Jo and I have woken up to find ourselves characters in a movie that started long before we arrived. Everyone else has established their roles and are deeply involved in their stories. They look at us and no one is quite sure what parts we are here to play. Their first response has been to welcome us. Brazilians are very gracious, hospitable people. The principal at the high school had us to dinner. We hold our evening English classes in one of his classrooms. The mayor's family invited us for lunch. We met his wife and children. We attended a birthday party given for a local doctor, though not the one who runs the clinic where we are supposed to work. The hors 'd oeuvres were delicious. I feel us being passed around among the town's elite as if we were some novelty, a curiosity discovered one day in the street.

Our central problem though is the *Posto de Saúde*, the health clinic. Someone, the mayor, the doctor, a member of the state's health department, someone, accepted an offer from the Peace Corps to have us work at the clinic here in Nova. It was all hastily done, this setting up a program in Bahia, you can bet on that. That's the way the PC works. Some bureaucrat decided they should move into Bahia. They found a man in the States to direct the project. He had to extract himself from his job and move himself and his family down here. In the meantime they sent Willie and one or two other veteran Volunteers up to Bahia to find duty stations for us, the newly arriving Volunteers.

I can imagine the scene. Willie blows into town on a bus or in a Jeep. He meets a few of the local dignitaries. Explains how these bright young Americans want to live and work in your town. And they've been trained, he tells them. They are, even now, getting more training in Ilhéus. Won't cost you a penny. Sound good? They come in single and double sizes. How many can you take, one, two? I got a husband and wife combination I can let you have. And for a clincher he probably threw around the name of John Kennedy, a good Catholic boy, who is wildy popular in Brazil.

So here we are.

Only the people at the *Posto de Saúde* were not prepared for us. They have no idea what to do with us. When we walk in the door, the staff members stop their work and greet us. They find us chairs and bring us *cafezinhos*.

Cafezinhos? Connie asks. She has taken a seat near him.
Hot coffee, very strong and syrupy, served in a small cup.
I see.

And we are encouraged to sit there and, and what? Smile? Drink the coffee? Hold the occasional crying infant so the mother can get some help for another sick child? The sense is they don't want to inconvenience us. At first we were celebrities to be set in chairs and looked after. But now our celebrity status has worn thin. We're beginning to look a little dusty and chipped, like statues of old gods no longer worshiped. We've become a bit of an embarrassment, I suspect, especially now that we've made clear we actually want to do something.

Then there is Doctor Nascimento, the man in charge of the *Posto*. The doctor is always friendly, back-slapping, hand squeezing, eager to see us. But he is seldom there, and when he is, he spends much of his time talking to us. The idea, his idea, is that by engaging us in conversation, our Portuguese will improve and we will be of more use. But when he is talking to us, he is doing nothing for the crowds of patients waiting to see him. So not only are we not performing any service, we are a hindrance. We take up chairs, we drink the coffee, we use up staff time and the doctor chats with us while the patients get sicker. It's very painful. We came to be of use but find ourselves in the role of guests who have overstayed their welcome, a burden more than a help.

And of what use can we be? The sense of stagnation is overwhelming at the *Posto*. The employees have narrowed their functions down to where they have plenty of staff to accomplish what they need to do. We know this by comparing it to Ilhéus where both the *Visitadories* and the *Auxiliaries* carry on active programs in the field. Here, they never leave the *Posto*. And since the doctor is seldom there, these minimally trained people, plus a nurse or two, are providing the health care for the poor.

There is another thing about Dr. Nascimento. He is completely unreliable with us. He says he will pick us up, and then he doesn't. He says he will be somewhere and then he's not. And all the time he is very friendly. One afternoon at the clinic he told us that the next day he would take us out to his *fazenda*. We didn't ask to go. He is very proud of his *fazenda*. He talks about it all the time and he insisted that he wanted to show it to us. We would have a meal there, he said. We would meet his family. He would come to our house the next day and we would all go out in his car. When exactly would he come we were careful to ask. Late morning, he said, before lunch. The next day we set everything aside and got dressed up and waited for him. Jo even wrapped a little present for his wife. The man never came. We sat around all day waiting because people are often late here. The day ended with no sign of the doctor. It was a difficult day for us. This man is our boss. We've been trying to measure up to his standards. He's made it clear that we are of no use to him because of our language skills. Had we failed him in some way? Was he angry with us? Had we misunderstood? Jo was devastated. She cried. Surely it was our fault. The incident actually made her sick.

A week later we saw him again. I wanted to know if we had done something wrong so I asked him about it. He brushed the whole thing off. At first he couldn't remember it at all and finally he said that we were supposed to have met him at the clinic and when we didn't arrive he left without us. A language problem, he said. But no big deal, we would do it again another time. But there has never been another time.

We are both certain he told us he would come to the house, though we also know that our language skills are imperfect and cultural differences are real.

Such things have happened more than once. They happen with other people, but not the same way. We have come to suspect that the Doctor is actually tormenting us, deliberately setting us up for disappointment, though I don't want to believe anyone would be so cruel, especially someone who has dedicated his life to healing others. And for what reason?

Well, the other night we concocted a theory. We believe the doctor wants us to quit and go home. We think he thinks we are spying on him. He has a government job. He's probably supposed to be on the job so many days a week, put in so many hours seeing patients in addition to his administrative work. Whatever the job description, it's pretty clear he's not doing it. We think word came down from the state level that he should take in a Volunteer and he suspects we have come to check up on him. So, I guess the question is this: Are we paranoid or is he?

Clint pauses and looks up at Connie. She has resumed pacing. She motions for him to continue.

Anyway the mayor seems more helpful and we may find our roles through him. He located this house for us to rent. I had some problems with the house because of its commanding presence on the hill, the fact that it is much too large for our needs (four of the rooms we are not using at all) and because it is near the *favela* but not really a part of it. Jo, though, was so eager to get out of the hotel and into a place of our own, that she convinced me to take it.

Working on the house has been our excuse to not go to the *Posto*. But really it's just an excuse, a little lie we tell ourselves. We don't have to lie to the doctor or to anyone else at the *Posto*. They don't care if we come. But in truth we could do both. The

Posto is only open in the afternoons. We could work on the house in the morning and then walk out to the *Posto*. I know this, and it weighs on me.

Last night Jo and I had a serious argument, at least it seemed serious to me. One thing that's happening has totally surprised me. Jo has started drinking at night. Not a lot, I mean she's not getting drunk. But she always has a glass of wine or two while she's preparing dinner. This never happened before. While we were in school, maybe once a month at a party, she would have a beer, maybe two. She might even get a bit tipsy. I'll admit I kind of enjoyed that. It made her sort of silly, a little flirtatious, and afterward, if I got her alone before she fell asleep, she was very affectionate. We both managed to keep our virginity up to the wedding night, but she was definitely more open, more playful when she had had a drink than otherwise.

That was sort of embarrassing, Connie says, stopping him. The whole thing about parents and sex is weird.

Of course, Clint says glancing up. Connie is standing at the window looking out. When she says nothing more, he asks if she wants him to continue.

She turns abruptly as if to say something. But then pauses, and with her hand sweeps the rebellious strand of hair back from her forehead. Yes, please, but I want to talk about Mom's drinking later.

We can do that.

But it's different now. We would go weeks when alcohol played no part in our lives. Even after we married and for the six weeks when we had the apartment in Springfield no booze entered the house.

I had no idea about the apartment in Springfield either, Connie interjects. But Aunt Connie told me that the summer my folks got married, before they left for training, they lived and worked in Springfield. I understood Mom had worked in Springfield but I always assumed it was before they got married. Anyway, please continue.

Now, when she drinks, her mood is sometimes the opposite of what it was before. Far from becoming cheerful and giggly, she might turn sullen, somber. Not every night. We've had some pleasant evenings and on a couple of nights I even had a glass with her. But what a strange thing this is! It started one night a few days after we arrived in Ilhéus. We were eating alone at the hotel and she ordered a glass of wine with her meal. I was shocked. I asked what she was doing. My question made her angry. "I'm an adult, aren't I?" she replied. "A married woman? Do I have to ask your permission to have a glass of wine?" Of course she didn't need my permission. I wasn't suggesting such a thing. I was shocked, that's all.

Then one day when were still staying at the hotel here in Nova, I came back to the room and found a wine bottle on the chest of drawers. I was surprised and disappointed. The bottle looked dull green and ominous as if some dark and sinister force had suddenly entered our world. At that time I was forcing myself to get out of the hotel. I wanted to explore our new town, meet people, make our presence known, and most important, practice the language. Jo was often sick those first days in Nova, and she was not going out as much as I. I knew she was having a rough time adjusting to our new and unsettled life. I assumed she was going through what the PC calls "culture shock." When you're in culture shock, all thoughts of home are dear and your present surroundings appear inferior, worthy of contempt, perhaps even hostile. It's a phase, you get through it. But when I found the bottle, I became reluctant to leave her alone. That wasn't fully rational, I'll admit. It wasn't like she was sitting around getting drunk. She just thought it would be nice to have a glass in the evening, that's how she explained it. But I saw alcohol as a threat in several ways. It threatened to damage the most important person in my life. It threatened to come between us. And it threatened to shrink my world as well as hers. Truth is, I believe in sobriety. Being alert in the world is enough of a challenge as it is. Alcohol just makes it more difficult. And there's another thing. People who drink want to draw you in. They want you to drink with them. Our room had became a refuge for her and her mind was always on her family. She wanted to talk about them, the little dramas that went on, the funny things her littlest sister says. And since we had gotten no mail, she worried about them. When she wasn't talking about her family or school, she searched the shortwave radio for English language stations. There are two, the BBC and the Armed Forces Network. In the evening she would want us both to drink wine and listen to the radio. She could be quite seductive about it when she wasn't sick. But I didn't want to drink and listen to English. I wanted to study Portuguese. At the same time I wanted her to be healthy and happy. I wanted our marriage to flourish. I wanted our experience here to be rich and satisfying for both of us. And I wanted us to work together as a team to do something about the terrible conditions that exist here.

So, we had this argument. Last night was the last night of *Carnaval* but in a way the whole thing started the week before. We had a difference of opinion about *Carnaval*. Jo wanted to go to Salvador and join the party. In Ilhéus some of the Volunteers had talked about meeting there for the celebration. It seemed to me wholly inappropriate. We've just gotten here. We've finally found a house and have tons of work to do. We've got no real job other than the English classes and no money. Until Clint arrived yesterday, the PC office in Salvador had been totally disorganized about getting us money, our mail and our air freight. We're still owed per diem for our time in Ilhéus.

Jolene argued that we could get our money when we arrived

in Salvador but she had to admit that might not work out. I argued that we could better use the time to build some shelves and start a survey of the neighborhood. This would give us a chance to meet people and discover if any sense of community exists in the neighborhood, any internal organization that we could work through to effect change. I want to feel a part of the neighborhood. I want the people to recognize us as neighbors. I want to help them develop a voice.

We can't wait around for the Brazilians to find a role for us. We've to go out and make it happen. So the *Posto* is not working. That doesn't mean we give up. The needs are everywhere.

Anyway, in the end we decided to not go to Salvador. Jo was not happy about it but she agreed it was the best decision. At least she agreed before *Carnaval,* but last night she acted like it had been totally my decision to not go. It was not a good week. The whole town seemed to go to sleep during *Carnaval.* Stores and offices were closed, the rich went out to their *fazendas,* the poor seemed to disappear. We did build the shelves but we took no steps toward conducting the survey. Jo would not go out and I was reluctant to leave her, or to venture out on my own. She turned sad again and passive. That's the thing that torments me, this sadness, this passivity. "What do you want me to do?" "Nothing, go ahead, I'll be all right." That sort of thing.

But it's not that simple. One day she might be passive but there's a balloon full of anger just below the surface. If I say the wrong thing look out. I get a diatribe. Everything I have ever done to annoy her comes boiling to the surface. And what a memory! Sometimes I wish we had a stenographer with us at all times so we had a transcript of what went on, who said what, and who agreed to do this or that. She sure remembers things differently than I do.

So that's the way it's been, sad and passive or angry and resentful, well, not all the time, of course. She can be very dear and sweet. She feels as bad after an argument as I do. And there are times when she is wonderful with the people here. It was a delight watching her during the vaccination day. She had great fun. And I love seeing her with the little kids. She's a natural around children. And in spite of her resistance and my diligence, her language skills, particularly her pronunciation, are better than mine. She has the ear, I have the determination.

But then last night she started drinking wine while cooking supper and the more she drank the more sullen and angry she became. Suddenly it was totally my fault we didn't go to *Carnaval*. And it wasn't because of the money, she claimed, or the work, or the house. It was because I did not believe in *Carnaval*. She insinuated that I had been dishonest. I had used the money and the house as an excuse because I didn't want to go to *Carnaval*. Okay, I'll admit I do have a philosophical problem with *Carnaval*. Let's face it, *Carnaval* is a giant debauchery. People get drunk out of their minds, spend money they don't have, dance themselves to exhaustion and who knows what else. The poor are tricked into thinking there is something wonderful in what amounts to a huge waste of money and time. People spend fortunes on costumes and floats and for what? For a few days of drunken partying and then it's all over for another year.

But that wasn't the reason I was opposed to going to Salvador. The fact is, we didn't have any money. We do have lots of work to do on the house. We do need to develop roles for ourselves, because we have no role at the clinic. I mean, we are here to serve, after all. Not to party. If we'd wanted to party, we could have stayed in the States.

Before the night was over it was also my fault that we were in Brazil at all. She described herself as a shanghaied sailor forced by me to come to Brazil against her wishes. It's not the first time I've heard this refrain, though never with such vehemence. The subject is very touchy for both of us. It is true that the PC was my idea and I have tried to be sensitive to that. It's also true, as she often reminds me, that she was in the middle of undergraduate school while I have my degree. And yes, as she also says, we were engaged and she was very much in love with me (as if I wasn't just as much in love with her!) and she wanted to please me. So what am I supposed to think about that? She admitted that she agreed to join the PC with me. At the time she even acted like she was excited about it, though she also admitted from the beginning that she was frightened. But now she was telling me that it was all my idea. That she only went along to please me!

I got pretty upset at that point. I have great respect for logic and internally consistent arguments. I have a major in philosophy after all. How can you possibly arrive at an honest understanding if you aren't being consistent and clear? On the one hand she was accusing me of being dishonest about *Carnaval* while at the same time admitting that she had been dishonest about joining the PC! Not only admitting but actually using it as an argument. As if it were my fault that I failed to understand that she really meant no when she was saying yes. What am I supposed to be, a mind reader?

She ended up sobbing, her face buried in her arms on the table, her hair scattered out around her. It broke my heart, but when I tried to comfort her, she brushed me away. It was the worst argument we have ever had and the worst night of my life, that's for sure.

She stayed like that for half an hour while I sat on a chair a few feet away. Finally she got up and went into the bedroom. I reached out for her as she passed but again she brushed me away. I spent the night alone on the floor on some bedding I put together from odds and ends of clothing and towels. All I wanted was to hold her in my arms, to comfort her, to feel her warm smooth skin next to mine.

In the morning though, we still hadn't made up. I was determined to get out of the house. It felt like a cage to me and I felt some resentment about having spent the night on the floor. She got up and made my breakfast. We didn't talk much, though we agreed we would talk later, and we embraced when I left. But then when I came back, I found a Jeep parked at the gate in front of our house. It was Clint and he had our air freight, a bundle of letters that had been sitting up in Salvador for weeks and some money. It was great to get it all and it changed Jo's mood from despair to joy. That was the best thing.

She wanted me to ride along with her and Clint to Jacarandá. It would have made her happy if I had. But the truth is, I wanted this time alone. I wanted to think things through. Spending time in Jacarandá might have felt good but serving our turn here in Nova is what will save us. I'm working toward a long-term solution, not a quick fix. I also have a strong sense of obligation. The US government put its trust in us. While I have my quibbles with the program, I still believe in what we're doing. We are not diplomats trying to promote America's objectives. We're not soldiers come to enforce America's will or missionaries here to convert the heathen. We have come simply to serve the people, to live simply and give of ourselves. I believe it is a noble calling. I feel a strong obligation to fulfil the mission we have been entrusted to carry out. I believe Jo does too.

It is now well after midnight and the neighborhood is silent. On the hillside below and around me a few hundred people are sleeping in rough beds, some probably on the floor, just as I did last night. Some went to bed hungry, many are sick, most if not all are uneducated, unread, untraveled. Meanwhile back home hundreds of other people sleep in comfortable beds with full stomachs, their cabinets filled with whatever medicine they might need. They have work, their children go to school, their houses are large and comfortable. They see an even better future ahead for themselves and their families. Side-by-side in the world, these two realities.

Enough sentiment. The long *Carnaval* holiday is over and it's time to get back to work. I went to the mayor's office this afternoon hoping to meet with him but he is taking Thursday and Friday off as well. It will be next week before I can see him. These delays are terribly frustrating. I am so eager to get started here. I refuse to sit home waiting. I'm going to force myself to be out and about, talking and listening to the people.

Chapter Ten
GREEN ORANGES

Clint closes the spiral journal and sits back in his chair. Connie stands at the far end of the room looking away. For a while neither of them speaks. Then she turns and looks at him.

She never gave it up.

What's that?

Alcohol.

I see. Did she abuse it?

No, I wouldn't say she abused it. It grabbed me by the throat, but not her. I never saw her drunk. But she drank wine every night. A glass while she prepared the meal, a second while she ate it. When they went out to eat, she insisted that the restaurant have a bar. And she would order something with gin, a gimlet, usually. Then wine with dinner. But I think there was always the temptation to have more. Sometimes she would sip on something stronger before she went to bed.

And Kyle?

She drank alone. It was like a silent statement she made every night. After she died, Dad said he regretted not drinking with her.

The things we regret.

Did she drink with you?

Clint looks at his notes scattered on the table before him. He picks them up and moves them closer to his chest in a manner that seems to Connie possessive and vaguely ludicrous, as if he were a fifth grader who had just received a love note in math class.

Yes, on occasion, he says. Like you I never saw her drunk and I have no idea if drink was important to her. I only knew her for a few short months. I'm happy to hear she had a full rich life. A good husband, two children. You say she was a teacher so she completed her schooling. That was one of the things she worried about. I think she had completed one or two years when they entered the Peace Corps.

She never converted to Catholicism either, Connie says. We kids were raised Catholic but she remained Lutheran. Sang in the choir, taught Sunday school. When you're a kid the strangest things seem normal. Every Sunday Dad, Phil and I would bundle up and head to mass while she set off on foot for St. Mark's Lutheran a couple of blocks from the house. Always walked, unless it was icy or the snow was too deep, then one of the ladies from the church would pick her up. We were home before her. Dad and I made Sunday dinner so she didn't have to cook. Yes, she did have a full life. Some regrets about how Phil and I turned out, and she died much too young, but a full life. I took her for granted, of course, the way kids do. After she died I missed her terribly. I wanted to talk to her, ask her questions, get her opinions, I still do. But that will have to wait.

Connie pauses. She glances briefly out the window again. Then she walks back to her chair and sits down.

Actually, she adds, as if revealing a confidence, in the first months after Mom died, I felt like I could talk to her. I felt her presence. Dad's health deteriorated in those months and I would talk to her and I felt she was helping me.

I see.

But then I lost touch. No more answers. As time has gone by she's come to seem more distant, more mysterious to me. But I had no idea she'd done anything like this.

More mysterious? Clint asks.

Yes. Connie takes up the journal and begins to leaf through its pages.

He waits but she does not elaborate. Did she ever do any acting? he asks.

Mom? She giggles. No, why do you ask that?

I just wondered.

No, no acting. Well, there was the circus. Mom was famous for her circus. She taught kindergarten you know. Thirty-two years in the same school. Every spring her class put on a circus. It was a performance presented in the gymnasium before the entire school and a flock of parents. In later years it always made the evening news. Mom made the costumes: lions, tigers, trapeze artists, clown suits. I was ring master my kindergarten year. A top hat, tall black boots, a whip and a cape. Every kid had a part to play. It took weeks to prepare.

Clint smiles. I'm not surprised about the costumes. She was practiced in the domestic arts, as we've discussed. Home economics, they used to call it when I was in school. She identified herself with that. Cooking, sewing. Later after they got a stove and refrigerator she would bake things. When she came to Jacarandá she would bring me a banana bread or some other baked treat that was familiar from home. And sewing was important. It became her work in Nova. She taught sewing and pattern making to girls in the *favela*.

There's references to that in the journal, Connie says. Apparently things never did work out at the clinic.

No, it only got worse, I'm afraid. But if you'd like I could tell you some things about my first visit to their house. That would have been the day I delivered the air freight and mail.

Yes, please. So, you did have a car? And you did go there?

Hardly a car. But for a few days a Peace Corps Jeep. A battered blue contraption that Vern and I drove back from Salvador after *Carnaval*. Vern and I were among the Volunteers Kyle mentioned. To be living in Brazil and not participate in *Carnaval* or at least observe it? Hard to imagine really.

Connie winces.

I don't mean to judge, Clint says. Kyle's decision was consistent with his goals and beliefs. Anyway, Vern and I did attend *Carnaval* in Salvador. We rode up with Eduardo. Eduardo's family had an apartment in the upper city not far from the cathedral and it was large enough, and with enough beds for all of us. Salvador is a very interesting city by the way. You might choose to go there sometime. Old colonial architecture set above a large bay with fortifications along the water. Its people claim that Salvador is older than Rio. It was more than four hundred years old when we were there.

Vern and I caught a break by having Eduardo show us around. He got us into a couple of private parties and clubs which gave us an opportunity to witness the celebration from the inside. But we also danced among what your dad would have called 'the people.' I remember being in a packed street following behind a flatbed truck filled with a raucous band. One incident was both curious and revealing, and it should be of interest to you, even though it doesn't involve your parents.

All right.

Vern and I were with a group of Volunteers. I don't know, five, six of us probably. One of them had an invitation to a private club. So we all went to this address hoping to get admitted. There was a wall in front of the building with a wrought-iron gate and behind the gate stood a doorman. The Volunteer explained who he was and who had invited him. The doorman surveyed the group of us standing outside the gate. He could admit us, he said, but not the *Preta*.

The what?

The man was pointing to Annette, a Volunteer, a nurse and an African-American.

Oh, gosh.

Annette was embarrassed, of course, and humiliated and I'm sure very angry. She urged us to go ahead. We refused, of course.

Good for you.

Hardly heroic, Clint says. Rather an obvious choice, I would say. But it's important that you understand the context. This was 1965 remember. Back in the States the civil rights movement was still in full force. Only a few months earlier President Johnson had signed the historic civil rights act that prohibited discrimination in public accommodations, restaurants, hotels, that sort of thing. There was not a Volunteer in the group who had not been told by a Brazilian that while prejudice was rampant in the U.S., it was non-existent in Brazil. Interestingly, the doorman himself had some African heritage.

Really? Connie asks, surprised.

Clint nods. And that's the difference, at least so far as I came to understand it. In the U.S. then, and still today, as you know, a person with even a small fraction of African ancestry is considered an African-American. In Brazil, by contrast, only individuals who were pure or nearly pure African, were recognized as different and set aside for discrimination. Not formal, legal discrimination as existed in the United States, understand. Not separate restrooms or water fountains, but a personal bias. Brazilians were proud of their mixed heritage, rightly so, but at least then, as this incident illustrates, Blacks did suffer unique problems.

Connie reaches forward, the metal rings on her wrist tinkling softly, and turns off the recorder.

Even today, she says, her voice somewhat conspiratorial.

I'm sorry?

When a white woman marries a black man in the United States. Or vice versa, I'm sure. Each of them is agreeing to be stared at. You're thumbing your nose at some people. That's just the way it is. I was prepared for that but I worry for my sons. Their identities are subject to fracture as they move out into the larger society.

I see.

Connie smiles at him and turns the recorder back on.

Anyway, I wish your parents had come to *Carnaval*. It might have helped them. Over the long weekend we ran into several Volunteers and through them got to finally meet Charlie Pell and his family. Pell was the PC director for Bahia.

The man my parents referred to as Mr. Pell?

Yes, good old Charlie. He had been an engineer with a large corporation in the Midwest, a farm equipment manufacturer of some sort. His wife was a great cook and they had a couple of boys in their early teens. He was happy to see Vern and me because of the air freight. Each of us had been allowed to ship a trunk before we left the states and now months later they had finally made their way to Salvador. Charlie also had some money and bundles of mail that he had been meaning to get down to us and your parents. He offered us the Jeep to haul the freight back to the southern part of the state.

So you did visit my parents?

Charlie instructed me to spend the day with them. I was supposed to deliver their things, check on them and get back to him. He hadn't heard a word since they arrived in Nova.

I'm sorry, but I thought you said you didn't remember going there. Her expression looks troubled to him, as if she's experiencing a loss of faith.

Yes, Clint says slowly, I guess I did say that. I was confused about the reference to my driving. I didn't normally have a vehicle. It's one of the things I missed.

All right.

Anyway, I did go there, but I had no practical way of informing Kyle and Jolene that I was coming. There was no phone service between our towns. I arrived in Nova Santana about ten in the morning. I parked the Jeep near the main plaza and asked a nine or ten year-old boy on a donkey where I could find the Americans.

The boy instructed me to follow him. 'No, no,' he waved his finger at me when I started to walk beside him. I was supposed to follow in the Jeep.

Clint pauses, smiling. He leans back in his chair, lifts the index finger of his right hand and waves it back and forth as if it were

a windshield wiper. A very characteristic Bahian gesture, he says
to Connie. 'No, no.' That's what it means.

All right.

So we made a bit of a procession, this proud boy on his
donkey with a propane tank balanced on the back of the wooden
saddle and me following in the Jeep. We left the plaza, passed the
church, climbed a hill, at the top of which stood the city hall,
went down the hill on the other side and started up another hill.
The cobblestone street became a dirt road and the road became
little more than a path. I'm trying to give you some impression
of the setting they were in.

Yes, I appreciate that.

On the plaza, and on the road from the plaza to the city
hall, some of the houses were hidden behind walls topped with
shards of broken glass set deep in the plaster. After the city hall,
walls became less frequent, though the houses were still brightly
painted with windows that could be shuttered and barred from
the inside. Where the cobblestones ended, the color began to
fade from the houses. Here many of the walls were built with
mud bricks or sticks and waddle. A few were painted, some were
whitewashed, others remained mud brown.

Our procession became more of an event as we bounced
up the rutted road. Women stared from doorways or stopped
beside the path to look, cans of water balanced on their heads.
A man riding a mule and dressed like a Brazilian cowboy with
a leather vest and hat paused as we passed. Girls clustered and
giggled, boys shouted and ran along side the Jeep. I remember
specifically one brazen lad who jumped onto the hood and lay
across it grinning in at me as I tried to see past him. The kid
on the donkey had become a Napoleon, waving his arms and
shouting orders to everyone in sight.

Connie smiles, nodding her head. For a man who did not
remember the trip at all, Clint's memory, it seems to her, has
experienced a remarkable recovery.

Finally the kid commanded me to stop. Ahead, the path ended at a gate. The boy slid off the hood and ran up the hill. He opened the gate and disappeared. Moments later he reappeared holding Jolene's hand and leading her down to the Jeep.

Clint lowers his chin and peers at Connie over his glasses. I can still picture her at that moment, he says, eyes glinting. She was wearing a pale green skirt and a white sleeveless blouse. Women Volunteers, incidently, had to wear skirts at all times. In rural Brazil at that time, a woman was not seen wearing slacks or shorts.

Okay.

Her hair was disheveled and she looked a little bewildered. When she saw me she let out a squeal and began to run. She threw her arms around me and we embraced for a long time. Her reaction was somewhat surprising. She didn't know me that well and she had never been affectionate with me in any physical way before.

Then why...?

Her behavior had very little to do with me as an individual, Clint adds. It could have been any American.

What do you mean?

I'll put it in terms with which I am most familiar, he says, resuming what Connie has already begun to think of as his professorial air. For the past two months Jolene had been swirling in a kind of vortex. Her environment had changed drastically and she was desperately struggling to adapt. The only person who spoke her language was Kyle and he didn't want to hear it. She'd received no word from home. The food was different and the water contaminated. She was often sick. Everyone was gawking at her, their jobs at the clinic were not working out. She was trying to fashion a comfortable home inside a bare building and she had very few tools to help her.

Wasn't some of that true for you as well?

The language part, of course. The food. We were all more

or less sick much of the time those first months. On the other hand, I had a place to live from the beginning. I had work, friends. No, I did not go through what your parents went through. Do you understand?

I do, yes.

Another factor is clear from what we read. Jolene was torn between her love and loyalty toward her husband and her reluctance to leave college in the middle of her undergraduate years and go off to Brazil. We're talking about the early 60's. It wasn't just that women couldn't wear slacks in Brazil. Her college dorm had had curfew hours, while as an undergraduate male, Kyle could come and go as he pleased. Now as a young wife, she was expected to follow her husband. So, her culture was imposing values on her. Even as she struggled to adapt, a part of her resented the obligation to adapt. You said of her later years, that her alcohol use made a statement. Well, even when I knew her, there existed a small private part of herself that Jolene insisted on preserving and expressing in her own unique way. I doubt she would have acknowledged my description in those terms, but that's my take on it.

Were you aware that she was in conflict?

Clint removes his glasses and rubs his eyes. He is conscious that Connie is watching him. She is capable of a cool clear gaze. In other circumstances, he thinks, she might have become a scientist herself.

Not in the way I have just described, Connie. You're hearing the benefit of hindsight.

Okay.

Anyway, Kyle was off somewhere and she was home alone.

The mayor's office, I think he wrote.

Right. She was deeply embarrassed because it was shortly before noon and she had been sleeping. We now know from the journal that the night before they had had an argument that was not completely resolved by the time I arrived.

Yes.

Another observation I would make: your mother had put on weight. Maybe ten pounds from when I first saw her in Rio. She was tall, as you know, so she did not look heavy, but she was a little rounder, fuller. It was as if her body had surrounded itself with a soft blanket of protection. She was embarrassed about that too, though the extra pounds did nothing to detract from her appearance. Female Volunteers typically gained weight. We males tended to become thinner.

Okay.

I should tell you about the house.

Yes, please, I'm very interested in the house. Dad drops clues but it was not his intent to describe the house and so I am left with more questions than answers.

Well, the path continued up hill another ten meters or so past the gate to a cement deck or patio that stood before the front door and went around to one side. The house had white plastered walls and a roof of red tiles, the kind you see throughout much of Latin America. When we got to the deck, I turned and looked back toward the east. The vista was across an orchard and over toward the city hall we had passed on the next hill. In the far distance, beyond the remainder of the town which was largely hidden by the intervening hill, was the river. The river bent and flowed past the east and the south sides of the town. Beyond the river was a long very tall forested hill that dominated the horizon.

It sounds beautiful.

A pleasant vista, all right. Your mother did indeed love that house and the grounds surrounding it. Orange trees, a couple of pineapple plants, some coconut palms. She was excited about the plants. Even before we went inside she led me to one of the trees in the side yard to show off the oranges. The fruits were large but green. She and Kyle had apparently waited several weeks for them to ripen before discovering they were ripe. The skin remained green but the interior was orange, juicy and sweet. It had something to do with the temperature or the hours of sunlight they thought. I've never looked into it. One of the luxuries when you came to visit them was fresh-squeezed orange juice.

Wow, Mom talked about green oranges! Connie blurts out. In her kindergarten classes! Also about bananas. How in the tropics there were several kinds of bananas but at home you could only get one. I always assumed she had learned these things in school or in a magazine.

Well, now you know, he says smiling. Her knowledge came firsthand from evidence found in her own yard. Let me tell you about the inside.

Yes, please.

The floor was composed of red hexagonal tiles set in cement. There was no ceiling. Looking up you saw supports and the undersides of the roof tiles. It was a rectangular structure divided into several rooms by plastered walls that went up seven feet or so and then ended. The walls were painted a light blue and a resident population of lizards hung out on them.

Lizards on the walls?

Yes, they were no threat. A good example of a symbiotic relationship, actually. The house provided them shelter and they helped control the fly population. There was also a pair of bats that lived in one of the back rooms that your parents weren't using. They hung from a rafter during the day and flew in and out a window at night. They too were not a threat.

One surprise after another, Connie says, shaking her head. You have no idea how fussy my mother was when it came to our house. That she lived in a place with lizards and bats absolutely floors me.

She explodes with a loud giggle that brings a smile to Clint's face. After it subsides she pours them both a glass of water and asks that he continue.

I was at your parents' house on several occasions and I'm try-ing to remember what it was like this first time. Kyle mentioned the table and chairs. I don't think they had much else in the way of furniture. I never got into the bedroom until after they left. Did he write that they had electricity?

Yes.

One or two bare bulbs on cords that hung down from the rafters, an outlet or two. They had a hotplate. It was later that they got the stove and refrigerator. The windows and doorways were open to the outside. The doors and the wooden window shutters were, I think, green, yes a dark green. They could be closed at night and barred from the inside.

When you say 'open to the outside,' do you mean no glass?

No glass, no screens. I handed Jolene the packet of letters and she took a few minutes to go through them. She had not received any word from her family since we left for Brazil in early December, apparently, and she was happy to learn that everyone was all right.

I was impressed by the house, of course. I wanted to know how they had gotten there from when I had last seen them, standing on the sidewalk in front of the *farmacia*.

Dad refers to the fact that they were in that hotel for a while, a month or something.

Yes. But more than *what* she told me, I want to first explain *how* she told me.

What do you mean?

I mean how giddy she was, how bubbling over with the shear joy of talking. It was a wonderful illustration to me of how im-portant language is to us as a species. Your mother had a physical craving to express herself that morning. To say familiar words, to spout her native tongue, and it came pouring out like a flood.

Clint pauses for a moment before continuing. I want to say this carefully and precisely. I hope you'll recognize before we finish that I developed a great appreciation for both of your parents. I felt respect even admiration for Kyle Henderson and I never lost that. But I need to say that Kyle drove himself relentlessly. He drove himself in all things, but most important was the language. If he was going to achieve the goals he had set for himself, he needed to communicate in Portuguese as comfortably and as completely as possible. To obtain that ability, he believed it necessary that he not speak or hear English. It was not his intention, I'm sure, but I suspect that he made Jolene feel guilty every time she said a word in English. And now alone with me, the dam broke.

I understand.

So, yes, they did spend some time, I don't know how long, in a hotel, but not the sleazy one. I think they spent only one night in that cheap hotel. Someone, the mayor or his assistant made arrangements for them at the other place. The place where Willy had been unable to get them a room. I understood it was a decent hotel, quiet with a small dining room. But I have no first hand knowledge. I never stayed there nor did I visit them when they were there.

Okay.

But I did get a vivid description of the sleazy joint, Clint says. Jolene called it a whore house.

Mom?

She might not have used that word, he admits, smiling. She might have said it was a house of ill repute or some other euphemism. She was probably wrong, incidently. If it had been a whore house, they could not have gotten a room. It was probably one of those places in Latin America where you can rent a room for an hour or two for a quick coupling. Maybe streetwalkers used it too, I don't know.

Oh, gosh.

He laughs. One of your mother's favorite words, and now I hear it coming from you.

Pardon?

'Gosh.' It is so Midwestern.

Connie is offended. Well, I am Midwestern and I try to avoid taking the name of our Lord in vain.

Clint apologizes and they both take another drink of water.

According to Jolene, it was a miserable place, Clint continues setting down his glass. The cheap place, I'm talking about now. Yes.

The toilet was just a seat with a hole above a pit, and it was located inside, across from their room, as I recall the story. It reeked and was thick with flies. They had brought some cleaner with them from the States. Several bottles, I believe.

That's in the journal, the Lysol supply. That is so Mom!

Right. Well, Jolene said she washed down the toilet and then their room and they hung up their mosquito netting. And oh yes, the lighting was miserable, a ten watt bulb or something. The way Jolene described the scene they spent the night huddled under the netting while from the other rooms came the sounds of giggles and grunts and bottles landing on the floor.

Come morning I would have been on the next bus, Connie says.

I think Jolene came close. And it wasn't just the place. It was the fact that they need not have stayed there.

What do you mean?

Well, that afternoon, after our bus had left, the mayor, or maybe it was his assistant, came and found them. He thought the accommodations were unacceptable and he made arrangements for them at the better hotel. He had more influence than Willie, obviously. He could get them in that night. Jolene told me all of this.

So, why did they stay?

Because Kyle had made a deal. That's the way she explained it to me. Kyle had agreed to rent the room and he was not going to demand his money back now just because something better had turned up. He felt their reputations depended upon it.

Dad did take his reputation very seriously, Connie says. That's one of the things people talked about at his funeral service. If he shook your hand on a deal, it was as good as done. It was a huge memorial service and several people said things along those lines.

Yes, well. He apparently thought it would set a bad example if the first day you arrive in town, you start going back on your word. They would look like ugly Americans. 'The Ugly American' was the title of a best seller that came out a few years before we went to Brazil. The term entered the language and represented an image we were trying to combat. Kyle was willing to move the next day all right. But he had made a deal for that night and he intended to honor it. Of course, at the time, he didn't know just how bad the place was. I assume it got a lot more lively after the sun went down. Clint chuckles. But Jolene did resent, I think, the fact that he insisted they stay. She felt a little betrayed that he had put her through that difficult night rather than risk tarnishing his reputation. As if he had put his own honor in front of hers.

I can see that.

And of course there was a similar problem with the house and then *Carnaval*.

Differences.

Indeed. So, anyway, Jolene was quite embarrassed that I had found her sleeping in the middle of the morning. At first she implied that she had stayed up studying language. Later she admitted that was a 'little fib.' She never studied language, she told me. Just trying to listen and speak it all day was as much as she could stand. Even that gave her a headache. I never knew the argument had been as sustained as Kyle described it, but I did understand that they had their differences about the house. Kyle thought it was too opulent for Volunteers though he liked that it was, if not exactly in the *favela*, at least adjoining it. I think his thoughts about the house were mixed. He wanted her to be happy in the worst way. And now that I think about it, I am probably giving you a false portrait of your mother as well.

What do you mean?

Jolene did feel resentment and she freely admitted that, but she also regretted the resentment.

I don't understand.

She saw it as a personal failing. One of the things your mother felt very strongly during the whole time I knew them was that she was holding Kyle back. That her needs were preventing him from becoming a great Volunteer. That she should have been studying the language, for example. That she should have been willing to live in a humble space in the center of the *favela*. That she should have been eager to help him do surveys in the community. Clint pauses for a moment. This point is very important, he adds quietly. Guilt was a crucial element of the conflict she was experiencing.

So, they were both torn.

Very much so. Anyway, I suppose we talked for an hour or more, waiting on Kyle to return. Finally, I decided to bring the airfreight up to the house. When I reached the gate, I saw Kyle standing by the Jeep talking to the boys I had hired to watch over it. There was quite a crowd admiring the old rig that had made its way through the *favela*.

The day was hot and Kyle had taken off his t-shirt and wrapped it around his head. Typical of a male Volunteer, he had lost weight. I could see the pattern of his ribs, the bones prominent along his shoulders and elbows. At that time he still wore boots and the grayish brown work pants the people in training had advised us to bring along. But with the thin bare top and the shirt curiously wrapped like a turban around his head, the image of Gunga Din came to mind.

Later he dressed differently?

Yes, but we'll get to that. He and I were happy to see each other, of course. We embraced and he greeted me in Portuguese. He knew the boys. The one on the donkey was probably the fellow he mentions in the journal. So we muscled the two cartons of air freight out of the Jeep and lugged them up toward the house. On the way he asked about Jolene. Was she all right? I assured him she was fine, that she was boiling water.

Clint hesitates. I suppose I should describe the water. It will give you a clearer idea of the conditions they were living in. They got their water from an open well on the property adjoining theirs. The well was very crude, more a hole than a well as we would think of one. It was located beyond a fence in a small cow pasture behind the house. I have some memory of the routine because I helped Kyle get water a couple of times. They had a bucket with a rope tied to the handle that you dropped into the water. If the bucket floated you had to tilt it with a stick so it filled. Then you hauled it out and back to the house.

The water was bright green with algae. So first they poured it through an earthen-ware filter they kept in the kitchen. The filter trapped most of the strands of algae, assuming you cleaned it repeatedly, but it was slow. Most every house had one of these filters. Many people erroneously assumed the filter purified the water. That was not true, as your parents knew. So after they filtered the water, they boiled it on the hotplate. Then it had to cool before you could drink it. Later when they got the stove and refrigerator, these processes could be completed more efficiently. Jolene had been running water through the filter and boiling it as we talked. When Kyle arrived I took them out to lunch.

Wait, Connie says, I want to know something.

Yes?

You probably don't remember, and I suppose it's silly, but do you recall how they reacted toward each other at that moment? I have this picture in my mind, okay? Mom is doing this thing you described with the water and you and Dad come in the front door carrying these, what, boxes or something?

Trunks, yes.

You set them down and what happened? Between them.

They've had a fight, right? He left in the morning and now they are together again. What happened?

I have no memory of that moment, Clint admits.

Clearly disappointed Connie says nothing.

I can tell you, though, that normally they were physically affectionate toward one another. Not lovey-dovey but they did touch each other. One image I have of them is from that first night at the reception in Rio. At one point Jolene and Smookie left the table, probably to go to the powder room just before we left for the restaurant. When they came back, Jolene stepped up behind the chair where Kyle was seated and crossed her arms over his chest and rested her chin on the top of his head. I was sitting across from him and she looked over at me with a warm friendly smile. I thought to myself, this is a happy couple and a lucky man.

That's nice, thank you for that.

She and Smookie were probably already plotting about the room. That's what the smile was about.

Mom had a nice smile, Connie says. She didn't need a plot to use it.

That's true.

You do have me intrigued about this Smookie though. You two were so hot for one another and then she ends up with this Vern guy.

Clint shakes his head. I won't bore you with the details. The three of us were close during training, as I mentioned. Vern and I were drawn to each other and to her and she was lapping up the attention, flirting with both of us in a very innocent-looking sort of way. That night, was just my lucky night. Vern undoubtedly had his. As an old and somewhat cynical man, I can't completely discount the possibility that she arranged to spend the night with me in part to make him jealous.

That would be sad.

Hardly sad. Joyous and frolicking to tell you the truth. But I can tell you this as one who is both professionally and personally somewhat knowledgeable about the subject. The process of sexual reproduction is endlessly fascinating. That is true of most every species that uses it as a way of reproducing itself. In *The Descent of Man,* Darwin spends a couple of hundred pages on the subject. We now know, for example, that tiny mites, mites so small that several of them at a time can catch a flight on one leg of a fly, that these tiny creatures have a courtship ritual. Can you imagine that? The males engage in antagonistic behavior in competition for the favor of a female. And the lucky male caresses the female as they mate.

Connie does not look impressed. Her expression, in fact, suggests disdain. Men have this bizarre obsession with size, she says.

Size? I'm not talking about their sexual organs.

No, size in general. Bigger cars, taller buildings, thicker bank accounts. Why is it any more remarkable that a small creature has a courtship ritual than a large one?

Clint looks surprised for a moment. Well, you have a point, he admits. Size and complexity are often related, but not inevitably. So, I accept your point as provocative, and thus interesting. His smile is genuine and open. It's the first time she has seen him that free with his emotions, and it pleases her.

So, where were we? he asks.

Going out to lunch, on you.

Right. Not much to say about that. Charlie Pell had told me to check on how they were and I figured he'd reimburse me for the lunch if it came to that. Truth is, I had more money than they did. My room and board were free. The stipend I got from the Peace Corps was pocket change for me. So we walked downtown. Kyle insisted we walk. He didn't want to be seen in a vehicle. He also wanted to talk Portuguese but I begged off, pointing out that being single I never got to speak the native tongue. Your mother appreciated that of course. Incidently, there is one other thing I want to mention about the entry we just read in Kyle's journal. What did you notice about the two of them and Portuguese?

Connie looks slyly at him, the daughter of a teacher recognizing the teacher in him.

What did I notice?

Yes.

Well, he seemed to study all the time and Mom admitted to you that she never studied.

Good. What else?

A finger comes up to the corner of her mouth. I'm not sure.

How did he describe the communication that went on between them and the woman next door? The one who did their laundry. Who kept swiping bits of chicken wing.

Mom did all the talking.

He nods. And the neighborhood kids who came to the door to beg oranges and coconuts?

They would laugh and chat with Mom but not with Dad, she says, a good student.

Exactly. Interesting isn't it?

Very, and why was that?

In part she had more natural facility. A better ear. You mentioned she sang in the church choir and I remember her having a good voice. That night in Rio as we were walking to the restaurant, Vern pulled out his harmonica and she sang along. Folk music was big at that time. In training, at conferences, we had hootenanneys. Kingston Trio, that was the era. So, I heard her sing, and I think her trained ear made learning a language more natural. But other thoughts come to mind.

Well, Dad's resilience and discipline for one.

That's true. He wasn't about to let a lack of natural ability hold him back. I admired that in him. But there is something deeper, something....

I don't know. Connie looks puzzled.

I wasn't questioning you, he says. I'm trying to formulate

how to say it.

Okay.

Here again I want to be careful. With the neighbor woman, that is easily explained. Given the culture and their status relative to one another, the woman next door would not be comfortable talking with Kyle. But the children. I think they perceived Jolene as more genuine somehow. More human. I'm not finding the right word.

Dad was more....

Well, more serious for one thing.

Right.

But also more doctrinaire.

He admits he's too serious, Connie says.

Yes, and willing to face it and work with it. But he was not aware, I don't think, that he came across as someone who was always trying to *improve* them. In effect, preaching to them.

Preaching? Connie asks, frowning.

Not the right word, he admits. But wanting to improve them. Thinking they or their condition needed to be changed. The problem never left his mind.

The problem of rich and poor?

The gap between them. In the journal he has referred to it. Not simply that it exists. But the tendency of people to accept it as a natural phenomenon. More than anything Kyle was aware of that tendency. He and I would talk about this. Our great gift as a species, you know, is our ability to adapt. But it can also be our curse. Given the right conditions and enough time, we can accept circumstances that previously we would have thought intolerable. As Kyle liked to point out, our history is pretty rugged. From the time we left the hunter-gatherer lifestyle and began clustering in larger units, most of us have been dominated by small groups of elite strong-men, priests, monarchs, military dictators. Kyle was aware of that predilection even in himself—the tendency to accept as normal, conditions that are neither just nor necessary.

And he fought that tendency with every ounce of strength he had. That struggle is what made him noble in my eyes. And in the end tragic.

Tragic?

Yes, Clint says, I'm afraid so.

So, yes, Clint says, we did have lunch at an outdoor restaurant located near the plaza in Nova Santana. The best restaurant in town, situated on a deck above the river, and famous for a giant scarlet macaw, a loud and arrogant bird that sat on a perch above the water. A most unpleasant creature, as I recall. A sign near the perch warned customers to not feed the bird. I wasn't tempted. One look at that beast and I knew he would prefer my fingers to anything else I might offer him.

Kyle had recommended a more modest establishment but I insisted on the best, inferring that I was carrying out Charlie Pell's orders, which in a way I was. Kyle even put his shirt back on. At lunch they told me about their difficulties at the clinic but Kyle described that in the journal so I won't go into it. The clinic was a real problem for them.

I can see it was a problem but I still don't get the impression Dad hated the doctor.

In time I'll develop that angle for you, Connie.

Yes, Doctor.

Clint, please.

All right, she says, giggling. Clint then.

It was early afternoon and very hot when we walked back to the house. At mid-day in summer there would typically be no breeze and the heat would settle like a thick blanket. The streets were nearly deserted. We were, after all, only thirteen puny degrees south of the equator.

What's our location here, Clint?

It occurs to him that she is not so much interested in knowing their latitude as forcing herself to use his first name. Shades of her parents, he thinks.

Well, the border between Canada and the U.S. is the forty-ninth parallel. So forty-nine north plus a few miles. A long way from Nova Santana.

I see.

Your shadow at that latitude in the middle of the day is so minuscule you step on your head with each stride. I was irritated at Kyle for insisting we walk. Finally a vehicle and he wanted to walk. And he always walked fast. It didn't matter what the temperature was, Kyle seemed in a hurry.

As kids we ran to keep up with him, Connie says. When the disease showed itself walking at all became a challenge for him.

Clint nods. Yes, I noticed the cane in the photos. And then the chair. I thought that an odd coincidence. Would you mind telling me what got him?

He passed on from a heart attack, Connie says. But the disease he had is called Kennedy's Disease. It didn't kill him but it sure slowed him down.

I haven't heard of it.

A rare slow-moving degenerative disease. The muscles atrophy and you lose control of them. Dad was in his fifties when the symptoms first appeared. He was not properly diagnosed until after Mom died. Sometimes its asymmetrical. For Dad it affected his left side more than his right. And swallowing became difficult.

I see.

So, Connie says, you were walking back to the house.

Yes, and when we got there I offered Kyle and Jolene a proposition. I proposed that they come with me to Jacarandá. They could spend the night and then return the next morning by bus. They had been talking about things they needed for the house. Of course, I was assuming both would come, or neither. It didn't work out that way.

Just Mom went.

That's right. She obviously wanted to go but Kyle was full of excuses. They had no money, but, of course, I had just brought them some money. Besides, the bus fare was next to nothing. They had no place to stay. But, as I pointed out, they could stay in an unoccupied room at the hospital. I knew Oscar wouldn't mind. But Kyle said he was hoping to meet with the mayor's assistant the next morning, and on and on he went with excuses. So your mom decided she wouldn't go either. I could see the disappointment on her face and so could he. You asked about physical affection, and this is one time I remember it. They had been holding hands and now he let go of hers and with his fingers he lightly brushed her cheek.

'I want you to go,' he said. And so she did.

And she stayed the night? That's in the journal.

Yes, in a room at the hospital. There was no way around that. Two buses made round trips between Nova and Jacarandá daily. You could come and go in a single day if you took the morning bus. But if you left in the afternoon, you had to stay over. By the time Jolene and I got to Jacarandá, the afternoon bus would have already left. So she had to spend the night. She didn't get to meet Oscar on that trip but I arranged a room through Orestes, his assistant. She did some shopping in the late afternoon and then took the bus back the following morning.

Do you remember anything else?

Several things, actually. On the drive to Jacarandá she was still bubbling over with talk for one thing. About her family, about Kyle, how they met.

On Christmas day, Connie says.

I don't remember the details.

Mom had gotten a new outfit and she wore it over to show my Aunt Connie. And Dad was there, he was home from Saint Bede's for the holiday.

I see. And she would have asked about Smookie, whether I had heard anything. She always asked about Smookie. Jolene had a bit of the matchmaker in her. Having helped set up the notorious evening in Rio, she was convinced Smookie and I were a match made in heaven. Turned out heaven had other plans.

As it often does.

I used the word as a figure of speech, you understand.

I understand how you were using it, Connie says.

Anyway, the road was terrible and I had to dodge potholes and change gears constantly. I was happy to have the conversation, and what Jolene talked about mostly was Kyle. I can't overstate the devotion, the admiration, she expressed for her husband. And I enjoyed having her talk about him. I was interested in Kyle. I wanted to know what made him tick. I had never met someone before who had flirted with the priesthood.

I don't think flirt is the right word, Connie says.

Perhaps not. Jolene explained that it had been traumatic for him at both ends, both going in and coming out. Anyway, I learned a lot that day about both of them. At one point, we passed a family walking along the side of the road. A father, mother and three or four small children. Typical of the poor people you would see along the road, they were sun-darkened, barefooted. Their clothing faded and loose about them. Their hands held clumsy bundles and they walked the unstable shoulder in a ragged line. We were still talking about Kyle and why he had made the decision to not become a priest. I wanted to know if it had been a loss of faith.

It hadn't, Connie interjects.

Yes, that was Jolene's impression as well. He was a good Catholic, she told me. But that meant little to me. In Brazil calling someone a good Catholic is ambiguous. It can mean nothing more than that you attend mass on Christmas and Easter, and raise your kids Catholic and donate when asked. In Jacarandá, the Protestants were called *Crentes* to distinguish them from Catholics. The word means believers. That tells you something about the state of the Catholic church in Brazil at that time anyway. So, I pressed for more information. Kyle went to mass every Sunday, she told me. He ate no meat on Friday and went to confession on a regular basis.

Practices he continued for the rest of his life, Connie says. Even though the church had changed the rules about meat on Friday. He liked having discipline in his life.

I knew him to be open to other ideas. He was not adverse to science, which I appreciated. In Ilhéus he had showed me a book by an Indian, a guy named Tagore, that he had brought with him. He wanted me to read the transcript of a conversation between this Tagore and Einstein.

Oh yes, he read widely about a lot of things including other religions. Buddhism, Hindu yogis, Native Americans. And he loved the King James version of the Bible. Every Christmas he would read us the Christmas story from Saint Luke.

Jolene thought he decided against the priesthood because he felt constrained by the church. He may have liked discipline but apparently he did not want to spend the remainder of his life struggling within the confines of a rigid order.

He told me he had come to realize he would not be a very good priest, Connie says.

That may be two ways of saying the same thing, Clint suggests. I remember an incident he described to me. He was flipping through the pages of a magazine when he came upon a full-page photograph of Mont San Michel. Do you know the place?

I don't think so.

It's a rock formation off the coast of Brittany in France. A craggy island at high tide but accessible by land when the tide is out. There is a very old building on this rock. In the middle ages it was a monastery. At other times it served as a prison. Anyway, Kyle reported that when he saw that image he experienced a sudden wave of nausea. The sensation he experienced was of being trapped. It was very powerful and he associated the nausea with the photograph rather than what he had eaten earlier in the day.

He thought he had been at this place in a previous life?
That was his take on it.

And you think that's silly, right?

I'd put my money on the cucumbers, Clint says with a grin.
Anyway, he gave up the priesthood but, according to Jolene, not
what had drawn him to it in the first place. She thought he was
searching for guidance on how to be a good person in a world
that is patently unfair in any moral sense. She referred to the
family we had just passed on the road. How does a Christian,
she said to me, a person who believes in the teachings of Jesus,
respond to the world as it exists? That was Kyle's challenge. She
thought that for Kyle life was a spiritual journey.

Wow, even then Mom saw that?

Yes, but her understanding came with a price.

What do you mean?

Well, as I said, she thought she was holding him back. 'Kyle,'
she told me emphatically with tears in her eyes, 'would never have
driven past that family without stopping. Never!'

As you might imagine, her words stunned me. I had given
no thought to stopping. They were just another family walking
beside the road. I said I was sorry, I felt I needed to apologize.
'Sorry?' Jolene exclaimed. 'Don't be sorry! I was scared to death
you were going to stop. Here we are having a pleasant conversation with a bit of a breeze coming in through the windows.
If they were jammed in here, smelling of sweat and whatever
they had in those bundles.... No I didn't want you to stop!' I'm
paraphrasing, of course, but that was the gist of it. She thought
Kyle was torn between what he saw as his work in the world and
his need to keep his wife comfortable and happy. She referred
to herself as a stone around his neck. That was her struggle.

I'm sure she really appreciated the chance to talk with you
about it.

I suppose. But the letters from her family had probably done
more to change her mood, that and the chance to speak Eng-

lish, ride in the Jeep, visit Jacarandá, which as I said, was larger, more lively than Nova. I don't think it had much to do with me personally. It could have been anyone.

But it was you, Connie says, glancing at her computer screen and her long list of questions.

Yes, it was, Clint says slowly. Anyway, there's one more important thing I need to tell you. That evening after we had done the shopping and I had arranged her room, I took her to Eduardo's restaurant for dinner.

The famous Eduardo.

Yes, the famous Eduardo. His restaurant was located on a corner.... Well, I want to give you the layout of Jacarandá. The river is running basically east and west at that point and the main part of town is located on a rise south of the river. There are several interesting plazas in Jacarandá, but the central one, which is called Plaza Dom Pedro Segundo, has a number of tall thin palms, newspapers stands and other small shops. The main church is located on the west side of the plaza. Behind the church is the bus station, which at that time was new and a source of local pride. The hospital, incidently, was located maybe a mile to the east and north of the plaza only a couple of blocks from the river. Eduardo's was in the other direction. A block past the bus station and a block north. The restaurant was on the corner of that intersection and it had both indoor and outdoor seating.

Where did you and Mom sit?

Outdoors, always, weather permitting. There was a roof of sorts, made with palm fronds. Japanese lanterns hung around the edge. Each table had a candle set in a glass bowl with red plastic netting. The preferred tables were closest to the street because from them you had a view down toward the river. Eduardo was big on views. The plaza would have been a better location for business but he wanted a view.

And the food?

The food was excellent. I don't remember what we had

that night, probably a steak. One dish I remember was called, *Churrasco Eduardo*, steak charcoaled with bits of sausage and covered with slices of hard boiled egg. Sounds like a prescription for a heart attack today but it was delicious. Eduardo did a lot with beef and with fish and prawns. He incorporated the traditional Bahian flavors, dende oil, *farofa*, And of course we had a bottle of wine. The best Brazilian wines came from the southern part of the country. I mention the wine because it gives me an excuse for what happened next.

An excuse?

When I introduced Jolene to Eduardo.

I'm confused.

Clint grins. Well, I'll explain. Usually, Eduardo greeted people at the door. He was a whirlwind in that restaurant. In and out of the kitchen, greeting people and taking them to their tables, straightening chairs, re-folding napkins, chatting with customers, pouring wine. But for some reason, that night he was not out front when we arrived. We were enjoying the last of the wine when he finally emerged from the kitchen.

I should preface this by saying that as the evening went on I had become increasingly uncomfortable about Jolene's position in this little outing. Here was a strange American woman dining out with me, her wedding band glinting in the candle light. How would Eduardo interpret this? Anyway, he spotted us and rushed over. I rose reluctantly to greet him. After the usual embraces and backslapping I turned and introduced him to Jolene.

'Eduardo,' I said, 'I want you to meet *Senhora* Jolene Henderson, my sister.'

Your sister? Connie asks.

Exactly. It just popped out of my mouth. I had given no thought to it. I had not said a word to Jolene about it. And like you, Eduardo was flabbergasted.

'Your sister, here in Bahia?'

'Yes, indeed,' I explained. 'She is also a Peace Corps Volunteer and she lives in Nova Santana with her husband.'

'Clint's sister! *Meu Deus do céu!*' Eduardo grabbed Jolene and hugged her. He kissed her on both cheeks. He hugged her again. He started calling people over, guests, waiters, cooks out of the kitchen. Everyone got introduced to my sister. And through all of this your mother projected the most astonishing calm. She never stammered, she never asked a question. She was gracious, friendly, warm, smiling.

Mom?

That's why I asked if she had done any acting. I swear to you, your mother may have been the greatest actress to never set foot upon a stage!

Chapter Twelve
THE BLACK SHEEP

Connie is suddenly full of questions but Clint refuses to talk any more. He tells her to shut down her contraptions and give them a rest. It's nearly five and he's tired. She starts to argue but then catches herself. They're silent while she disconnects the recorder, turns off the laptop and stows everything away in her bag. The beret is back on Clint's head and he's preparing to leave when he has an inspiration.

Come to dinner, he tells her. At my condo.

Oh, no, you needn't.... She's stammering, realizing that she would only be making more work for him.

But he insists. He gives directions and after a brief struggle Connie agrees to arrive at seven.

You can count on traffic, he warns her. There is always traffic. Any allergies I should know about?

She has none.

Do you eat fish at all? Some salmon? You're in the Pacific Northwest after all.

Salmon would be wonderful, she says. It's just oysters. But please, anything. Don't go to any trouble. I can bring some wine.

Just bring yourself, he says. I have plenty of wine. He doesn't trust her to pick out the wine. And the recorder, he adds. You never know.

She arrives ten minutes late, banging on the door. He waits a moment and shouts for her to come in. The door is unlocked.

You're right about the traffic, she says when she enters out of breath. Then seeing the windows she goes directly to the view and looks out at the river. Oh, this is marvelous! What a marvelous view! And it's clearing up. I had this picture in my mind, I'll admit it. Stereotypes, who can escape them, right? Portland, Seattle, Vancouver. Rain, rain, drizzle, gray, more rain. And then I got to the airport and sure enough it's raining! Then today, pretty cloudy. Pretty gray. But now a blue sky. And what a view!

More coffee, Clint thinks. She's been drinking more coffee.

And I should tell you, Connie continues, that airport in Vancouver? That is world class! That entrance. The Indian things. The dioramas, totem poles, canoes, green and growing plants. And the waterfall! Riding down the escalator beside that waterfall, I thought, this is world class, this is marvelous. Then I get outside, and sure enough, it's raining.

Maybe we should put that in the freezer, Clint suggests, pointing toward the 500ml of vanilla ice cream she holds in one warm hand. In the other is a small basket of fresh strawberries.

As he makes final preparations for the meal, Connie walks around the apartment examining everything. Yes, he says, those are my sons, Michael and Devon. Michael's the one with the wife and kids. They're in Singapore.

And Devon's the surfer?

Yep, the wave guy.

She picks up the photos and studies them closely. Handsome, both very handsome men. And a beautiful wife and two lovely little girls. Granddaughters, what a treasure. You're a lucky man, Clint. But too far away, don't you think? You need to seduce them into coming here. I'm sure they'd love it. I've only been here twenty-four hours and I've already seen hundreds of Asians, maybe thousands. Michael's wife and those little girls, they'd feel right at home. A little cold maybe. Singapore's probably pretty hot, huh?

Yes, pretty warm, Clint says. I prefer a coarse salad, by the way. I hope you don't mind. Collard, kale, chard, spinach, arugula, that sort of thing.

I'm sure it's delicious.

Farmers' markets are sprouting up all over BC much to my delight.

We have them too. In the suburbs, in the city itself. Chicago is a city of neighborhoods, you know. 'Sprouting up.' I like that. Very clever.

She stands beside the spindly philodendron looking at the contents of his desk.

'The Problem of Consciousness?' she asks, picking up an article.

Yes.

Connie giggles. I never thought of consciousness as being a problem.

Being conscious is not a problem. Explaining it is.

I can explain it, she says dropping the article back on the desk. The soul is conscious, see. The soul inhabits the body, wears it like a suit. Looks out through the eyes. Like they say, the eyes are the windows to the soul. We're all souls, Clint, consciously walking around in our bodies.

The body as burka, Clint thinks but doesn't say. He keeps his focus on the rolled collard greens he's cutting. Scientifically I mean.

I see. And you have a thing about crows, I take it.

Crows and ravens. In the door of the fridge you'll find a bottle of Pinot Grigio and another of sparkling apple juice. I believe the cork screw and glasses are on the counter. Would you pour us each a glass?

Edgar Allen Poe, she says as she begins to fulfil his request. 'Tapping, tapping.' That's all I know about ravens. Big black birds. Don't know that I've ever seen one, maybe in Lincoln Park Zoo.

You wouldn't in your neck of the woods. Maybe if you've traveled in the Appalachians, they're local there, or north near the border. Common in the north and west, of course. She has, he observes, restricted herself to apple juice.

What got you started on ravens?

It was crows, actually. My wife and I, my first wife that is.

Pamela, I think you said. The mother of your sons.

Yes, that's right. She and I were camping on Vancouver Island the spring of the first year we came up here, that would have been, let's see, 1970. She was pregnant with Michael. We discovered a family of nesting Northwestern crows. Mother, father and two newly hatched little ones. We watched them for some time. Those wide open mouths! Just about 180 degrees. One parent always at the nest. The other would fly off for food, come back and feed the three of them, first the other parent, then the two little ones. Why do they do that? I wondered. Why do they come back at all? And why share? Why don't they keep the food for themselves?

It's love, she says with a grin, handing him his glass.

She's teasing him, and he knows it, but he's too much the teacher to let it go. What we think of as altruistic behavior in animals can be explained genetically. Some animals are genetically predisposed to behave in such a way that the family unit stays together at least until the young have fledged. Others are not. Among crows, or their predecessors, those that were multiplied. The others disappeared.

That sounds so cold to me. So lifeless. She leans toward him, elbows on the counter, the curl of hair falling to her forehead. You might as well be describing a wristwatch or some other mechanical thing that has no life, something just running on automatic.

Clint turns from his work. I couldn't disagree more. The word mechanical suggests a static condition. A device set up to operate a certain way until it runs down, wears out or is modified from without. The biota, by contrast...

The what?

Living things. Life. Life is internally dramatic, ever changing. And lifeless, you say? Just the opposite is true. To study evolution is to study life. Its intricacy, its complexity, its precise interconnectedness and ever-adapting vitality. The more I've learned, the more I stand in awe of it. The more humbled I am by it. The more precious it seems to me. My own existence and that of every other organism that shares life with me.

Beautiful thoughts, Connie thinks sipping her juice, and yet in his mind, it's all just a series of random, blood-drenched accidents. None of this does she express to him. She is in no mood to go head to head with this man. Far from argumentative, she feels playful, almost flirtatious. An epiphany had come to her back in the hotel room. She had taken a shower and had already selected the gray slacks and the black blouse with its thin vertical streaks of jagged white that remind her of lightening, and she stood before the full-length mirror trying to determine if the red scarf worked. Worn outside the blouse, she decided, it was too much. She untied the knot, fitted the scarf inside the blouse so it followed the neckline and posed again before the mirror, hips slightly cocked, right leg forward, the palm of her hand touching her thigh, head tilted to the left, unaware that the pose she had assumed mimicked perfectly the one her mother utilized when selecting an outfit. Better, she thought, but not tonight. Out came the scarf and onto her left wrist slid a simple red porcelain bracelet. The pose again, this time with her left hand on her hip. She liked its loose fit, its flash of color, the angle it assumed against the back of her hand. At that moment she felt herself emerge from the grieving waters of Kyle's death. She could breathe! Breathe in a way she had not breathed since the day she found him slumped on the floor beside his bed. And she was on vacation and far from home. Someone else had responsibility for the boys, others were weighted with the endless office details. These realizations stunned her, made her laugh out loud. It felt delicious and a little risque, maybe dangerous. The danger part came back to her when she poured Clint's glass of wine: the feel of the moist cold bottle in her hand, the pale glowing color, the bouquet rising from the glass. Seventeen years, she thought, and still there.

She smiles now at her host in a way he has not seen her smile before.

I can see you have a gentle side, Clint, she says, though I must say it wasn't obvious to me this morning.

He's ridiculously touched by her words. Embarrassed, he turns back toward the salad, squinting in a futile attempt to prevent his eyes from tearing up. Don't be fooled, he mutters. You haven't faced me over a Scrabble board.

After dinner, Connie clears the table, rinses the dishes and sets them in the washer while Clint cuts up the strawberries. They decide to wait on the dessert.

The sister thing, he says when she has wiped down the counters. She recognizes the cue and he waits while she sets up her computer and recorder. The conversation, the wine and food have relaxed and revived him. He feels like talking.

The sister thing is the way I came to think of it. One rash moment and there it was, a solid feature in the world, as real as a rock face, not about to go away. And it didn't take long for word to get around. The next morning, Orestes, Dr. Oscar's secretary, approached me in the hallway. Oscar wanted to talk with me.

Oh, oh.

Oscar sat behind his desk smoking a cigarette. But I should describe Oscar, my friend and mentor. He was a short man with a large round nearly bald head. He had a thick salt and pepper mustache, a flat nose and eyebrows that came to points half way along their length. He hated his glasses and was forever pulling them off and banging the earpieces against one another as he talked. With the mustache, the pointed eyebrows and the large bald head he looked like a gangster.

A gangster? Connie asks in a teasing manner. Did you ever tell him he looked like a crook?

Clint frowns. Of course not. I was twenty-three years old. The man was my boss. No, I would not have suggested to Oscar that he resembled a crook. So, anyway, I went to his office and found that sitting across from him was Don Alfonso da Costa, Eduardo's father. I've described Don Alfonso, I believe. You said he looked like a lizard. Yes, I suppose I did. Connie giggles. So, we've got these two men. One looks like a gangster and the other like a lizard.

Clint pauses, sipping his wine. I see I have been unfair to them, he says, if that is all you remember. No, I'm being silly. That's not all I.... They were two very powerful men, he adds. Each a formidable presence. Yes, I'm sure.... So, I entered the room and Oscar jumped up and embraced me. He was honestly hurt that I had not informed him that I had a sister living only a couple of hours away. How could this be? Naturally, I apologized to them both. Fortunately, Oscar had been out of town for a couple of days so I could not have introduced her to him. Had he been available, such a failure would have been unpardonable. And I had introduced her to Eduardo. Right.

They also inquired about Jolene's husband, of course. I assured them that Kyle would come to Jacarandá and when he did I would introduce him to both of them. It turned out I was wrong about that. Oscar later met Jolene as I will describe, but I have racked my brain and so far as I can recall, Kyle and Oscar never met.

Don Alfonso was Oscar's friend, but their relationship was not simply a friendship. As the town's richest man Alfonso was also a frequent donor to the hospital. After we had finished discussing Jolene, and I had offered all the necessary apologies, they wanted to know if I visited the little garden across the alley from my room. I knew about this garden. I had walked through it on a couple of occasions. It was an attractive little enclosure, nicely landscaped. Oscar explained that Alfonso had built the garden. He acquired the land and designed the landscaping and had overseen all aspects of its construction.

Alfonso sat quietly in his chair, listening to this.

'Alieta,' he said finally. 'Dona Alieta.'

Alieta was Alfonso's first wife, Oscar explained to me. Alieta had died in childbirth. The garden had been built by Don Alfonso in her memory.

'In honor of all mothers,' Alfonso added. 'And fathers. A place for them to wait, as I had waited.'

That is so sweet! Connie says, drawing out the vowels.

This Alieta was Walter's mother. After her death Alfonso had married Dona Neyde, the one with the massive hips, the mother of Eduardo and the other children. Alfonso described Walter as a good son. Married. He had given Alfonso a grandson and more recently a granddaughter, also named Alieta.

'You are Eduardo's friend,' Alfonso said to me. It was a statement, not a question. Still, I assured him that I was.

'This restaurant business, what do you think of it?'

I thought it was an excellent restaurant and told him so. The food was delicious, the atmosphere wonderful. Eduardo was a great cook just like his wife, Dona Neyde. I thought I was being complementary as well as honest, but my words did not please Don Alfonso.

'A waste,' he said simply.

I looked at Oscar. I did not understand.

'His fiancé is a beautiful girl,' Oscar suggested.

'Yes, yes,' Alfonso shot back, 'and how long has that been going on? He should marry the girl if he is going to marry her. Does he think we live forever? Walter has two children and he knows *cacao*. He knows men, he knows markets. Eduardo needs to marry this girl and start a family. He needs to forget this restaurant business and get back to the family business. Doesn't he know where money comes from? Money comes from *cacao*, not from cooking fish and selling it to people under colored lights. Talk to him. He needs to understand what he's doing.'

It was quite a rant, and after he finished Oscar tried to assure him. 'Clint will talk with Eduardo,' he said.

I promised I would and Oscar smiled and patted me on the back. That had become my role, you see, a minor functionary in the hospital administration. I worked under the direct control of Dr. Oscar who took it as his challenge to keep me both busy and entertained. Sometimes, I think he enjoyed this. Other times he found it a burden.

Did this man boss you around? Connie asks.

I wouldn't say he bossed me around. No. He kept me busy though. When he went to meetings he often took me along. Later he would ask for my analysis of the participants. Other days I delivered supplies to a field clinic in an outlying neighborhood. Who's working? he would want to know. How busy where they? I picked up his cigarettes and his Scotch. I delivered messages in sealed envelopes. I provided a talk at his Rotary Club. I helped prepare orders for medical equipment and translated the manuals into Portuguese. I once accompanied him when he bought a bull for his *fazenda*, which he seemed to think was a wonderful way to spend a day.

That sounds like a lot more fun than what Mom and Dad had going, sitting in that terrible clinic with nothing to do.

Yes, Clint says. I'm glad you understand that. But Oscar was serious that I talk to Eduardo. Keeping Don Alfonso happy was part of his job description so it was also part of mine. So, one night a couple of days later, when Eduardo and I were alone together, I brought the subject up. Well, two subjects: his father's displeasure with the restaurant and his extended engagement that seemed to be going nowhere. I'm going into this because you know about Eduardo, and because Jolene was very fond of him.

Oh, yes, Eduardo is a suspect, Connie says.

A suspect?

Connie blushes. I mean a person I'm interested in. I gathered from your letter, the one I found with the journal, that Mom liked him a lot.

Yes, very much. Anyway, it was late. The restaurant was closed. We were sitting at a metal table in the kitchen with a couple of glasses and a half empty bottle of *pinga*.

What's that?

That's slang for *cachaça*.

That's no help at all, Clint.

It's a liquor distilled from sugar cane. Not a substance to be indulged in lightly by the way.

I'll remember that, Connie says. If I ever fall off the wagon. On the other hand, off the wagon I don't remember much at all.

I see. Well, Eduardo would be very tired. An evening at the restaurant was a production for him, a performance piece. He was the maestro, the master of ceremonies, the impresario, and by closing time he was drained. I regretted bringing the subject up at all, especially at a time like that, but he responded graciously. His father, he said, was a man who could never get enough. 'More grandchildren, more land, more money. If I went into *cacao*, it would justify even more land, more trees. If I gave him a grandchild, he would want another one.'

I apologized but Eduardo assured me that I had done the right thing. His father and Oscar had wanted me to speak with him, and so it was proper that I did so. He told me that unlike him, I was a good son and my father should be proud of me. 'You keep your promises,' he said, 'and you look after your sister.'

Sister? Oh, right! Mom!

Yes, I thought that was pretty funny at the time. Eduardo didn't blame Oscar either. Oscar had the hospital to run and there was always a new piece of equipment or a new addition that needed funding. Eduardo sighed and said something poignant. 'In this family, Clinton, I am the black sheep.'

He called you Clinton?

Yes, everyone there called me Clinton.

But not here.

Never here. With the black sheep remark, Eduardo was referring in part to the fact that Flora, his youngest sister, had just become engaged. He said it would be a great wedding and I would be invited. Flora had made a perfect match. A doctor in Salvador. A family of landowners who had a *fazenda* that adjoined his family's. Eduardo was hoping the marriage would take some pressure off him. Flora was made for reproduction, he told me. She would produce a load of grandchildren. But it would probably not be enough. It was never enough. He took up the bottle and poured more *cachaça* into each of our glasses. He studied them, then got up and came back a moment later with a couple of lime wedges, some sugar and a tray of crushed ice. He stood beside the table, mixed the drinks and stirred them with a long handled spoon. Even exhausted Eduardo could never just pour some booze. He always had to make it right. Always with a bit of a flourish, taking the tail of his apron to wipe from the table surface any trace of lingering moisture. Does that give you some impression of who he was?

It does, thank you. Did you meet his fiancé?

Once or twice, Clint says. She was young with a pretty face, very shy. She never said more than a word or two in my presence. She attended a finishing school in Rio, so she was seldom in Jacarandá, though her family too had its *fazenda*. I don't even remember her name.

Did my parents meet her?

No, neither of them would have met the fiancé. I'm not sure Kyle ever met Eduardo.

Really! That surprises me.

Getting your dad out of Nova was like pulling teeth. It's hard to imagine that Kyle didn't have lunch once or twice at the restaurant, but it's very possible they never met. Anyway, the next big thing that happened with your parents, at least so far as I am aware, was the defining incident with Nascimento. On that occasion your dad did come to Jacarandá. He came alone, though at the time he was in no mood to have lunch.

Before you go into that, there is something I want to ask you. If you don't mind.

Of course.

You said you took Mom to the bus station the morning after...

The sister thing?

Right.

I would have. We probably had some papaya, bread and coffee in the hospital dining room. We did that when she stayed over. Then I would have walked with her to the bus station.

And you must have talked about the....

The sister thing?

Yes.

I suppose we did, yes.

I was just wondering how Mom felt about it. The morning after, so to speak. It put her in a bit of a pickle too, I should think.

I know exactly how Jolene felt about it, Clint says. Jolene felt guilty about it.

Guilty?

She sensed, correctly, that I had done it to protect her reputation. So she felt guilty. She thought she had made life more complicated for me by coming to Jacarandá without her husband. Maybe, indirectly, I introduced that idea to her. If so, I regret it. But in her mind, it was another example of her selfishness. Rather than blame me, she blamed herself. And I could not convince her otherwise.

They're quiet for a moment. Then Connie says, When you were talking about the breakfast...

Not much of a breakfast, really. Some coffee, some fruit, one of those little loaves of bread.

...that you and she did that when she stayed over. Does that mean Mom stayed more than once at the hospital in Jacarandá?

Yes, Clint says after a moment. Jolene stayed at the hospital more than once. Several times, as a matter of fact. But you will forgive an old man. There is a sequence.

Of course.

Chapter Thirteen
NASCIMENTO

They take a break. Connie gets up, spoons out the ice cream, tops it with the strawberries and brings the bowls back to the table.

They're eating and quietly when Connie says, I'm a peeker when it comes to books. Mom was too. Dad never peeked. He thought it was cheating.

A peeker?

Yeah. I read the first chapter, see if I like it. Then I take a look at the ending. Sometimes, I'll try to resist. Maybe I'll go four or five chapters before I have to peek at the ending.

That's cheating all right.

That's not cheating! Who am I cheating? Tell me that, who am I cheating?

The author, I suppose. Maybe yourself.

Same arguments Dad would make. They don't wash with me. The author got her money. The publisher got its money. It's my book and my business. Besides, what is it? Like I'd tell Dad, a book is a bunch of sheets of papers with black marks on both sides all stuck together on one end. Nobody cares if I buy it or don't buy it. If I buy it nobody cares if I read it or put it on the shelf. If I read it at all or only part of it. That was another thing with Dad. Once he started a book he had to finish it. If he hated the book, he'd read it all the way through just because he'd started it. 'How can I criticize a book if I haven't read the whole thing?' he'd say. Dad wouldn't even read the stuff on the back. He wouldn't read the jacket or the blurbs on the inside. He'd start with the first word the author wrote and read straight through to the last just the way the author intended it to be read. The author was god to Dad. Now Gilbert used to say to me, 'I don't care if you read it backwards or forwards or standing on your head. Just you don't go telling me a word about it 'til I've read it.'

Clint smiles. Well, you can't cheat here, Connie. The last chapter doesn't exist until I tell it to you.

I know and it's driving me nuts. Do you mind if I make some coffee?

Of course not. He explains where things are. He feels pleasantly indulged. She has given him more ice cream than he would have allowed himself. He likes ice cream. He wishes he didn't but he does. He likes it enough that he never keeps any around. It's devilishly hard now to keep the flab off. In his mind it has come down to ice cream or wine, which in a way makes the decision easier.

A treat, he says. Thank you.

My pleasure. The meal was wonderful.

Strawberries were a problem in Brazil, he says as she gets out the old grinder that had belonged to his parents. The rule was, if you didn't cook it, then you shouldn't eat it unless you could peel it. No room there for strawberries. Of course, your parents craved ice cream. Well, we all did. That which is rare, you know.

And you? she asks smiling. What did you crave?

Me? Well, diving a car, as I may have alluded to. Hamburgers. American hamburgers with ketchup and pickles and the inner surface of the bun lightly toasted. The air in autumn. The crunch of snow when you walk on it. He chuckles. I used to write letters to Smookie when I was feeling lonely. Usually late at night, midnight or later. That's when it got to me. Alone in the hospital, most everyone, even the guys in emergency, asleep. There was an outside door down the hall from my room. The door through which the janitors hauled trash out to an old truck they kept there. The doorway had a landing covered by a metal roof. I could sit on the landing even if it was raining and if I kept the door ajar, I had enough light to write by. Poor Smookie. Sometimes, my letters consisted of lists of cravings. Weeks later I would get her response. Popcorn, she would write. Good candy bars. The smell of burning leaves. Toasted marshmallows. A really cold, clear morning. Skis running over powder. Did I say she was from Colorado?

Yep.

To which I would respond: taffy apples, the smell inside a library, the sound of skates on ice. We were tormenting ourselves, and each other.

You two. So what happened anyway? Connie slides a cup of water into the microwave.

Clint shrugs. Vern was writing as well. Maybe he had more interesting cravings.

He pours himself more wine. I know it's getting late and you're probably still tired from the flight. It's been a long day. But if you're up for hearing a little more, I'm ready to proceed.

A cup of this and I'll be on point for an hour or so. Like I used to tell my motorcycle buddy, If your motor's running, man, I'm ready to ride.

Clint frowns slightly as he glances down at his notes. We've come to the incident with Dr. Nascimento.

Yes, that's what you said a few minutes ago, Connie says returning to the table with her coffee.

He doesn't remember saying that a few minutes ago. Lapses. They've started to happen more often. Faces, names, little gaps in the record.

He sighs and sips the wine. So, let's see. One afternoon, it was probably three weeks or so after Jolene's visit, Kyle showed up at the hospital. That, I think, was the next contact I had with either of them. His costume had changed again. Now he wore a locally-woven straw hat, the kind you could buy at any market, and he had a pouch hanging on a strap from his shoulder, the pouch you later found in the attic. But he still wore work shoes, a shirt, the slacks he had brought with him from the States. If anything he was thinner than the last time. I commented on the hat and pouch in a joking sort of way, but he was in no mood to talk about clothing. He insisted we go straight to my room. When your dad got tense, the skin on his face seemed to shrink drawing it tighter against the underlying structure. His skin was tight as a drum when I met him that afternoon.

Dad was intense at the best of times, Connie admits. Sometimes tense, but always intense.

'I need to telephone Mr. Pell,' he said to me in English when we were inside my room. 'You can do that from here, right?'

It was true the hospital had a radio phone that could reach Salvador. I had called Charlie after I returned from Nova. But the phone was notoriously unreliable. Some days you could get through, other days not. And who knew whether Charlie would be in the office? Why the call? I asked. Kyle said he wanted to report a doctor to the authorities.

Here it comes, Connie says. Dr. Nascimento.

But what authorities? I wondered. And why?

'The Secretary of Health,' Kyle said. 'Maybe the police. That's why I need to talk with Mr. Pell.'

Kyle didn't have much time. He had caught a ride with a truck driver but the trucker was going on to Jequié and not returning until the next day. The bus back to Nova was leaving in an hour and he had to be on it. 'I left Jo back there and I'm worried about her.'

I asked if she was sick. Not sick, he told me, but very distraught. He refused to give me the details. He would explain after the call. But he had to call.

As we walked back toward the office, I realized that I too had a problem. I was about to introduce Kyle to Oscar and Oscar would know Kyle as my brother-in-law. But had Jolene informed Kyle? I started stammering around but he was in no mood to hear it. 'I know, I know,' he said. 'I have no time for that now.'

It turned out Oscar was away, and as I said, I don't know that the two ever met. Orestes let us into Oscar's office where the phone was located. I dialed Pell's number and handed the receiver to Kyle. Of course I could only hear his side of the conversation which went something like this.

'Mr. Pell, I have some serious bad news to report. You know Dr. Nascimento? Yes, the director of our clinic in Nova Santana. That's right. Well, I want to report him to the authorities.'

'...I don't know what authorities. That's why I'm calling you.'

'...in Jacarandá. At the hospital with Clint.'

'...because he killed a woman today, that's why!'

Connie gasps.

Those are the exact words Kyle spoke to Charlie Pell. Then he handed me the phone. And he dropped down in a chair, holding the leather pouch in his lap.

Charlie Pell was not a happy man, I can assure you. 'What the hell is going on down there?' he demanded. Of course I knew no more than he did, as I explained to him.

'Is there anyone in the room hearing this? This could get the whole program kicked out of Bahia!'

I assured him that we were alone in Dr. Oscar's office. That Oscar was not there and the door was closed. This was not totally true, but Kyle got up, closed the door and then it was.

'Well, calm him down, you hear me? Calm him down!' Charlie was not calm himself. In fact Charlie was shouting. But then, so was Kyle: 'She bled to death! She died in Jo's arms, does he understand that?'

Finally, I heard Charlie Pell take a deep breath. 'Okay, let's start at the beginning. What happened?'

Clint smiles. So, Connie, at that point, an interesting conversation took place. Charlie Pell asked questions that I repeated to Kyle who gave the answers to me which I then conveyed to Charlie Pell. Neither of them, it seemed, felt comfortable speaking directly to the other.

'Go back with him,' Pell told me before we hung up. 'Have him write a report about what happened. Then call me as soon as you get back. And keep a lid on him!'

So I did take the bus with Kyle back to Nova and on the way to the station, he gave me the full story. Apparently, a woman who lived in the *favela* just below their house had gone to a second woman in the neighborhood for an abortion. During the night she started bleeding. In the morning one of the woman's children came and got Jolene. When Jolene saw what was happening, she sent the child back for Kyle. Kyle was not permitted to enter the house, which was full of woman from the neighborhood, but was instructed by Jolene to fetch a doctor. Kyle ran across town to the clinic where he encountered Nascimento. The doctor was sitting behind his desk chatting with a couple of clinic employees. Kyle told me he begged Nascimento to go with him to the woman. When Nascimento refused, Kyle ran back downtown to the pharmacy which was owned by another doctor, an elderly man who no longer had an active practice. This man drove Kyle back to the *favela*. When they got to the house, the doctor determined that the woman was dead. She was a young woman with three children.

Oh my. Connie has closed her eyes.

I have a vivid memory from that bus ride, Clint adds. The bus was full and we were standing in the aisle when we left Jacarandá, gripping the overhead rail to keep from getting tossed around. Seated below me was a heavy-set woman and on her lap sat a little girl of four or five. The little girl was staring up at me with a fixed expression. She was staring of course because I was a tall foreigner. But in my mind this little girl was connected somehow to the three children whose mother had just died. That's why the memory is so vivid, I suppose. I knew she was a girl because the tiny lobes of her ears were pierced with studs. She was naked but for a pair of shorts. Her hair was dark brown, long and wavy but mussed up. Her smooth clear skin had the color of coffee with cream and she was staring up at me with the most surprisingly blue eyes. A beautiful example of the mixing of races in Brazil. A pacifier hung from a dirty cord around the child's neck. She made sucking sounds on the pacifier for a few minutes. Then the pacifier fell from her mouth and bounced off her stomach and all the time she stared at me with those large blue eyes. I was sort of in shock, looking down at this little girl. I still remember the impassive expression on her face.

Anyway, it was late afternoon when we arrived at Kyle and Jolene's house where a bit of a scene was in process. A sharp line of shade ran from the far corner laying a wedge of shadow across the patio and front steps. And there in the shade, facing the closed green door, sat a group of seven or eight children. They were silent, unmoving. Kyle stepped over them and tried the door. He found it locked. He asked the children if Jolene was inside.

She was, the oldest child said. This was a serious, somber child of maybe eleven or twelve, and she spoke softly, her voice little more than a whisper.

It wasn't just the children who were quiet, I now realized. No noise came from anywhere in the neighborhood, no music, no laughter, no children being called, no lilting conversation between neighbors.

Kyle tried the door again but it had been barred from the inside. He seemed perplexed for a moment. He turned back to the children and repeated his question.

The children nodded their heads. The two of us turned back to the door and stood staring at it. Then the oldest child said something that neither of us understood at first.

'*A morte tocou-a.*'

What does that mean?

I'll get to that, but what we heard and understood was only one word: *morte*, the word for death.

'*Morte?*' we stammered.

'*Sim,*' the girl assured us. '*A morte tocou-a.*'

'Jolene!' Kyle yelled suddenly. His voice was so urgent and loud that I jumped back. He pounded on the door. 'Jolene! Jolene!'

He jumped off the patio and ran toward the back of the house, shouting her name. Seeing him some of the younger children began to giggle and then to laugh, but the oldest girl hushed them. '*A morte tocou-a,*' she repeated somberly.

I was standing on the patio with the children crowded behind me when I heard the bar being removed from the door. The door opened and Jolene stuck her head out. Of course she was very embarrassed. Here I was again in the middle of the day, and once again she had been sleeping. Her hair was a mess. A reddish checked pattern marked the left side of her face as if someone had slapped her with a finely patterned waffle iron. Meanwhile I could hear Kyle at the back of the house yelling and pounding on everything that would make a sound. The younger kids started giggling again and this time there was no stopping them.

A few moments later the three of us were inside with the doors and windows again shuttered. Jolene had insisted on closing everything. Kyle brought out his portable typewriter and set it on the table. He started drafting the report on Dr. Nascimento that Pell had asked for.

'I can't stand them staring at me,' Jolene said. 'They stand in the doorway and stare at me. If I close the door, they come to the windows.'

I asked her what they were saying and she shuddered slightly as if she were cold. 'They're saying that Death has touched me. I was holding Maria in my arms when she died. They think that Death brushed against me as he pulled Maria out of her body.'

Oh my.

Your mom had had a tough go all right and was in a bad way. One of the women claimed to have actually seen Death enter the room, but Jolene had not seen or felt anything. 'We couldn't stop the bleeding, that's all. She just got paler and weaker and then she died.' Jolene's body was quivering as she explained this. 'It was everywhere! I just couldn't make it stop!' And with that, she covered her face with her hands and started sobbing.

Poor Mom, Connie says softly, staring into her cold coffee.

Yes, it was horrific for her and I know it tore Kyle's heart to see her like that. But his response was to keep saying the fault was Nascimento's. And to continue typing out the report. He wanted to make Nascimento pay for this terrible thing that had happened, not only to Maria, but also to Jolene.

'I don't want to be here,' Jolene said after she stopped sobbing. 'I wasn't trained for this. I was trained to teach mothers about nutrition and breast feeding. Not this. Why did they come for me? I'm not a doctor. Why did they think I could help her? And now I'm somehow special because Death has touched me? No, I don't want this. I can't live with this!'

In a motion that surprises Clint, Connie reaches out and grips his arm for a moment.

Well, nobody said anything for a long time. Then Jolene excused herself and went into the bedroom and Kyle started typing again. I slept that night on a grass mattress on the floor in the front room beneath a window. I woke up in the night and I heard the drums for the first time.

The drums?

We will talk more about the drums later. But that night was the first time I heard them. I got up and opened the shutters. The air was warm and humid and the sky filled with stars. A bat wheeled among the orange trees feeding on insects. Yes, it was definitely drums, and not far away. On the other side of the hill, maybe, beyond the pasture behind the house.

Connie is looking at him out of the corners of her dark eyes. You're not going to tell me one thing about those drums, are you?

A bit of melted ice cream remains at the bottom of Clint's bowl. He reaches in with his finger, sweeps it up and places the finger in his mouth.

Of course I will, he says. In good time.

In good time.

Yes. So, anyway, the next morning when I caught the bus back to Jacarandá I had Kyle's report in my hand. A version written in English, by the way, and a second in Portuguese. Kyle had been awake typing long after I fell asleep. The first thing I did back at the hospital was telephone Charlie Pell. You'll never guess what he asked me.

Probably not.

He asked if Jolene had performed the abortion.

You're kidding!

Well, we all say foolish things now and then, don't we? I've spent years in bureaucracies, so I understand better now than I did then why he felt he had to ask that question. Charlie Pell, remember, was an organization man. He had served his turn in the Navy. He had a degree in engineering, a discipline that rewards caution, precision and redundancy, and he had escaped to Bahia from a mid-level executive position in the bowels of a large corporation. His decision in mid-career to uproot his family and transplant them to Salvador had been a brave, if not a desperate one. But the idea that Jolene Henderson of all people had set up an abortion clinic in Nova Santana was beyond absurd.

I should hope so! Though I have to admit something right here. Mom and I did not see eye to eye on the abortion question. She believed in a woman's right to choose. I believe in the sanctity of life. I knew her position and she knew mine. We didn't talk about it. She stayed on one side of that chasm and I stayed on the other.

I see. So, of course, I told Charlie there was not a chance in the world that Jolene Henderson had performed the abortion.

I guess!

'Thank God for that.' Charlie said when I had set him

straight. 'That's all we need. Some Volunteer out in the sticks performing abortions.'

Clint sips his wine and chuckles. It really was pretty funny now that I think back on it. But Charlie had other problems and one of them was the report that I had on the table before me. That and Kyle's insistence that it be presented to the proper authorities. 'I know one thing,' Charlie said. 'I can't go marching into the office of the Secretary of Health with a report that accuses a Brazilian doctor of murder. A report written by a twenty-two year old American kid who's been in the country for a couple of months.'

He was probably right about that, Connie says. That's just the kind of problem a manager runs into. You want to support your people, but you've got the whole organization to think about. Yeah, I know where he was coming from on that one.

Yes, he did have the project to think about. The Peace Corps was in Bahia because of the Secretary of Health. Oliver Burke, the Peace Corps director for Brazil, had sold the program to him. If Charlie pursued Kyle's agenda he would appear a bigger fool than Kyle. But that didn't mean the problem was going away. Kyle was very determined. He wanted to go to the mayor. He wanted to go to the police. He talked about sending a copy to Ollie Burke in Rio. I made him promise he wouldn't do anything until he heard from Charlie. But he was ready to go and I made that clear to Charlie.

'What a mess!' Charlie said to me. 'Hold on to that report and don't show it to anyone. I'll be there by noon tomorrow.'

I thought that an exaggeration. Salvador to Jacarandá was a seven hour drive. But Charlie was true to his word. He was at the hospital by eleven, which meant he left home around four. First he did the political work. He sat for an hour drinking coffee with Oscar and me, talking about cigars and horses and airplanes, anything but what was foremost on his mind. The whole experience was terrifying for me because it was only after we were in

Oscar's office that I remembered the sister thing.

The sister thing! Connie squeals. Here it comes again. That's the problem with lies.

They have legs all right.

More than legs. It's like a wad of stale chewing gum in grade school. Remember that? It's making you sick and you can't find a place to put it 'cause it'll stick to your hands and everything else it gets close to.

Clint thinks about that for a moment, glancing at her over the rim of his wine glass. It had not occurred to me, honestly, that my little lie would involve Charlie, but obviously it did.

Sure it did!

Yes. Well, fortunately, Charlie was being a bit secretive himself. He never mentioned the Hendersons to Oscar or that he was going to Nova Santana, and Oscar never brought them up either. As we were walking back to my room, I decided the time had come to confess. But once inside, all Charlie wanted to do was read Kyle's report. He grabbed the papers, sat on the bed and insisted that I close the door, as if the words themselves might jump off the page and spread like a contagion. After that I chickened out. I could have told him told then and there but I chickened out.

Was it because of Nascimento? Connie asks.

Was what because of Nascimento?

That they got sent home. That would be my bet. Word got out somehow. The whole kit and caboodle was at risk. To save the deal this Pell guy sent them home.

Clint smiles. Save your money, he says. And have patience.

Not my strong suit, Connie admits.

Over the next few days, Charlie Pell did what he had to do. He refused to let me ride along to Nova though I pressed pretty hard on that. And he didn't stop by the hospital on his way back, though I thought he might. He pulled Kyle and Jolene out of Nova and hauled them up to Salvador. He put them up in a spare bedroom at his house. He fed them one of his wife's delicious dinners. He gave them a personal tour of the city. He got them all the money the Peace Corps owed them. Jolene and his wife went on a shopping trip.

Finally, he set them down and presented Kyle with the facts of life. The woman's death had been a tragedy. Their attempt to save her had been noble and brave, and he was sure they would remember the experience for the rest of their lives. But the doctor had not killed the woman. The woman had died from a botched abortion. The doctor might be arrogant and lazy but he worked at a clinic and he had a room full of patients waiting to see him. It was not his responsibility to go running around town with Kyle making house calls. Finally, the Peace Corps does not involve itself in the politics of the country or the agencies in which it serves. He would put the report in his file but it would go no further than that. He might talk to the Secretary of Health some time about Nascimento in a general way, but not about this incident in particular.

End of story?

End of story. I learned it from Kyle and Jolene three days later in Jacarandá. I was crossing the central plaza on my way to pick up some smokes for Oscar when I saw them. They had taken the bus from Salvador and had a short layover before their connection left for Nova. I walked with them back to the bus station and learned that Charlie Pell had given them three choices. They could go back to Nova, do their jobs and forget the whole thing. He could transfer them to another town. Or he would put them on a plane for the States. They chose to go back to Nova.

How was Mom, do you remember?

Considerably recovered, I would say. Kyle had done a clever thing, I think.

What do you mean?

He told Jolene it was her decision. If she thought they should transfer to another town, they would transfer. If she thought they should go home, they would go home. She chose Nova. It was an important moment for her, I believe. She had loved Salvador. It had been her first visit. Your mother loved to shop.

Tell me about it! She never lost that.

She kept a list of names with her at all times. I don't know who they were. Her family, I suppose. Kyle's family, friends. It gave her an excuse to browse around in shops, markets. She wanted to take back some special present for each of them.

That's so like her, Connie says, yawning.

Check when you get back to the States. You'll probably find little clues hidden in the homes of all your relatives.

That's funny.

It was very complex, you know. Each purchase had to be appropriate to the person in some way yet not too heavy or too bulky or too expensive. And now that I was a member of the family, whenever I tagged along as she shopped, I would get a play-by-play of who and what and why.

A member of the family?

Her brother, Connie. I had become your mother's brother.

Oh yes, her brother, I had forgotten. She feels tired. Oh my, it is late, she says, glancing at her watch. I've taken your whole day, and half your night. She clicks off the recorder. Thank you so much!

More to come, Clint says. But we have done a lot of talking, and I see the bottle is nearly empty.

And with the juice and coffee I'll be up several times. She begins to assemble her things. And I still have to drive.

You're welcome to the futon, if you wish. I understand it's quite comfortable.

Oh no, it's not that far. Besides, there's something I want to look at. There is an entry in the journal, one of the final ones. If I remember right it must have been written shortly after this incident with Nascimento.

What's it about? Clint asks.

Connie smiles coyly. I'm afraid you'll just have to wait until morning, Doctor.

Clint, please.

Yes, of course. Clint.

Chapter Fourteen
HUMDINGER

When Clint arrives at the hotel the next morning, Connie is already in the conference room. She's standing by the window with a large cup of coffee in her hand. The journal and other paraphernalia are arranged neatly on the table. Also awaiting him is a large glass of grapefruit juice. He had let slip that he liked grapefruit juice. A good thing he does because he had emptied a glass with breakfast and now he would be having a second.

I watched you drive in, she says as they shake hands. That is so neat, that van! Hand controls for everything, right? Brakes, clutch, throttle?

No, clutch, Clint says.

Oh, duh, of course not. Why a clutch? Automatic for sure.

Yes.

And power everything, right? The sliding door, the lift?

Yes, he says again.

That is so cool! But wait a minute. There must be a trick from the outside.

Clint smiles. Not exactly a trick, Connie. A key.

Okay a key. Gotcha.

Turn the key, the door unlocks and that activates the power source so the door opens and the lift slides out and lowers to the pavement. I reversed the sequence this morning when I exited the vehicle. The lift rose and entered the van, the door closed and locked.

I saw that! Wow! That really is cool! Independence, that's the thing.

Yes, he says slowly. That's the thing.

A caseworker talked about a van for Dad, but it wouldn't work. His arms were affected as well as his legs. He wouldn't have had the control. Connie seems to ponder the possibilities for a moment. No, she adds almost to herself, that wouldn't have worked.

I see.

Then she brightens, pushing the hair back from her forehead. I got out and about early this morning. Up to your old stomping grounds.

My...?

The campus. U.B.C. My gosh that place goes on forever!

Yes, it is quite extensive.

And what a morning! Clear as a bell. Warm. I walked for almost an hour. I don't suppose I saw half of it.

Clint asks if she has a map of the campus. She doesn't.

The hotel might have one, he suggests. If not, they're available at several places on campus. I can direct you.

Oh, good, Connie says. But it seems to him that her tone of voice contradicts her words. She isn't particularly interested in having a campus map.

You're given to mystery, he observes.

Mysteries? Sure, when I get a chance.

No, mystery. Singular.

I am? She has dimples. They're more pronounced when she's puzzled than smiling.

Yes, that's why you don't really want a map. You're like Michelle in that way. My second wife. By not knowing the names of the buildings or their functions, you're free to people them with your own imagination. If you had a map, everything would be defined. Here are the arts, there the sciences, that's student services, these are the botanical gardens.

Connie sips her coffee. She watches as he makes his way to his spot at the end of the table, continuing to talk.

Michelle is devoted to mystery, let me assure you. She grew tired of my need, my apparently endless need, at least in her eyes, to classify, understand and explain. Michelle believes that mystery is the fundamental truth of the universe. It is the ground before which all knowledge, all certainty comes and goes. This difference between us was probably present from the beginning, perhaps that's what attracted us to one another in the first place. I remember when we met she had a glass pyramid in her bedroom in which she sat to meditate.

A pyramid?

Yes, a small glass pyramid built for one. That should have been a clue, I suppose.

I should think so!

But who knows? It seems to me that her passion for mystery grew stronger as her passion for me and our marriage dissipated. By the end, evolution, that is, my life's work, had become just another creation myth. In her mind it was no different than say the Adam and Eve story or Raven popping open the clamshell. Evolution, she once said to me, is the creation myth for the age of science. And like all such myths, it will have its period of glory. Then it too will pass and the eternal mystery will once again be visible. 'But evolution can be distinguished from these myths in that it is actually correct,' I suggested. To which she replied with a rather haute certainty, 'My dear, all myths are thought correct in their season.'

Clint laughs. Who can argue with that? It is true that I desire to classify and explain things. That's the work of a scientist and my natural inclination. When some phenomenon appears mysterious, it represents a problem to be resolved, the way a symptom represents a disease to be diagnosed and cured. My own view of mystery is similar to Darwin's who lamented the poor fossil record that would explain the emergence of flowering plants, by calling it an 'abominable mystery.'

When he finally pauses, Connie surprises him.

Sorry, but this mystery idea doesn't appeal to me. I don't think I'm like Michelle at all. In fact I'm the opposite of Michelle, I like answers. That's what my faith gives me, answers to every question. If I don't have an answer I pray on it and the answer appears. Maybe we're more alike than you think, you and me. We both like answers.

Clint shakes his head. We're the opposite, he says. It is possible for three people to all be opposite from each other, you know. We form a triangle, you, Michelle and I. You and I both want answers but we seek them in the opposite way. You go to your Bible or pray on it. I study the mysterious thing itself. I study it without preconceptions. I break it down, analyze it. The answer comes from the object, not from an old book. It doesn't pop into my head while I'm praying or sitting in a glass pyramid.

He stops and she says nothing. They have approached an edge neither of them desires to cross.

It's Connie who finally breaks the silence. Anyway, I would like a campus map. Then I could find my way around. If you mark the building where you work I can check it out. That might be fun, to stoll through the building where you have worked all these years.

Then we'll find you one, he says, pleased. You'll want to visit the botanical gardens. The anthropological museum is another treasure. At the new library and learning center you can peek in the ground-floor windows and watch robots retrieving books.

Connie laughs. Robots! What happened to people?

Well, the robots aren't alone. People work there as well.

Well, I do like books, though with the business and the two boys I have little time for them.

And when you do have time, Clint says with a smile, you are, I believe, you called it a.... A peeper?

A peeker.

Right. A peeker. Have you peeked into any of Jorge Amado's books?

She's not familiar with the name.

Bahia's most famous author. Gone now, but alive when we were there. A friend of Angelica, Oscar's wife. I recommend *Gabriela, Clove and Cinnamon.* A very entertaining portrait of Ilhéus, the town where your parents and I trained. The story is set fifty or more years before we were there, back when *cacao* first became king. Angelica was a nut for literature, by the way, forever bringing me books. I made the mistake once of telling her that I happened to be driving through Idaho the day Hemingway killed himself in Ketchum. After that she would introduce me to people by saying that I was with Hemingway when he died.

Clint thinks the story is funnier than Connie does.

He watches as she recharges her coffee and feels himself relax. A fondness for the color black. That's typical of her generation, he thinks. Dressed less like the professional woman this morning, but the color still dominates, black slacks, a gray and white blouse loose at the waist, black sandals and no socks. A red scarf at her neck.

Well, now, she says, speaking of literature. She takes up the journal and waves it around. I did re-read that entry last night and I would like to go through it with you this morning. Is that okay?

That's why we're here, Clint says. Who reads?

I wrestled with that. It's not easy reading for me. But it's my turn. And I feel guilty for asking you to read yesterday. You've been doing all the work while I sit and listen.

I can do it, I'm familiar with his handwriting now.

No, I'll take it, she says, opening the notebook.

Wednesday March 31, 1965

Earlier tonight I forbade Jo to return to her job at the *Posto.* It was not something I wanted to do. I was upset at the time. Otherwise I like to think I would have handled it differently. Not a different result, just a different way of reaching it.

Our marriage is a partnership, as any marriage should be in

my opinion. We make our decisions together. But I remember something her minister said when he met with us before the wedding...

I would have guessed they were married by a priest, Clint says interrupting her, not a minister.

They were married twice. Once by the priest and once by her minister. Mom used to say it was like double-knotting your shoelaces.

A practical girl, your mother. So, read on, please. I want to hear this minister's advice.

The minister told us that most of the time a marriage is a partnership, but sometimes a marriage is more like a ship in a storm, and in a storm, a ship must have a captain. Decisions have to be made. Orders have to be given and carried out. Jo was upset with the minister, and I tried to comfort her afterward. This minister was pretty old, maybe fifty or more. He had been a chaplain in the Navy during the war. He comes from a different generation, I said to her. He had his say, but we know who we are. Now though, I understand a little better what the minister was talking about.

We are definitely in the middle of a storm. And in the middle of a storm any port looks good. But the *Posto* is one port neither she nor I will enter again. The storm, of course, is our situation here. We are alone in this small town in the middle of Bahia and we have literally nothing to do but teach an English class a couple of nights a week. The PC in its wisdom sent us here. It assigned us to a *posto* run by a *médico* who not only has no use for us, but has put us through hell rather than interrupt his morning coffee. In the process he took the life of a young mother. And the PC is not willing to do anything about it. Nothing! A forgotten report in a folder in a file cabinet sealed away in an obscure PC office in Salvador, far from the eyes of anyone who could act on the information it contains. But maybe it's not in a file cabinet in the PC office. Maybe Mr. Pell is so afraid of that report and the truth it contains that he keeps it under lock and key at his house. He wanted to make certain I had no other copies, that's for sure. He asked about carbon copies and I gave them to him. So, he has all the copies. Maybe he has even destroyed them by now.

I could always type it again, of course. Every word is burned into my memory. But that's all right. Nascimento has won. It's over. Maria is dead; he's still in charge of healthcare here in Nova. But that doesn't mean we go back out there like sheep returning to a fold, returning to beg for something to do. Jo was proposing that. She thought it might be different now. Our language skills are more advanced. Nascimento might feel bad about what happened. But I know better. Nascimento feels just fine. Maria's death and Jo's suffering mean nothing to him. It was never our language skills, not really. He wants us out of there. He has wanted us out of there from the beginning. And he has power, that's obvious. Even the PC is scared of him and the more we go back the more chance he has to humiliate us. So, no, we are not going back to the *Posto*, but we aren't going to be run out of town either. We're needed here. We have a mission.

And that is the surprising news! Today more than any other day I know that I am supposed to be here. It is no accident we are here, and although I turned the decision of whether we would stay or go home over to Jo, and I truly did turn it over to her and I was terrified when I did, there is no possibility that she could have made the wrong decision. The decision wasn't hers to make, not really. The decision had already been made and there is no way she could have made the wrong one. I know that now even though I did not know it then. "Oh ye of little faith!"

Connie pauses and looks up. Last night you used an interesting word. You said Dad was being 'clever' when he gave Mom the power to decide if they should stay or go. Do you think it was a trick?

No, I never thought it was a trick. But it did cross my mind, that he knew how she would respond. So it was safer than it might have looked. He says here though that he was terrified. I think we have to take him at his word.

Yes, Dad's word was good. Dad's word was always good. She turns back to the notebook.

All of this came clear to me on the bus as we were pulling into Nova. The road from Jacarandá comes in along the river. You come down a hill out of the dense forest and there suddenly is the river on your right and then the first scattering of shanties. Soon out the window I saw families walking with their bundles. A short time later I spotted the milk boy on his donkey, a five gallon milk can hanging on either side of his wooden saddle, his ladle banging against the animal's shoulder. His work was done for the day and he was headed home. If all had gone well, his cans were empty and his satchel stuffed with ragged filthy cruzeiro notes of small denominations that would be taken out and flattened and carefully counted by his grateful parents. The houses came thicker and faster. The bus driver blasted his horn. I saw chickens scattering to get out of the street with that matronly scolding manner they have. I saw children running alongside yelling with excitement. I saw the blind old man sitting as always in his doorway with his staff across his lap, nodding his gray head as if to say, yes, you are right on time. I know that boy, I thought, that boy with his donkey and his milk cans. I have bought milk from him. I know that toothless old man, his eyes milky and pale. I stopped to chat with him once. And the closer into the town we got, the better I felt.

Jo loved Salvador and our time with Mr. Pell and his family. She is drawn to cities as she is drawn to the sea. The streets, the crowds of people excite her. She loves to sit in a restaurant. She loves to poke around in the little shops. She always has her list of people for whom she must buy some gift, some memento of our time here. "Your Aunt Rita might enjoy this," she says, holding up an embroidered cloth. She can spend hours in this endeavor. I am grateful she possesses the talent for I have none of it. Were it up to me, I would probably be desperately looking for a few things the day before we get on the plane.

Did that remain true? Clint asks. Her love of cities?

Mom loved Chicago. We lived in the suburbs but nothing gave her more pleasure than a shopping trip to the city. Some of my most pleasant memories are Christmas shopping with her, just the two of us.

But she never saw the sea again?

Not so far as I know. She liked walking the beaches on Lake Michigan, the lakes in Wisconsin. I could of sworn she had never seen the ocean. But I've come to see that she had more secrets than I could have imagined.

I'm sorry for interrupting.

No, that's fine, Connie says, turning her gaze back to the journal.

Still, it is odd how differently the two of us envision this experience. For her our time in Brazil is a detour in her life's course. A side trip. Her mind dwells on the before and the after. She's collecting things and experiences to take back to her "real" life. But for me, this is my "real" life. What has come before, has been a preparation for this. And I have no interest, at this stage at least, in what comes after. Riding the bus into Nova today, I knew that I was coming home. Well, not home exactly, I can't say that it's home. But it is where I am supposed to be. Where I have to be at this moment in my life.

In Jo I sensed a hesitancy as we approached our town. Maybe she was asking herself if she had made the right decision. Maybe I should have hugged her right there on the bus. Maybe I should have promised her that everything was going to be all right. But I was scared, to tell the truth. I didn't want her to reconsider the decision. The decision has been made. We can't spend the entire two years wondering if we should stay or go, or should have come in the first place. If I pushed the first decision, that is the decision to join, she made the second decision, that is the decision to stay. We're even and we're here, that's the way I see it.

Downtown was busy, crowded with life. Our luggage was light, a single bag with the few things we had packed in a hurry when Mr. Pell insisted on taking us to Salvador, and then another couple of bags with the items we had purchased there.

What Jo and I felt when Mr. Pell told us to pack for Salvador was very complex and difficult but it can be boiled down to the simple fact that we were made to feel like children. We had no choice in the matter. We were not free agents. We were Peace Corps Volunteers, that is we were in the employ of the United States Government, and Mr. Pell is the project director, which is to say, our boss, and he was hauling us to Salvador, and that was that. Of course he didn't put it that way. He couched it in terms of a reward. We had been through a traumatic experience, he said, which was certainly true, and he wanted to give us a few days away, a rest, so we could collect ourselves.

But I knew the game. If I had any doubts while we were still in Nova, they were dispelled once we reached Salvador. It was all handled rather cleverly when you think about it. First he got us out of our home base where we might have had some power. (A petition signed by neighbors? A rounding up of supporters?) Then he had us in his house in Salvador surrounded by his family and his things, where all we had to our name was a toothbrush and a change of clothes. There he lays down the law: the report is going nowhere, the incident is over, you go along or you go home.

The Peace Corps has this sense of invisible power about it. You think you are a free agent. You volunteered after all. You

are an adult. You are on your own in your town. You build a
life, you try to do your work. Mr. Pell even refers to himself, his
secretary and his assistant, as support staff. And it's true, they
get us our money, belatedly usually, they got us our mail (again
belatedly) until we could inform our correspondents of our local
address. They saw that our airfreight was finally delivered. But
then something happens and suddenly you notice the strings. A
string is pulled and your arm goes up. Another string and you
begin to dance. Refuse to dance? All your strings are yanked and
you are gone and the puppet show goes on without you. That is
exactly what happened in training, both half way through and at
the end. Strings were pulled and you looked around and people
were missing. "Deselected," a bureaucratic word if ever I heard
one. Gone is what it means, out the door. You were lucky to
have a chance to say goodbye.

I have to admit that I resent the presence of the Government's hidden power. I had the same problem with the Church.
The parallels are striking. In both cases you devote yourself to
service. But if you think you define what service means you're
being naive. In both cases an orthodoxy must be recognized and
adhered to. You think you're finding your own path but in truth
it is more like a channel, and while its course may not be clearly
defined, certainly it exists within a set of parameters. You step
beyond them at your own risk.

Okay, I am compromised. I need to recognize that. It is also
true that I am a man of my word. I have made my promise and
I will stick to it. There will be no more talk from me about Nascimento or the incident itself, though we are not going back to
the *Posto*. Of that much I am clear. It is also true, that we are a
long way from Salvador. There is much to be done and I have
some leeway in what I do and how I do it.

Connie stops reading. Looking up, she says, I was not surprised to read this part. So far as I know, Dad never let himself

become part of a large organization again. He started his own business.

I can see how he would succeed in running his own company, Clint says. He was very disciplined. Disciplined and determined and bright.

At first it was just him alone, Mom helping when she could. Later he had a staff and agents who worked for him. He hired engineers and lawyers, contractors, accountants. He worked with banks and lenders. But he was the boss. He set the rules and established the direction he wanted the company to take. He never sold stock or had a board of directors. He treated his people very well and they were loyal to him. It was something he preached to me. Stay in charge, he would say. You have to live with your own mistakes. You don't have to live with the mistakes of others, not if you plan it right. I learned a lot from him and I have tried to follow his example.

Are you still working in retail?

Oh gosh, no, I run the family business now. Really running it, now that Dad is gone. She smiles and it is clear to him, how proud she is to say those words. I came home when Mom got sick. My marriage had broken up and I brought the boys with me. I felt called to be with Mom at that difficult time of her life. With Dad too. His heart was broken seeing her go through what she did. After she died, he began to deteriorate more noticeably. It was very hard for all of us. Dad had been troubled when I left the Catholic church, but he accepted me back now. He saw that I had my faith. And it was my faith that got me through. He brought me in to help with the business.

How fortunate he was to have you, Clint says. And Phil? Is he involved in the business?

Connie laughs. No, thank God. Phil has no head for business. His mind is in the clouds. He teaches a few philosophy classes at the junior college and grows a big garden. His wife teaches yoga. And he will have his inheritance.

I see.

I would like to continue now, Connie says.

Of course.

A curious thing happened as we were walking to our house from downtown. I realized that in a certain sense, Nascimento has tainted the downtown for me. The people there are his friends and neighbors. I don't want to overstate this. I want my thinking to be very clear on this point. I love Nova. I love all of Nova and people from all strata of the society have been kind and generous toward us. But as we left the downtown with its businesses and its walled-in middle class homes, and as we approached the *favela* where we live, I felt better and better. Those shops, those middle class houses, represent the attitude of complacency, the acceptance of the gross inequality that I find so reprehensible. In a sense the *favela* represents the same thing. It too represents the inequality. But in another sense the two are opposite. The *favela* represents the burden of the inequality, downtown represents the profit. Profit is light, it lifts. Burden is heavy it weighs down. In a fair society, the burden and the profit are spread across the spectrum and thus a kind of balance is achieved. But here, the weight rests upon the poor. The scale is indeed a proper symbol for justice.

My goal now is to avoid the downtown as much as practical. I haven't spoken with Jo about this and I don't intend to become doctrinaire on the point. I will accompany her to the market if she wants to have me along. The basket can become quite heavy. Nor am I going to insist that we never visit a restaurant or accept an invitation to a party or other social event. But my thinking has changed. In the beginning, I was thinking integration. Not racial integration, though skin color darkens as you descend the social ladder in this society, but class integration. I wanted to involve the more prosperous in helping those who have less. There is a group at the church, for example, that wants to work through the hierarchy to make our church a distribution point for Food for Peace. The local Baptist church is doing this already and the Catholics don't want to be left behind.

Fine, I respected the impulse and I was working with them on this project, indeed I was the catalyst that got it beyond empty fantasy. I met with the group a couple of times and finally we approached the priest to discuss the possibilities. Everyone thought that since I was an American and this was an American program that my participation would be crucial. The priest, unfortunately, is a huge disappointment. He mutters platitudes but does nothing. He is, I suspect very lazy and sees everything in terms of whether it will mean more work for him. If it does, he is against it. This man is neither well liked nor respected. The strangest rumor, and I stress that it is only a rumor, is that the priest has a twin brother in Salvador, that he goes there regularly, dons his brother's clothes and lives his brother's life, complete with drunken debauchery. I find the rumor hard to believe but he is unquestionably an evasive, furtive man who avoids eye contact and mutters his words and refuses to commit himself or his parish to anything. The meeting happened only a week ago and it had been my intent to convene the group again and to work with them to compose a letter to the bishop in Ilhéus. Not about the priest, but about the Food for Peace program. Now, I think, I will not convene the meeting.

There are two independent reasons for this decision. First, I have come to realize that getting the rich to help the poor is folly. (By rich I simply mean the people downtown, because relative to the people in the *favela* they are rich. And some of them are rich by American standards as well.) If the Food for Peace project worked, for example, it would be a feel-good thing, nothing more. The rich would think that they had provided some great service to the poor, and thus would need do no more. The small weight of guilt that rests upon their shoulders would be lifted and they could rest content in their prosperous lives.

Secondly, the Food for Peace program is itself fatally flawed. It reeks of hypocrisy, being little more than an incidental byproduct of a vast subsidy to the agricultural interests back home. What does it accomplish? It gives surplus food to the poor. Certainly the poor need food. Their diets are abysmal. In some emergency situations, after a flood say, or a massive earthquake, the program might be helpful and actually save lives. But to think of giving food to the poor as a solution to the endemic problem of wealth distribution in a society is both absurd and counter productive. It insures continued poverty by strengthening the poor's dependancy. What a travesty! The rich walk away smug while the poor become welded to the whim of a fickle United States Congress. The American farmer feels noble, the Congressmen feel noble, the rich ladies in the church feel noble and absolved and the problem has gotten worse. And how aptly named it is! Food for Peace. A farce, a fraud, a reeking hypocrisy! Give the poor a little food and they won't come banging on your door machetes in hand. Isn't that what it comes down to? A small bribe to keep the revolution at bay. Give them something to lose and they will huddle in their shacks content with a few mouths full of rice that were it not shipped here would have been thrown into the ocean just to keep the prices stable.

What could I have been thinking? Well, I know what I was thinking. I knew from the beginning that the program was a fraud, but I thought if I could help the church ladies with this I might spur them to do other things. It was naive on my part and perhaps I am guilty of the same sin I now charge the ladies with: the idea that doing something, anything, is better than doing nothing at all. Not true, it turns out. Doing something can be worse than doing nothing if what you do solidifies the status quo. I must never underestimate the power of my mind to justify its actions. Rationalization, a classic defense mechanism, is subtle and devious and endlessly attractive. The ego never rests in its struggle to make itself feel comfortable in the face of horror.

This is just one example of why I intend to avoid the downtown. Would it not cause me to choke on my own words I might actually thank Nascimento for bringing this lesson to me. I could not believe that he would do nothing! I could not believe that he would sit there and let Maria die and Jo suffer the horrible pain of those who stand helpless in the face of death. But he cared not a wit. That is the truth of the matter. And what I recognized as the bus pulled into the plaza is that Nascimento is different from the others only in degree, not in kind. At their core, none of them care. It comforts them not to care. It prospers them not to care. They simply do not care!

But if my heart lightened and my step quickened as we walked toward our house on the hill above the *favela*, Jo's heart, I am sad to say, grew heavier. Isn't this but another irony! That the house I once thought too ostentatious now reached out to comfort me while the same house she once longed for and insisted upon should now sadden and depress her.

"It's going to be a mess," she muttered. "All that mud the day Mr. Pell was here. Oh, I miss those showers already!"

Salvador like a worm had worked its way into her heart. It wasn't just the city with its beautiful vistas of the bay. How she loved those hot showers we enjoyed daily at the Pells! The clean and pressed sheets! How she enjoyed the sumptuous food Edith Pell cooked up in her kitchen with the help of Aliva, the servant girl. Yes, the Pells have a servant! It really was like becoming a child again. The Pells had become our parents. They fed us, they housed us, they showed us a good time. And in the end, just like parents, they told us what we could do and what we couldn't do. And Jo loved it!

But Salvador was gone now. Gone were the romantic buildings with their arched doors and windows, the wrought-iron balconies, the narrow cobblestone streets, the *capoeira* dancers, the costumed ladies selling hot spicy prawns on the sidewalk. The street too had ended and once again we were walking on familiar dirt up the winding rutted path to our home. I was bubbling with energy but when I looked at Jo I saw tears in her eyes. "What are we going to do?" she asked. Her voice was that of a little girl. I was carrying our luggage but she had the packages of precious things she had picked up in the city, and they seemed to weigh her down.

Do? I thought. What do you mean, do? We will get to the house and put our things away. We'll straighten it up and make some food and get ready for the coming day.

I expressed this after a moment and she was suddenly angry. "You never understand, do you?" she said, sharply.

So there we were walking along silently toward the house. I didn't know what to say and apparently she had nothing more to add, content to sniffle and try to wipe her eyes without dropping the packages, all the while attempting to smile and be polite to the people who greeted us along the path. And the poor do greet us, they treat us with respect, now more than ever. It has not escaped them what we tried to do for Maria. Jo had feared that being touched by death had been a curse, but in fact it had been a blessing, a grant of authority.

But that wasn't the end of it. Soon as we had a private moment, she said, "Not tonight. Tomorrow, and the day after tomorrow. What are we going to do for the next seventeen months? Seventeen months!"

Coming from her lips it sounded like a prison sentence. But I saw now what she was driving at.

"Maybe Dr. Nascimento doesn't want us out there after all of this," she added. "Then what are we going to do?"

Mr. Pell had mentioned the problem when he was trying to interest us in moving to another town. He even had a town in mind. He was going to drive us there directly to have a look but we voted against it. After we decided to return to Nova he asked if we could continue to work with Nascimento. I was noncommittal. I was worried, frankly, that if I told him the truth–that I had no intention of working with Nascimento—that he would insist on moving us. But then Jo mentioned how it might be different now that our language skills had improved, etc. It grated on me to hear her laying responsibility for the problem on us when really it was all Nascimento's fault, but again I held my counsel, and the subject soon changed.

Since I had not responded when Mr. Pell brought the subject up, it was reasonable for Jo to assume that I was willing to give Nascimento and the *Posto* another try.

"We're not going back out there, Jo," I said now. "Not after what he did to you. Not after what he did to Maria."

We talked about it some more. I explained my thinking.

"But what are we going to do?" That child's voice again.

"Look around," I said, waving my hand. "Isn't it obvious there is plenty to do?"

Well, that was the wrong thing to say. It made her angry and when a person is angry they can't hear what the other person is saying.

We were both in bad moods when we finally reached the house and went inside. The place was a bit of a mess. We had left in a hurry and we had no usable water. Jo began straightening up and I got some water from the well, cleaned out the algae that had dried in the filter, ran the water through and put some on the hotplate to boil. We made some dinner and Jo started drinking wine. I don't mean to say she was getting sloshed, but she had a glass or two and I think it is not unreasonable to assume it had an affect on what happened later.

I was washing dishes and she was sitting at the table with her glass when she said, "Well, I guess I can understand why you don't want to go out there. I know how you feel about him. But we have to do something. We can't just sit here and subsist! There's the conference coming up in a few weeks and we have to show that we're doing something! Like you say, you can talk to the mayor. But maybe I should just go out there, not with you, alone. I should just go out there, act as if nothing happened, and tell him that we want to be of use. I can talk with Rosanita. She knows our speech is better and she has always tried to be helpful. Maybe she will help us get back into Dr. Nascimento's good graces. He's our boss, afer all. He's the man we came to work for."

"I don't want to be in Nascimento's good graces," I told her. "I want nothing to do with the bastard."

It was quiet for a moment. I had my back to her, washing dishes. I heard her pour some more wine into her glass.

"Okay," she said after a while. "I didn't say you. I said you could talk to the mayor about other things we might do, like you said. And I could go out to the *Posto*. After all we did decide to come back here and..."

"Not we. We didn't decide. You decided." That's what I said. And, okay, I shouldn't have put it that way. As I write the words now, I can see that they were a mistake.

"So now it's all my fault, is it?" she said, angrily. "I'm the cause of all of this?" She was crying again. I am so tired of her crying.

I calmly explained that obviously I was not saying that. We are in this together, of course. But I had given her the authority to make the decision, and I was very happy she made the decision she did.

"You're talking like whatever happens from now on is my fault."

Of course that wasn't true, either. She wasn't really listening to my words. I hadn't meant anything like that. I was trying to compliment her. She was brave and loyal and she had done the right thing.

But she was hearing none of it. "You act like you have been absolved of all responsibility! Now we're here because of me and whatever goes wrong is all my fault!"

By that point I had had enough. I admit I felt a lot of anger. I put the dish towel down, well, maybe I threw it on the floor.

At least that's where it ended up. I picked up this very notebook and I tore out a page and wrote in large letters: NOTHING IS YOUR FAULT! I TAKE FULL RESPONSIBILITY FOR EVERYTHING THAT HAS EVER HAPPENED IN OUR MARRIAGE!, and I signed my named at the bottom and put the date under my name. Then I got the hammer and a couple of nails and I nailed the sign on the wall beside the water filter, where it is at this very minute.

Jo very gently set down her wine glass and stood up.

"And since I am responsible," I said. "Fully responsible, I have the right to make a few decisions around here. And one of them is that you are never going to set foot in that *Posto* again. Not with me, not alone. This family will have nothing more to do with that man or that place! Do you hear me?"

"Yes, I hear you," she said, and then she went through the door and into the bedroom.

That was two, maybe three hours ago. I haven't heard a peep since.

Connie closes the notebook. Clint thinks maybe she will reach for the packet of tissue but instead she says, Well, that was a humdinger wasn't it?

Chapter Fifteen
THE RAIN IN NOVA SANTANA

Should I get you some more juice? Connie asks after they have taken a fifteen minute break.

I'm fine, Clint says.

Are you sure? Something else? Coffee? I haven't seen you drink coffee. How do you get through the day without coffee? She gets out of her chair and reaches for an empty cup. It seems she is about to pour him a cup of coffee whether he wants it or not.

Clint holds up his hand like a cop stopping traffic. I had a cup with breakfast, he tells her. I've grown more sensitive to caffeine over the years. It won't let me alone if I consume more later in the day.

Connie sets the cup down and begins to pace. Oh gosh, she says, I hope that doesn't happen to me when I grow old! I'd be so helpless without coffee. Then suddenly she freezes. She is facing the window with her back toward him. When she turns her face is bright red. It almost matches the scarf around her neck. I am very sorry. I am really sorry.

Pardon?

I didn't mean...I didn't mean to suggest...

Clint chuckles. That I am old?

I am so embarrassed!

I know how old I am, Connie. I have some idea of how old you are. I know how old your sons are and how old my Aunt Mabel is. Mabel is the last of my parents' siblings to be alive. Aunt Mabel is old to me, I am old to you, and to your sons, well guess what?

I really am sorry!

Sit down, please. Turn your recording device back on. I want to tell you about the Pennsylvanians. The visit of the Pennsylvanians caused a bit of a stir.

Does it involve my parents? she asks returning to the table.

It was Kyle who caused the stir.

Oh, oh.

Besides, Clint says, studying his notes, if I remember correctly the next time I saw Kyle and Jolene was when I went to Nova Santana with the Pennsylvanians. Kyle's comments to the Pennsylvanians made him sort of famous among the other Volunteers. I don't think anyone ever found out about the confrontation with Nascimento. Pell swore me to silence and he kept a lid on it himself. But there was an American reporter traveling with the visitors from Pennsylvania. He passed along the gist of Kyle's remarks everywhere they went.

All right, Connie says without enthusiasm.

It was a few weeks after the crisis with Nascimento. You need to remember that weeks passed when I had no contact with Kyle and Jolene Henderson. I had my work and my life and they had theirs. We did not correspond or communicate regularly between meetings.

That makes sense.

Well, one day, probably in April, I know it was before the conference which was in May....

Dad mentions the conference.

Yes, I'll get to the conference. But one day a woman and a couple of men from Pennsylvania came to the hospital. Accompanying them was the reporter I mentioned. He was from an American national newspaper. It might have been the *Los Angeles Times*, I can't remember. There was also an embassy man who represented the Alliance for Progress. The Alliance was a foreign aid program established by the Kennedy administration. The Pennsylvanians were in Brazil on behalf of an organization set up by a group of service clubs. They had come in search of small aid projects that individually were not large enough to justify funding from the Alliance but were worthy and could be funded by one or more of the service organizations. In other words, they were looking for ways to spend money and Oscar and I were happy to help. We suggested screens for the windows in the operating room. Months later the screens arrived and were installed. I didn't have much to brag about when I got back to the States, but at least I could claim that the countless flies inhabiting the hospital in Jacarandá had to find their nutrition someplace other than the exposed organs in the operating room.

A grimace from Connie. I can't imagine an operating room with windows and no screens.

Screens inhibit the flow of air. We had no air conditioning. The surgeons complained about the screens but Oscar brought them around. Anyway, after our meeting at the hospital the group was driving to Nova Santana. Oscar let me go along to help show the way. It was April, as I said. We were moving out of summer and into fall. We had started getting some rain and the temperatures were a little less intense. That was my first visit to Nova after a rain and the cobblestone streets were slick with manure and the soggy rinds of jack fruit. The Pennsylvanians were expected by the mayor. He had a tour scheduled to show them a few of his favorite projects. He and his entourage welcomed us at city hall with coffee and biscuits. Among the honored guests was your mother.

And Dad?

No Kyle at the social. And hearing that last entry we can imagine why. Kyle had lost faith in the town's movers and shakers. He was placing his loyalty with the poor.

Right.

The mayor's name was Almondo. We called him Doctor Almondo because he was a lawyer. Dr. Almondo was happy to have Jolene at the meeting. He took pleasure in introducing her to everyone. Oscar had been the same way. The Brazilians thought it would increase their chances of getting American aid money if they could parade out a Volunteer or two even though we had nothing to do with other government programs. We also know from the journal that by this time your parents were no longer working at the clinic, though working is a misnomer. Apparently, they never were able to do any work at the clinic. Anyway, Kyle had started a new project with the help of the mayor's office.

The garden project?

Yes, establishing a garden and teaching gardening skills to young boys. I don't remember where your mother stood at that point with her sewing project. That day with the Pennsylvanians was when I first met Dr. Almondo. I would see him again later under very different circumstances, as you shall see.

He was a bit of an odd duck, this Almondo, but he turned out to be very helpful to your parents. Obviously, their rejection by Nascimento had a profound influence on them. They had come to Bahia to be of service and Nascimento did not want their help. Hardly the reception they had expected or prepared for. It seems to me, though, by going to the mayor's office Kyle had been resourceful. He persisted through what had certainly been a bureaucratic fog, and eventually enlisted the mayor's support for the projects they or perhaps the mayor envisioned. I credit the mayor as well for being open and willing to provide support.

Well, the help was free, Connie says. Why turn it down?

You'll understand when I explain that in some ways this was a precarious time in Brazil. A few months before we arrived there had been a military coup. A left-leaning government had been ousted and a cabal of generals had assumed control. In the wake of the coup there were investigations. The investigation resembled, though on a much smaller scale, the anti-communist McCarthy investigations in the fifties in the States. The former mayor in Nova had been removed from office a few weeks before we arrived and this new mayor had replaced him. The former mayor was seen as too populous, too closely aligned with the old regime, which in the minds of many meant communist. You missed the fifties of course but being linked to communism then was analogous to being linked to terrorism today.

I understand.

And you didn't have to be caught walking around with a Molotov cocktail in your throwing arm. A new school in the *favela* might be enough to put you under suspicion. So, the old guy was out and this new guy, Almondo, was in. Though in this case, the new guy was rather old. And yes, I'm being consistent here, Clint adds smiling. By old, I mean older than I was when I knew him. In his fifties, probably. But it wasn't just age. He was also old in style. Every time I saw him he was wearing a suit and tie. A thin man with soft hands and dark glasses, an intellectual, very proper and formal. I always thought of him as having stepped out of the nineteenth century, the perfect person to comfort the junta. But underneath he was quite progressive. He was kind and helpful, not only toward your parents but also toward the poor. He took risks, I realized later, but was quite sly about it. Several of the projects we visited that afternoon had been initiated by the dynamic former mayor. Dr. Almondo kept them in place but changed their names to make them sound less threatening. A cluster of new houses, for example, constructed for the victims of a flood two years before and formerly known as the *Bairro de Democracia,* was now called the *Bairro de Republica.* The garden where we found Kyle digging a post hole, previously called the People's Garden was now officially the City Garden.

So, Dad...?

Yes, there he was, straddling the post hole, his bare feet sunk in the mud, shirt thrown off and lying in the grass, his skinny torso brown from the sun, pant legs rolled up, digging away, while five boys aged ten to fourteen or so, stood around watching him. The scene begged for a photograph and the reporter jumped out and shot several. I have no idea if they were ever published.

No question though, your dad was in his element and more than happy to give a little speech about the new project.

'These boys are learning to take charge of their lives,' he told the visitors. 'Instead of giving them food, we teach them to grow their own food. Instead of asking for a hand out they are reaching out for a higher rung on the ladder.'

He spoke in English for the benefit of the guests so I'm not sure how much the mayor and his entourage understood but they were beaming. The Pennsylvanians were lapping it up as you might imagine, and Jolene was blushing with pride. But then everything changed. It took just one question from the Pennsylvanians. It was a simple question and well intended. 'Tell us,' one of the men asked, 'how can we help you?'

I don't....

Well, it wasn't the question, Clint says. It was Kyle's answer that caused the problem. He said they couldn't help. In fact whatever they gave would only hurt.

But why...?

Clint lifts his hand again stopping her. He peers mischievously at her over the rim of his glasses. I can tell you that everyone got real quiet at that point. The visitors looked at each other and then they looked at the guy from the Alliance for Progress. The guy from the Alliance explained to Kyle that the Alliance had seeds they could get to him. Then one of the Pennsylvanians suggested tools. They could assemble a package of spades and rakes and ship them down. Everybody was nodding their heads, thinking this was an excellent idea.

But Kyle would have none of it. 'You don't get it,' he told them 'You think you can just show up here and help? You can't help. Seeds, shovels? What's the lesson in that? That some rich American might show up some day and solve your problems? Fat chance.'

Oh my. Connie looks toward the ceiling.

That wasn't the end of it. He introduced the five boys, and

he announced their names as if he were introducing an all star sports team. 'These young men are learning the only lesson worth learning. That they are in charge of their own lives. That nobody is going to solve their problems for them. They are human beings living on this earth and they have as much right as anyone to a good and rich life. It is their right and they don't have to beg for it and they certainly shouldn't wait around for someone to hand it to them. They have the right to *demand* it! And they have the right, if necessary, to *take* it!'

Clint chuckles, nodding his head. So, there we stood, quiet and a bit embarrassed. The mayor and his assistants may not have understood the details but they knew Kyle's words would not lead to money for the city's coffers. The Pennsylvanians were ticked off. They didn't appreciate being told that their mission was doing more harm than good. The guy from the Alliance for Progress was furious. And the reporter, a rather cynical fellow who I found very entertaining, could barely contain his amusement.

What a mess!

You've been married, Connie, so I think you'll understand when I describe something significant that happened next. I've tried it twice, you know.

What?

Marriage.

Well, we're a pair of losers then. Two for you and one for me.

Hardly losers, Clint replies. Just not married.

Connie laughs. Yes, now I like the sound of that!

Anyway, he continues, it was your mother who broke the silence. Here's what she said: 'Hon, these people are only trying to help.'

So? Connie's dimples return to her cheeks.

I submit that was the wrong thing to say.

It was true, wasn't it?

It most certainly was. Kyle had been a fool on his high horse giving that little sermon. But what she said was also false.

I guess I don't understand.

False because she didn't say it to convey the obvious fact that the Pennsylvanians were trying to help. She said it to cover up her own embarrassment.

Now, I really don't understand

This was an exciting day for Jolene and she had dressed for the occasion. Earrings, perfume, a nice dress. All these important Americans in her town and one of them a woman, the mayor proudly introducing her at the social, the chance to speak English, get the latest news from the States, be the center of attention.

Yes....

And now here was her nearly naked husband, standing in a pasture up to his ankles in mud, telling these important people exactly what they didn't want to hear.

Okay, I understand.

Kyle was Jolene's hero. Probably had been from the first time she met him. So far as I know he was her hero to the end of her days. But at that moment, she saw Kyle Henderson in a different light and she was embarrassed. She spoke to cover that embarrassment. In that sense, it seems to me, her words were a betrayal. I'm not going to sugar coat anything here.

I understand.

I picked up on it at the time, and so did your parents. Jolene regretted her words the minute she spoke them. I saw it in her face and when I looked at Kyle I saw that her words had cut him like a knife.

Connie winces.

For all Kyle's arrogant self-righteousness he recognized, I think, that he was alone at that moment. He had angered the mayor. He had annoyed his fellow countrymen. He'd been injured by his wife. But don't get me wrong. Kyle wasn't backing down. Skinny, bare-chested, standing alone on a pathetic patch of ground with five scruffy boys, their skin various shades of brown, their shorts colorless, their shirts ragged. He had spoken the truth as he saw it, and he had taken his stand. Yes, that was your father, and that is one of the finest memories I have of him. From that spot of ground Kyle Henderson was going to leverage a change in the world. And he was going to be true to himself and to his beliefs while he did it. I felt great admiration for him at that moment, even affection. At the same time, I thought him ridiculous.

The two of them are silent for a moment and Clint feels vaguely vulgar and corrupt. Who is he to make these observations? What does he know about marriage? Connie's right. He had failed twice and however he may try to cover it over, the dark sense of failure lingers.

So, what happened?

We left, Clint says. We returned to the vehicles and we left him there. I think your mom stayed, but we left. The mayor had other projects to show. After the tour the Pennsylvanians would be traveling on to Itabuna and I had to catch the bus back to Jacarandá. I don't think I saw the Hendersons again until the conference a few weeks later.

This conference. Did my dad present a paper or something?

I wouldn't call it a paper. Charlie Pell selected him to give one of the presentations. At every conference, a couple of Volunteers made presentations. I was rather surprised that Charlie gave him a forum. In my mind Kyle was still the super Volunteer. But I was also beginning to think of him as a loose cannon.

Did he do something strange at the conference?

Not at all. The session he led was motivating.

I think there may be a draft of his presentation in the journal. It's one of my favorite entries. Much of what I read in here.... well, I know Dad wrote the words, but it doesn't sound like the dad I knew. But this speech or whatever you call it has his charm, his humility. She opens the journal and begins to glance through the pages.

Wait, here's a reference to it. Oh, I remember this. This was another one I liked.

Monday April 5, 1965

Mr. Pell has asked me to present a program at the conference that's going to be held in Salvador in the middle of May. I am surprised and flattered and a little nervous. He didn't suggest a subject. The letter simply said that I would have an hour on the last day, that I should prepare a brief presentation on a subject that is of interest to me. One that would provoke a discussion among my fellow Volunteers.

Also, Jo's idea of a sewing class went over well with the mayor, once she finally got in to see him. More than a week went by between the day she first tried to set up an appointment and the day the meeting actually took place. He was impressed that she makes most of her own clothes, that she is skilled not only at hand-stitching and machine work but also pattern making. He agreed with her that these are skills young poor women would benefit from learning. He offered to find a treadle machine for her, and Salvador, his assistant, offered a building in the *favela* as a classroom. The sewing class, like the garden project, will be part of the vocational school the mayor is trying to start. I am very proud that she has taken the initiative on this. We'll see, though. The mayor has a way of saying things that don't end up happening.

The garden project is moving very slowly. Some days it just rains and the ground is soggy and the boys don't show up and I get saturated and frustrated out there trying to put in the fence. The fence is the first step. We have to secure the area from the goats and mules. They will eat everything we grow if we can't keep them out. Bahia is a fencing-out culture rather than a fencing-in culture like we have at home. If you want to protect something you put up the fence.

The mayor has promised me posts and wire fencing but neither the posts nor the wire has been delivered. I'm digging the holes even though I have no posts to put in them. When the posts do arrive we'll be ready to set them and string the wire. When the boys are present I try to get them to help. And like everyplace else in life, some are more willing and capable than others.

I try to not let the rain stop me. I want to set an example. I have to say, these people are put off course by most everything that comes along. Take this week, the week between Palm Sunday and Easter, known here as the "Week of the Saints." The grade schools are closed all week, the secondary school only goes through Wednesday. The mayor's office will also be closed Thursday through Sunday and even on the days it's open, no real work gets done. Everyone is content to meet and greet and drink coffee. The whole week takes on the flavor of a holiday. I have no hope that my posts and wire will arrive by week's end, or the sewing machine show up or the building become available. What to do? I go to the mayor's office. I pester, I remind them of my presence. Sometimes I feel like Sisyphus, condemned to be forever pushing his rock up the hill.

Today it's raining again, and I have to say I go out in the rain not just to set an example. The fact is, I would go nuts if I stayed in the house day after rainy day. When the rains first began this fall I tried to stay in. I used the wood we had lying around to construct some more furniture and shelving. I drew out the garden plot and designed the size, the number and location of the raised beds we will need to construct. I decided what crops to grow and where each variety would be placed among the beds. I made a list of the tools we needed and hiked down to the local hardware store to find out what seeds and tools are available and how much they cost. I made lists with prices and delivered them to Salvador who is ostensibly in charge of the vocational school. I studied the language books. I wrote an article on the open-air markets for the newspaper back home.

But it gets old, and it gets old in a hurry. The weather is not cold, it's just wet and muddy. I sit in the open doorway and look out at the rain. I'm thinking I only have a few months here and what am I doing sitting in this doorway watching rain fall on the trees? Pretty soon Jo is speaking English to me. She wants to talk. If I say something in Portuguese, she comes back in English. The rain has depressed her too and she wants to relax and make the best of it. She turns on the radio, finds the BBC or Armed Forces Radio. She sits at the table drinking tea and listening to English programming while sewing something for the house. When evening comes she puts away the tea and the sewing and brings out the wine. She makes dinner, dancing around the hotplate singing along with the radio.

Mostly though she wants to talk. She tells me that life is going on at home and she is sitting here in this house with the rain falling down and she has nothing to do and is not helping anyone. She's afraid that she's missing out and she will never catch up. She's getting fat, and old and ugly, but mostly fat. And it wouldn't be so bad if she was actually helping someone, but who are we helping? "Really, who are we helping?" And she's right, who are we helping? But that's our responsibility, I think to myself: find what needs to be done and do it!

She goes on. The people back home are going to school, getting jobs, getting engaged, having children. Her friends from the University write us. They tell us over and over how much they admire what we're doing. Then they start talking about their classes and the sororities they're pledging, and who is going with who.

She wants to talk about her family, about my family. She goes into all the intricacies of both families. What children are favored by what parent, and what children are not favored. And how that relates to where the particular child is located in terms of age. How oldest children have a different life than the middle kids and how the middle children are different than the youngest kids. She wants to talk about her oldest sister's husband and the other guy her sister dated in high school and what happened that she didn't marry the first guy and did marry the second, even though everybody in the family liked the first guy better. And she wants to know what I think about all this. Did I know the first guy? I must remember him. He rode around town in a 1950 Ford that had an ivory cue ball as the handle on the gear shift, and the car was never really painted. It was that gray color, what do you call it? Primer? I suggest. Yes, primer, You must remember this guy, she tells me. He got drafted and now he's in the Army.

She wants my opinion on all kinds of things. Should she change her major when she gets back to school? And if so, to what? And her sisters. Isn't her youngest sister the funniest person in the whole world? She reads her letters out loud to me so I can get the full affect of the humor. Her youngest sister and her sister's best friend have developed a language of weird words and the letter is full of these strange words and all kinds of funny gossip, most of which is probably less true than you might think.

She tells me about her aunts and uncles, and how her mother had an older sister who died in the flu epidemic in 1918 and her father had an older brother who was killed when lightening struck the steel-wheeled tractor he was driving one summer weeding corn and how the storm came up suddenly behind him like some malevolent creature and killed him with a single bolt of lightening and how this uncle of hers was scorched black and didn't know what hit him. And how on Memorial Day the families still place flowers on the graves of these children. And talking about this makes her feel vulnerable, because things happen and we are so far from everyone.

Her grandfather too on her mother's side. He died from dropsy when her mother was a teenager. How huge and bloated he was in the photographs taken in his later years, though he was quite handsome in his wedding picture. I do remember that wedding picture, right? The one hanging in the hallway on the way to the bathroom in her parents' house? Oh, I must remember, her grandparents look so stern and formal, the way people did in the photographs taken in those days. The grandfather is seated in a chair and his bride is standing beside him with her hand on his shoulder. Her grandmother was quite beautiful. Oh, you must remember, and of course I do, I say, vaguely remember. In the hallway, right?

"That's what I just said, in the hallway, near the door to the bathroom. Are you listening at all?"

"Yes, I'm listening."

Then she wants to know if I know what dropsy is? I pretend I don't, though really I do since she told me once a long time ago when we were dating. Congestive heart failure, she tells me, is what they call it now. The heart grows weaker and weaker and bigger and bigger, which sounds like a contradiction but isn't, and it becomes less and less capable of circulating the blood and as a result fluids build up in the cells and the person seems to become fat, though really they're just full of fluids.

"I see," I say.

Her poor grandmother, she reminds me, never remarried. She lives alone on High Street. She's very sweet and her house always smells like flour, and tucked away in a cedar chest in her bedroom is a newspaper with a headline announcing the death of George Washington. "Really! A real newspaper from 1799! You should see the classified ads!"

Thinking about her grandmother, my wife becomes sad and afraid. Her grandmother is in her eighties. Jo is worried that her grandmother will die before she gets home.

And I'm thinking, as I listen to this endless monologue, that I will die sitting in this house. And she's right. We are accomplishing nothing. And if I don't die, I will go home without leaving a single mark in this small town in Bahia, especially if I wait until it stops raining.

So I say I am going out, even if it is raining. But she has other plans. She wants me to take the bus with her to Jacarandá. We received word that our book locker had been delivered to the hospital there. The PC provides a book locker to each Volunteer or couple of Volunteers and she thought we could go pick it up. I declined, though probably I should have gone since it is raining and there isn't much I can accomplish in any event. She was upset that I didn't go, and probably I should have. Instead I went out and walked around. I visited the shop of the man who made my leather pouch. I sat and talked with him for a while. I don't know what he thinks of me. He's a dour fellow who's hard to understand. Then I went to the shop of the family that made our table but they were closed, probably for the holidays. I walked around the *favela* looking for people to talk to and sort of observing things. People nod and greet me but it is showery and finally I come home and write this entry in my journal and work on my paper for the conference.

Chapter Sixteen

MASTER DETECTIVE

They sit quietly for a few moments after Connie has finished reading.

What is your sense of Kyle at this point? Clint asks her.

I don't know what to think, she says not looking at him. Well, maybe that he's making himself very narrow.

Narrow?

Drawing inside himself, narrowing his focus. Turning away from the larger community, even Mom. And that made it harder for Mom. I don't know. I'm just rambling. I have no idea really.

No, that's good. Narrowing.

Connie stands and walks along the length of the table. She reaches the far end and turns. In my office I walk. I hope it doesn't bother you.

No.

In meetings, on the phone. It's a nice thing about cordless phones.

Yes.

She turns again and starts across the far end of the room. Maybe it's from my days in clothing stores. Prowling was part of the job. Keeping an eye on customers. You want to discourage theft but at the same time offer assistance and encourage purchases. The idea is to make the customer think you're there to help while also reminding them that you're watching. Not put them off, mind you, not irritate or intimidate them but watching. It's subtle. You want to watch them, and you want them to know you're watching them without making them think that you think it's necessary to watch them. She reaches the corner near the window and stops. Well, that made a whole bunch of sense, didn't it! Anyway, where are we?

The book locker, Clint says. It was a wonderful thing, the book locker. A small library with something for everyone, from history to literature to science fiction. I was thinking the book locker trip followed the conference but now I see it proceeded it. The trip Kyle refers to, the one when your mom came over to get the book locker, that's when Jolene met Oscar for the first time.

Excuse me, Connie says, turning back from the window. The description Dad gave of Mom talking? Did that ring true to you?

At that moment Clint remembers the photo album. Red leather, small and thick with a zipper so you could close it up. One snapshot per page, maybe twenty, thirty in all. Photos of her parents, her siblings. She brought it in the big bag she carried on the bus from Nova to Jacarandá and she flopped down on his bed at the hospital with her legs crossed and handed the album to him and looked over his shoulder at the photographs telling him jokes and stories about the people as he turned the pages. Her breath soft and warm against his neck and ear. He would be embarrassed and aroused and made sure the door stayed open and sometimes her skirt would ride up and he couldn't help but see the pale and lovely curve of her inner thigh.

She needed to talk about her family, he says to Connie. I was reminded of your mother, when you brought out the family album. She too had photos to show. Photos of her parents, that would be your maternal grandparents, and her siblings your uncles and aunts.

One uncle, Connie says, from my mother's side. Three aunts.

I don't remember those details. She talked about them now and then. Kyle's family as well. Mostly when I tagged along as she was gift shopping.

Aunt Connie is the one I'm closest to. Though at the moment I am feeling a little estranged from the lot of them.

Once we realized there was no going back on the sister thing

Jolene wanted to invent a common history. My idea was that we would be half brother and sister. The same father say. Then we could live in different places. That made a lot of sense to me but she didn't want to have anything to do with a broken home, not even in fantasy.

I'm not surprised. My parents were devastated by my divorce. Divorce wasn't an option for them.

No, they stuck it out.

They didn't just 'stick it out,' Connie says, starting to walk again. That's not right. They were very close in their way. They loved each other. They stayed together because they wanted to.

Clint apologizes. I'm sure you're right. You grew up with them, and I never saw them again, so who am I to say? All I know is that when it came to our 'imagined' family, your mother drove a hard bargain. She wouldn't go for a twice-married father. And she wouldn't accept having my father as 'our' father and her mother as 'our' mother. No, no. Jolene insisted we have same parents and our parents would be her parents. I had gotten us into the mess so I didn't have room to argue. She would haul out the photographs and give me long biographies so I would be able to discuss 'our' parents with anyone I met.

I keep wondering about Dad, Connie says. What did he think about the games you and Mom were playing?

Clint hesitates. Your dad encouraged them as I will explain. But first I want to say more about Oscar. He was a great fan of Sherlock Holmes. Did I tell you he had studied in London?

You might have mentioned it.

Well, he did. His English was good but he never wasted it on me. He took his responsibility seriously. In exchange for the services I was providing the hospital, he wanted to give me a Brazilian experience. That meant I had to learn the language. Except in one or two emergencies, he never spoke English to me.

Yes, you mentioned that, too.

Okay, well Sherlock was his role model. He fancied himself

the keen observer, and from those observations he liked to make clever deductions.

All right, Connie says, returning to her chair.

So, one rainy day—this was almost certainly the day your mom came to pick up the book locker—I was surprised to find Jolene standing inside the front door of the hospital chatting with Oscar. Oscar had a way with women and she was laughing happily. Seeing her standing next to Oscar I was aware of her height. Your mom was tall. Taller than Oscar by an inch or more. As tall as Angelica his wife.

Five-eight, I think.

Jolene would dress her best when she came to Jacarandá. It was an outing from the mud and poverty surrounding their place in Nova Santana. Her reddish brown hair pulled into a ponytail fell in sweeping waves to her shoulders. In Nova she often wore a scarf on her head, but not in Jacarandá. A sleeveless blouse, one of the bright wrap-around skirts she made. Her legs were long, her calves lovely.

Connie motions him to stop. She presses a finger against the narrow bridge that separates the nostrils of her nose. It doesn't work. She sneezes twice, squinting her eyes tightly each time and then takes a tissue and wipes her face and hands.

I'm sorry.

Are you all right?

I'm fine, it was just dust or something. You were saying....

I'm trying to describe what happened the first time Oscar saw Jolene.

Yes.

The two of them were standing in the hallway outside his office.

I think you said Mom's legs were lovely.

She smiles at him, those intense dark eyes, but Clint feels annoyed. This is a favorite part of his story and he wants to tell it well. Oscar's voice is in his head and it wants to come out.

It was more than forty years ago, Connie. What I'm simply trying to say is that Jolene dressed her best when she came to Jacarandá. She wore jewelry, for example. Like the necklace I sent home with the journal. My point is that your mom cut a figure when she came to Jacarandá and Oscar was impressed.

I understand.

'I saw the *Senhora* approaching the building through the window of my office,' Oscar explained to me when I came upon the two of them. 'I recognized her immediately as your sister. To a scientist the family lineage is obvious.'

Oh my, Connie says, covering her mouth.

Clint is grinning now. That's exactly the way Oscar talked. And he went on from there.

'Most men do not train themselves to observe people,' he would say. 'Women in general are more observant than men. Men look quickly at all women of course, but only so far as is necessary to fuel their lust. Then if their lust is excited, they lock their attention on those specific qualities that sustain it. But as a scientist it is my responsibility to study the whole person. I studied the whole woman as I watched you coming up the walkway, *Senhora*. Your height, the breadth of your shoulders, your gait. You may not be aware but your walk is strikingly similar to your brother's. Both of you, for example, are slightly pigeon toed. This will serve you well over the long term, incidently. A slightly pigeon-toed walk preserves the knees. It is true that your pace as you approached the hospital was slower, more hesitant, than is characteristic of my friend here, but I attributed this to the fact that you were about to enter a large and intimidating structure not knowing if you would find your brother inside. And perhaps, if I may say so, as you approached the building you still experienced yourself as living in a foreign country even though, as I have now learned, your command of Portuguese is admirable given the time you have been with us. In any event, these were the qualities that first captured my attention. But as you drew closer I noticed other, more delicate features. While it is true that your coloring is different from my friend here, I confirmed my conclusion by the shape of your ears.'

Her ears? Connie asked.

That's how your mother reacted. She was blushing rather dramatically at that point. Incidently, that is a quality you share with your mother, as you're probably aware. A tendency to blush. Darwin made a study of blushing, you know. He was quite interested in all aspects of life. Even blushing. Truth be told, I believe he is one of the most maligned of our great minds. I am often saddened by how little he is appreciated, given the contributions he made.

Wait, Connie says This thing about coloring that Oscar mentioned. Did he mean hair?

Probably. Why?

Was your hair darker or lighter than hers?

Darker, Clint said, though as you can see, the color is long gone.

Like mine, she says. I mean, mine is darker than Mom's was too.

Yes, I've noticed that. Anyway, Oscar went on about the ears, saying that it was not surprising that Jolene should be unaware of how similar our ears were. 'Most of us are relatively ignorant of our own ears,' he told her. I say 'told her' because he was primarily talking to her. My job, and it was not infrequently my job when I was around Oscar, was to serve as his admiring audience. 'We normally see our ears only from the front and then hanging there on the periphery of our attention. We are drawn naturally to the eyes when we study ourselves in the mirror, and also, and this is true particularly of females, if you will forgive me, *Senhora*, to the real or imagined defects that we see before us. It is also true that like most women you have somewhat camouflaged the size and shape of your ears. The tops are covered with your lovely hair and from the lobes hang those attractive earrings, which I note are secured by clasps rather than posts, a feature that reveals that you are not native to our culture. But as to the ears themselves, upon close observation, the family similarities become obvious.'

Your mom and I found ourselves gazing at each other's ears. Then the doctor instructed us to stand side by side in profile.

'The ears are not identical of course. Yours, *Senhora,* are more petite, more delicately formed, and Clint's, in addition to being larger, and if I may say, cruder—Oscar delighted in teasing me—are more forward-facing as would befit the male hunter. But when one examines the shape as they taper toward the lobe, and the lobes themselves, both of which hang well below the point where they attach to the cranium. Yes, the similarity is striking.'

At that point Oscar asked to examine our hands. As usual when she came to Jacarandá, Jolene's hands were full. Since it was raining she would have had an umbrella. And she always carried a large woven bag with circular wooden handles. And then, either in the bag or separately she would have some treat she had cooked or picked out at the market to bring to me.

She would bring you a present?

Always, some token or other. Maybe it was a couple of oranges, or some other fruit she had gotten at the market. Later after they got the stove and refrigerator she would bake things, cookies, pineapple upside down cakes, banana bread. Familiar food from home.

How many times did she come to see you?

Clint pauses. Several times, as I will explain to you in good time.

All right.

Oscar, always the gallant, seeing your mother's hands were occupied, would have taken the objects from her hands and set them on a bench. Then he took our hands in his own. His own hands, incidently, were not the hands you would expect to find on a hospital administrator. They were the thick callused hands of a rancher and horseman. Somewhere along the way he had lost the final segment on the little finger of his left hand. The injury looked old and forgotten. The calluses notwithstanding, his hands and fingernails were always immaculate, the cuticles cleanly defined. Like many male Brazilians, he regularly visited a manicurist. So Oscar took our hands and studied them carefully, backs and palms. Then without comment he let go of my hand while continuing to hold hers. I didn't know what to think. Was he suspicious? Oscar was a very smart man and his reluctance to talk about our hands had me worried. The truth is, Jolene and I did not look at all alike other than we were both tall.

I was going to say.

Your mother, on the other hand was not worried, or at least she did not appear to be. She was enjoying the whole thing, not only the sham we were endeavoring to pull off, but also the attention she was receiving from Oscar. Before he could comment on our hands, she had a question for him. 'So, Doctor,' she asked rather coquettishly, 'you have had an opportunity to examine us both, who do you think is older, me or my brother?'

I was not happy to hear this question, Connie. I didn't know her exact age or her birthday and I was afraid Oscar might put me on the spot. But my fear was unjustified. Oscar was not about to surrender center stage by asking me a question.

'Your question is a profound one, *Senhora*,' he said quite seriously. 'Age is a delicate matter, especially when it comes to a beautiful woman, and normally it is best left undiscussed. However, since you have asked, I will attempt to answer. As between siblings, girls tend to mature both emotionally and physically faster than boys, thus they can appear older relative to their brothers than in fact they are. Girls at certain ages are often both taller and younger, for example. A girl may also enter puberty sooner than her older brother. On the other hand after a certain age, men tend to be larger and heavier than women and to the casual observer this may lead to an erroneous conclusion.

Similarly, when a man develops facial hair this can give the impression of age. Then again, later in life, in the forties or fifties, for example, a man who may have produced children but has not had the burden of bearing and raising them, may appear more vital than a woman of the same or even a slightly younger age. Finally, as we know, near the end of life, we men tend to die off while women not only endure but may reassume some of the mannerisms they possessed as children.

'Perhaps later Clint will take you on a tour of our facility. If so, you will visit one ward that houses the elderly and the infirm. We are quite proud of the program. These elderly people have no families, or have been abandoned by them, yet we have found a place for them here. The patients, you will notice, are almost all women and often when I visit, I see in these old women patterns of movement, facial expressions, the manner in which they hold their hands, that I suspect they utilized as children, then gave up during their mature years, only to once again adopt at the end of their days. I note this particularly when they are made to feel shy about something or other. But all of this is quite beside the point, isn't it? You have asked a difficult question, and I must attempt to answer it.'

Oscar released Jolene's hand. He stepped back and studied the both of us as we stood side by side, looking first at one and then the other. His fierce eyes had lost all hint of a smile. Perhaps because of the duplicity we had entered into, I had a sense of myself standing in a police lineup.

'You may have noticed,' he continued after a moment, 'that I made no comment earlier as I observed your hands together. Were you native to Bahia, *Senhora*, your hands would confuse me, given your beauty and status in society. They are obviously not the hands of a poor woman. They bear no deformities such as my own, no scars that I noticed other than the small one on the ring finger of your right hand. They are scrupulously clean and adequately well maintained. And yet, they are not the hands of the typical upper class Bahian either. You notice I said, "adequately maintained."' He pointed out where a couple of her nails were chipped and irregular in shape. Also that her hands were stronger, the muscles better defined then those of upper class Bahian women. Having explained all this he continued, 'I had to assume that your life here in Bahia may involve more labor than you experienced at home, still what I saw in your hands suggests a familiarity with physical labor of longer duration than the few months you have been here. I was further confused when I compared them to your brother's hands. The two hands do not look like the hands of a brother and sister. Clinton's hands are soft and puffy, except of course for the calluses on the tips of the fingers of his left hand which I attribute to the beautiful music he provides us on the violin. So, my confusion was this: what sort of family would raise two children in such a way that the daughter's hands showed a history of labor, while the son's did not?'

Good question, Connie says.

Yes, that's what I was thinking at the time. Anyway, the doctor paused and looked at both of us intently. 'But thanks to your question, *Senhora*, I now have the answers not only to your question but also my own. Your ages are close, allowing enough time between them of course for impregnation and gestation. However, my determination is that you are the older of the two, most likely the oldest child in the family. The oldest child tends to mature the fastest and is most likely to mimic the physical activities of her parents. While the activities of a younger child are more governed by his siblings or playmates. Thus I conclude that you are the oldest child, that you enjoyed helping your mother and perhaps even your father around the house while Clinton here was hidden away in the library playing chess and practicing his violin.'

Oops, Connie says. You were older, right?

Yes, by a couple of years. But Oscar was quite pleased with

himself. His analysis had been both charming and erudite. His pleasure quickly disappeared, however, as he looked at Jolene's expression. She wanted so much to believe in this charming man but she could not bring herself to confess to more years than she actually possessed.

Which is not to say she was daunted, mind you. She admitted that Oscar had been wrong about our ages but she was flattered that he had thought her more mature than her brother. A brother she added, looking at me with a scowl, who had always lorded his age over her.

Mom said that?

Did I tell you she was an actress? She went right on flattering Oscar. He had been right about everything, she said. She did love work, even physical work like mowing the lawn. But I, her lazy older brother, refused to do anything useful around the house.

That is so funny.

Oscar was swept away. He took both of Jolene's hands in his own and squeezed them happily. She was absolutely charming, he said. He welcomed her to the hospital. She could stay over whenever she wanted and he instructed me to make sure she had the best room available. So that was that. So far as Jacarandá was concerned there was never any doubt but that we were brother and sister.

Did she stay?

Not that night. She had come to get the book locker which was an impossible mission. It probably weighed seventy-five pounds and was as large as a shipping trunk. There was no practical way for her to transport it by herself to Nova Santana even if I helped her drag it to the bus station. So she picked out a few volumes to take back and after a tour of the hospital I walked her to the bus station. We probably stopped by the restaurant so she could say hello to Eduardo. She always wanted to see him. And by now the rain would have stopped and the sun come out. Sometimes after a rain, when you walked through Don

Alfonso's little park, the air was full of butterflies, as if they had been waiting pent up for the sun. It's images like the butterflies that have been coming into my head lately.

I can see why she was attracted to Jacarandá, Connie says. Going there gave her a chance to feel like a woman.

Yes, Clint says, I think she needed that.

Chapter Seventeen

MAKING A DIFFERENCE

Connie wants to talk about her mother's hair. You said it was long?

Yes. To the shoulders and had some wave in it, which I assume was natural. No curling irons in Nova Santana. I notice a similar tendency in your hair. The curling strand has sprung loose again and is back on her forehead.

I was wondering if you have any photographs from your days in the Peace Corps?

Clint shakes his head. I did have a camera in Brazil and I took a few rolls of slides but I haven't seen them in decades. I know they're not in the condo and the chances are slim to none that they exist at all. I instructed my latest ex to get rid of everything I didn't take with me and she expressed an eagerness to comply. They may have disappeared with the first marriage.

Would it be an inconvenience to ask her?

Michelle? To ask, no. To obtain a helpful answer probably. To go over there and paw through any old boxes that remain, a considerable inconvenience, I'm afraid.

Connie blushes. I'm sorry. Yes, I understand completely. And do forgive me, I shouldn't have asked. I can be pushy. I was the same as a child. Dad reminded me of that a couple of times when he watched me with my boys. I was a challenge and apparently I made life pretty miserable for Phil growing up. Now I have two of my own.

Why do I feel uncomfortable? Clint asks himself. Do I think I really owe this woman something?

I could probably call her, he says.

Please don't bother. It was just a thought. Mom and Kyle have become a mystery to me. Take Mom's hair. You saw the pictures in the album. All of my life it was never long. In high school photos, in their wedding pictures her hair was like you described. She had beautiful hair! As a kid I would pester her to let it grow out, but she never would. Too much bother, she would say.

It was a bother for her in Nova but she never cut it.

Keeping it clean was difficult I suppose. You mentioned the scarves.

Yes, in Nova she often wore a scarf. Adequate clean water was a problem as I've described. At the hospital in Jacarandá she could shower. It wasn't great. Just a pipe coming out of the wall with no nozzle, but the water was clear and modestly warm. At Nova I suppose they washed themselves with water in a pan. What we used to call a sponge bath.

But in Jacarandá, you said, she didn't wear a scarf.

Not that I remember. Nor in Salvador when I saw her there.

Do you think it's significant that she kept her head covered in Nova Santana? A covered head is not insignificant for a woman.

Nor is cutting the hair. Or keeping it cut. But it's also possible to read too much into these things. That's a problem my profession contends with when studying the fossil record. We even have a phrase for it: paleo poetry. Which means creating more narrative than the facts justify. In Nova, remember, it was usually either hot and dusty or humid and muddy. I took a pair of contact lens with me, but almost never wore them. The dust and pollen turned them into discs of sandpaper against my corneas. And like I said, the water.

Of course, you're right. So, where were we?

Last night after you left, I realized that I needed to introduce the idea of community development to you. It was the saddle Kyle strapped on his back. And indirectly, at least, it led to his downfall.

You already told me about this. The project had to do with public health and community development.

Yes, and I described the public health side of training. But I haven't said much about community development.

No, you have. You talked about how it was subversive.

I did?

Yes. How the Peace Corps sold the idea of public health to the Brazilians but stressed community development with the Volunteers. I don't know what community development is, but that much I remember.

All right. Well, I guess I did then.

You said you were trained in public health and that some of you had more training than others. Smookie was a nurse, I believe.

Yes. Clint looks a little flustered.

What was your major by the way?

My major? It started off pre-med, but then I met a biology professor and all was lost. Not even Oscar could turn me around.

Connie smiles. A good teacher can do that. Mom had kids graduating from high school, a couple even from college, who sent her invitations to their graduations. And she had been their kindergarten teacher!

That must have given her great satisfaction.

Of course, but to her, it didn't mean she was exceptional. It just meant she had been doing her job. She was exceptional though, Connie says, her voice falling off, she really was.

I'm sure you're right. He hesitates. So, did I talk about Kyle and community development? How he in particular saw it?

I don't think so.

Good. Perhaps I'm not completely losing my mind. So, as I was starting to say, for Kyle community development was a radical concept. His understanding was not inaccurate, but it was an extreme interpretation of what we had been taught. He thought the concept of community development embodied a fundamental truth, a truth that other words people use when they talk about social progress, words like 'education,' and 'public health,' and 'being of service,' fail to acknowledge. As Kyle saw it, the situation in Bahia, or any society for that matter, was not an accident.

What do you mean?

The gap between the rich and poor was not an accident. Not in Kyle's eyes. Adequate food, good housing, safe water, decent schools. These things were missing from the poor communities of course. But not missing in the sense of having been mislaid or forgotten or left somewhere inadvertently.

I still don't understand.

Then I will try to argue the point on his behalf. Assume for a minute, he would say, that everyone in Nova wakes up one morning and suddenly realizes that the people living in the *favela* below our house—I'm speaking for him now—are drinking water that makes them sick and kills their children. I would have responded, well, many of them do understand that. And he would have said, yes, they understand it, but what if they realized it was unacceptable? And I would have said, that most of them probably would agree that it is a bad, or at least an unfortunate thing.

Then Kyle would have slapped his fist on the table. 'That's it!' he would shout. 'That's it exactly! They might say it's bad. They would certainly say it was unfortunate. But they would not say it was unacceptable. If they really believed it was unacceptable, they could change it in a few weeks.' He'd be talking pretty fast by now. 'What's it take after all? Some pipes, a well or two. The technology is available! It doesn't change because they don't want it to change.'

That's weird. Who doesn't want it to change?

Good question. Now you are playing my part and I am free to play his. The people who aren't doing anything about it, that's who. The rich, the middle class, the church, the municipal government, the list in his mind was extensive. He was not suggesting these people created the gap, or caused it to happen. But he did believe that those people, that is the people who were not poor, did benefit from the situation. They benefitted from acting as if the gap were a natural and unavoidable condition of life. Along the lines of 'The poor will always be with you.'

Jesus said that, Connie says.

Really? One of Kyle's heros, but he certainly did not accept that part of the teaching.

It's taken out of context, she adds. So what did Dad mean by 'benefitted?'

The non-poor benefitted by not having to worry about it. By choosing not to pay the cost of changing it. By utilizing the pool of cheap labor that poverty guaranteed. Are you familiar with the Iron Law of Wages?

I don't think so.

One of your father's favorite examples. And not one of our species's finer moments. The Iron Law of Wages was formulated at the beginning of the industrial revolution. It suggested that the price of labor should be set by the market place rather than by laws, such as laws that would guarantee a minimum wage, or limit the number of hours of work, or restrict the use of child labor. The Iron Law of Wages dictated that the price of labor would always be near bare subsistence because if laborers earned more than subsistence they would produce more children, and thus there would be more laborers and their individual value would go down. Conversely when the wage fell too low they would have fewer children and in time there would be less laborers and the wage would go back up. So there was no reason to help the workers because it would not really help them in the long run but would only hurt the rich. The rich, of course, were the people who formulated the law and benefitted from it.

Nifty.

Your dad thought that a similarly cosy situation existed in Bahia. The status quo didn't change because people benefitted from it. And that's where community development came in. Community development is an approach to addressing community problems by organizing the community to work together. Not the community downtown. The community on the hill. The community on the suffering end of the problem. The idea was to get involved in that community. Figure out who the natural leaders were. See if there were any existing organizations that had community support, and then listen. Try to learn what the people were concerned about. You weren't the overt leader and you didn't tell them what you thought the problems were even though they might seem obvious to you. You were in the background, learning, making suggestions, organizing, prodding. The idea was to lead without leading, to encourage a community of people to recognize the strength they had in numbers and in organization.

Sounds like jujitsu, Connie says. My boys are into martial arts, like their dad.

You could say that, viewing it from the organizer's perspective. Using the other's strength. But not in opposition, in support. You want to create or strengthen an organization that will continue to function after you have left.

It sounds very difficult, especially for a foreigner.

It was virtually impossible, Clint says. Totally naive. But that was the standard set for us. Our mission was to access the community through public health but our goal was to create lasting change through community development. If all you did was public health, you were not operating at the highest level. This challenge obsessed your father. He thought the condition of the poor was intolerable and the way to address the problem was through community development.

I understand. And you said it was impossible?

Clint doesn't answer immediately. I'm trying to avoid generalizations, he says finally, straightening his back. I want you to draw your own conclusions from the details I provide you.

It was a word you used.

I acknowledge that. But that was my opinion. I doubt your father ever thought it was impossible. And I'm not sure his obsession with community development is what destroyed him in the end.

He wasn't destroyed, Connie says. They may have come home early, but they lived a productive lives. Their marriage was strong. They raised two children and they were both very successful in what they did.

He apologizes. You're right, of course.

So, I don't think destroyed is the right word. You said you wanted me to feel admiration for them.

Clint nods. Obviously it was not the best choice of words. But I must say, this obsession did lead Kyle to some strange conclusions. Take medicine, for example. Your dad had strange ideas about medicine.

What do you mean?

I'll be happy to explain, but first I have to tell you about a conversation I had with Oscar. I told your dad about the conversation and then he told me his ideas about medicine.

All right, Connie says without enthusiasm.

One day I went to see Oscar about doing some different work. Being around Kyle had convinced me that I should be doing more to change the world. To make a difference.

Change the world?

Clint laughs. Going out for Oscar's cigarettes. Sitting with him in boring meetings. Delivering supplies to the clinics. This was not community development, not in your dad's eyes. Of course, Kyle never judged. He never said I was not doing enough. But he did set a standard of commitment. And he was interested. He wanted to know exactly what I did. And he would listen and ask questions. The implication was obvious. I was living a plush life. I had my own room at the hospital, free meals in the cafeteria. I was on a soccer team and I played classical music with Eduardo—

Eduardo fancied himself a piano player. I was hanging out with the 'haves' and enjoying myself. Without saying a word directly, your dad prompted me to believe that I was not doing enough.

Dad was very good at that kind of thing, Connie says, smiling. The indirect nudge.

Agreed. So one day, I went to see Oscar about being more directly involved with the poor. He listened to me and then said that I had to accompany him to the agricultural exposition going on at the edge of town. He would do things like that. I would get all worked up about something and he would say we could talk later but meanwhile we should go to this or that other thing. So, I went with Oscar and his family to the exposition. I saw the animals, beautiful horses and bulls and cattle brought in from all over. Oscar took me to the cockfights where he bet on all the wrong roosters using keen observations and clever deductions. It was there, incidently, that I met the famous Dr. Nascimento. He had brought a bull to the exposition and was at the cockfights. I saw him as a braggart, a powerful man with heavy thighs and a hairy chest. He carried a whip with him, the kind jockeys use. I still remember one part of our conversation. He asked if I went to the cockfights in the U.S. I told him cockfights were illegal in the U.S. He made a joke about that. He said–and he said this loud enough so that everyone around us could hear–that maybe the Americans should make cockfights legal and then they wouldn't find it necessary to get involved in other people's wars. He was referring to Vietnam, of course, which at that time was just beginning to become news.

Anyway, that night I had dinner with Oscar and his family. After the meal he and I retired to his library where he began pouring shots of Black and White.

Excuse me, but I thought the subject was Dad's ideas about medicine.

We're coming to that, I swear. But first the conversation with Oscar.

All right.

So, we were talking and drinking and Oscar brought up the subject of my being assigned different work. He asked me what I wanted to do, and I said that I wanted to make a difference.

A difference?

Yes, I told him I wanted to leave Brazil a better place than I found it.

I see.

The poverty is shocking, I told him. The small children with distended bellies and protruding navels running around naked. Children living in the street with no homes. I told him about the group of boys in Ilhéus who lived in the crannies of the hotel where we stayed.

The ones who sang, Connie interjects. Dad wrote about that.

Yes. And it wasn't just children, as I said to Oscar. Poor women particularly seemed aged beyond their years. They are worn down, used up, living in shanties, defecating in banana patches, washing their clothing in the river, carrying water for blocks, producing litters of children. Men too with injuries and deformities. Even young men with few or no teeth. It was quite an outburst and when I had finished I was afraid that maybe I had offended him. After all, it was his country I was talking about. A country where I was a guest. Then after a minute Oscar began to grin. 'You are a very lucky fellow,' he said to me. I agreed because I thought he meant that I was lucky to come from such a prosperous country as the United States. But that's not what he meant at all.

What did he mean?

Well, here's what he said, and I will never forget it. He said, 'You have come to the perfect place to get help for your problem.'

Your problem?

Yes, *my* problem. And I didn't understand his response any better than you did. 'We must decide,' he went on, 'what is the best way to solve this problem you have, this problem of misery.'

I don't get it.

Of course I didn't either, being the young naive kid I was. And standing at the bar in his library drinking his scotch, I had no option but to hear him out. Yes, Oscar continued, I had a problem of misery and there were three basic ways that he could help me solve this problem that he thought I had. In one scenario I would be surrounded by misery but not necessarily be miserable myself. He looked at me carefully. I still had no idea what he was talking about. Then he shook his head. No, that wouldn't work, he decided. I was already living and working in the hospital, and the hospital was filled with misery. Since that was not enough to make me feel as though I was making a difference, we needed to move on to the second choice. With this option, he said, I would be miserable but the people around me might not themselves be miserable. His face brightened. 'How about digging holes for people to shit in?' He was confident this would make me perfectly miserable. The sun was hot, the ground hard. And the holes needed to be deep, a couple of meters at least. Would I then feel I was making a difference? I could see now that he was toying with me. I tried to get him to stop, but there was no stopping Oscar.

'No, no,' he said, 'we must think this through.' He was sure I did not want to return home thinking that I had not made a difference. He had a third alternative. In this scenario I would be miserable but so would the people around me. Maybe I could work in a leper colony. Yes, that was probably the way to go. A leper colony. I was sure now I had offended him. I started to apologize but again he ignored me. He tore off his glasses and tossed them on the bar. His eyebrows arched, his eyes looked fierce, his mustache thin and dark.

'*O Brasil é, oque é!*' he shouted. '*O Bahia é, oque é!*'

Which means?

That Brazil and Bahia are what they are, and fundamentally they will never change. There was a joke in Brazil. It said, 'Our

country is the country of the future, and it always will be.' Maybe
he meant something like that. If so, he was wrong, obviously.
Brazil is rapidly becoming a world economic power.
Anyway, I apologized again but he waved it off. I hadn't
offended him. He had just seen himself in me, that's all. 'Do
you know why a man becomes a doctor?' he asked me. 'Do you
think it's to make money? To get free peeks at tities and pussies?'
Pardon the language. 'No,' he said, 'a man becomes a doctor
because he wants to heal the world. He wants to be like a mother
or a father who kisses the scraped knee and makes it all better.'
'But you have made a tremendous difference,' I protested.
'The hospital is one of the best in the state. You are well known
everywhere, *Senhor* Pell tells me this.'
Oscar shook his head. He looked tired suddenly. I noticed
patches of darkness beneath his eyes. It frightened me to think
that a man as strong and fierce as Oscar would grow tired, that
he would age and die. I was only twenty-three but in Oscar's
face I saw my own mortality. I knew then that one day I would
be where I am now, an old man confined to this chair talking
to you, and Oscar who was younger then than I am now, would
be long dead. But around Oscar nothing was pathetic. Nothing
morose. I asked him why I had come to Brazil if there was really
nothing for me to do, nothing that would make a difference.
'Everything makes a difference,' he shouted. 'Do your work!
But more importantly live! Cockfights, food, music, sex, smells,
family, horses, friendships, parties, plants, dogs, life!' He gave
me a bone crushing embrace, then stepped back. 'And laughter,
Clinton. Always laughter. These are the only antidotes known
to my profession.'
'But nothing changes?' I asked.
'Not the way we would like,' he said. 'You will change by
knowing me, I will change by knowing you. But *'O Brasil? O
Brasil é, oque é. 'O Bahia é, oque é.'*
His story ended, Clint feels embarrassed, surprised it still has

an emotional pull on him. To cover himself he says to Connie, The question you are supposed to ask now is: So, what does any of this have to do with Dad's idea of medicine?

So what does any of this have to do with Dad's idea of medicine? she asks obediently.

Good question. But unfortunately, or rather, fortunately, it's time for fish and chips. Pack your stuff, and if you have sun screen bring it along.

Clint drives them south a few blocks to Steveston Village near the wharf along the Fraser River. The day is clear and warm approaching twenty-five degrees, and they park in the shade of a tree. From the side door of a small establishment a block back from the water, they order their halibut which comes wrapped in fake newsprint, his with a proper dose of vinegar and hers with a cup of tarter sauce. They make their way to a bench on the boardwalk where she can sit and they can spread out the food and drinks. She has her black leather bag which she sets on the ground between her feet. She is careful about the bag. In it are her father's irreplaceable journal and her equipment including the computer that contains most every word they have said to one another since they met the morning before.

A gentle on-shore breeze, the water green and still. Out in the channel some commercial traffic moves slowly. Closer in a few sailboats and several fishing trawlers are moored in their slips. Just below their bench a family of tundra swans cruises about in stately procession, two white adults and four nearly-grown but still brown offspring. Families stroll on the boardwalk, pausing to take a photograph or two. Clint is recognized by a couple on bicycles. They stop and chat with him briefly. He introduces Connie as a friend from the States.

You rode, I take it, she says after they have left.

Along here, he says. All over really. Unless the weather was terrible. I commuted to the University on my bike. It was a big part of my life. In the summer I did some touring. The San Juan Islands. The Oregon coast was a favorite.

Connie can't resist glancing at his legs. The shoes jut out somewhat awkwardly, the ankles bone thin, the tan slacks baggy and shapeless. When she looks up, he's watching her. His expression does not appear angry or pained and for this she feels a rush of gratitude. Still, she looks quickly toward the water, feeling heat rise off her cheeks.

Ever ride the Ragbrai? she asks after a moment.

Across Iowa? No, I've read about it. Quite the party they say. Do you cycle?

Not me. Gilbert rode it a couple of times. Anything athletic, Gilbert's up for it. We would meet him mid-week in one of the towns along the way. The boys were very young then.

Does Gilbert still ride?

No, the work, the new wife, the new baby. They've got him tied down.

But you? he asks. You haven't remarried?

Connie shakes her head. No time for that so far. The two boys, then Mom, then Dad. Now it's the business. I've been blessed with challenges, and I don't mean that cynically. But speaking of work, there was something that struck me when you were talking about the Pennsylvanians. You described a scene when you came upon Dad working in the garden. I think he was digging holes for the fence.

Yes.

You described him as working and the boys standing around watching him.

You noticed that. It was often the case when I saw him with the boys. He led by example, you could say.

That never changed. After Mom died he decided to bring me into the business. He knew his time was limited, I suppose. Still, I was grateful and surprised. I always thought he saw me as a screw up, which for a number of years there I was. But he had a hard time delegating. It went against his instincts. The business was his creation. He wanted the weight of every decision to be on his shoulders. That's just the way he was. He invited me in, but I had to push to really get in, if you know what I mean.

Was he active in caring for Jolene? I assume she needed care before the end.

Was he? At first he wouldn't let anyone near her. It created a terrible dilemma for him. The business and her care. And it caused Mom to worry about him. He was starting to have symptoms and Mom thought the symptoms came from the stress. She was wrong about that, as it tuned out. But the stress was real. Mom and I were on the phone a lot. I could tell she was concerned about him but he kept telling me that everything was under control. I prayed about it for days. Finally, I just told them I was coming home and bringing the boys with me. He was upset. He didn't want me to come and he had lots of reasons. Everything was fine, he insisted. Having the boys in the house would just make more worry for Mom. The decision was very difficult for me. I had to quit my job, uproot the boys from their school and friends. And he certainly implied that my coming would do more harm than good. But I wasn't hearing that in Mom's voice. I felt called so I went ahead anyway. In the end he was very grateful. He developed a nice relationship with the boys, too. That was a bonus. He became their grandfather in a way he hadn't been before.

Gulls seeing the food have begun to gather nearby.

Connie throws them a fry.

You'll only encourage them, Clint says.

They're already encouraged.

He is in no mood to argue. The sun feels warm and wonderful on his face, his chest and arms. He could fall asleep sitting here. He does that more often now. A short nap in the afternoon.

That's the way Jolene was with the pigeons, he says, rousing himself. In the central plaza in Jacarandá just down from the bus station. She always wanted to feed them.

Good for her, Connie says, tossing another fry.

I admire what you did for your parents, he says. I've known people, men in particular, who had a very hard time caring for their wives when they were sick. Good men, responsible men. Not with the flu or something. I mean terminably ill. It's a special skill. Some of us aren't cut out for it.

Dad was willing and able. That and the business were just too much for him.

I don't know about myself, he admits after a while. Fortunately, so far I have not been called upon to provide that service. I was surprised, though to see who showed up after my accident.

Your ex-wife?

Of course everybody stopped by. But it was the surfer who came and stayed.

Your boy?

Devon, the younger one. No kids, no long term relationships. I always thought you couldn't hold him down with an anchor but he was here within twenty-four hours and he stayed for six months.

Good for him.

Yes, in addition to healing and recovery there is a lot of adjustment that has to go on. Training is involved, reorganization of one's life and surroundings. And the rage. One has to come to terms with the rage. It is Clint now who glances down at his legs. So, having Devon here was very helpful and I understand something of what you've been describing. I'm sure Kyle was grateful that you insisted on coming home.

They finish eating and take the short path out to Garry Point Park. When they reach the ocean, Clint instructs her to turn and look back up the river. Her gasp brings a smile to his face.

Mount Baker, he says. It's actually across the line in Washington.

That is so beautiful! It's like a ghost mountain. Everything is so flat and then suddenly there it is.

They find a free picnic table and Connie gets out the recorder and sets it up.

So you told Dad about your conversation with Oscar?

The next time I saw him. Your parents had just gotten the stove and refrigerator along with a few other household items. Kyle rode the bus to Jacarandá to purchase an adaptor for the gas cookstove. The coupling on the stove didn't match the propane tanks in Nova. The propane dealer in Nova had the adaptor but he demanded an exorbitant price, so Kyle came to Jacarandá to get a better deal. I'd say the incident with the propane dealer further alienated Kyle from the people downtown.

How did they buy all these appliances? I thought they were broke.

They didn't buy them. The story I heard was that among the first Volunteers to come to Brazil had been a married couple stationed in the far west of Bahia on the Rio San Francisco. Apparently, the Peace Corps had set up households for the married couples in the first contingent, and after they left, the appliances had been stored out there. By this time, Charlie Pell had an assistant, a Volunteer named Manny. Manny picked up the appliances and delivered them to Kyle and Jolene along with the remainder of their book locker. Kyle thought the conveniences set them still further apart from the people he wanted to work with. But they were indeed conveniences and made life a lot easier for Jolene and him.

Mom didn't come to Jacarandá?

No, I remember being alone with Kyle in the cafeteria. Then later shopping with him for the adaptor. It was on that trip that he expressed his ideas about medicine. We were talking about Oscar and the hospital. I probably gave him a tour. As usual, he was very inquisitive about my work, my living conditions, my life in general. A conversation with Kyle was never idle or totally casual. He wasn't nosey or gossipy but his intensity led him to ask questions that other people with a stronger sense of deference might not ask. He wanted to know if I did my own laundry, for example, made my own bed.

Did you? Connie asked with a grin. If I'm not being too nosey.

When it got made, I was the one who made it. I ate most meals in the cafeteria and I took advantage of the laundry service for my clothing, linens, towels. A young man mopped the floor of my room now and then. But nobody made my bed.

It sounds like a college dorm.

It did resemble dorm life except I was the only resident not there because of a medical condition. It could get lonely. My room, and the one your mom stayed in, were not on the wards. The hospital was an old building that had gone through a number of modifications over the years. These rooms had once been patient rooms but now they were in the administrative wing and after hours no one was around. Kyle told me he would not have wanted my assignment. It reminded him of life in a prison or a monastery, comfortable but deadening. That's probably when he told me the Mont San Michel story I related earlier, the one about...

Yes, I remember.

Kyle had hoped to meet Oscar but Oscar was away. In my memory they never met, as I may have said. Anyway, at some point I related what Oscar had said about Brazil, how it would in essence never change. Kyle interpreted Oscar's remarks differently than I had. He thought Oscar sounded defeated. That was the word he used. Defeated. In my mind that was an interpretation you could entertain only if you had never met Oscar. The opposite was true, as I explained to Kyle, Oscar was full of life, the most vigorous of men. I tried to describe what he was doing for medical services not only in Jacarandá but also in the outlying areas.

'When a person is in pain,' Kyle told me when I had finished, 'or when something is happening to their body that they don't understand, no one is more welcome than a good doctor.' He described an incident that happened in Ilhéus. On Christmas

Eve he had gotten really sick, nauseous, throwing up, the room turning. He had terrible diarrhea. His temperature was 103 or more. Somehow, Jolene got in touch with one of the doctors training us at the clinic and this doctor came to the hotel that very night. He gave Kyle a shot, a shot which, according to Kyle, had him feeling almost normal an hour later. The transformation had been so sudden that Kyle thought it almost miraculous. He told me he had never been so happy to see someone as that doctor. But then he said that for him, medicine was 'a status quo sort of thing.'

Did you understand what he meant?

His perspective was that health is normal and sickness abnormal or below normal. The job of the doctor, according to Kyle, is to get you back to normal. Thus, to his way of thinking, medicine doesn't change anything. It just returns you to the status quo. He would always be grateful to the doctor who left his family on Christmas Eve to come to his aid, but for Kyle, personally, he could not be content with bringing people back to the status quo. For many if not a majority of the people in Bahia the status quo was intolerable. He wanted to change things in the larger context.

He would have been overjoyed to have Mom returned to the status quo, Connie says, looking again out toward the water. Truth is, he thought the doctors killed her.

Really? Clint asks, surprised.

Not intentionally, of course. But, yes. She had radiation. She had chemo. It was probably already too late, though we didn't realize it at the time. Mom went through the usual stages and finally came to accept it. But Dad had a harder time. He flew her to Mayo's. He flew her to a place in Houston. He was filled with that terrible sensation that comes when responsibility is combined with helplessness. Anyway, according to some markers, she was improving, but her doctor decided to apply another dose of radiation. She died four days later. Dad thought the radiation killed her.

Yes, I can understand that, Clint says slowly. Kyle felt responsible to do whatever he could, and it didn't work out. I'm sure it was awfully difficult for all of you.

Connie nods.

I want to ask you something, Clint says after a pause. Since we're on the subject of your parents' illnesses. It's very personal. Please understand, you have no obligation to answer. Of course, you know that. You're strong, I can tell you don't get pushed around. But I mean it. The fact that I've spent a couple of pleasant days with you does not create an obligation. You understand? The question doesn't even have anything to do with Brazil. Which is why you're here.

She has turned from the water, those dark puzzled eyes study him.

Agreed?

Well, you've got me intrigued, she says with a half smile.

This morning before I came over I went online. You said it was Kennedy's Disease that Kyle had, right?

Yes, that's correct.

Well, I did a search. Genetic based, and very rare.

Yes, it's very rare.

I am concerned about your boys.

Ah.

And you.

Neither of the boys carry the gene, Connie tells him. We had them checked as soon as Dad was diagnosed.

Whoopie! Clint shouts, shaking his fist in the air.

The sudden eruption of emotion, and the joy on his face makes her break out laughing.

The odds were fifty percent for each of them, right?

Yes, that's what we understood.

I'll be damned. What a relief that must have been. And you?

I have no symptoms, Connie says.

That's wonderful! That is truly wonderful. From what I read, the daughter carries the gene a hundred percent of the time, but only rarely exhibits any symptoms.

You're a good student, Doctor. You got it exactly right.

I am so happy to get this news. I have been struggling with whether or not to ask. It's none of my business, really. But I couldn't get the photographs of those boys out of my mind. And, of course, you.

Thank you for asking, Connie says. She leans toward him, touches his shoulder with her hand and brushes her lips against his forehead.

He feels embarrassed now and his eyes flush with tears. Fortunately, he has on his sunglasses. But the glasses are not necessary, Connie has already turned her attention to the bag at her feet.

There is something I want to read to you, she says, taking out the journal. It's less personal than some of the entries. I think maybe it ended up as one of the articles he sent home to the newspaper.

Please, he says, happy to move on.

Monday May 17, 1965

Mostly what I write about any more are holidays. The week of the saints finally passed and now we have lost another week between a three day festival called *Micareta* that began on Sunday, a week ago yesterday, and ended on Tuesday night, by which time we were on our way to Salvador for the conference. We finally returned this afternoon. So, the combination of the holiday and the conference, cost us another week, actually, eight days.

Between the week of saints and this lost week most days have been rainy. Still in all some progress has been made. The small one-room building finally became available for Jolene's sewing school and we spent a Saturday cleaning it up. Tables and chairs were found, a dependable old Singer treadle machine arrived with most but not all of its attachments. Rumor is it belonged to the mayor's late mother. Jo held her first classes a few days later. She has fifteen students.

In the garden, the posts finally arrived and the boys and I got them set, and the wire strung. Then just before the holiday we began preparing some ground for seed beds. I had hoped to have seeds in the ground before we left so germination could take place while I was away. But I hadn't counted on *Micareta*, which seemed to pop up out of nowhere. On that Friday I explained to the boys that we would be planting on Monday and they looked at me like I was crazy. "*Micareta!*" they exclaimed in unison. Of course I had no idea what they were talking about.

I could have planted the beds myself over the weekend or on Monday, but the planting, it seems to me, will be interesting and instructive for the boys so I decided to wait. I like to think I made a good decision although it went against my natural tendency which is to do everything myself just to get it done. So far as the boys are concerned, doing it myself is the simplest and fastest way to get a project completed.

So he was aware of this tendency, Clint says.
Yes.

Take setting the posts. At first I assigned them to work in pairs, each pair with a post. The process was not complex but there were several steps you had to follow. First, they had to scoop out all the loose dirt that had fallen back into the hole between the time we dug it and the time the posts arrived. Then I wanted them to place a few small rocks in the bottom of the hole so the post would not be sitting in water and rotting from the bottom up. Then they had to place the post in the hole without knocking in a lot more dirt. They had to set the post in the middle so they could pack dirt around it. It needed to be plumb, of course, and they had to fill the dirt in slowly and carefully, tamping it down as they went. When complete the post had to still be plumb and secure enough to support the wire and resist the efforts of a hungry mule to push it over.

The boys could not accomplish this task on their own. Even if I kept my attention on them, so they were actually working rather than goofing off, the posts stuck out at weird angles and could be wiggled around at will. The goal, as I had to keep telling myself, was not to simply get the fence built, but also to teach the boys something about pride of workmanship and sharing a task. Finally, we went at it as a group, working one post at a time and after three weeks and not a little frustration, the fence is up and secure.

Building the fence revealed a lot about myself and also about the strengths and weaknesses of the project. The best thing is that I am developing a close relationship with five poor boys in Nova Santana, and if the mayor has his way the project will soon expand to ten boys. The schools operate on a half-day schedule. My boys go to school in the afternoon and work with me in the morning. The mayor wants me to also start working with five other boys in the afternoon who attend school in the morning. One of the requirements, and thus one of the benefits, is that the boys stay in school. Another is they receive a modest wage, paid now by the mayor's office, though my goal is that the garden will eventually be self supporting. I hope they will learn some skills that prepare them for adult life. I try to engage them in practical and philosophical conversations as much as I can. All to the good, it seems to me. Jolene fears I want to turn them into social activists of some kind but that is not really the case.

First I want to learn how they see the world and their place in it. Only when we know and understand each other better will we talk about other things.

On the other hand even if I do develop a close relationship with these boys and have some lasting influence on them, I didn't come to Bahia just to teach five or ten boys. I prefer doing the garden just in the morning and having the afternoon to pursue other goals. If I follow the mayor's recommendation and take on an afternoon crew, and I don't see how I cannot–he has in fact been very kind and helpful to us–that will give me less time to work on the larger projects.

What do I mean by larger projects? Well, I started by trying to learn how things work in the neighborhood around our house. Where does the water come from? (A scattering of shallow unsecured wells that animals drink out of and defecate into.) Where does the waste end up? (Food waste, what little there is, is eaten by domestic and wild animals. Dead animals are quickly devoured by the squads of circling vultures. Animal waste ends up wherever it is dropped. Human waste, mostly in the bushes, though some families have outhouses.) Is there any evidence of law enforcement? (Not that I can see, at least not in the sense of patrols) A truant officer? (The concept does not seem to exist) How do folks cook their food? (On simple wood stoves mostly and a few men seem to eke out a modest livelihood cutting and delivering wood, though many families, it appears, cut their own.) Clothes are washed in the river and dried on the rocks and bushes. People seem to share tools and equipment but I have not noticed any formal structure regarding this. I have yet to understand how chickens are owned or kept track of, though the few pigs seem to be watched pretty closely by their owners. I have no idea where the turkeys that occasionally wander through our yard are coming from or going to.

Some enterprise goes on. A mule and driver can be hired out. A neighbor makes small manioc cakes that she sells at the market. A man makes beautiful wooden bird cages. His cages are found in many houses but I don't know where the birds come from. Are they caught wild? Raised by someone?

Even learning a simple thing can be complicated. I wanted to know, for example, whether the people rent or own their homes. If I ask someone if the house we are sitting in or standing beside is theirs, they say it is. But that, I assume, simply means that they live in this house rather than one of the others. Whether they own or rent is a more invasive question, and if they own it, whether they also own the land it sits on is a difficult concept to communicate given my knowledge of the language. Downtown there are streets and houses in neat rows lining them and here too the houses tend to face in certain directions and are spaced in ways that suggest an awareness of eventual streets or at least common paths or trails but I doubt it was planned out in any advanced way. It all seems very organic. I suspect the neighborhood began as a squatter development, perhaps not more than a decade ago.

My real goal, of course, is to learn the structure of the *favela*. Who are the natural leaders? What formal or informal organizations exist within the community? Is there group decision making going on? So far I have found scant evidence of any structural organization though I suspect I have not yet arrived close to the heart of the community.

Community development, Clint says.
Yes, I can see that now.

I have made this study indirectly by talking to people. I wander the neighborhood, chat with folks, look at things. One of my excuses for initiating a conversation is the garden. I'm known as the guy who is planting the garden with the boys. If I see something growing in a backyard, I stop by and ask about it. I talk with men building walls and women washing clothes. I know the cobbler and the furniture maker, the boy who sells the milk, the men who make roofing tiles.

None of this is easy or natural. We are viewed as foreign. Our speech is odd, our hair and skin coloring not quite normal. Jo and I are both taller than many of the men. Our status is strange and undefined. We are the *Americanos*, the people who talk funny and ask odd questions. At first some older women laughed openly when they saw us. One woman expressed amazement that I was as old as I was and still could not speak well. She seemed to have no concept that other languages exist and that I was just learning this one. This phase has passed. We are accepted now in a certain way. People greet us as we pass. Still we are not members of the community in any normal sense. There is one old man I meet on the path now and then. Our relationship reflects the way we are seen here, I suppose. If I greet him as *Senhor*, he responds by calling me *Doutor*. If I greet him as *Doutor*, he responds by calling me *Patrão*. There is an element of resistance in this patronizing attitude. He is a cunning old man, I suspect. A man who has spent a lifetime learning how to survive in an unequal and unfair society. I would love to be his friend and listen to his stories, to hear from his heart how it has been for him. But that will never happen. He has learned his tactics so well that they have become a part of him. He will not deviate, certainly not with a person in my position. His manner, in other words, not only provides him with a convenient cover, but also serves to keep me at a certain distance.

This sense of separation bothers me. At first I thought it was just language that kept me apart and I worked to improve my language skills. Then I cast off my old clothing and adopted theirs. Still, I am not one of them.

This past week, Jo and I began a kind of survey of the community. We visited nine homes over three days. The idea was to formally introduce ourselves, the sewing school and the garden. Having Jo along was a great help. Not only does she have a better ear for the language, but women are much more comfortable talking to her than to me, and more comfortable talking to me when she is present. And women are more common in the homes than men. We visited with women in each of the homes but with men in only two of them. In a third, the woman gave us the name of her man but he was not present.

We suspect no men live in the others, though we did not press to learn for certain. Children are everywhere. Each of the nine homes have children. One has eight, three have seven, one six, one five, (and she is also caring for two nephews), one has three and the last two have two each. So 49 kids counting the nephews, or an average of five and a half kids per home.

These visits are not easy, even with Jo along. Sometimes it is hard to know what if anything they accomplish. We are not at ease and it's awkward for the people we visit. We talk about families or schools or children or gardens, and of course the weather. We also spend time staring out the windows or at the dirt floor and finally we say goodbye and leave.

Initially I wanted to talk about outhouses. I wanted to know how many of the houses have them and explain a little about how important they are. In the end though I stayed away from the subject. Given the uncomfortable formality of the situation, it seemed inappropriate to begin talking about toilet habits and trying to explain in my broken Portuguese just how important they are. Still that does seem the way to go. I had an example last week when the woman who does our laundry was at the house with two of her nine children. I'd became so disturbed at the sight of those children's huge, worm-filled bellies, that I flat out asked if she had an outhouse, although I already knew she didn't. She admitted the truth and I stumbled through my explanation about those big bellies. I could see her maternal instincts well up on her face. She believed me. When we explained the mayor's plan which is similar to the one in Ilhéus, she said she wanted to participate. Later, I got a note from the mayor's office authorizing her family to have one of the platforms. I don't know yet if her husband has dug the hole or picked up the platform, but some progress seems to have been made. Still, we know this family better than the others. We have an ongoing relationship with her and the discussion was part of a larger conversation that took place in our home, rather than hers. I did not feel I could do the same in the initial visits. Still, with that success in mind, I think it is important that we continue making the visits, even if they are uncomfortable, and on the surface accomplish little or nothing.

Chapter Nineteen
MISTAKES

When Connie looks up from the journal, she sees Clint Estergard scratching the back of his head in what seems to her a furious manner.

I'm surprised he didn't mention it, he says. That was after the conference, right?

Yes, I believe so. Mention what?

Clint ignores her question, responding instead with one of his own: Did you say there's a draft of his conference presentation in the journal?

Yes.

Read it to me, will you?

She opens the notebook again, flipping through the pages. He gave it a title. He called it 'Mistakes.'

Fine, read it please.

It's undated.

That's all right.

I made a mistake the other day that I want to tell you about. I make a lot of them actually. I suppose you do too. I make mistakes with the language, for example. I mis-speak it, I mis-understand it. I assume I heard something when I didn't. I assume people understand me when they don't. I think I have a meeting arranged and the person I had planned to meet doesn't show up. I sometimes pretend to understand when in fact I don't.

I also make mistakes that are cultural. I get upset if someone doesn't show up, or is late, whereas my Brazilian friends seem to shrug if off. I would prefer a simple 'No,' to what seems to me the evasive '*Amanhã.*' And I still can't remember if you're supposed to unwrap a present when you receive it, or later.

At a more basic level, I tend to run into people on sidewalks. I mean literally run into them. I read somewhere that we unconsciously learn certain cues to help us navigate in crowded places and here, apparently, the cues are different.

Anyway, lots of mistakes, some large, some small, but the particular mistake I want to tell you about happened a few weeks ago. I have started a small garden project with five boys who are my students. Soon I may have ten. In our town the children go to school half days because there aren't enough classrooms or teachers to accommodate them full time. My wife, Jolene, incidently, is doing the same thing with a group of girls, though she is teaching sewing and pattern making rather than gardening.

The deal I made with the mayor is that he would pay the boys a few cruzeiros a week in exchange for helping in the garden. When we are up and running and selling produce, we will pay him back, and after that the boys will keep the profits. That's the plan.

So, anyway, the mayor loaned us a plot of ground near the *favela* and we are slowly putting in a garden. I want to describe how I met three of the boys I am working with and the mistake I made the day I met them.

I know some of you who are stationed in small towns get your electricity from community generators that operate only part of the day. Nova is lucky to be connected to a central power source. One of the blessings of centralized power, a recent phenomenon in Nova, is that Senhor Silvera and his wife Justina have opened an ice cream parlor just off the plaza. Jolene and I both love ice cream and I know our P.C. doctors say we shouldn't eat the local ice cream but I confess that we have been to the ice cream parlor more than once. One day we were sitting inside enjoying our cones when I saw three boys standing in the doorway looking in. Fortunately for the boys we actually had some money that day. Not only had a Peace Corps check arrived but the bank was actually open and we could deposit it and withdraw some cash.

So I went out and invited the boys in for ice cream. I have to tell you, what those boys said to me that afternoon, broke my heart. They said they could not come in. They said they were too dirty to come in. Try as I might, I could not get those boys to step through the door. I even suggested they go over to the plaza and wash their hands in the fountain, but they only shook their heads. You see, it wasn't the dirt on their clothes or their skin they were talking about. It was a stain on their spirits, a mark on their souls that kept them from coming inside the ice cream parlor.

Of course, we bought three ice cream cones and took them out to the boys. And that day, Vincente, Jose and Giberto enjoyed ice cream cones and now they are working with me in the garden.

So, what was my mistake? you ask. My mistake was that I lost track of my responsibilities. I thought, erroneously, that the objective was to get them ice cream, but that wasn't the real objective at all. Our job, I hope you will agree, is not to make sure the boys get an ice cream cone now and then. Our job is to get those boys, and all boys and all girls, to recognize that they have the value, the self worth, indeed they have the right, to step into the ice cream parlor, or into any building or business in this country. They do not need to stay on the outside looking in. They belong!

Amazing, Clint says, when Connie has finished.

I was moved as well.

Effective story all right, but that's not what intrigues me. What you read is not the presentation he gave at the conference.

It isn't?

Well, let me qualify that. I'm sure his talk included everything you have just read. But the central event, the focus of his presentation, does not appear in this draft. The draft must have been written before the event happened.

What event?

And the curious thing, Clint continues, it's not described in the other entry either, the one we read earlier, the one written after the conference. I find it odd, that's all, because in my memory that event changed Kyle's life.

Are you going to eventually tell me what the event was? Connie asks, looking frustrated.

Clint smiles and apologizes. Falling back on old lecturing habits, I suppose. Trying to build a little suspense to keep the students awake.

Well, you've succeeded.

Good for me. It was simple enough and apparently it happened just before the conference. I wasn't present at the time, of course, but this is what I remember from what he described. The garden was located in a little swale and as you know Kyle had been busy constructing a fence around it. At the top of the swale he had put in a gate. One morning as he and the boys approached the garden they saw something lying in the path in front of the gate. It was a strange object. I think he described it as shaped like a horn of plenty, something fashioned out of leaves and vines. It was fairly large, as I recall, maybe two feet long. Protruding from the open end of the horn were some dried grasses.

Had someone dropped it?

Not accidently. Kyle and the boys were convinced someone had placed it there deliberately. It lay directly in front of the gate. And it frightened the boys because they recognized it as a sign left by a witch doctor.

A witch doctor?

Have you heard of *Macumba* or *Condomblé*?

No.

Both terms designate the same thing. In other parts of Latin America you will hear different names. It's a religion with African roots and it's quite popular in Bahia. Anyway, the boys were frightened. As Kyle told the story, the boys wanted to leave. One even took Kyle's arm and tried to prevent him from approaching the object. The poor in Bahia are quite superstitious. They saw this object as a bad omen. So the emphasis of Kyle's presentation, as I remember it, was his description of what he did when he and the boys came upon the object, why what he did had been a mistake and what he should have done instead. And finally how he was going to make up for his mistake when he got back to Nova Santana.

Okay. So, what did he do?

He kicked the object out of the way. He saw it as a threat, not just to him, but to the boys and through them to the garden project itself. Whoever placed the object before the gate was trying to scare the boys away from the garden. That was his thinking at the time and he wanted to show the boys that they need not be intimidated. He kicked it aside and opened the gate and led them in. His actions were consistent with the empowering theme he talked about in the draft.

Did the boys follow him?

Yes, they did.

So, why was it a mistake?

I'm not sure it was, Clint says, but Kyle thought so. That was the point of his presentation. He said he should have picked the object up and held it to his chest. In other words he should have treated it as a gift.

I see.

His talk led to a lively discussion about black magic and how to relate to it. That's part of what made the presentation so special. Kyle announced that he was going to try to find the person who had placed the object before the gate. He would apologize for his failure to accept the gift. He intended to ask for forgiveness.

I see, Connie says again.

That was our first conference. I think we had three all

together, but your parents were gone before the second one happened.

Connie stands abruptly and begins to walk back and forth between Clint and the water. She's carrying the journal in her right hand and waving it about as she walks.

So something dramatic must have happened, she announces. Something between the first conference and the second. They seem to be getting along rather well. Not perfect, of course. But the sewing school and the gardening. There's nothing in what I just read to suggest they would suddenly leave.

No, you're quite right. I think they were doing well at that point. At least they had work. And I believe for Jolene life was somewhat better. The stove and refrigerator made her domestic responsibilities easier. And with the sewing school she felt she was making a contribution. But it was still rainy and muddy and when Kyle was not working in the garden he was probably out in the community.

So, she was lonely.

Very much so, I would say.

So, that's it? That's why they came home?

That's not why they went home. We were all lonely.

Connie feels a surge of anger and she starts walking faster back and forth. It had to do with Mom, I'm sure of that. Something happened to Mom.

As a matter of fact, Clint responds calmly, the conference was a treat for Jolene. I spent most of my time with Vern, of course. The single Volunteers tended to hang out with each other. But your parents, Vern and I probably had dinner together one night and I saw them at breakfast and during the meetings. All of the conferences followed a similar format. Three or four nights at the Hotel Plaza. A private consultation with a PC doctor. We got a TB skin test and had several cc's of gamma globulin shot into our posteriors as a defense against hepatitis. We turned over stool samples and the doc would remind us of what we should and should not eat. Oliver Burke, the PC director for Brazil, flew in from Rio with the big picture of Peace Corps projects throughout the country and the world. Usually we had a party at a beach outside of town and a steak dinner complements of Charlie Pell. We got money and pep talks from Charlie. One or two Volunteers gave presentations. Mostly though we reveled in restaurants and bars, comfortable beds, private baths and unlimited hot water. Jolene got to dress nicely and she probably spent several hours shopping. It was a pleasant break for her.

I don't care about the conferences, Connie says, waving the journal. I'm feeling very frustrated. I want to know what happened.

I'm getting to what happened.

Connie pauses in front of him. Promise me one thing.

All right.

Promise me that you do know what happened.

I do and I will tell you, but you must understand the context.

The context, Connie says, walking again. Well, I want to say this to you: I know one thing you don't.

All right.

And it's about my mom and it's about Brazil.

All right.

And it's important. And this time Connie does not turn. She just keeps walking, as if she has suddenly decided to walk to Mount Baker.

Nothing appears to have changed when she returns, red faced, a half hour later. Clint is still sitting beside the picnic table facing the water. He appears to be dozing. She sits down beside him.

I am very sorry, she says.

No need to apologize.

But I want to apologize. That was totally uncalled for.

I understand this is personal for you. Incidently, I turned off the machine. I assume you don't need a record of my snoring.

I just needed to settle down. I needed to walk.

I understand.

I promise to be more patient.

You don't owe me any promises, Connie. Are you ready to continue?

I want to read something.

I thought we had finished the journal.

I think I said almost finished. This entry may have resulted in an article sent home.

All right.

Wednesday April 13th

On Monday I went looking for the house of a certain Geraldo. I wanted to return a crowbar he had loaned me when the boys and I were putting up wire for the fence. I knew approximately where his house was. It's in the *favela,* not too far from here. He had described it well, saying it was surrounded by growing corn and rambling bean stalks. Geraldo was seated at the table eating a small amount of meat with a large amount of *farofa,* or manioc flour. On the table sat one of his daughters, three or four years old. Now and then she would plunge her hand into his plate for a fistful of food. Geraldo is one of the poor, uneducated in any formal sense. Yet, it's impressive to see how well he cares for himself and his family.

The house is clean and cool with a cement floor and a low tiled roof. He built the house himself, adding rooms as his family has grown. Now in his middle forties with streaks of gray in his black hair, his house has grown to five rooms including a long sleeping room, and his family consists of himself and his wife and four children. He is one of those people who can do most anything and he hates waste in any form. He gave me a tour of his yard which was as dense as a jungle but as well cultivated and maintained as a royal garden. He said he could not leave any spot of ground vacant. Although his property is probably less than a third of an acre, he has two good stands of corn, the older with tassels and young ears. He also grows okra, beans, leaf cabbage, a banana tree, a coconut tree and several young orange and tangerine trees.

He ordered coffee as we stepped out to see the yard and when we returned the pot was hot and waiting. The coffee was very Brazilian: black, strong and syrupy with sugar. With the coffee we enjoyed cigars, which his wife makes. To cut off the tips, he pulled from his belt a clean, stainless-steel, bone-handled hunting knife. As we enjoyed the coffee in tiny cups and the large sweet cigars, he told me that he had been born in an industrial town near Aracaju, Sergipe. Aracaju is where our friends Polly and David Lehman are stationed so I was curious about it.

Geraldo says that the people of Sergipe work harder than the people in Bahia and are more independent. But he left Sergipe as a young man and works here in Nova as a handyman for the city, doing whatever is needed but specializing in mechanical things. Among the relative poor, he is the only one I know who owns a motor vehicle. He built it himself. It has four wheels. It's open and consists of a flat bed like a raft and is powered by a Model A engine. One day, he and one of his children gave Jo and me a lift in the thing. It has one long seat on which the four of us sat, I to the left of the driver. Geraldo's ability to assemble and maintain this vehicle speaks to his mechanical genius.

As I was leaving the house, I mentioned that I liked the cigar. He asked me to wait and soon returned with a fistful of them. Then we waited until his wife found some paper. A present must be wrapped after all. Then she went and found string to tie the wrapping since I did not have a pocket in my shirt. Finally, I left. After yet another cup of coffee. Walking back to the house, I felt I had encountered a noble uncommon man.

You had to be careful, Clint says. Careful about offering a compliment when you were in a Brazilian's house. If you told the host that you liked the vase on the table, he would offer to give it to you. That's what happened with the cigars.

I feel he was happy and relaxed when he wrote those words, Connie says. Happy to know that man, happy to visit that man's house. Happy writing about it. That's what's driving me nuts. Good things are happening to them.

Yes, at the same time, Kyle is filled with frustration. He's trying to penetrate to the heart of the community and he can't. He's experiencing a sense of exclusion. He sees himself as an outsider, not welcomed beyond a certain point. His inability to locate the community's center, the power and the organization that lay behind it, is frustrating his effort to bring about change. Already, you notice, the garden project is not enough for him. He wants to bring about change, real change. He thinks community development is the way to accomplish that. And to do community development he needs to find where the energy is, the center.

I understand.

What Kyle came to believe was that *Condomblé* was the very thing he had been searching for, the hidden heart of the poor community.

I see, Connie says.

They are silent for a moment and she adds, Unfortunately, that entry is almost the last one in the journal.

Clint sighs and touches his forehead. The skin on his face has tightened and dried out from the sun. Yes, he says, that is unfortunate. We are left with just my old and faulty memory.

It is so frustrating for me, Connie says. Things seemed to be going pretty well and then he stopped writing.

Yes, I understand.

Chapter Twenty
DAIQUIRIS AND DRUMS

Clint has a rehearsal in the late afternoon with the string quartet in which he plays second fiddle. Strictly amateur, he explains to Connie. His fellow musicians are grayed and graying, present and former members of the faculty from various departments. Three men and one large-boned woman, an experimental psychologist, who grips her cello by the neck and wears surprisingly strong perfume.

Connie hints that she might like to come along. She wants to hear him play.

I'll play something for you, he says, if we get the chance. In fact, I'm working on a project with the violin that I can try out on you. But you wouldn't enjoy this rehearsal. Come back in the fall if you want to hear the group. We usually pull together a program. Perform it once here and a couple of times among the rustics, in Hope and somewhere on the Sunshine Coast.

He drops her at the hotel and promises to be back at seven-thirty. They will go out for dinner. She apologizes again for walking off and leaving him there in the sun and she promises to be waiting at the door when he returns.

He doesn't linger after the rehearsal. Usually he and Jeremy have a beer but he finds himself eager to get back to Connie. Traffic is unusually light and he reaches the hotel ten minutes before their appointed time. He's waiting in the van when she steps through the side door and into the parking lot.

She apologizes yet again, this time for not being there when he arrived.

I was early, he tells her.

I know, but I could have anticipated that.

They head up Marine Drive toward the city. Well, you can't come to Vancouver and not eat some Chinese food, he says. If you're not comfortable with chopsticks use the western weapons. The idea is to get the stuff inside where you can taste it.

I use chopsticks. My sons can too. They love Chinese food.

I'm impressed.

You must think we're real rubes, she says, poking his shoulder.

No, I didn't mean to imply...

She laughs. It's all right, Doctor.

Clint, please.

Yes, Clint.

He sits hunched forward over the wheel. It happened right about here, he tells her a few moments later as they're passing the south side of the campus. Mid-morning. Fall term about to begin. Traffic heavy. Cars were parked bumper to bumper all along here. People unloading things to take into the dorms.

Were you driving?

No, I was on my bike. And moving pretty much with the traffic. Probably thirty kilometers per hour, maybe more. That's part of the fun when you're in condition. You're keenly aware of yourself and your surroundings. The cars, pedestrians, the other cyclists. You feel like you're part of a larger organism, a flock of birds say. Ahead I see a man standing in the street beside his parked car. He's short, balding, an East Indian, reaching up, his belly against the side of the car. Ironically, as it turned out, he's unloading his son's bicycle from a rack on the top. I know there's a car following on my left but there's room for both of us to get past. Then, just as I reach him, the man steps back. I swerve but hit the calf of his leg with my front wheel and I'm flying through the air. That's all it took.

There's nothing that can be done?

No. Some animals can do wonders, as you may know. Lizards can grow a new tail, crabs a new claw. Darwin describes cutting a worm in half and ending up with two complete worms, each with all the implements necessary to have a front and a back. But in this case, the lines of communication are confined within a narrow channel inside the vertebrae. A lot of people think the spinal cord has to be severed, but that's not what happened in my case. The trauma was such that a lesion formed constricting the channel and the impulses cannot get through. I'm sorry, he adds, about the chopsticks remark.

At the restaurant, she places her recorder on the table between them.

Are we working? he asks.

If you're up for it.

Clint pulls the sheets of paper from the pocket of his jacket. They have become quite wrinkled and he smooths them out and studies them for a moment. Good thing I triple spaced, he says. I keep adding notes. Often it comes to me while I'm practicing. Nothing like running through scales to free the mind.

We can just enjoy the meal if you prefer.

Oh, we'll enjoy the meal all right. Service is slow here but it's worth the wait. So, let's see. We covered the conference and Kyle's presentation. The next thing... Okay, I received a handwritten note from your mother.

A letter?

Just a note. Jolene had given it to the bus driver along with some money so he could hire a kid in Jacarandá to deliver it to me. I got it on a Friday. The note instructed me to come to Nova the next afternoon, but didn't indicate why. Plan to spend the night, the note said. Nothing bad had happened, she assured me, but I should bring the promised bottle.

The promised bottle?

That was a bit of a joke. She was referring to a bottle of rum. Among the appliances they had inherited was a blender. When I heard about that at the conference, I told them the next time I would bring a bottle and we could make daiquiris.

I see.

It was hard not to tease Kyle now and then. He was so serious. When Vern and I heard about the blender and a refrigerator with a freezer compartment we accused him of becoming a party animal. We asked if Hugh Heffner had stopped by yet for a drink. Your dad didn't find this particularly entertaining but he took it all right. Jolene, though, was serious about the daiquiris. She had never had one, and was eager to try. She promised to have limes and sugar on hand the next time I came. She was waiting at the bus stop, wrapped in a sarape and holding an umbrella. She called me brother and threw her arms around me. We were leading a double life and it was kind of fun. With Brazilians, both in Jacarandá and in Nova, we were brother and sister.

I can tell you were having fun, Connie says.

Winter had come to Nova, if you can get your mind around the idea of winter in the tropics. The rains had set in, that was the main difference. I've described the route up through the *favela* to your parents' house. During the dry season it was a wide uneven dirt path. But with the coming of the rains the residents had to be more careful where they walked. This resulted in narrow undulating routes resembling game trails. To get over the depressions where water was flowing or the chocolate-colored earth gathered in pools, the people placed stones and boards forming precarious foot bridges.

Jolene refused to explain the purpose of my visit. She was being coy. 'A secret,' she teased. She had promised Kyle not to tell until the three of us were together.

Kyle wasn't home when we arrived at the house. The interior had changed considerably from the last time I had been there. The refrigerator hummed. The stove gleamed beside the water filter. They had built more shelving to store food and utensils, and Jolene had sewn curtains from a red and white checked fabric and hung them in front of the shelves. The walls she had decorated with practical items you could find at any market:

brooms, sieves, baskets. It was creative. Seeing them displayed like works of art, you noticed the craftsmanship that had gone into those most utilitarian of objects. You would have enjoyed their house. It really was quite charming. Mom had a sense of design and color, Connie says. Dad was in charge of the yard and garden, but the interior was her bailiwick.

Well, she had made it a home all right. But characteristically she shrugged off my compliments. Fixing up the house was what she did when she was hiding out. And according to her, she hid out a lot, though it didn't sound that way to me. She was still teaching English classes and now she had two sewing classes that met four days a week each. But Kyle set the standard. According to Jolene, he left the house early and did not return until evening. So, she was alone or with students most of the time. The tension between them was ongoing. She wanted him home more but she also felt guilty that she wasn't as driven as he was. Jolene enjoyed the English classes while he thought they were a waste of time. Most of the students were young bank employees taking the class to improve their resumés. Middle class kids, you might say, and Kyle had given up on the middle class. The division between the poor and the not poor dominated his thinking and he refused to accept it as natural the way the Brazilians did. In the evening he would insist on describing every terrible thing he had seen or heard during the course of the day. He was forcing himself, and thus her, to listen to every wailing child, to look at every distended stomach, to notice every festering lesion, to report every injustice he saw. It was, I guess, his way of shoring up resolve.

That must have been hard for her, Connie says, saddened by what he is describing.

For both of them. But yes, particularly for her. Conflict. On the one hand she might quite reasonably have thought the descriptions he forced on her were unnecessarily brutal. On the other hand, she knew both that he wasn't exaggerating and that he needed to see and express these things. And she probably considered it her job as his wife, to dutifully listen to every word he felt compelled to speak.

Yes.

The most recent episode had involved the death of a man named Lagosta. It occurred the week before I arrived. This man died at the Saturday market. He was a drunk. Not old. Jolene described him as thirty-five maybe forty. He was sitting on the sidewalk at the edge of the plaza with his back against a wall. Jolene said she hadn't noticed him at all. She was busy shopping, but Kyle came and got her. He took her hand and led her across the plaza until they were standing only a few feet in front of the man. Jolene described his face as being the oddest gray.

Lagosta was a nickname probably. It's the word for lobster. So I suppose he once had a ruddy complexion, but now it was gray. Like the ashes of a campfire, according to Jolene. His eyes were vacant and his loose clothing hung half off him. His arms, his face and his chest were covered with flies.

Kyle told Jolene that Lagosta was dying. She didn't want to believe it and she was very embarrassed to be standing in front of the man talking about him as if he were some inanimate object. But Kyle held her there for a moment. He had been talking to people, he explained. They had told him the man's name, that he was a drunk and that he was dying.

Then Kyle put his hands on Jolene's shoulders and slowly turned her in a circle. 'See,' he said, as she was slowly revolving, 'it's just another day at the market. There's the man who cuts the thick pork chops for you. There's the family that has the good tomatoes. There's Adi's mother with her manioc cakes and next to her the man who always tries to charge us extra because we're foreign. And see the rich women shopping in their bright dresses with their servants carrying the baskets? It's just another day at the market except that Lagosta here is dying. They know

Lagosta is dying, Jolene. They all know, but they don't see him. They simply choose not to see him!'

Connie places her hands over her mouth.

Your mother was terrified, as you might imagine. She thought she might throw up right there. She was sure that Kyle wanted her to help carry Lagosta to a doctor, but she knew she could not do that. She could not touch that man. She could not be holding another person when death came. She was shaking and starting to cry. But then Kyle took her in his arms. He told her there was nothing she had to do. Nothing, except carry the basket home herself because he was going to stay at the market. He was going sit there with Lagosta. Then Kyle sat down on the sidewalk beside this man. He removed his hat and waved away the flies. He took Lagosta's hand in his and held it.

Connie has tears in her eyes. He wanted to make them see.

That's right, Clint says slowly.

So, what happened?

Well, your mother grabbed up the basket and went straight home, at least that's the way she described it. Later Kyle told her what had happened and she told it to me. The people did notice of course. They couldn't help but notice that the American was sitting on the sidewalk beside the dying drunk. Kyle could see them looking and whispering to one another. A few people finally came over and talked with him. A couple of teachers your parents knew, the wife of a doctor. They were embarrassed. Kyle thought they were embarrassed because of Lagosta. Because he had the indecency to die on a Saturday at the market in front of the Americans. But Jolene thought that was not fair. She had a good relationship with some of the wealthier women and she liked the vendors at the market. She thought they were kind and decent people.

Anyway, Lagosta did die that afternoon, but not in the market. The man who owned the hotel where your parents had stayed that first month offered Kyle a room. He and Kyle carried Lagosta across the plaza to the hotel and he died there in bed. Kyle was holding him when he died, apparently.

I'm proud of him. Connie takes the napkin from the table and wipes her eyes. I'm proud of them both.

As well you should be. I remember thinking as I heard that story that Kyle Henderson threw a shadow on us all. It wasn't jealousy. I had no desire to behave as he did. I knew in my heart that I would have walked away from that sorry drunk as soon as I saw him. If I had felt any guilt, it would have passed through me and dissipated like a muscle spasm. It also crossed my mind that Kyle might himself be teetering along a fine edge; fall one way and he would be a hero, fall the other and he would be considered out of his gourd as we used to say. But he stood apart, no question. I had to respect him for that.

When did Dad return to the house?

Late. I remember he was not there when we went out to watch the sunset.

So you and Mom were alone?

Yes, so I suggested we try out the new blender.

The daiquiris.

There you go. And in volume, I must admit. Your mom and I shared a weakness for daiquiris. Would you like one yourself, by the way?

No thank you.

Would you mind if I ordered one? I haven't had one in years. Sort of a salute to those days?

No, of course not.

But I can't tempt you? Something else?

You can tempt me, she admits, but I won't have one.

Clint orders the drink and smiles across the table. Your parents and I had some fun, when I think back on it.

Good.

Anyway, by the time Kyle got home it was dark and the cuticles on my fingers stung from having squeezed so many limes. The short-wave radio was blaring. Back in those days, the BBC still had programs that echoed from the old empire: Mrs. Hutchinson-Smith in Kuala Lumpur, the announcer would say, is sending out this request in honor of Mr. and Mrs. Nigel Farnsworthy of Nairobi and the big band would start another tune. Your mom and I were pretty well lubed, singing along and sauteeing onions when your dad finally came through the door.

Kyle had taken to using a walking stick, a staff-like thing that stood as tall as his shoulders. And he still had the leather pouch and straw hat. The coming of the rains had forced him back to wearing boots. But if you'd have seen all his paraphernalia set in the corner beside the door you'd have thought Johnny Appleseed had just arrived. Jolene had carefully saved a couple of the precious ice cubes from the small freezer and we spun him up what I took to be a world-class daiquiri with a double shot of the rum. Like most of us, alcohol loosened your dad up, but it did not noticeably alter his pace or change his direction. I had the impression he had great respect for it, like a man who had learned to never turn his back on the ocean. This daiquiri he sipped slowly, looking bemused, content to watch us peeling and chopping and singing along at the table.

I was in a mood to tease him a little. 'Give your wife a turn on the dance floor there, Henderson,' I suggested at one point, bringing forth my best British accent.

'Yes, Henderson,' Jolene seconded, 'give the lady a twirl.'

Kyle resisted. He didn't want to take Jolene away from preparing the meal. No, no I insisted. Finally after a lot of talk about how he couldn't dance and how he had crushed Jolene's toes dancing at their wedding reception, finally Kyle Henderson reluctantly danced with his wife.

He danced with me at my wedding, Connie says. That's the only time I remember.

It made Jolene happy and I know he wanted her to always be happy. He wanted her to be happy because he loved her. But it occurred to me that Kyle had a selfish motive as well. If Jolene were happy she would give him the slack he needed to do the job he felt he needed to do. But, of course, it would take more than a dance or two to accomplish that.

Did you dance with Mom?

The daiquiri arrives. Clint sips it carefully and then shakes his head with disgust. Nothing like the ones we used to make, he whispers across the table. A decent daiquiri requires fresh-squeezed limes and plenty of rum. You want some bite in there. He sets the glass on the table. You were smart not to order one. This threatens to ruin my memory rather than enhance it. The daiquiri has fallen into disrespect, I'm afraid. It's become just another excuse to pour you full of sugar. A drink for people who are really looking for dessert.

So, did you? Connie persists.

Did I what?

Dance with Mom.

Maybe once. Once or twice. She was a good dancer. I knew of course that she was musical. I had heard her sing.

Yes, you've told me.

She had a good sense of rhythm. And our heights worked well together. The top of her head came to about the bridge of my nose. I used to enjoy dancing.

Do you think it bothered Dad that she danced with you?

Not at all. We were brother-sister, remember.

Well...,Connie says, not really.

That's the way we thought of it. And as I suggested, whatever made your mother happy, Kyle was for it.

Okay. So why had they summoned you? For daiquiris?

Not for one of these, surely, he says, taking another reluctant sip. I wouldn't have come for that. No, I finally learned the answer over dinner. They had made contact.

Contact?

With the *Condomblé* people. Kyle informed me that the thing lying in front of the garden gate had been a message from Oxossi, one of the deities in the *Condomblé* religion. I don't know where he learned that.

Did he really believe it?

You mean literally? I have no idea. But given what happened, possibly.

What do you mean, what happened?

I mean eventually, which we'll get to. But on this night they had been invited to a *Condomblé* ceremony. And they thought I might enjoy seeing it.

I see.

Kyle said that after the drums started...

Finally, the drums!

Yes, Connie, we have finally gotten to the drums. Anyway, at dinner Kyle explained that after the drums started, a man would come to get us. So, I asked what seemed to me a fairly obvious question. One that would be good to have answered before we went off with this man. What had actually been the message that had been left in front of the garden gate? Had it been a kind of greeting, or had it been a curse?

Yes, I see what you mean.

Kyle and Jolene looked at each other and Kyle said, 'We have no idea.' But he was grinning.

Dad was?

Clint nodded. Maybe it was the daiquiri, but if there was ever a time that Kyle Henderson was teasing me, that was it.

The first of the appetizers arrive and Connie turns off the recorder so they can concentrate on the meal.

No MSG, Clint says, his mouth half full. That's one of the reasons I like this place. Even the sauces are made here. You have to watch the sauces if you're sensitive to the stuff.

After they have eaten Connie is concerned about the batteries in the recorder. Clint speaks with the headwaiter and he moves them to a table in the adjoining bar. A quiet spot against the wall and near an outlet.

Connie orders a chocolate mousse and he a gin and tonic. Perhaps he'll do better with something British, he says, nodding toward the bartender.

He doesn't look particularly British to me.

Oh no? See the lady in the photo on the wall behind him?

Yes, now that you mention it. I've been seeing that photo in a lot of places.

You're in the old Commonwealth, Connie. So, anyway, the drums began a short time later and all the ice was gone and the daiquiris had begun to wear off. When the drums started we found we had little to talk about. Your parents had no sink, did I tell you that?

No, but by the way, did they have a toilet?

Yes, but don't ask me where it all ended up. As to the dishes, since they had no sink Jolene did them in a metal bowl set on the table. The kind of thing you might set a baby in to bathe. My job was to take each soapy plate and pan outside, rinse it with a small amount of precious boiled water and then wipe it dry with a towel. Meanwhile, Kyle brought more water in from the well, poured it through the filter and set it on the stove to boil.

We finished cleaning up and the drums continued. Jolene went into their bedroom to change and Kyle and I stood outside on the dark patio. The sky was enormous. A quarter moon, a scattering of voluptuous, bright, well-defined clouds. The air had a warm density some evenings. It smelled of things rooted and alive and announcing themselves with their scent. The near trees of the orchard were massed darkness, distinguished only by their tops silhouetted against the lighter sky. Somewhere nearby, a bird endlessly repeated its five-note riff as though playing off the rhythm of the drums.

You have an excellent memory, Connie says, smiling.

It must be the gin, he says, grinning. It certainly wasn't the daiquiri. Anyway, Jolene joined us a few minutes later. We were all a little nervous anticipating what might lie ahead. In my mind I engaged in the never-ending debate familiar to every Volunteer in Brazil: the man was supposed to come for us after the drums started. The drums had been beating for an hour. Obviously the man was not coming. That was one side of the argument. But the other side would come back: You might have developed some patience by now. Bahians experience a more flexible time than we. An hour spread fits well within the standard deviation. Then: We are fools standing out here like Easter Island statuary when Brazilians would be inside eating, drinking and engaging with one another. When the man finally arrived, if he did, they would invite him in for an hour before they set off together. Their now is larger than our now, I told myself. We live within the beam of a flashlight. They beneath an enormous moon-lit sky.

That's a nice thought.

Funny, but I remember noticing Jolene's freshly re-applied perfume that night.

My mother liked expensive perfume.

Yes, but she never over did it. Not in my experience. And I thought it was curious how women and plants adopt a similar strategy.

What do you mean?

Emitting attractive smells.

Unlike your cello player.

Yes, unlike the cello player. Who's a fine person, by the way, and a good cellist. Just a little heavy with the spray. Anyway, after what seemed a very long time standing there in the dark, we heard the gate creak. What we saw first was the brilliance of his outfit: white slacks and shirt, a pale blue sash around his waist. Then the whites of his eyes. He stepped onto the patio and into the thin spill of light spreading out through the door. He was very dark and his black skin glistened. His full lips smiled, revealing a few surviving teeth. On his gnarled and knobby feet were thongs.

Did you know this man?

I had never met him, but he and Kyle embraced. Amadeo was the man's name, I believe. He was maybe ten years our senior. His manner was formal, bowing. I was *Senhor*. Jolene was *Dona*, the lady of the house. So, how's the mousse?

Delicious. And the gin?

Very British. Jolene was a good hostess. She had set out a plate of fresh-baked cookies. She invited Amadeo in for the cookies and some juice. The prospect presented a quandary for Amadeo. He was shy about entering the house of the Americans and yet intrigued, maybe fascinated. Plus he wanted to be polite. We sat in the front room on kitchen chairs around a small table. Amadeo declined the juice when we offered it to him, but when Jolene suggested water he accepted.

He worked as a janitor at the school where Jolene taught English. He was there in the evenings to open the classroom door, returning at the end of the class to close things up again. Accepting the plate of cookies from Kyle, Amadeo said, '*Obrigado, Senhor.*'

'My name is Kyle,' your father chided. '*Senhor* is for older richer men.'

Amadeo smiled and nodded but did not volunteer to pronounce the name.

Kyle probed him with gentle questions. He was good at this. He wasn't looking for information so much as trying to make Amadeo comfortable. Amadeo had come to Nova, we learned, from the interior a couple of years before the flood. He had come because of a woman but that had not worked out and he lived in the home of his cousin and her husband. His Portuguese was soft and slurry, melodic with a diminuendo in the middle vowels of the last word of a phrase. He was thin but had strong cheek bones and a square forehead. Maybe it was just the night or the booze but I felt drawn to this man. He had been born with shiny dark skin and African features on a continent where neither was an advantage, yet he had amassed a strong personal dignity. I remember his hands. The lighter skin in the palms gleamed with the energy of old ivory. It was an energy he protected, keeping his hands loosely cupped and in his lap.

I think of my sons.

Yes, of course. As I said, great personal dignity in this man. Polite, but not obsequious in any way. Kyle asked him about the flood. Yes, he had witnessed the flood. No, his home had not been destroyed. Yes, he knew a man who had drowned. He did not elaborate.

Kyle related a story he had heard from the boys he worked with. During a religious procession held shortly before the flood, some men dropped the statue of the patron saint of the town. This, one of the boys, claimed, had caused the flood.

Amadeo nodded solemnly but did not commit himself. 'A *gente*,' he began, meaning the people. 'The people say many things.'

During a pause in the conversation, Jolene reminded us of the drums. Moments later we were descending the dark path toward the gate. Beyond the gate we turned left onto a path that climbed the hill past the pasture behind the Hendersons' house. We walked for ten or fifteen minutes, mostly up. Amadeo was probably happy to be out of the house. He produced a flashlight and shined its light solicitously on the ground in front of Jolene, sometimes stumbling himself as he stepped off the path to make the way easier for her.

We came to an open area and saw above us a building flooded with light. On either side of the path leading to the building was a row of lanterns. It was from the building that the drumming came. Figures in dark silhouette passed in front of the open windows and doors. The sound was much louder here and the rhythm seemed faster, more intense. We reached the door and stopped. A dozen persons stood outside watching the dancers within. The spectators turned at our arrival. They greeted Amadeo softly, glancing at us.

The colors Amadeo wore, the white and pale blue, the blue

of robins' eggs, were everywhere in and around the building. In addition to the clothing of the dancers and bystanders, the walls had been painted white. Blue crepe paper streamers hung from the rafters; poles supporting the roof were swirled in it. Standing in the light pouring from the door it occurred to me that the three of us looked pale and out of mode.

Connie is interested in the building. Was it like a church? A house?

More like a roller rink, as I remember roller rinks in the 1950's. An open rectangular room with no ceiling. Along one side on a platform sat several drummers. Beside them rose a large eclectic altar that seemed to welcome any object that had significance to anyone, be it the painted figurine of a saint, strips of bright cloth, dried plants, the shiny end of a tin can. I remember cigar smoke. The floor was thick with dark sweat-gleaming dancers all dressed in outfits similar to what Amadeo was wearing except that the women, of course, were in full skirts.

Yes.

I would have been perfectly happy to have observed from the obscure dark outside the doorway. Amadeo, however, had other ideas. He began to part the crowd and turning back motioned us to follow. We hesitated. The idea seemed preposterous. What were we doing here anyway? I asked myself. This had nothing to do with us. Besides, the dancers were mashed together flesh against flesh. Amadeo motioned again eagerly. It was Jolene who first pressed forward squeezing sideways between the gyrating bodies. Kyle waved that I should follow her.

I was very uncomfortable. As we moved slowly toward the platform, I felt every inch an ugly American, injecting myself into a transaction where I had no currency other than my foreignness. It got worse; looking over the crowd I saw on the platform three empty metal folding chairs. Our arrival had been anticipated. We were going to be treated as guests of honor.

Just then a scream exploded from a large dark woman to

my immediate left. Her mouth was inches from my ear and the scream registered both as sound and as a physical blast against the side of my face.

Clint stops talking. He takes a sip of gin and looks intently across the table. I want you to experience the full impact of that scream, Connie. That scream was unlike anything this middle class boy had ever heard. It rose up without restraint or hesitation from our collective origins.

Was she screaming at you?

I had no idea. I fell back. I might have fallen to the floor had hands not grabbed me, held me up and pulled me out of the circle of space that was appearing now around the woman. The drumming and dancing continued without pause. But into the pattern of the dancer's motions there came now a nodding gesture toward the woman who was twitching and muttering and frothing at the mouth. Across the circle I saw Jolene. She was frozen in place, her skin pale as flour. Then I spotted your father. Kyle Henderson, the thin solemn one. Kyle Henderson, the man who a couple of hours before had been reluctant to dance with his wife. Kyle Henderson was dancing! Awkward, clumsy, eyes closed, your father was dancing!

Did you and Mom dance?

Absolutely not. Kyle danced until after midnight. But Jolene and I? Not at all. We took our seats on the platform and watched. You need to understand. We were not seeing a dance as we typically think of a dance, at least not in the current western sense of the term. True, people were moving about in time with the drumming but as part of a ceremony, or a service, to use a word more closely associated with a religious meeting. We were on the outside watching. And we were truly outsiders. We had been invited as guests, not as participants. I was angry at Kyle, and embarrassed by his behavior. I thought his participation ignored differences that were real and deserved our respect. I believed he was making a mistake and I resented that I was unavoidably associated with it. I also thought his actions would alienate him from the very people he was trying to get closer to. More than forty years have passed since that night and I still can't say whether my assessment was right or wrong.

What do you mean? Connie pulls the journal from her bag and begins riffling through the pages.

Well, he did make inroads into that part of the community, so in that sense he was right and I was wrong. But as you'll see, the outcome was not favorable and I continue to believe he would have been better off had he taken a different course.

Okay, she says, looking up. I want to read this. It's brief, it's weird and it's undated. I wonder if it applies.

I'm sure now the garland was a greeting. Our efforts have been recognized. Not our works. Our works had not yet justified recognition, but our efforts. Such a mistake I made! How simple to have reached down and picked it up. To have treated the gesture with a fraction of the respect with which it was offered. I have punished myself a hundred times for that rash act! As they say, it is the ego's impulse to rush. Out of fear or anger or lust, the ego wants to grab or hit or push away. And the blunders pile up like boulders. Had I been able to hold myself still for a moment. To have found that still center within where all wisdom lies. Had I just taken a deep breath. But no. With a joyous rush of power, I kicked. How wonderful it felt at that moment! I must confess how superior I felt! I, the western, educated mind, displaying its contempt for crude superstition. Power! The raw joy of disdain! I see now how it is possible that a man could in the moment of the act feel perfect pleasure even in murdering a fellow human being. That is the paradox of our lives. Our moral challenge. How something so wrong can feel so good!

But perhaps we have received a second chance. By inviting us to their ceremony they have shown remarkable tolerance. To my credit, I did put the word out. I have expressed my regrets.

No one responded, of course. No one has revealed knowledge of anything. Then out of the blue came this invitation. And shy wonderful Arnando. His was a position of great honor. Chosen to deliver the message to us. Chosen to deliver us to the ceremony. It was a great responsibility and a great honor. He is a foot soldier. But the leaders, if there are leaders, have their eyes on him, that's obvious. Tonight his status is risen. He has performed his duty with dignity and honor. But I must admit to myself that I know nothing about this organization. Perhaps there are no leaders. But there is organization. Events are planned, decisions made, activities carried out. Where else among the poor have I found any semblance of organization? This is of the people. It belongs to them. Perhaps tonight I have found my home.

Maybe I have the man's name wrong, Clint says when she has finished. Arnando, did he say? It could have been Arnando.

Yes.

Kyle probably wrote the entry that very night. Long after I had fallen asleep a few feet away.

Chapter Twenty-one

RUMOR OF SORCERY

Would you mind if I have another?

Connie studies him for a moment. Earlier that afternoon when they were leaving Garry Point Park he had done something that surprised her. While she was putting away her equipment he had removed a pair of old cycling gloves from his pocket, the kind that protects the palms but leaves the fingers exposed. He asked if she would be able to find the boardwalk where they had eaten. When she said she could, he promised to meet her there, and then he took off as fast as he could move, spinning the wheels with his gloved hands. He moved fast, faster than she could have walked and soon he was out of view. When finally she reached the bench where they had eaten, he waited, face flushed, still breathing heavily, a smile on his face. At that moment he looked young, pleased with himself. But then tonight he had chosen a spicy Szechuan dish as one of the entrees. It was very hot, too hot for her unless she mixed tiny portions with generous helpings of rice. He claimed to love the food but eating it had caused his eyes to tear up and sweat to break out across his forehead. The episode had struck her as ridiculous. As if he were forcing himself to endure pain for some obscure reason and all the time claiming to love it. And now he seems older to her. His nose reddened from their afternoon in the sun appears even larger, the marks of age on his cheeks and temples more vivid. And those ears! Hairy and gigantic! How could that doctor have possibly equated those ears with her mother's?

It's not my decision, she tells him.

Well, you have a vote. Or should have. I'm driving and you're a passenger. Your life will be in my hands.

I trust you to know.

Thank you, I appreciate that. He motions to the waitress and when she arrives, orders a second gin and tonic. Before she can remove the empty glass, he fishes out the wedge of lime with his fingers, places it between his lips and peels off the pulp.

Watching him, both Connie and the waitress wince.

It's just that I'm in a mood, he says, dropping the green skin back in the glass and handing it to the waitress.

I'll have coffee, Connie says.

He watches the waitress walk away. Then turning to Connie and using a tone of voice that suggests he is revealing a confidence, he says, Up to this point we've been setting the scene. But now we're coming down to it. Things changed rapidly after that. I never saw Kyle again in Jacarandá, for one thing.

Did you see him again at all?

Oh yes. Yes, indeed, but not in Jacarandá. Always in Nova. Your mom, though, started coming to Jacarandá most every weekend. She would arrive on the bus Friday morning and spend the afternoon shopping by herself. After work I would I meet her downtown. Typically we sat on a bench in the Plaza Dom Pedro Segundo across the street from the Catholic church and she would pull out her little treasures...

Treasures? Connie asks.

The things she had purchased.

I see.

She'd take them out one by one from the large woven bag she carried. Each item would be wrapped in a rough gray paper the way the shopkeepers often did in that place. This wasn't expensive stuff, trinkets really. She was very careful about money. Often they were little things for her students: thimbles, a spool of thread of some sought-after color, a yard or two of fabric. She believed in giving gifts.

Yes.

Once or twice she led me to a store. There would be some item she had been unable to decide upon. I learned to not rush her through these little dramas. The decisions were important to her. It took some restraint on my part because buried in that huge bag was a treat for me. A half-dozen cookies or some similar freshly-baked goodie.

Are you saying this happened every Friday?

Most every Friday for a while there, and she always poked around in the shops, and she always brought me a treat. She was a tease. The treat would be the last thing removed from the bag. I began to count on it like Pavlov's dog. But first, each little purchase had to be removed and unwrapped and displayed and discussed and carefully re-wrapped and stowed away. Only then would she pull out my treat.

So, what did the two of you do?

We went to movies, Clint says. There was one cinema in town and the movie changed every day or two. We ate out. We talked, we walked around. She shopped, of course. On Saturday mornings we went to the market. And don't forget we were doing theater the whole time.

Theater?

I mean staying in character. She was my sister. I was her brother. She had come to Jacarandá to see her brother. Even when we were alone, sitting on a park bench, she would insist on it. 'Now, save these for later, bro,' she would say. 'You don't want to spoil your supper.' She did use the word 'supper,' incidently, to designate the evening meal. The mid-day meal, what I think of as lunch, she and Kyle called dinner. Midwestern terminology, I assume.

I guess, Connie says, frowning.

Anyway, I was uncomfortable with the constant brother-sister dialogue. It reminded me that a lie formed the sub-flooring of our relationship. The more frequently we brought it up, the more likely we would say something that gave us away. But Jolene could not bring it up enough. In conversation with Eduardo or Oscar or some other friend, my childhood imperfections and wrongdoings formed a major theme in her discourse. She was having fun with me. She portrayed me as lazy. My room at home was a mess. I avoided work, or like Tom Sawyer bribed someone else to do it. One time, I think it was when I introduced her to Oscar's wife Angelica, I learned that I had run away from home at age eleven. I was astounded to find out that I had spent the night in a shed, driving my parents frantic with worry. All of this happened because they refused to let me keep a stray dog.

Connie looks at him astounded. Her mind had wandered for a moment. She had been thinking again about Clint's ears and her mother's, how different they were. It had just occurred to her that Clint Estergard might be a compulsive liar, that all this time he had been making most everything up. It was obvious that he was at the very least embellishing things, but what if he was flat out lying? How would she know? Then came the story about the dog.

What? he asks, surprised by her expression.

That's a story about Uncle Steve! Mom's brother. It's a family story, that story. The kind that gets repeated at Thanksgiving or Christmas. The dog's name was Vladimir.

Forgive me, Clint says. I didn't remember the name of the dog.

You're forgiven, she says, laughing.

Another favorite subject was Smookie Collins. According to Jolene, all my problems could be reduced to the absence of this young lady. I was in love with Smookie, she insisted, and Smookie loved me as well. The evidence was dubious in both respects. But Jolene was certain. The fact that she had spent only a single evening with Smookie, and that several months before, did not deter her. Every week she wanted an update. I did get letters now and then and I would read them to Jolene. I played my part too, of course. Smookie was living with a rich family in Cuiabá. She had met an even richer guy named Ramon whose family owned a huge ranch. Ramon took her flying in his family's plane. I suspected that Smookie was falling for this Ramon, but Jolene would challenge me. 'Why is she telling you all this? she would ask. 'Well, because that's what's happening in her life.' I would answer. 'Don't be naive, brother! She wants you to know she's attractive, that other men are paying attention to her. It's obvious to any girl that she loves you!'

So, here was another role she played. Counseling me on my love life, or the lack thereof. And it wasn't just for my benefit. Everyone learned that I was in love with a Volunteer whom I had met in training and who was serving in Mato Grosso. 'If Clinton is ever sad,' she would explain, 'it is because he is missing his Smookie.'

When Clint pauses Connie asks if her mother would spend the night.

Of course. She became a regular at the hospital on Friday nights. And always we had dinner, or should I say, supper, at Eduardo's. More than anything about Jacarandá Jolene Henderson adored Eduardo and his restaurant. Some days, when I couldn't find her in the plaza or in the shops, I would track her down to Eduardo's. The two of them would be in the kitchen gutting and scaling fish, or doing some sort of prep work. And why shouldn't she adore Eduardo? He was charming and clever, almost six feet tall, thin, suave as the flat side of a razor. He spent a fortune on soft pastel shirts and linen slacks and fancy Italian shoes that he went all the way to Rio to purchase. He drove a Karmann Ghia. He looked like he belonged on a yacht or at a roulette wheel in Monaco. And of course, he adored her as well. They shared the sacred fellowship of those persons who love to prepare and share food. He treated her like a professional and insisted on explaining every ingredient in every dish he delivered to our table.

Connie nods her head. So long as Mom had the strength, she kept cooking. Even after her own appetite was gone, she still wanted to cook for everybody else.

Maybe at that point it was just obligation, he says quietly. Not that she didn't enjoy it. I'm sure she did. The pleasure of doing your duty. Being of use. There's something worthwhile in that. She took cooking seriously all right. One night she put me in my place. I complained about Eduardo having to describe everything while the food got cold. Not to his face, of course. After he left. 'You're a musician,' she scolded me, 'you must recognize how important the audience is to your performance. You want them to be attentive and patient and appreciative. Well, here in Eduardo's we're the audience and we must show the same respect you would ask of him if you were performing.'

Good for her.

Right. Of course unlike food, music doesn't get cold. Anyway, as I may have told you, we had a favorite table. It was outside, beneath the frond-covered roof in a corner away from the entrance. We would sit on the same side of the table facing the street so we could comment on the passersby and enjoy the view. Across the street the town sloped gently down toward the river and beyond the river was a range of hills and often beyond the hills an array of clouds that would fill with fire when the sun set. Beautiful cloud patterns form in Bahia. Did I mention the Japanese lanterns?

Yes.

As evening came on you noticed them more. In the center of the table a candle burned in a small bowl of red glass. The flame caused the bowl to glow like a ruby caught in plastic netting. Cigarette smoke mixed with the smells of cooking food and bougainvillaea. We always ordered a bottle of red wine, and the bottle was empty when we left. When night came on, we would move to the other side of the table and watch the action in the restaurant. She knew all the waiters. She would tease them and insist they try the wine and get them to talk.

None of this sounds like my mother, Connie says. Not the

mother I knew. My mom kept a pencil and a scrap of paper on the counter beside the refrigerator. Not good paper even, the back of a flyer, an old envelope. On it was her list of things to do. She spent her life working through that list and never got to the end. Literally, never got to the end.

I see.

What you describe sounds so romantic. I can see why a young woman would love being there. But Mom was a married woman. She had a husband back in Nova Santana. I have a hard time justifying why any married woman would be in that situation.

Clint stops. His eyes scan the room for a moment before coming back to hers. You're misreading the situation, Connie. You're misreading it badly.

But...

Jolene was a twenty-one year old girl coming to Jacarandá to visit her brother. That's the way she saw it. That's the way everybody in Jacarandá saw it. A totally innocent thing.

Connie looks at him but says nothing.

Clint smiles. But I must say these were more than just casual visits. She involved herself in everyone's business. Take Eduardo's love life. She had an opinion based on her observations of Eduardo and her questioning of me. She never met Eduardo's fiancé but I had once or twice. Jolene would press me for details. What was she like? How did they relate? Were they physically affectionate with one another?

So, were they? Connie asks.

Not at all. But that didn't mean anything. They were formal, that's all. They were around his huge family. She was very young, seventeen maybe, with a pretty face. But shy, polite, smiling.

How old was Eduardo?

Twenty-seven or eight, if I remember correctly. I may have mentioned that she was attending a finishing school in Rio. So, she was not around very often. I knew very little but Jolene wanted to know everything. Had I ever seen them talking privately, or heard them laughing together? Did they seem happy? Did they?

Happy enough. The occasions were happy family occasions. Jolene said that Eduardo never spoke of his fiancé. 'Eduardo is more enthusiastic about the salad he's putting together than about his fiancé,' she would say to me. 'The poor man. There's something very sad behind the polite and happy front he sets before the world. I worry about him. I think he regrets the decision to marry this girl. Maybe he loves someone else, some girl from the lower classes. I'm sure he was pressured by his family to marry this girl.'

Ironically, in the most gentle of ways, Eduardo expressed a similar concern. 'Your sister almost never mentions her husband,' he would say to me. 'I think about her and I wonder if she is happy.'

What did happen to Eduardo? Connie asks.

Clint hesitates. Eduardo hanged himself. He hanged himself in the back room of the restaurant late one night after closing. They found him the next day. It happened shortly after your parents left.

Yes, I read in the letter that he had hanged himself. But why?

He and his fiancé had broken up. She had left him. That was the word at the time, which may have been true. Later I came to have a different take on it.

Really? What was that?

I think Eduardo was gay. It was not a good society in which to be gay. I think the engagement had been his attempt to go straight and it failed. When the girl backed out Eduardo felt very exposed and alone. He ended his life. It may have been a sudden, rash act. But maybe not. Maybe he had planned it for a while. I don't know. His death shook me to the core, I have to say.

I see. It makes sense, I guess. Had he ever...?

No, not with me. He even took me to a house of prostitution once. He called it a cultural experience. He had his girl and I had mine. But I think that too was a fake. He probably just paid the girl to sit and talk. When Vern and I stayed with him in Salvador for Carnival he took us to several private parties. One of them, Vern and I realized later, was all men. He knew these guys, they knew him. I mean it wasn't overt. Nobody was making out or anything but it was all guys.

I see.

But he and your mom adored each other. They shared a special closeness. When I would walk her to the bus station on Saturday afternoons, she always wanted to stop by the restaurant to say goodbye to Eduardo. Sometimes she would stop there when she arrived as well. And they always asked about one another. That letter I wrote to your parents was a difficult one. I was devastated by his death and I knew the news would devastate her. And, of course, she and Kyle were already going through a difficult adjustment, returning as they had to the States. But I have to say, I was disappointed, even angry, that they never responded.

They didn't answer your letter?

No, they never did. I must have written two or three letters altogether, thinking perhaps the first had been lost in the mail.

There was only one in the pouch.

They didn't answer any of them, Clint says.

The waitress delivers their drinks. Clint watches as Connie pours cream into her coffee.

Ah, youth. If I drank that I'd be awake all night.

Hardly youth. Youth is what we're talking about. My parents were so....

Am I boring you? he asks.

Pardon?

You just yawned.

No, not at all. This is what I have come for.

The story. That's what you came for. We're getting ahead of the story and I promised myself I wouldn't do that. Let's breathe some life back into Eduardo. He has a few more weeks to live and he might as well enjoy them.

Oh yes, please. I want him to live forever.

I agree, Clint says, sipping his drink.

But I'm sorry, I still don't understand why Mom suddenly started coming to Jacarandá every Friday. She wasn't doing that before, was she?

No, this was new. Clint thinks about it for a moment. Kyle encouraged it, I know that.

Really? I was thinking maybe she was trying to make him jealous. Like Smookie and that guy with the plane.

Ramon? Well, maybe. Who knows what motivates people in the end? Most of the time we don't know for sure even about ourselves. But I can tell you what they told me, both Kyle and Jolene. Start with the basics, okay? Kyle wanted to stay in Nova and do the work he thought he was destined to do. At the same time, he had a strong obligation to Jolene. He wanted their marriage to work. He wanted her to be happy. He also wanted her off his back. He was gardening both mornings and afternoons. He had discovered the *Condomblé* thing, which he thought was a way into the community and he wanted the freedom to explore it. He was overjoyed that I had introduced her as my sister. She needed family and I had generously offered to provide it.

He told you that?

In so many words. Not only me, but Charlie Pell. Remember how worried I was that Charlie Pell would get the news from Oscar or someone else?

Yes, I remember.

It worried me sick but I kept putting off telling Charlie. Then one weekend Jolene told me she would not be coming the following week. I don't remember why. A wedding or something in Nova. So I took the bus to Conquista to see Vern. It's a long story and I won't go into the details but when I got there, Vern had sprained his ankle a couple of hours before in a soccer game and was on a pair of crutches that were way too small for him. Not a happy fellow. To complicate matters he had the old blue Jeep and Charlie Pell was flying in that afternoon to pick it up. Vern was supposed to meet Charlie at the airport but he couldn't drive so I drove us out there and we met Charlie. By this time, Charlie had a pilot, a guy named Alberto, who flew him around. Alberto landed, dropped Charlie off and then flew back to Salvador. Alberto was a dashing figure, by the way, with black hair, dark wrap-around glasses and shirts with epaulets.

But that's another story, Connie says, smiling.

True. So, we had dinner that night, Charlie, Vern and I, in a restaurant on the second floor of an old hotel there in Conquista. Well, I should tell you that before Charlie arrived, I had been talking to Vern about my problem with Jolene.

What problem with Jolene?

The sister thing.

Oh.

Vern didn't think I should tell Charlie anything. He recommended that I make up a story that I could tell Charlie if Charlie ever asked. 'File it away in the back of your mind,' Vern advised me. 'It's like having a savings account.' But I decided that I was going to tell Charlie anyway. Come hell or high water I was going to muster up the courage at dinner and confess all.

So, did you?

Shh, Clint says, putting a finger to his lips. All in good time.

Yes, Doctor.

So, we had dinner in this stuffy place where Pell was staying the night. Probably steak and surely a good amount of wine. Charlie Pell was fun to be around. He had great stories and behaved like a wise older brother. You got the impression he was giving you glimpses into some secret inner circle. He entertained and inspired us with gossip and tales of the small successes of our fellow Volunteers. He made you believe that we Volunteers were part of a spirited team, well intended but very human young men and women struggling against great odds. Our mission was noble, our successes finite but concrete. He spread success stories like grass seed, Charlie did, but failures he kept quarantined in his briefcase and the back of his mind. No Volunteer other than myself ever knew about your parents and Nascimento, for example. So, I admired him, and that admiration coupled with the wine and companionship, had brought the sister thing to the tip of my tongue. Meanwhile though, Vern was looking out for me. Whenever I started to talk he would kick me under the table with his one good foot.

Why was he doing that?

Clint laughs. That's the kind of guy Vern was. As an army vet he believed it was always a mistake to admit to anything. Then, out of the blue, Charlie Pell asked, 'Well, what do you hear from the Hendersons?'

So there it was, my golden opportunity. But before I could say anything, Vern burst out with 'Well, I hear Kyle's become a *bruxo*.'

A what?

A sorcerer. Vern had met this traveling salesman. Met him in a bar in Conquista and the salesman asked if he knew the American in Nova Santana. He told Vern that the American in Nova Santana had become a *Condomblé* sorcerer.

Really?

Clint smiles. I wouldn't lie to you, Connie.

Connie blushes. No, I'm just surprised. Dad?

That was something to see, I tell you. The expression on Charlie Pell's face. In a matter of seconds I watched it go from good-humored collegiality, to confusion, to shock, to horror, to professional reserve.

'Can you shed any light on this?' Charlie asked me.

I told him the idea was ridiculous. The three of us had attended a *Condomblé* ceremony and that's probably where the rumor started. Charlie was dubious. A number of Volunteers had attended such ceremonies but no one had accused them of being sorcerers.

'Well, Kyle did dance some,' I admitted. 'Maybe that's where it came from.'

Charlie scowled. 'And I'm not comfortable with this other thing the three of you cooked up.'

Clint pauses. He looks at Connie and smiles.

The sister thing?

Yep. Kyle had written Charlie a letter weeks before. Probably right after the conference. Jolene needed a break now and then from Nova, he wrote in the letter, and in order to protect everyone's reputation, Kyle had come up with the idea and I had gone along to help them out. Kyle placed all the responsibility on his own shoulders. Charlie Pell was almost apologetic to me. Neither he nor the Peace Corps would lie to protect us, he explained. If the thing blew up all three of us could end up going home early. He knew that would be unfair to me since I was just trying to help, but that was the way it had to be.

Is that what happened?

What do you mean?

Is that why they were sent home? Connie pauses. If they were sent home. Or did they quit? I still don't know anything!

That's not true, Connie. You know a lot. What do you think we've been doing the last couple of days?

Yes, you're right. I'm sorry.

No, that's not what happened, though I do have a confession to make. I did not straighten Charlie Pell out. I let him think I was innocent, the good guy. Vern, of course, almost choked trying not to laugh.

So, Dad told Charlie Pell that the sister thing was his idea but that still doesn't explain why Mom started coming to see you every weekend. Do you think Dad actually pushed her into it?

I doubt he pushed her. It was complicated as most things like this are. She loved being in Jacarandá so it was not difficult for her to come. She was lonely at home with Kyle gone all the time and it still rainy and muddy. On the other hand she felt that by leaving every weekend she was failing him in some way. Failing to meet his high standards. Not being there to cook his meals. She talked about the survey they started and never completed. They were supposedly living the simple life with the 'real' people, and here she was having a good time in Jacarandá most every weekend. But for a few weeks anyway, I think she made peace with herself. She did have her work now. The sewing classes were going well. She needed time away if she was going to continue the work, that's the way she saw it, I suppose. And then the supplies she bought. Maybe, in her mind, the visits to Jacarandá made her a better Volunteer, and if they helped her to not complain so much at home, a better wife. And it took some weight off Kyle. She believed in Kyle. She thought he was a great man. Have I made that clear? If he thought he was fulfilling his destiny, she believed it also.

I see.

At the same time she resented the burdens his greatness placed on her. That's my take on it.

So, tell me, did you enjoy her visits? They must have interfered with your life in some ways.

Clint pauses. In his right hand he holds his nearly empty glass. He studies it for a moment and then looks at her.

What do you think?

What do I think?

Her visits were a torment.

I don't...

You think I was not looking forward to them?

Well, I don't know, I...

I was becoming obsessed by your mother. I would have thought you might have guessed by now.

No, I...

So, yes, I enjoyed her visits. My whole week revolved around her trips to Jacarandá. At the same time they were a torture. Clint swallows what remains of his drink. He pulls out the lime and strips it clean. That's the way it was, he says. Finish your coffee. We should go.

Chapter Twenty-two
THE RAIN IN JACARANDÁ

On nights when Jolene stayed over at the hospital, Clint could not sleep. Their rooms were close but not adjoining. His was against the outer wall, hers across the hall and a couple of rooms away with a small window open to the courtyard. He had to pass her room coming to and going from the toilet. It wasn't just lust that kept him awake. He knew that because masturbation did little to ease the agitation. But the longing was intense and it struck him as cruel and barbaric, that the two of them, they who found themselves so comfortable, so at ease and happy together during the day, should at night have to sleep alone in two empty rooms a few feet apart. Did these thoughts flood her mind as well? Passing her closed door in the night he could feel himself trembling.

On the outer wall just below the ceiling in his room was a row of cement blocks with openings that allowed air to pass between the room and the out-of-doors. When it rained, the sounds had an immediacy and a complexity he would have missed had the wall been solid. Sometimes he would lie awake trying to isolate and identify the different elements that together meant rain: the dampness on his bare skin, the sound of water hitting the edge of the distant tile roof a story above, drops brushing against the wall itself, others striking directly on the pavement below, the musical note from large heavy drops that rolled down the roof and bounced off the metal lid of the oil drum set against the wall beneath his window, the swish of drops that seemed to caress the leaves and tree branches in Alfonso's little park on the other side of the alley. Lying alone in the warm night, naked and damp with Jolene Henderson sleeping down the hall, he came to notice something new about the rain. The complexity of noises suggested a release of tension. The atmosphere, he imagined, weary of suspending all that moisture in the air, was letting it fall to the earth with a sigh. In that sense, the rain was synonymous with crying. Though, as he tells himself now, lying alone in his bed in the condominium, that was hardly a scientific assessment.

Chapter Twenty-three
WALLS

They agree to meet at the hotel the following morning at nine-thirty. Connie is down at the room and has her apparatus set up shortly after nine. She crosses the street to the coffee bar she discovered the first morning. Again today she rose early, grabbed a cup of generic coffee in the lobby and took a walk, this one through the streets of Richmond. Then she came back and showered and checked her email and now she is looking forward to a treat. She enjoys the rare freedom she has had these last few days to schedule her own time. The barista has come to recognize her. He smiles a greeting. She orders a tall latte with two-percent milk and a double-shot of espresso. She sips the foam chatting for a few moments and then carries her cup back to the hotel.

Nine-thirty comes and Clint is not there. She watches the parking lot and through the double doors keeps an eye on the lobby. There is no sign of him. It crosses her mind that he is not coming. The thought irritates her. Part of her is angry at him and part is angry at herself for doubting him. Another part is angry at herself for getting angry. She decides to wait until ten before telephoning his condo. He has told her with some pride that he does not possess a cell phone.

A few minutes before ten a woman from the front desk appears at the door. Clint called. He's running late but he is on his way. When he arrives a few minutes later, he apologizes. He had phoned his ex-wife. Michelle told him there were some boxes she had never gotten around to throwing away. So he had driven to her house to see if by chance the slides he had taken forty years ago were still around.

She thinks I'm going off the deep end, he says to Connie, positioning himself at the end of the long table. First I insist she throw everything out. Then years later I come searching for something I hadn't bothered to look at for decades. Michelle was quite amused. She told me about a woman whose talk she recently heard at her social club. The lecture concerned time and clutter management. Everyone, it appears, is buried in clutter. This woman apparently makes a decent living advising people on what to keep and what to throw away. She will come to your house and work with you to organize your drawers and files, make room in the garage for your car. The general rule, according to Michelle, is if you haven't worn an item of clothing in six months, throw it out.

Six months?

It must be global warming, Clint says. I remember Canadian winters as being longer than that.

I'm glad Mom and Dad didn't hire this woman.

Yes, no journal. Of course, then you wouldn't have to listen to me blathering on. Anyway, no luck. Not a slide to be found. No bolo, no old Portuguese stirrup, no maté gourd. *Nada.*

I feel guilty.

No reason to. It wasn't that much work.

No, I was angry at you for not being here, and all the time you were on a mission to help me.

A useless one, unfortunately. He notices something now that brings a smile to his face. Come closer, he says beckoning with his hand. I want to see it up close.

She too is smiling. She starts to take it off.

No, no. In its natural habitat, please. She leans toward him and the necklace dangles away from her throat. He cups his hand behind it. Blue sapphire, just as I remembered. Probably from Minas Gerais.

I was wondering if maybe you bought it for her.

Oh no, that would not have been appropriate, he says. The question surprises him. What would a man be saying, he thinks, if he bought jewelry for a married woman who was not his wife? I don't know where she got it. Salvador, probably. She never traveled south through Minas, so far as I know.

Aware now of Connie's perfume, Clint releases the necklace. He leans back and she straightens up. She goes to her chair and sits down facing him, pleased with her little surprise.

So, class, he says, let's check the syllabus and see where we are. He pulls the notes from his pocket and glances at them. Ah, yes, the wedding of Eduardo's sister Flora. Yes, that's where we are, and that's where I next heard a rumor about this father of yours. The wedding was near the end of August or early September if I remember correctly. So a couple of months had passed.

Did Mom or Dad come to the wedding?

They did not. They would have been invited, Jolene directly, and through her Kyle. But they did not come. Kyle remained a mystery in Jacarandá and I can't remember why Jolene was not there.

All right.

Flora married a man named Cicero, a young and upcoming doctor in Salvador. The wedding took place in the Igreja de Nossa Senhora on the Plaza Dom Pedro Segundo and was performed by the bishop himself. A series of social events preceded and followed the wedding. In addition to the actual ceremony I attended a dinner the night before and a reception that followed the ceremony. Eduardo and I played some music at the reception. That was my contribution. These invitations, especially to the dinner, were generous offers to a young foreigner who had only a passing relationship with the bride and her family. Throughout my stay in Jacarandá people thought to include me in the events and ceremonies that marked their lives, their birthdays, their weddings, their holidays. These occasions revealed to me the generous, social nature of the Brazilian people.

I see.

The events surrounding the wedding were community not just family events. Even the dinner preceding the wedding, which was a sit-down affair ostensibly restricted to the families of the bride and groom, had to be served in shifts. It took place at the long table in the home of Eduardo and Flora's parents, Don Alfonso and Dona Neyde. The one I described earlier.

Right.

Besides the people at the table, there was a crowd that gathered in the doorway and spread out toward the street. I have no idea if they were crashers or had received a second class invitation of some kind. The guests seated at the table seemed impervious to those witnesses who stood silently in the open doorway a few feet away. But Dona Neyde, who as you might imagine commanded the dinner like a sea caption, did not forget the crowd on the front steps. Every now and then she instructed her staff to deliver them another tray of hors d' oeuvres.

Late in the day of the wedding, near the end of the reception, Don Alfonso took me aside. The crowd had thinned. The bride and groom had left as had Cicero's parents. I was about to leave myself when Don Alfonso approached the group where I was standing and asked to have a word with me. This surprised me. Alfonso had always been polite but he had never spoken more than a few words to me. I knew him through Oscar, of course. And I was a friend of his sons. But I was also thirty plus years his junior. Compared to him and his circle, I had no wealth and less status. Thus the invitation to meet personally one-on-one seemed odd.

The reception had been held in a banquet room at a social club. The walls were lined with chairs. A bar stood in one corner with a few tables. Alfonso led me first to the bar, which had been abandoned by the bartenders, though several bottles remained. He poured us both some *cachaça* and began to lecture me on the drink. 'You must learn to enjoy our national drink,' he told me. Of course I had already had *cachaça* several times, even with his own sons. But Don Alfonso was not the kind of man who appreciates learning that you already know what he wants to tell you. So I thanked him, sipped from the glass and expressed my satisfaction.

'You Americans only want to drink whiskey' he told me, 'but *cachaça*, good *cachaça*, is also an excellent drink.'

I agreed of course. Don Alfonso was an important man, the richest most powerful man I knew.

The man had strong opinions about most everything including alcohol. '*Cachaça*,' he pointed out, 'is produced from sugar cane so it is made for our tropical climate. A man is shaped by the climate where he is raised and so for me *cachaça* is the best drink. It is natural for me just as whiskey is natural for you. You should try it often so you can learn to like it.' Of course I did like it, though I had learned the hard way to enjoy it only in moderation. I had already told him several times that I liked it, but that did not deter Don Alfonso. 'You were not raised in this climate so *cachaça* will always taste somewhat foreign to you. But still if you treat if fairly you will come to appreciate it.' I agreed that this bottle in particular was very good *cachaça*. 'But it must be good *cachaça*,' he went on as if I hadn't spoken. 'Bad *cachaça* will poison you.' Don Alfonso pointed to the chair he wanted me to sit in. 'You must stay away from bad *cachaça*.' I agreed to stay away from bad *cachaça*.

Don Alfonso sat beside me. He gave me a cigar and lit one for himself. He told me he was tired and he looked it. He had just delivered his youngest daughter into the hands of a rich Salvadorian family. It had been, he explained, a satisfying but exhausting and very expensive delivery. If I ever had daughters, he suggested, I should raise them to elope. As it turned out, I didn't need that advice.

We smoked and sipped our drinks. Don Alfonso asked me about my work. I told him briefly what I did with Oscar. He nodded and started talking about the family his daughter had married into. I only understood parts of what he said. Don Alfonso was hard to follow. He spoke much faster than Oscar, for example, and was not as concerned as Eduardo, to give another example, about choosing his words carefully and watching my expression to see if I understood. Don Alfonso spoke and he left to his listener the responsibility for understanding what he had said.

So, it is possible that my mind may have drifted somewhat but then I thought I heard Don Alfonso make some comment about my sister and her husband. He also used the words *Ligas Camponesas*.

What does that mean?

I had no idea at the time what it meant. And I was confused at first about the reference to my sister and her husband. I couldn't figure out who he was talking about. I tried to clear the booze out of my brain. He was explaining that Cicero's parents had a large *fazenda* not far from his own lands. He leaned forward and said, as if in confidence, that although they were a fine upstanding family who's lineage could be traced back to the colonial era, they were not good *fazendeiros*. The land, I learned, had been cleared by Cicero's great-grandfather. That man's son, Cicero's grandfather, left as a young man to get an education and had remained in Salvador. A brother had stayed on the *fazenda* but he died childless. Cicero's father knew the property only marginally and Cicero himself had probably not visited the place more than a half dozen times, though another brother had apparently shown more interest. They had an overseer who managed the *fazenda* and who brought reports to Cicero's father in Salvador every month or two.

This mode of operation was, in the view of Don Alfonso, no way to run a *fazenda*. He, that is Don Alfonso, took an active role in the operation of his *fazenda* and he expected the same from his sons. Then, as you might imagine, he returned to the familiar theme of the wayward Eduardo. Yes, he could entertain himself with this restaurant adventure but Eduardo knew as well as Walter, who had gotten a degree in agronomy, that their family's wealth was based on the *cacao* raised on the *fazenda*. The raising, harvesting and curing of *cacao* was a complicated business, Don Alfonso informed me. It was labor intensive and required great skill. You could not live the good life in Salvador and expect some hired hand to run a successful *fazenda* on your behalf. In time the hired hand would cut corners. He would care little for the land or the people who lived on the land, and in the end he would probably rob you blind.

Alfonso was going full steam at this point. 'The management of a *fazenda*,' he told me, 'is very complex. It is in reality a small town. More than three hundred people live on my *fazenda*. These people have to be fed and housed, and looked after. You have good workers and bad. You have good families and others who are not so good. You don't need all of them year around but you need all of them at certain times, and some of them at other times. Still, you cannot kick them off the land when you don't need them, or even when they become old and no longer useful. No, if you want to have good workers you have to house and feed them all year around to the end of their days, whether you need them or not. And of course the families have children and the children too must receive some education. It is a very complex operation.'

I agreed that it sounded very complex, though I had no idea why he was bothering to explain it to me, unless he was hoping I would talk to Eduardo again. I was also worried that I had missed something important at the beginning.

Meanwhile, Alfonso was marching on. 'Life on a *fazenda* can be dangerous,' he told me. 'The men work with machetes, with machinery, with horses and cattle. We have five hundred head of cattle on our *fazenda*. We have dozens of horses, mules, donkeys. Just last year a man was killed when a mule kicked him in the head. Your brother-in-law needs to understand this.'

Dad?

That's right. He was talking about Kyle. I had finally figured it out for myself.

What did Dad have to do with this?

I had no idea and Don Alfonso was not about to explain. 'A *fazenda* is like a small town. But it is not Rio or Salvador or Jacarandá or even Nova Santana. A *fazenda* cannot have a hospital like the one in which you work. It cannot have schools like we have here in Jacarandá. A *fazendeiro* cannot build a super highway from his *fazenda* to town. A *fazenda* is by its very nature rural, remote. The people who live and work there are simple people. Their wants are simple, their needs are simple. We cannot give them fancy houses, they don't want fancy houses. They are simple poor people. Your brother-in-law needs to understand this.'

Finally, Don Alfonso glanced at the ash on his cigar 'My wife is waiting for me,' he said. 'I must get back to my family.'

We stood. I shook his hand. I told him I understood, though in fact I understood very little. Alfonso gave me an embrace and a slap on the back as was the custom, and left me standing there. I was confused, as you might imagine. Afonso was the most important man in the region. And he seemed to know more about what Kyle was up to than I did. So, I decided I had better get over to Nova as quickly as I could.

You hadn't been seeing Dad during this period?

I hadn't seen your father in two or three months, not since we attended the *Condomblé* ceremony. Your Mom had been in Jacarandá six or seven times but there had been no sign of Kyle. And Jolene had changed.

What do you mean?

What I mean is that when Jolene first started coming regularly to Jacarandá, she would talk about Kyle or her family most of the time we were together. But now she spoke less of him, less of home. She was developing a life in Jacarandá. She had acquaintances, favorite shops and shopkeepers, Oscar, Eduardo and everyone who worked in the restaurant.

And you.

Yes, and of course, myself. I was her friend. She trusted me, I believe. I thought she was happy but later I came to realize that all this time she was worried about Kyle. She just wasn't talking about it.

Connie is puzzled. Why is that? she asks. If you were her friend, her brother, as it were? And if she trusted you, like you said. If she was seriously worried, I would think she would be pouring her heart out to you.

Yes. All I know for sure is that she didn't, Clint says. I went through some pretty heavy seas after your parents left Brazil. It was, to be frank, one of the most difficult times in my life. I had lost Jolene and Kyle. Then a couple of weeks later we lost Eduardo. His suicide and the events following, his funeral etc., were, as you might imagine, traumatic for everyone. So sudden, so tragic, so unnecessary. In some ways I felt excluded from his family. He had been my connection with them and now he was gone. I even entertained the idea that they held me partially responsible for his death, though I knew that to be irrational. I felt lost and alone. And, of course, irrational or not, you do blame yourself. What signs had I missed? What could I have done to prevent this? Then, to top it off, a planned vacation didn't turn out as I had hoped.

You got vacation time?

Yes, probably six weeks during our tour.

Did my parents take a vacation?

No, I'm sure they didn't. Kyle was not the vacation type And then they were gone. Forgive me for going off on this tangent but I really am thinking about your question. That is, why Jolene did not talk to me about Kyle if she was so worried about him.

Okay.

But first I need to tell you about the vacation. Vern and I had planned this trip for some time. It was going to be our big trip. Four weeks in the south of Brazil. We were going to take a bus to Rio and then on to São Paulo where the Mato Grosso contingent had scheduled a conference. We would meet Smookie and a couple of other Volunteers at the end of their conference and take a bus to the famous waterfalls at Iguaçu. Then down to Porto Alegre and back up to Rio. After Rio, Smookie and the others would return to Mato Grosso and Vern and I would return to Bahia. That was the plan.

I see.

But I couldn't leave at the scheduled time. Eduardo had hanged himself two days earlier. Vern went ahead and I followed a couple of days after the funeral. By the time I got to São Paulo the conference was over and everyone had left for the falls. By the time I got to the falls, it had happened.

What do you mean it had happened?

Vern and Smookie.

I see.

Clint falls silent for a moment. I had a great deal to think about after that. And a lot of time to do the thinking. A hundred and fifty-some hours on buses all told that trip. Much of it at night. We would take overnight buses to save on hotel rooms.

I see, Connie says again.

Vern and Smookie tried to be helpful. They were my friends. They knew about Eduardo, of course, and about your parents. But they were a pair now, snuggled together in the seat in front of me. Eduardo, dead, hanging in the back room of his restaurant where I had spent many pleasant hours. Kyle deeply troubled, and he and Jolene gone home and out of my life. A lot to think about, and a lot of time to do it.

I'm sorry. What did you say about Dad?

I believe I said that Kyle was troubled.

Yes...

And I will get to that. But at the moment we are talking of Jolene, and why she did not discuss her concerns with me.

Yes, Connie says again.

Your mother was a master at creating walls, that's what I decided.

Walls?

Yes. Walling off one part of herself from other parts. Take Smookie. I came to believe that Jolene used Smookie as a barrier. Whenever she felt herself attracted to me, or me to her, she would place Smookie between us. Reminding herself and me and everyone we met how important Smookie was to me.

I see.

In a similar way, when she came to Jacarandá she walled off what was happening in Nova Santana. She created two separate lives to meet the complex needs she had. And the needs had changed. Before she needed to talk. Now she needed to not talk. She just wanted to live. To be happy in her new Jacarandá life. She was worried about Kyle, but during the weeks she was coming regularly to Jacarandá she locked those worries away, locked them away even from herself, that's what I came to believe. Finally, though, as you shall see, the walls came down.

But...

Yes, that's right, Clint says again, the walls came down.

Chapter Twenty-four
A CONVERSATION WITH KYLE HENDERSON

So, back to the wedding and my talk with Alfonso, Clint says. And following that, my urgent desire to see Kyle.

Yes.

It was Wednesday before I could get away from the hospital and take the morning bus to Nova Santana. I ran into Kyle right away. He had come downtown for a haircut and was passing by when my bus arrived.

I accompanied him to the barber shop where he introduced me as his brother-in-law and I waited while the barber did his work. The barber was chatting with a couple of friends and Kyle sat silently without moving. I can picture him there. He would put the pouch on his lap with the straw hat on top of it. They made a large bulge beneath the sheet that the barber had draped over him. There was something patriarchal about Kyle by that time. Even though he was small and thin, he looked dominant, serious. His face was the face of a farmer, with a line above his eyebrows separating his sun-darkened features from his pale forehead.

To pass the time I would have thumbed through a copy of *Seleçãos*, the Brazilian edition of *Reader's Digest*. Not the articles, the jokes. Humor is one of the toughest things, you know. When you start to understand the humor, you know you're getting the language. This magazine had a special meaning for me. Oscar had told me that at the time of the military coup people had placed copies of *Seleçãos* on their coffee tables to indicate that they were not sympathetic to the communists. The word "communist" at that point applied to anyone who did not support the coup and since the magazine was associated with the U.S., its prominent appearance in the home inferred you were anti-communist. Thus even the presence of a trivial magazine can be adaptive in certain circumstances.

Clint chuckles, pleased with himself. But then seeing Connie's expression he says, Sorry, have I said all this before?

No, but you have talked about the coup.

If I start repeating myself hit me with something, okay?

It's a deal, Connie says.

Yes. Well, assuming the same principal applied to barber shops, Kyle apparently had a pro-American barber and his neck was not in danger of being cut.

What? Was there really a risk...?

Sorry, a bad joke. The fact is, I have never felt so safe in my life as I did in Brazil. Well, maybe when I visited Michael in Singapore. Singapore is safe, assuming you know the rules. In this regard, though, things have changed in Brazil. Now, you have to be careful where you go.

Anyway, soon enough Kyle was trimmed and we were back on the street. It had rained during the bus ride but now the sun had broken through. Along the main street the grates were being raised on the shop fronts, awnings lowered. Here and there people swept the sidewalk. The brooms, incidently, were different from what we know. Crude, round constructions, bundles of stiff straw tied around the handle. The streets were drying off, the air fresh; the smells of wood smoke and roasting coffee. A public address system blared music from speakers hung on power poles. Once again I am trying to give you an impression of the world your parents inhabited.

I appreciate that, though I'm at a loss as to why they never wanted to return to it. Or at least to some place that resembled it.

Yes, well, Clint says. Unfortunately you're pondering a question to which I have no answer.

I understand.

It was a Wednesday that I went to see Kyle, and Wednesday was a market day in Nova. A minor market, but there was more activity on the streets than usual. Kyle said his boys were at the market selling a few cabbages and mustard greens but it was at another plaza and we did not see them. Instead we headed toward your parents' house. Kyle assumed his usual fast pace, rapping his staff on the pavement as we walked. He greeted most everyone we met. The elderly, young children, it didn't matter.

He and the boys had been having trouble with thieves in the garden. 'It's frustrating,' he told me. 'They're stealing from the boys, quite literally taking money out of their pockets, though the thieves might not think of it that way. Maybe they think they're stealing from me.'

I asked why they would steal from him.

'They're stealing for the food,' he said, 'that's the motivation. But why not steal from me? I'm astonishingly rich in their eyes. And of course they're right. I am astonishingly rich compared to them. Folks at home think we're making a sacrifice by living the simple life among the people, but from the perspective of the poor, we are rich Americans. In their eyes there is little difference between us and Liz Taylor, Frank Sinatra or the other famous faces that appear in the scandal sheets. We belong to the rich, Clint, you and I. So lock your doors, my friend. Guard your purse. We may have come to play the part of the poor person but we have been cast in the role of the rich. And the job of the rich is the same everywhere: try to keep those who are not rich from taking your riches away from you.'

Your father laughed when he talked this way. Such thoughts seemed to please him. I saw him as a happy man that Wednesday morning. His hair was trimmed, his pace buoyant. His stroll through town was a performance given for my benefit and his own pleasure. And he was enjoying our conversation which we carried on both in English and Portuguese. He had come to relax his rules about speaking English. We encountered two women crossing the street with large bundles of laundry balanced on their heads. Kyle tipped his hat and greeted them with a warm and respectful formality. The women addressed us as *Senhores*, carefully nodding their heads in return.

Jolene, I learned, was home sick with the runs. He had gotten her some medicine the previous afternoon and he thought she was on the mend. He thanked me for welcoming her in Jacarandá. That seemed like an opportunity to address the subject at hand. So, I asked when I might see him again in Jacarandá. I told him he was becoming famous. People were talking about him.

Your father stopped walking. He turned and looked at me. I still remember the suspicious expression that came onto his face at that moment. Part of it might have been the intense light. A rough line of shade caused by the brim of his hat crossed his face at a rakish diagonal. One cheek and his mouth were in the sun. But the mouth was pinched, the lips thin and hard; his eyes, his nose and other cheek were hidden in deep shadow.

'Famous?' He wanted to know what I meant by 'famous?'

I was uncomfortable so I made a little joke about how he seemed to have picked up a new line of work. He still didn't understand what I was getting at. No reason he should have, of course.

'As a sorcerer,' I said finally. I related the story Vern had heard from the traveling salesman. The idea sounded so absurd to me, no less absurd than Jolene performing late-night abortions, and I thought Kyle would at least see some humor in it. But I was wrong, the news had the opposite affect. His manner now was smug and insular. Put upon. Who are these people? his expression seemed to say. And he was angry. He saw it as an injustice, a false accusation, and nothing enraged Kyle more than injustice.

Yes, that's true.

I explained that there were other things I had been hearing. Kyle looked into my eyes for a moment and turned away. He studied the vultures circling between us and a line of distant thunderheads. He suggested we go back down town. He didn't want Jolene to hear the conversation. He didn't exactly say that, but that was his thinking, I assume. At the time, I had no reason to believe he was hiding things from her. He just wanted to hear what I had to say before she heard it. Perhaps he could explain or temper it in some way. Besides, she had enough going on with the cramps and diarrhea. I understood that. I knew very well what dysentery does to you. A war was raging in her gut. The mere thought of food sickened her, the smell of it could bring waves of nausea. She would look pale, drawn out, hunched over. And being the good hostess she would feel compelled to make me coffee or serve me a snack.

Wait a minute, Connie says. I'm interested in something you just said. You said that 'at the time' you didn't believe he was hiding....

I did, yes.

And later you changed your mind?

Clint thinks about that. In the end Kyle lied to Jolene, he says slowly. As you will see. But he did it for her benefit. In his mind he was shielding her, to keep her from worrying. Understand, his high regard for her never changed. But at the time of our conversation he was not anxious for her or anyone else to know what he was up to, though, as I said, I was unaware of his thinking.

I see. And you are going to tell me what he was up to aren't you?

I'm going to tell you everything I know, Connie. But I'm trying to tell it to you chronologically.

She blushes. I'm peeking aren't I? The voice of a little girl.

You're trying, Connie. So anyway, Kyle and I walked back toward the center of town and after a while we stopped at a little shop and bought sodas. Kyle and Jolene knew the man in this shop and they often stopped there. It was a tiny little store, more like a closet with a white-washed interior. Along the back wall was a shelf. And on this shelf were samples of the candies and sodas the shopkeeper had to sell. The proprietor himself sat on a stool in front of the shelf. Beside him was an ice chest and boxes of the candies, his inventory. The door was a Dutch door, the top half open, the bottom half closed. We stood before the door and made our selections. The man removed two bottles from the chest, popped off the caps, took two straws from a box and placed one in each bottle. He set the bottles on a narrow counter built onto the top of the half-door and accepted our payment which he placed in a cigar box at his feet. I was impressed by the efficiency. The transaction was completed without the man having to get off his stool.

And the vendor was proud of the straws. He grinned when he saw us looking at them. He thought the straws added a touch of elegance to his product. But, of course, as soon as we were away from his door we removed the straws and threw them away.

Why?

Because the man had touched them. We also wiped the rims of the bottles with the tails of our shirts. Jolene's condition was on both our minds you see.

Yes.

Unlike Jacarandá, in Nova's central plaza there were no merchant stands. It was pleasant with tile-work walkways separating patches of garden. Some trees, some benches, the smell of jasmine. The town was small enough that the plaza really did serve as the center of town. On a Saturday night teenagers would walk around the outside, groups of boys, groups of girls, some couples, lots of chaperones. Music piped through a public address system. Kyle described this for me as we found a bench in the shade. 'It's like our drive-ins,' he said. And he was right, both were platforms for courting rituals. It's curious, how different they were. One private and cut off, the other open and communal. But that's far from our subject, isn't it? You missed the drive-ins, I suppose.

Yes, Connie says.

So we drank our sodas and I asked him if he knew what *Ligas*

Camponesas meant. He had no idea. He asked if I had looked it up. I had looked up the words but the dictionary provided little guidance. *Ligas* meant leagues. And a *camponeso* was a peasant. 'Maybe it's like a minor soccer league or something,' he suggested. 'In baseball we have farm teams.' He wanted to know why I was asking.

I described the conversation I had had with Don Alfonso and the difficulty I had understanding him. But I was pretty sure that Don Alfonso had not been talking about soccer.

Kyle listened carefully and when I had finished he wanted to know Alfonso's last name.

'Da Costa,' I said.

Kyle got very excited. 'Alfonso da Costa! You know him?'

I explained that he was Eduardo's father.

'Wow, he's one of the biggest landowners around!' He asked if I had been to the *fazenda*. I hadn't though Walter had offered to take me some time. Then I asked if he had been there.

'No, not really.' His manner was vague. He paused. He seemed to be thinking. 'There's this man,' he finally said to me. 'His name is João that's all I know. He's a Negro, his coloring is very dark. He's short but thick with muscles like a god. He's a hunter, a lone wolf. He shows up, he disappears. Sometimes you see him on the periphery of the *Candomblé* thing. He wears a leather vest, a pair of slacks, a leather hat. That's all, except for the gun and his leather pouch. It's like mine, the pouch. The same man made them both. You remember the man who took us to the ceremony?'

I did, of course.

'I told him I wanted to see the *fazendas* and he introduced me to this fellow João. There might have been a communication failure because what I wanted was to go onto the *fazendas* and meet the people working there. I wanted to see what the conditions were like from the perspective of the people living on the *fazenda*, but Arnando probably thought I just wanted to see the country, the land. He knows that João goes everywhere. He's a hunter like I said. You might say he's a poacher. He crosses boundary lines without thinking. No not without thinking. João doesn't do anything without thinking.'

I asked Kyle if he had gone into the country with this João. He nodded and started to speak but then stopped. His attention had been captured by the appearance of a man on the other side of the street. The man was coming out onto the sidewalk through a metal gate in a wall. The man looked vaguely familiar to me.

'Nascimento,' Kyle muttered.

'Your friend the doctor?'

'He's not my friend, not close. That's the place I really want to go.'

'His *fazenda*?'

'Exactly,' Kyle said.

The doctor was about to get into a bright blue Willys when he spotted us. He crossed the street and entered the plaza with strong quick steps. In his left hand he carried a machete in a leather sleeve.

'Some of us have work to do,' he said, waving the machete, 'but I see the leisure classes are enjoying a morning on the plaza.' The doctor laughed loudly, implying that his comment had been a joke. It was a pleasant, back-slapping encounter, all grins and greetings, at least on the part of the doctor. Kyle managed to be cordial. The doctor remembered me from the agricultural exposition. He asked about Jolene. When he learned she was sick he offered to pay a house call. Kyle explained that he had gotten her some medicine and that she was getting better.

'Well,' the doctor said before he left, 'you Americans have weak constitutions. We Brazilians have grown up with these bugs. We swallowed them with our first glass of water and we've been feasting on each other ever since.'

'Now that's a pleasant thought,' I said, after he had left.

Kyle didn't respond. We had finished the sodas and he decided to check on the boys.

We walked to the market but the boys were not there. So we walked out toward the garden which was a mile or so away. It was late morning by now. The sun was hot and I had not brought a hat. Seeing Nascimento had transformed Kyle. His buoyant friendliness had become determined intensity. I noticed it in his speech. Portuguese spoken by most Brazilians is a beautiful language. Some *Baianos* by the way they speak—the 'g' ing of 'd's, the 'd'ing of 'r's, the little riffs and retards they build into phrases—manage to distill the very essence of where they live and who they are. Earlier, Kyle's speech had attempted to imitate that musicality. Now, after the encounter with Nascimento, he still greeted the people we met, but his manner was clipped, less lyrical. It had an almost military tone and his smile only a suggestion of what it had been.

Of course I wanted to know what he had been doing on the *fazendas*. But he was not interested in explaining any further. He said he needed to find out what the boys were up to.

We reached the gate at the top of the hill where we could look down on the garden. I could see five or six boys down there. Each had a hoe and they seemed to be having a contest to see who could throw his hoe the farthest. Those hoes were dangerous weapons. The blades were heavy slabs of iron secured to long wooden handles through a hole in the steel. The boys would grip the end of the handle in two hands and spin like a discus thrower swinging the hoe around them and then heave it as far as they could. The game looked very dangerous. As we watched a blade flew off its handle, almost hitting one of the boys.

'Oh, my gosh!' Kyle said, and started to run down the hill.

By the time I reached the garden all the hoes were on the ground. The boys were lined up in a row while Kyle marched back and forth in front of them like a drill sergeant, yelling about safety. The boys were interested in me but Kyle would have none of that. 'Look at me,' he kept saying. 'I want you to look at me!'

An hour or so later after the boys had left, Kyle was clearly depressed. They had not sold much of the produce he and they had picked early in the morning. The baskets they had used to carry the greens to the market lay abandoned in the grass, the unsold vegetables wilted and ruined. Not all the money they received could be accounted for. The group appeared to have devolved into a sullen non-communicative mass.

'The little bastards,' I said. We were gathering up the hoes and the baskets so Kyle could take them to the house.

'They're just kids,' your dad replied without rancor. 'Poor kids. They make a few cruzeiros doing this. To get their money, now and then they have to let a rich American yell at them.'

I never saw Jolene on that trip. When we got to the house lugging the hoes and baskets we found a note. She felt better and had gone to visit one of the girls in her sewing class who had just had a baby.

It was a while before the bus left, but I never got Kyle to talk with substance about the *fazendas*, or what he was doing out there. He thanked me for coming to Nova. He appreciated my report. But nothing had changed, he assured me. He was doing the garden. Jolene had the sewing school. Yes, he was going into the country some. Yes, he had gotten to know some people in the *Candomblé* community, but the stories I had heard were absurd rumors. They were inevitable, it seemed to Kyle. A couple of Americans suddenly appear in a small town in Bahia. They start living and working there. People see them coming and going. What are they up to? Rumors were inevitable.

Clint glances down at the sheets of paper on the table in front of him. There is a long silence but finally he says to Connie, The thing is, I believed him. As I sat on the bus back to Jacarandá, I replayed the conversation in my mind and I believed him. I looked up to him. I thought he was our most talented Volunteer. The most dedicated, the most sincere, the most capable. I knew he was up to something. I wasn't totally naive, and I knew he wasn't letting me in on everything. But deep down I believed in him. I believed he knew what he was doing.

Connie has turned her gaze toward the window and the parking lot on the other side. When Clint stops talking she says, I feel like we're getting close to the end.

Yes, he says. We are.

Chapter Twenty-five
THE PHONE CALL

Clint spends a few seconds looking at his notes. I can't remember how many weeks passed between the meeting with Kyle in Nova and the emergency phone call I received from Jolene. Probably three or four. I remember she came to Jacarandá one time after that bout of diarrhea.

A phone call? Connie asks. Are you telling me they had gotten a phone?

I'll get to the phone call but first I need to describe the visit she made to Jacarandá. It was her last visit and I remember it for a few reasons. For one thing I had begun to suspect that the pigeons who hung out in the Plaza Dom Pedro Segundo had come to recognize us. As I told you she always brought me something to eat, something she had baked, and we usually opened the package while seated in the plaza. When we did that, the pigeons came around and she would insist that I share the goodies with them.

You've mentioned the treats, Connie says. Several times.

Sorry, old memories of your mother's cooking, I suppose. Anyway, I went to the plaza a couple of times by myself and sat alone on our regular bench and the pigeons paid only scant attention to me, no more than they did to anyone else who sat down on a bench. But I suspected that if I sat there with Jolene or if Jolene sat there alone, they would quickly come around. So that Friday, I met Jolene at the bus station and had her go into the park alone. Sure enough, within a couple of minutes, the pigeons were clustered at her feet. After a while, when she produced nothing, they wandered off. But then, as soon as I arrived, they rushed back. At that point she pulled out the oatmeal cookies and we all had a treat, including the pigeons and a group of boys who had learned the same lesson as the pigeons.

So, the young biologist was already on the job, Connie says without enthusiasm.

Correct, Clint says. But it was not just an idol curiosity. Research has confirmed these findings. We know, for example, that my good friends the crows have a remarkable ability to recognize individual humans. But more to the point is another thing. Your mother told me she had been sick. I already knew she had been sick. But now I realized from the way she described her illness that Kyle had not told her about my trip to Nova. I assumed he hadn't because if he had he would have had to tell her what Alfonso had said to me, and for that matter, what the traveling salesman said to Vern. I still had no idea what he was up to, but I now began to suspect that Kyle was not being totally forthright with her.

Did it occur to you that Mom might be hiding things from him as well?

I had no reason to think that. It was Kyle not Jolene who was undergoing the transformation. But at the time, the explanation seemed simple enough. I thought the rumors were absurd and I assumed Kyle hadn't passed them on to Jolene because he thought they would cause her needless worry.

Okay. Did you ever find out what that word was, the one that Eduardo's father had used?

Ligas Camponesas? Yes, Oscar explained that to me. It referred to a land reform movement. Landless peasants demanding that the large holdings be broken up and distributed to the people. Pre-coup these leagues were a political force in the northeast. Post-coup they were equated with communists and silenced. I have no evidence that your dad was involved with such a group, though he probably would have agreed with the goals. It was just a term someone like Alfonso would throw around. And I can't say with any certainty what Alfonso actually said, the context, I mean. I don't know that he was connecting your father with these leagues. I explained all this to Charlie Pell later, after your parents were gone.

So, did you tell Mom?

That I had been to Nova?

Yes.

That was a dilemma for me. Telling her would be disloyal to Kyle who had obviously chosen to not tell her. On the other hand, if I did not tell her, I would be disloyal to her.

So? Connie asks again. Did you?

Clint smiles. Yes, I told her. I told her everything. But later. After we had eaten and gone to the movie. Your mother was different on that last trip. As I mentioned I met her at the bus station. That in itself was unusual. Normally, she would arrive and spend the afternoon shopping and I would meet her after work. But on this Friday I arranged to be uptown on an errand when the bus arrived, so I could meet her and conduct the little experiment I have just described.

Is that the only reason? Connie asks with a slight smile on her face. The experiment?

You're right, of course, Clint admits. While the experiment was important to me, the errand was carefully timed. I didn't even know she was coming for sure. But the truth was I didn't want to wait until after work to see her. I wanted to be with her as long as possible. So I arranged my schedule so I could be at the station when the bus came in. That's the way it was. However, that's not the way it turned out.

But you met her?

Yes, and we did the thing with the pigeons, all right, but then she asked if she could have some time alone. Well, I could understand that. We all need time alone now and then. I even flattered myself into thinking it had something to do with me.

What do you mean?

Maybe she wanted to buy me a present, or something. I had no idea. But it was disappointing. I had arranged to have the rest of the day off and now I was headed back to the hospital. I honored her request, of course, but it felt different.

I understand.

So, yes, I left her there on the plaza and returned to the hospital. Several hours later, after work, I came back downtown and we went to dinner and then to the movie. Oh yes, another usual thing...

I'm sorry, but had she gotten you a present?

No, not that I remember. But she did ask if we could eat at some place other than Eduardo's.

Really? Didn't that surprise you?

Of course it did, at first. We ate at a restaurant on the plaza, one that specialized in steaks and then we went to the movie.

Please, Connie says, interrupting him again, I am sorry, but wasn't this a really major change?

The change in restaurants?

Yes.

Clint shrugs. Jolene explained it. She thought she was getting into a rut, that's all. Going to the same shops, seeing the same people. Eating the same thing on the menu. She said she wanted a change. Perfectly reasonable, it seemed to me. I just mention it because it was a change.

All right.

So, anyway, that was the night we watched *La Ronde*, a French film with Portuguese sub-titles starring Jane Fonda. Most films I saw in Brazil were American. Films in a language other than English were tough because I could not read Portuguese well enough to fully understand the subtitles. I don't know if I explained this, but we learned Portuguese without reference to a textbook.

You did.

All right. Anyway, it was believed that you developed better pronunciation if you learned the words by hearing rather than seeing them. So my reading ability lagged behind my speaking and listening skills.

I understand, Connie says. She stands up and begins to pace back and forth beside the table.

It was after ten, Clint says, watching her. When the movie let out, I mean. It was after ten and Jacarandá had shut down. The shops were grated, the windows shuttered, the streets empty. Jolene had not enjoyed the film. She thought it was frivolous. I pointed out how handsome the young soldier had been. But he was cruel, she said. That was the kind of mood she was in.

Okay.

Eventually, we reached the little park next to the hospital, Alfonso's park. It was a pleasant spot, that park. Narrow paths beneath a canopy of small trees, a couple of cement benches. I remember the trees as having thin, fern-like branches. I always enjoyed going in there, especially at night. It was dark and quiet. We had been in the park on other evenings. I think we were drawn to its seclusion.

Wait a minute, Connie says, pausing in mid-stride. Why did you and Mom want seclusion?

Because we were foreign and a constant object of attention, Connie. If you've never lived in a non-urban third-world community, it's hard to explain. But attention is drawn to you. Maybe you experienced that somewhat when you were with your husband. As a mixed-race couple.

Yes, in places, that's true.

Even the movie theater was not really a private space for us. Many of those around us had never sat in a movie theater with two Americans. To them we were part of the show. This is especially true when the film is in English and you're laughing when they aren't because the subtitles are lousy and the translator didn't get the joke.

I see.

So anyway, we sat down on one of the benches. As I said, it was dark enough that we could hardly see each other. Sometimes we would just sit there and listen. You could hear a faint rustling on the nearby branches as birds and lizards adjusted to our presence. After a couple of minutes, though, I heard another sound and I realized that Jolene was crying. I reached over and touched her arm. Was she tired? Was it something in the movie, something I had said?

After a while she spoke. She told me she was betraying Kyle.

She said that? She used those words? Connie is standing now at the far end of the table, her hands on the back of a chair. '

Those, or words to that effect. She was referring, of course, to her habit of coming to Jacarandá every weekend.

Are you sure that's what she was referring to?

Yes, I'm positive. She said she was going to have to stop coming to Jacarandá. I tried to convince her otherwise of course. She admitted that Kyle was away from the house most weekends. Before she had used that fact to justify her trips to Jacarandá, now she turned the analysis around. Maybe her coming to Jacarandá was causing or at least encouraging Kyle to go off with this João character. I thought that unlikely, but there was no dissuading her. Of course she was very apologetic about crying and unburdening herself on me. She kept repeating that I was the greatest brother a girl could have. That sort of thing. In the course of the conversation I described my visit to Nova. And as I suspected, Kyle had not told her of my visit. Of course, she wanted to know why I had gone there.

Did you tell her?

Yes, I told her everything. It was very difficult because I knew my news would further disturb her. I also felt I was being disloyal to Kyle. There's another thing too. In a certain sense I no longer trusted myself.

What do you mean?

Well, as I said, I wanted her to keep coming to Jacarandá. I knew I would feel alone if she stopped coming. So, I could not be sure that I would think or speak objectively about her situation. As a person trained in the sciences, I am sensitive to bias, my own as well as others.

I see. Did you tell her what you were feeling?

No, Connie, of course not. That would not have been appropriate. But I did tell her about the trip to Nova and my reasons for going there. The news released a whole new bundle of emotions in her. I told you earlier about the walls she had put up.

Yes.

And how they would come down.

Yes.

Well, the walls did come down. That night, in the park. She had been very worried about Kyle but she had been trying to deny this even to herself. My report confirmed her worst fears and brought them rushing to the surface. At the same time she hated herself for worrying. Her worry was part of the betrayal she was talking about. It meant she didn't trust him in a certain fundamental sense because Kyle kept telling her not to worry.

So why was she so worried?

I think that's obvious. Her husband's life had become a mystery to her. He mentioned new friends, people he had met through the *Candomblé* community. She didn't know these people. He was gone a lot, sometimes overnight.

Overnight? Connie has resumed pacing but with these words she stops and spins around so she is facing him.

Yes, Connie, overnight. That's what she told me. I had no idea, of course. And he did not want her to go with him. He would come back exhausted, scratched and even thinner than before. He would drop into bed and sleep for ten, twelve hours at a stretch. At the same time he seemed happy, almost ecstatic. His eyes were bright, he was full of talk about this fellow João, about the animals he had seen, about the *fazendas* and the people who lived there. And he told her not to worry. He kept telling her not to worry. He had found his path. That was a phrase he used with her. He had found his path. So, you see, Jolene was in the same place I was. We admired him. We wanted to believe him.

Yes, I understand.

So, we deferred to him, even though we, or at least Jolene, was very worried about him.

I understand. And that was a mistake? Do you believe now it was a mistake to defer to him?

In retrospect, clearly, Clint says. Though even now I can't imagine what either Jolene or I could have done to produce a different outcome. He had found his path, as I said.

Yes.

So, the phone call.

Yes, the phone call. Connie returns to her chair and sits down. The call came early on a Wednesday afternoon a couple of weeks later. I was in the cafeteria eating lunch when someone from Oscar's office said a call had come in for me. Other than one or two from Charlie Pell, I had never received a telephone call before. It was Jolene. She was calling from the mayor's office in Nova which had only recently gotten a radio telephone. I knew something serious must have happened.

Jolene explained that Kyle had not come home for four, no, I think five days and she had no idea where he was.

Five days?

Correct. And Jolene could not stand the strain any longer. That morning she had told the mayor of Kyle's disappearance. The mayor had insisted they call the office in Salvador and Charlie Pell was flying down. She wanted me to come as well. I agreed to get there as soon as I could. That she was in crisis was evident from our conversation. Even after these many days, she had doubts about sounding the alarm. Should she have gone to the mayor's office? Should she have called Charlie Pell? Was she betraying Kyle or helping him? All this she expressed to me in our brief conversation.

Poor Mom.

Yes, yes, indeed. Clint sighs. Unfortunately, the bus to Nova was not scheduled to leave for three hours. Oscar had driven up to Salvador that morning so his car was not available. I filled my duffel bag with toiletries and a change of clothes, thinking that I would hitchhike and if no ride turned up, catch the bus when it came past. But when I got to the front door, Orestes ran out of the office and stopped me. He had called Eduardo. Eduardo was coming over. He would lend me his Karmann Ghia or drive me there.

Eduardo was also very worried about Jolene. He tried to be delicate on the ride over, but he suspected something I hadn't even thought of. In Brazil, as in most places in the world, when a man suddenly disappears, it is usually with a woman.

'But Clinton,' he argued, 'I know he is your brother-in-law but is it not possible....' Words failed him.

'No,' I said flatly. 'That is not possible.' But in the back of my mind, I did begin to wonder. What if Kyle had met some women? It could have happened.

Yes, Connie says. Their marriage sure did seem to be in trouble at that point. And anything can happen. But I can't imagine that Dad would have just abandoned her. Not under any circumstances.

No, of course not. But it is funny you should say that about the marriage. Eduardo had the same take as you. That the marriage was in trouble, which is ironic when you think about it. The marriage lasted another, what, thirty years? And Eduardo would be gone in less than a month.

They had been married thirty-seven years when Mom died.

Okay, well, in any event, Eduardo certainly thought your parents' marriage was on the rocks. Where he got that idea, I don't know. I had never suggested it. Something Jolene said to him, I suppose. He had a favorite phrase he liked to throw around and he used it this time: 'We must acknowledge, Clinton, the human heart is a mysterious thing.'

Connie shakes her head. The idea of Dad running around seems beyond mysterious to me. But I don't know what to believe at this point.

Well, Kyle's heart was mysterious all right. But as I explained to Eduardo, Kyle's mysteries were not of the usual strain. Kyle was spiritually mysterious, perhaps psychologically mysterious. But I could not imagine him being sexually promiscuous.

So, it wasn't that?

No, Connie, it wasn't that. But Eduardo was not convinced. It turned out that he, too, had heard stories about my *cunhado*, my brother-in-law. What I learned over the miles remaining between Jacarandá and Nova Santana, was that my *cunhado* was surprisingly famous, or to be more precise, notorious. Some thought him a sorcerer, a practitioner of black magic. By others he was said to be a communist.

Clint pauses looking at Connie.

Go on, please.

I just need to catch my breath. I guess even professors run out of hot air at some point.

Would you like some juice?

Yes, that would be nice.

I'm sorry. I forgot about it this morning. Connie leaves the room and comes back a few minutes later carrying a tray with a large glass of grapefruit juice and some pastries.

She pours herself a cup of coffee and they sit quietly for a few minutes. Outside a delivery woman is removing boxes of food items from a truck, loading them onto a handcart and wheeling them into the lobby and through to the restaurant.

Tell me something, Clint says after they have watched the woman make a couple of deliveries. You hear stories about police officers, you know.

Yes.

Your ex-husband. Gilbert, I believe. Does he like donuts?

Loves them, Connie says, laughing. One of the major food groups for Gilbert.

Really. And oysters too? I believe you mentioned he likes oysters.

Yes, he's crazy about both. Though not at the same time.

Yes. Well, that's good I should think. Not at the same time.

Clint finishes the glass of juice and the better half of a Danish. He wipes his lips with a napkin.

Better. Thank you.

It is I who should be thanking you. I am so grateful that you have taken this time. Really, I am.

He smiles. We've gotten on all right, haven't we?

I was hoping you felt that way.

He sighs. So, anyway, Eduardo and I drove straight to the city hall. There was no word on Kyle. Charlie Pell's plane, they told us, had just made a couple of passes over the town and the mayor had driven out to the landing strip to pick him up. Eduardo had to return to the restaurant but before he left he wanted to see Jolene. So we got back in the car and drove up to the house.

A dog lay stretched across the doorstep of the Hendersons' house. He rose stiffly as we approached the door. I expected to find Jolene alone, but two shy young women were with her. Two of her students, their dresses faded but clean, on their feet brightly colored plastic shoes. Jolene held a plate of food on her lap. When she saw us she ran and hugged us both. Eduardo explained that he had to get back to Jacarandá but Jolene walked with him down to the car while the two young women and I tried to make small talk.

Jolene was gone for a while and when she came back she was sobbing.

Why was she sobbing?

Why shouldn't she be sobbing? Her husband was missing, and had been for the better part of a week.

But you didn't say she was sobbing before.

No, she wasn't tearful when we arrived. I suppose she had assumed a brave front for her students. But seeing me there, her brother as it were, she felt she could let herself go a little. In any event, the students left soon after she returned, their dog trailing after them and the two of us were alone.

'The word is out that I have been abandoned,' she told me. 'My husband has run off. They come and sit with me. They don't speak of it directly, but that's what they're thinking.' She pointed toward the table where I could see two other platters of untouched food.

I felt somewhat awkward. We sat down in the living room across from each other.

'Kyle hasn't run off,' I said, trying to assure her.

She shrugged her shoulders. I remember how obedient she looked, like a good student unexpectedly chastised. Her back straight, her eyes toward the floor, tears on her cheeks, her hands formed into fists on her lap. Her mouth worked but no words came out.

"Do you think that's possible?' I asked, confused by her response.

She shook her head. 'Not with another woman,' she said.

What did she mean by that?

I didn't have a chance to find out because just then Charlie Pell and the mayor of Nova Santana arrived at the front door.

Chapter Twenty-six
SHRINE

G ood old Charlie Pell, Clint says. He was at that moment
a very happy man.

Happy? Connie asks, surprised.

No doubt about it. His rusty disobedient hair, his square
jaw, served him well in moments of crisis. He exploded into the
room, hugged Jolene, slapped me on the shoulder and set about
to make things right. As I watched him pace back and forth, I
thought to myself, it was for moments like this that Charlie had
left the big corporation with its massive farm implements and
brought his wife and sons to Brazil.

An action junkie, Connie says. Gilbert is into the martial arts
with his cop buddies. Some of them are like what you describe.
He calls them action junkies.

Maybe that's a little strong for Charlie, but the good old
American can-do spirit was in full flood. By way of contrast, we
had Dr. Almondo, the mayor of Nova Santana. Dr. Almondo
was a different sort of man. Reserved, proper, salt and pepper
from head to toe, conservative in speech and manner.

Yes, you described him previously. The guy that came in
after the coup.

Correct. You got the impression that Dr. Almondo was committed to preserving an ordered dignified way of life, a way of life
that he thought had once been prevalent but was now threatened
with extinction. He wore gray suits, white shirts and dark narrow
ties. He was thin, slight, with thick glasses, small smooth hands,
the nails pink and manicured. Dr. Almondo looked like he belonged in a library. But for all his propriety, this man had gone

the distance for your parents. He took them in after Nascimento had rejected them. He established worthwhile projects for each of them and now he stood in the doorway willing to help. And what he got in return, if you don't mind my saying so, was more trouble than he deserved.

You sound angry at my parents.

I was quite angry at your dad for a while. Not then, of course. Then I was only worried. But later, after they had gone, anger was part of what I felt. His alienation from the power structure prevented Kyle from appreciating what the mayor had done for them.

I see.

Meanwhile Charlie Pell was talking about establishing a command center. From the patio, the mayor graciously offered the use of his office. Jolene suddenly realized that the poor mayor was still standing in the doorway and not about to enter until formally invited to do so. She rushed over, took his hand and ushered him to a chair at the kitchen table. The food left by the students would come in handy now. She put water on to make coffee.

As I've told you, Charlie Pell was a father and although he had no daughters of his own, he tended to treat all the female Volunteers as members of his family. He stopped pacing and put his arm around Jolene's shoulders literally taking her under his wing.

'You make the coffee,' he commanded me. He led Jolene over to the single bed that served as a couch in the living room. The bed was another thing they got along with the stove and refrigerator. It had two long pillows that she had made and covered to serve as a back. 'You poor, girl,' he said to her as they sat down, 'how brave you have been. But the mayor and I are here now. There's an explanation for this and I'm going to find it. And I'm going to find Kyle too, and bring him safely home. What we need now is to set down the facts. We need to narrow the search, determine a course of action, assemble the available manpower. Tell me everything you know.'

Slowly the facts came out. Kyle had left shortly after lunch on Friday or Saturday, I can't remember which, saying he would be back on Sunday afternoon. It was now Wednesday. He had left several times before but had always returned when promised. She wasn't sure where he had gone, though he said he was visiting some people on a *fazenda*. He had left the house alone though it was possible he had met someone on the way out of town. He had taken with him a blanket, some food, a jug of water and his machete.

The basics of her description were translated for the benefit of the mayor. Have I said that Charlie Pell spoke passable Portuguese?

I don't think so.

As a child he had lived with his parents in the south of Brazil. I don't remember the details. Anyway, the mayor hearing this information asked if Kyle had mentioned which *fazenda* he intended to visit. Jolene shook her head.

'The town is surrounded by *fazendas*,' the mayor explained to Charlie. 'They spread south and east to Ipiaú and north and west to Jacarandá. We can send men out to inquire at each of them. I have been reluctant to spread an alarm until you arrived, but if this is your wish, we are prepared to do so. Perhaps it would be helpful to know Kyle's intentions. What, if I may ask, is he engaged in on these journeys?'

The mayor had popped the central question all right. The three of us looked at Jolene.

'He wants to meet people,' she said.

Meet people? Connie asks. Clint sees that her eyes are closed. The palms of her hands are pressed against the sides of her face.

Yes. Her response was so vague, so inadequate that it seemed obvious to me, and probably to Charlie Pell and the mayor as well, that she was hiding something. But if Charlie thought that he didn't let on.

'He's probably conducting a survey of some sort,' he explained to the mayor. 'We train them to do surveys, Doctor. My guess is he's trying learn more about how local people grow their crops. Yes, that's probably it. Educating himself about the local farming practices.'

I doubt Charlie believed that any more than the rest of us did. But the mayor didn't press further. When the coffee was ready we sat at the table and he explained how he and his staff would go about contacting the *fazendas.*

'Very good,' Charlie said when he had finished. 'We're grateful for your cooperation.' He shook the mayor's hand. 'I think just inquiries for now. No reason to set off any alarm bells just yet.'

After the mayor had left the three of us sat at the table and ate more of the manioc cakes left by the students. After a few minutes of casual chatter about his wife's cooking and Alberto's flying, Charlie returned to the business at hand.

'I need to know the truth, Jolene. The complete truth. All of it, even if it hurts. Is there any chance....'

'That he's involved with another woman?'

'I have to ask.'

'He has every reason to be,' Jolene suddenly blurted out. 'And I couldn't blame him. I have been a terrible wife. I have failed him at every turn. And you too, Clint. I've been such a burden to you.'

It was quite an outburst, but Charlie read it correctly, I think. 'This is no time to be hard on yourself,' he told her. Have you any evidence? A woman intuits these things. Have you had suspicions before now?'

Jolene admitted that she had neither.

'Has he said anything to you?' he asked, turning to me. 'Anything at all that would suggest he was running around?'

The idea seemed preposterous and I told him so.

'So, I think we can discount that for now. I'm sorry but we need to get through this, Jolene. If not that, then what the hell is he up to?'

'I don't know. He left to visit the *fazendas*, that's all I can tell you. He stays with the people not with the owners. I think he sneaks on to the properties. The owners probably don't even know he's there. He says the conditions are terrible, the housing, the schools, if there are schools. The people are serfs, that's the way he describes it. And he said he would be back on Sunday. That was days ago and he's not here!'

Charlie suddenly got it. 'You're saying that Kyle is trespassing on these *fazendas*?'

Jolene winced but nodded.

'So if the mayor checks with the owners, they're likely not to know anything even if Kyle has been on their property?'

Jolene admitted that was true.

Charlie Pell pondered the implications. The day was hot. Flies buzzing everywhere. A lizard or two waited on the living room walls, toes spread on the vertical surface, eyes hard, tongues ready. We sat at the table. There was surprisingly little to do, really. Either you sounded the alarm and called in the Marines or you waited. Charlie had a lot to think about. A Volunteer gone missing, a distraught wife. A Volunteer up to no good, at least not in the eyes of the local establishment, not in the eyes of the program, not in Charlie's eyes either.

Clint stops for a moment. He removes his glasses and rubs his eyes. Are you all right? he asks.

Yes, Connie says looking up.

You want to take a break? Some coffee?

No, I'm fine.

Clint reaches for a tissue and begins to polish the lenses of his glasses. Okay. So, at that point I thought I had to bring up what seemed to me an obvious possibility. I asked Jolene if Kyle had ever talked about going to Nascimento's *fazenda*.

'The doctor at the clinic?' Charlie Pell roared. 'That Nascimento?'

I nodded and we both looked at Jolene. She had turned pale.

'He promised me he wouldn't,' she said simply.

'And if he really wanted to?' I persisted. 'And if he wanted you not to worry?'

'What?' Charlie Pell roared again.

'It's possible,' she admitted.

'What?' Charlie roared yet again.

I waited for Jolene to say it.

'That he didn't tell me.' Her voice was soft and low as if it were sneaking past a censor.

'And went anyway. Okay, I get it.' Charlie stood up. He slapped one fist against the palm of the other. I heard the slap and then I heard an intense interrupted buzz. A lizard had moved slightly. Its head bounced a little as it swallowed.

'He hated that man!' Jolene said, and then suddenly she threw her hand over her mouth and ran to the bathroom.

Charlie was pissed. He had assumed that with the garden and the sewing classes everything was going well. 'What's he doing out there anyway?' he demanded of me. 'The fool! And leaving her alone here. Is he off his rocker or what? Tell me!'

'She thinks Kyle's dead,' I said to Charlie Pell. 'Did you notice? She used the past tense.'

Mom did?

Yes, she talked about Kyle in the past tense. She had said that Kyle 'hated' that man. Normally, she would have said 'hates.'

I see.

The possibility that Kyle had been murdered or injured in some way was in the back of all our minds, of course. It's reasonable to consider the worst in a situation like that. But the other thing is that magical thinking threatens to take over. You come to fear your own thoughts. As if thinking something will make it happen. So we become reluctant to express those thoughts for fear we will give them more power. That's magical or superstitious thinking and it's not based in reality.

You don't think thoughts have power? Connie asks.

Clint chuckles. That thought had the power to send your poor mom running to the john with her hand over her mouth. But no, thinking or expressing what we fear will not make the feared thing more likely to happen. I don't believe that, and I hope you don't either.

Our beliefs shape our experience, I believe that.

Saying it might rain before you go on a picnic will not make rain more likely. Can we agree on that?

Yes, Connie says, smiling. We can agree on that.

Good. Jolene couldn't bring herself to express her deepest fears but they broke through when she said that Kyle had 'hated' Nascimento. Hearing herself say those words made her sick.

I see.

As it turned out, I spent the remainder of the afternoon at the house, much of the time alone. I thought we should contact Nascimento, but Charlie said it was pure speculation that Kyle had gone anywhere near Nascimento's place. He had promised he wouldn't, after all, and we could not just barge in on a doctor and start making demands, especially in view of the history between him and Kyle. No, Nascimento's *fazenda* should be treated just like the others.

Jolene agreed, but I could see the decision tormented Charlie. His analysis made sense, but the thought lingered in my mind, and perhaps in his as well, that he was avoiding an uncomfortable confrontation for political reasons and placing Kyle at greater risk.

Jolene had mentioned João the hunter and now Charlie decided that our next step was to find this mysterious hunter. The problem, you see, was that we could not institute a reasonable search because, if we disregarded Nascimento, there was no one place Kyle was more likely to be found than any other. There were dozens of *fazendas,* miles of roads, hundreds of miles of dirt paths and game trails all scattered over a vast area of forests, fields and orchards. We needed to narrow the search and this

João might hold the key.

Charlie and I decided we could not leave Jolene alone. Nor could we leave the house unattended in case Kyle or some messenger should arrive. So, I was assigned to house-sit while Charlie and Jolene walked the neighborhood making inquiries.

There was nothing for me to do but wait. I sat on the couch for a while. I tried a book from the book locker but that didn't help. I wandered into their bedroom. It was the first time I had been in there. It was a small room with a tiny make-shift dressing table. Much of the space was taken up by the large wood frame they had built as a bed. On it lay two straw mattresses covered with a sheet, all shrouded in a web of mosquito netting that hung suspended from a rafter. I remembered Kyle describing how at night they would lie beneath the netting and watch the bats fly in and out the window. I might have mentioned the bats.

You did, yes.

They lived in an unused room at the rear of the house and since the house had no ceiling they could move from room to room by flying above the dividing walls. Kyle had once showed me the empty room and the bats hanging from a rafter.

Yes, you have mentioned the bats, Connie says again.

Anyway, I walked back there to have a peek at them. I opened the door. The window was boarded shut but I could make them out hanging in a line on the same rafter as before. They hung head down, their wings wrapped around them, looking fleshy and dullish black. Beneath them the floor was splattered with guano that glistened in the thin light entering beneath the ceiling tiles. I was about to re-close the door when I saw something new in the room A small platform in the far corner to the left of the boarded window.

On this platform, which was a sort of wide shelf, stood a collection of odd objects, religious statues, metal crosses hanging from ribbons, a couple of bottles with dried flowers, two small wooden boxes with lids on tiny hinges, containing inside what looked to be dried grass ground to powder. Also on the platform, the hoof and foreleg of what I took to be a goat. The jaw bone of an animal, teeth still in place. Suspended from the rafter by a long string was the shiny top of a tin can. Any significant movement of my body disturbed the air enough to cause the can lid to turn and glint. As I stepped back from the display, I noticed something else. On the wall to my left hung the stretched and dried skins of four snakes, each of them a meter or more long.

Clint puts his glasses back on and glances at Connie. Her eyes are closed again.

When I closed the door and turned back toward the front of the house, Jolene was standing a few feet away watching me. The experience had shocked and angered me. I demanded to know what the hell was going on with the shrine.

'It's not a shrine,' she stammered. 'They're just souvenirs, things he wants to ship home after our tour.'

She was deceiving herself or trying to deceive me. I felt I had to confront her. 'Those are not souvenirs, Jolene, and you know it. It's all arranged. I mean, it is weird.'

She slumped and I thought for a moment she might collapse and fall to the floor. She asked that I hold her, and that's where we were when Charlie arrived twenty minutes later, standing in the middle of the kitchen, holding each other and swaying slowly back and forth.

'Don't tell him,' she whispered, 'Please, don't tell him.'

Did you tell him? Connie asks, looking up.

Clint shakes his head. No, Charlie never knew about the shrine. No one knew. I dismantled it shortly after they left as I will explain to you.

Was it really a shrine?

It was a shrine all right, lovingly assembled. Anyway, Charlie had no news. He had gone to the city hall but the mayor was away, and no one had anything to report. He and Jolene had not tracked down the hunter either. Charlie compared this João to a ghost. 'People don't want to talk about him,' he told us. 'I get the feeling they're afraid of him.'

Jolene agreed that he was very mysterious. He never spoke to her and would not enter the house. When he wanted Kyle, he would stand at the gate and clap his hands. Kyle told her that João lived out of doors. They had also asked about Amadeo, or Arnando, I guess it was, the man who had taken us to the ceremony, but he too was away. It was almost dark by now and the day had been a bust. No Kyle and no leads. Jolene offered to cook some food but Charlie insisted on taking us to the restaurant with the macaw.

Did you think he was dead at that point? Connie asks.

I was thinking all kinds of things, but, yes, that was one of them. But now I'm thinking Charlie's idea was a good one. Food, that is. How about some lunch?

Should I bring the recorder?

No, let's just eat. I'm contemplating a salad. What about you?

I'm thinking about Mom.

Ah.

Chapter Twenty-seven
THE HUNTER

They have a quiet lunch in the hotel dining room at a table near a window. The restaurant has floor-to-ceiling windows styled like those in the conference room, only these look out on a busy intersection. People on the sidewalk in sandals, in shorts and T-shirts. Another day bordering on hot. Clint is hungry and the salad is delicious, fresh mixed greens, cubes of beet, slivers of carrot, a scattering of salty sunflower seeds, generous lumps of goat cheese, a lively dressing.

Are you all right? he asks, wiping his lips. She has restricted herself to a cup of Thai-carrot soup. And for a while now has been watching the street.

Yes, I'm fine.

The soup was all right?

Yes. Delicious.

You've been patient, he says. I was worried about that at first. We'll wrap it up this afternoon.

I was thinking we could go back to the park, but now I'd rather not. I'll be more comfortable in the private room. She motions to the waiter and insists on paying for the lunch, pulling a card from her wallet. Then she stands. I'm ready if you are.

They settle themselves in their familiar places and Clint studies his papers for a moment.

Well, that was a long night for all of us, he says when she turns on the recorder. Charlie Pell, being the boss, got the bed in the living room. Jolene loaned me Kyle's pillow and set me up on the floor a few feet away from Pell with a lumpy mound of mats and blankets. I slept badly. It wasn't just the bedding of course. We were all worried sick and feeling powerless.

At first light I opened the front door and stepped out onto the patio. There I found Kyle Henderson.

Connie places a hand over her mouth, a mannerism that reminds him of her mother.

He lay on the cement with his head resting on his leather pouch. His thin hair was scattered about his forehead, his bare feet jutted out from the peasant slacks Jolene had made for him. His feet were dirty, scratched and exposed. His shoulders and mid-section were covered by a damp blanket. I feared for a moment that I had found a corpse wrapped and delivered in the night, but when I bent down, I could see he was breathing. Beside him lay his straw hat, his sheathed machete. No staff, but next to the machete a strange thing: a sapling, freshly cut, five or more feet in length, its branches trimmed away, its bark peeled off to expose a moist yellowish-green surface, its tip sharpened to a point. Your father had made himself a spear.

Both hands are at her face now.

As I straightened up I heard a sound down near the gate. I turned and saw a man standing in the shadows. He acknowledged my look and reached for the gate. I asked him to wait and went to him. He was a black man, surprisingly young, only a little older than Kyle or myself. Short but muscular with broad shoulders. His feet and his legs from the knees down were bare and dusty. The man wore a battered leather hat with a thong knotted below his chin. The brim was low against his eye brows. Across his back hung an old small-bore, muzzle-loading shotgun. The stock's butt-end appeared from behind the leather pouch at his hip, the tips of the barrel and ramrod were visible above his left shoulder. His dark skin in that early light had a reddish gloss.

The man told me that he had waited until someone found Kyle, but now he had to go.

I asked if he was João the hunter.

'I am a hunter,' he said. His voice was very soft. He appeared reserved but I could tell he was pleased that I recognized him. A hint of pride crossed his face. His weight shifted again toward the gate. I asked if Kyle was all right. He told me that Kyle had become afraid and he had brought him back. That's all he would say. He opened the gate and walked away. I watched until he passed between two houses and disappeared from sight. When Kyle woke a short time later Charlie Pell, Jolene and I were standing a few feet away. He sat up and looked around.

'Mr. Pell?' he said.

'Good morning, Kyle. How are you?'

'I'm fine, Mr. Pell.'

He said he was fine?

Yes, and he denied that João the hunter had brought him home. He had returned alone in the night, he said. He had found the door bolted shut from the inside, which was correct. We had bolted it closed. Thinking Jolene was alone he did not want to scare her so he had lain down on the cement to wait until she got up. He must have fallen asleep, he said, just before it got light. According to Kyle the man I described was not João the hunter. João, he said, was older, as old as Charlie Pell. Jolene confirmed this with a nod. Kyle said he did not recognize the man I described, though physically he was similar to João, and yes, João did have a shotgun and a leather hat.

So who was the man you saw? Connie asks.

We never came up with an identification. Our concern was not the man, but Kyle who sat on the pavement before us. Charlie asked him how long he had been away.

'Two nights, Mr. Pell. Why?'

He said two nights?

I'm relating this as accurately as I can, Connie.

I'm sorry, please continue.

Yes, two nights. To which Charlie responded very cleverly, I thought, by saying, 'Well, I'm thinking you must be hungry.'

'I am hungry, I'm very hungry.' Kyle stood up. He slipped

the pouch over his shoulder and put on his hat. He picked up the machete and the spear and walked in the front door leaving the three of us standing outside.

My, God! Connie says. Dad?

Jolene rushed in to start breakfast and Charlie asked me if there really had been a man by the gate. I assured him I had both seen and talked with the man. I knew what Charlie was thinking but I didn't want to accept it.

What do you mean?

I didn't want to believe that Kyle was experiencing some sort of psychological trauma. I wanted to find other explanations. I argued that the man might have followed him home without Kyle's knowledge, which seemed obvious to me. He was probably João's son or an apprentice or some sort. This João may have had disciples. For all I know Kyle may have been one of them.

Connie is smiling smugly.

You want to say something?

I know who the man was, she says.

Really? So who might he have been?

You'll think I'm being silly.

Don't let that stop you.

He was some sort of guardian angel.

Clint thinks about that. I see, a guardian angel. With a shot-gun no less.

He assumed a form appropriate to the occasion.

With a shotgun?

A hunter.

All right, Clint says. Charlie, anyway, wasn't in the mood for explanations.

'He's been gone five nights and he says two. A guy brings him home and he says he came alone. He's a Peace Corps Volunteer and he's walking around barefoot with a spear. What does that tell you? I'm not a shrink but I know what it tells me. I have to get him out of here immediately.'

That was the thinking at the time, incidently, and may still be. You get them out of the environment where they've lost it as quickly as you can, and you get them back to the States and into more familiar surroundings. Kyle wasn't the only one this happened to. I heard of two other guys they rushed onto planes and sent home.

No women? Connie asks.

Only males in my experience.

Interesting.

Anyway, Charlie instructed me to get down to the city hall as soon as it opened. We needed to tell the mayor that Kyle was safe. I had to call Charlie's office and tell his secretary what was happening so she could arrange for Alberto to fly down in the four-seater. With a Peace Corps doctor on board if possible. Then she had to make arrangements for Kyle and Jolene to fly to Rio and on up to the States. But the mayor's office wouldn't open for a couple of hours and in the meantime Kyle wasn't supposed to know the plans.

We were still talking when Jolene came back out onto the patio. Coffee was heating for all of us, she said, and she was preparing a large pot of oatmeal. She needed someone to squeeze orange juice and someone else to run down the hill for a liter of milk. Her voice sounded surprisingly light and musical. I could tell that the nightmares crouching at the back of her mind had vanished. Her husband might be disturbed, but he still walked the earth and once again was within her sight.

Of course.

Charlie volunteered to do the juice. Kyle came to the door and said he would get the milk. That made the three of us nervous but no one was prepared to confront Kyle at that point. So, Charlie told me to go with him, and not let him out of my sight.

So, I did. I walked with Kyle down to meet the boy on his donkey who sold milk at a small plaza below the *favela*. The one he wrote about in the journal.

How did he seem to you?

Kyle? Surprisingly normal.

Really. Did he still have...?

The spear? Most definitely. The whole outfit. He used the spear like a staff, the butt end tapping the earth each time his left foot hit the ground. On the way he told me that Nascimento kept slaves at his *fazenda*.

So he had been to Nascimento's?

Apparently. He claimed he had. He said that he had talked with several people who lived and worked there.

And they were slaves?

That's the word Kyle used. And it was not unheard of. Slavery is a somewhat slippery term. We think of slaves as people in shackles bought and sold at a market place but Kyle was using the term to describe people who might have begun working voluntarily and who might earn some modest wage. But the situation was set up so they became indebted to the owner and couldn't leave. The owner sold them food, tools, housing, all on credit against future wages. If they wanted to do a garden they had to rent the land. Kyle described it as trap. If the worker tried to leave owing money, Nascimento tracked him down. Not because he was a *slave*, mind you, but because he was a *debtor*.

Clever.

Yes. But remember, all this is based on what Kyle told me. I don't know what was real and what was delusion. But according to Kyle the situation was very dangerous. He said that if Nascimento had found him on the *fazenda* he would have killed him. He even claimed that Nascimento knew he was snooping around, that he had seen Nascimento and a couple of his men the day before on horses. He claimed they were looking for him but he had kept himself hidden. He also told me that he had heard from a number of people that the year before Nascimento had beaten a man to death as an example to the others. The people lived in fear of him and his two goons. According to

Kyle, some of the workers even believed that Nascimento had magical powers. That he could take on different forms like that of a pig, or a snake.

So we got the milk and then we had breakfast. At the table, Kyle sat with the spear across his lap. You've probably never had the occasion to sit at a table with a man who has a spear across his lap. Fortunately there were four sides to the table and only four of us having breakfast. Oddly, he never asked me or Charlie Pell the reason for Charlie's visit. Charlie filled the silence with gossip about other Volunteers. A new wave was due to arrive in a couple of weeks. He was arranging in-country training for them, and looking for sites where they could be stationed. He thought he had a nurse, he said, for the hospital in Jacarandá. This woman, Janet, later became a friend of mine.

Clint pauses. He studies Connie for a moment across the corner of the table. I'm going to tell you something now that I hadn't planned to tell you. Something that even after all these years brings a sense of embarrassment.

Is it important?

It's important to me that I tell you and perhaps the incident will help explain or justify your mother's failure to respond to my letters.

Well, all right.

After the breakfast, Kyle said he was tired and went into the bedroom to sleep. I left the dishes to Jolene and Charlie and walked to the city hall to carry out the instructions Charlie had given me. When I got back an hour and a half later, the flies were up and buzzing. Charlie was pacing back and forth on the patio. There had obviously been some discussion while I was away. I was not privy to that, so I don't what was said.

I understand.

I didn't see Kyle but Jolene had packed a couple of suitcases. They stood by the door and she sat on the couch, dressed for traveling, her eyes bright and swollen from crying. As I came through the door and saw her there it suddenly struck me that I would never see Jolene Henderson again. Charlie was only a few feet away but I could not contain myself. I sat down beside her.

I spoke in a whisper. But Jolene did not want to hear my words. She squeezed her eyes closed and shook her head violently.

I insisted. I knew this was my only chance. 'Listen to me,' I said to her. 'If this doesn't work out... You know that I...'

'No, please!' With her hands she made pushing motions as if she were physically shoving me away. She knew what I was saying but she didn't want to hear it. Charlie was still outside on the patio. His mind was elsewhere, but the force of her words pulled him back and he leaned in from the doorway.

'What's the matter now?' he asked, glaring at me. Before I could say anything, Kyle spoke from the kitchen. At some point he had gotten up. What he had seen or heard I don't know. He was standing by the table with his spear in one hand and a glass of water in the other.

'They love each other, Mr. Pell.' He said this quietly and serenely.

But Charlie was neither quiet nor serene. 'What?' he shouted.

'They're brother and sister. We told you about that.'

'Oh Christ, that crazy scheme. I had forgotten all about that.'

I looked at Jolene. She was gazing at her husband with such admiration and desire that I knew my case was lost.

You loved her, Connie declares triumphantly. And not as a sister!

Here we go again.

It's so obvious!

Needs, Connie. My relationship with your mother existed within a field of swirling needs, not just hers, not just Kyle's, but mine as well. Now the poles had shifted. Before, she needed me and now I needed her. But more importantly, for the first time since they arrived in Brazil, Kyle needed Jolene. That's what changed. Her husband really needed her. That put the music into her voice.

Love. Needs. Call it what you want. It wasn't brother-sister needs.

You're right, he admits.

And Dad trusted you.

Yes, indeed, he trusted both of us. His trust was absolute as I have just described. And he was right about that, he was right to trust us.

Connie cocks her head and studies this large old man. She is confident that he is lying, that he is the one. But she forgives his lie, appreciates it even. He's lying out of respect for her mother. For Kyle. And for her. Now she must show the same respect, the same restraint.

Connie smiles at Clint in a new and generous way. So, you think that's why she didn't respond to your letters.

That's always been my assumption, Clint says. The woman had a way with walls. Now a wall had gone up on me. Anyway, a short time later a plane came in low over the town, rattling the air and tilting its wings back and forth. It was Alberto, a sky god, announcing himself.

A sky god? Connie says, laughing. You've got no room for guardian angels but you're okay with a sky god?

You got me there, Clint admits. Vern and I made up a pantheon of Brazilian gods one afternoon while waiting for Charlie Pell's plane to come in. At the very top, we decided, was the immortal Pelé, the world's greatest soccer player. Beneath him were all the other professional soccer players, and beneath them your run-of-the mill singers and film stars. Most accessible to the common person, though, were the inter-city bus drivers. These guys with their sunglasses and officer-type caps possessed great power and authority. They had sole command of their craft; they traversed great distances over perilous roads; they had access to a powerful horn; their pattern of arrivals and departures created both expectation and longing. But in a galaxy above the bus driver (though far below Pelé and the lesser soccer gods), more rare than the bus driver, more aloof and unpredictable, more daring and death defying, was Alberto, the pilot. Here was a being possessed of magic, free of schedule, capable of severing himself from the thick heaviness of earth with its stones and thistles, its snakes and heat and insects. Alberto was a god who appeared from nowhere. He descended to pass briefly among us and then rose again to disappear with a roar.

You're sounding uncharacteristically romantic, Clint.

He laughs. I'm paraphrasing Vern. He was the romantic as it turned out.

At least so far as Smookie was concerned.

You got that right. So the plane passed over and turned and flew out toward a pasture on the other side of town. Charlie Pell sent us from room to room shuttering the windows and bolting the doors. When we got outside Jolene removed a key from a pocket of her skirt. She stepped forward without a word, slid the key through a rough hole in the door, turned the lock and handed the key to me.

We made an odd little parade walking down the path to meet the mayor who had agreed to drive us out to the plane. Charlie led the way with one of the Henderson suitcases and his own duffel bag. Jolene and Kyle followed side by side, she dabbing at her eyes, he barefooted with his pouch, his straw hat and spear.

He still had the spear?

Indeed he did. There is a part left for the spear. Meanwhile I lumbered along behind lugging my bag and their other suitcase, a heavy locally-made box with a skin of thick yellowish cowhide.

A leather suitcase? I never found anything like that in the attic.

They must have gotten rid of it because I sure remember carrying it. Word had gotten out that the Americans were leaving. People stood in doorways watching us. Children ran alongside. Women and girls came up and hugged your mom. No one touched Kyle, though some men nodded toward him as he passed. A few of his boys greeted him and he them. I can't tell you what the people thought. They may have stood in awe of him or maybe they just saw him as a kook. I don't know.

But they hugged Mom?

Yes, many of the women hugged your mother. That was one of the ironies. In the end it was Jolene the people felt closest to. Like her, they were wiping their eyes. Actually, as I think about it, an extraordinary thing happened on that walk. I had forgotten about this.

Are you going to tell me?

Of course, I'm going to tell you. It happened as we approached the plaza where the mayor was waiting with his car. A woman. A woman who obviously knew your mother came up to us. She was crying and holding a baby. Not a newborn, a baby boy three or four months old with chocolate colored skin. The woman thrust the baby into your mother's arms. She wanted your mother to take the little boy with her.

Are you sure it was a boy? Connie's voice is urgent.

Yes, Clint says calmly. The evidence was there for all to see. Why?

Nothing, she says, looking away, it's just kind of bizarre that's all.

Hardly bizarre, Connie. Genetically speaking it makes perfect sense. The squirming little rascal that Jolene suddenly found herself holding was carrying half of his mother's genes. Those genes had a much better chance of reaching reproductive age in an American home than in a Brazilian *favela*.

Connie grabs her throat and fakes a gag. Clint, that is ugly! That is really ugly. 'Genetically speaking' you say? What about a mother's love?

It's...

Imagine what that woman was going through, she continues, cutting him off. The torment that went into that decision. And you say, 'genetically speaking.' Give me a break.

The two are not incompatible, Connie. I am not saying the mother was just a robot in service of her genes, though some may argue that. But does what we call a 'mother's love' serve the gene's impulse to replicate itself? Absolutely. Indeed it is virtually necessary.

Connie shakes her head. 'Genetically speaking.' So, where was Dad in all this?

Standing by, spear in hand.

He came along willingly?

He seemed to. I never knew what Charlie Pell had said to him. Whatever it was, I heard no complaint from Kyle and he did not need to be forced, though he made no offer to help with the luggage.

Jolene gave the baby back, tears flowing all around. Charlie climbed into the front seat of the mayor's car and the three of us piled in back with Kyle in the middle. It took a while to position the spear so it fit between the seats and passengers, the butt end beneath the dash, the shaft resting on Kyle's shoulder, the tip protruding behind the back seat. Kyle performed this task carefully, making sure he did not rip the mayor's upholstery or break or dull the spear tip. There was something in the care he took, the patience, the respect, that moved me deeply. Seeing we were ready the mayor set off for the airstrip where Alberto waited in his shades and khaki shirt.

I was hoping the Peace Corps doctor would be there, in part because then Charlie would have remained behind with me. But Alberto had come alone.

Dr. Almondo in his gray suit, ever gracious, ever correct, insisted that we take a moment to acknowledge the importance of the occasion. He asked that we form a line before the airplane and he then addressed us. The tone of his proclamation was exemplified by his uplifted hands and the opening words: "*A Senhora e os Senhores....*" We learned that the people of Nova Santana would always be grateful for the gifts of youth and dedication that this young couple had brought to the city in the spirit of President John Kennedy who had cared deeply about the people of South America. We learned that the contributions of Jolene and Kyle would not be forgotten and that the people of Nova Santana and the people of the United States would always remain friends and partners. He walked along the line shaking our hands and exchanging expressions of gratitude. It was an absurd thing, that little speech, and yet, I have to admit, it brought tears to my eyes.

It brings tears to Connie's eyes now.

Then, as the rest of us stood by, Alberto and Charlie managed to get the suitcases and Charlie's duffel into a narrow space behind the back two seats. When they were finished, I saw Alberto take a long slow look at the spear in Kyle's hand. Charlie saw the look too, and sensing a problem, led Alberto away to a spot twenty yards or so in front of the plane where they appeared to engage in an intense but to us inaudible conversation.

Finally, Charlie came back and said in English, 'Kyle, there's a problem with the staff.'

Kyle said it was not a staff.

'A staff, a spear, whatever you want to call it. Are you willing to leave it here with Clint?'

In a movement that I thought was both child-like and dignified, your father leaned the shaft of the spear against his chest; he crossed his arms over it and hugged it to his body.

Oh my.

So, Charlie returned to the front of the plane and began a further conversation with Alberto. They were still talking when we saw a blue car hurrying down the road toward us. It was moving with reckless speed raising clouds of dust. I was standing beside Kyle and I felt him stiffen at the sight of it.

Was it?

You've probably guessed. It was indeed Doctor Nascimento, and he seemed to leap from the car before it had completely stopped. He was a dynamic presence with his boots, his thick thighs, his slicked hair, his thin mustache, his hurled flatteries. He rushed to embrace Jolene. So sorry he was to hear they were leaving. Her work at the clinic had been, 'irreplaceable, irreplaceable.' Jolene stood limp, looking embarrassed. But then when Nascimento turned and opened his arms toward Kyle, he got a different response.

'No closer, Doctor!'Kyle shouted. He extended his right arm and leaned the spear point toward Nascimento. The butt end was against the ground, anchored between the large toes of his right foot in precisely the way the old black man had controlled the tiller of the boat the day we first arrived in Ilhéus months before. The tip was in line with the base of the approaching doctor's throat at the point below the Adam's apple where tracheotomies are performed.

Your dad looked very frail and tense and desperate as if all his tendons were taut, his muscles in spasms. Violence did not become Kyle Henderson. It was foreign to his very nature and to every principal he held dear, but I think he would have tried to kill that man rather than endure his embrace. It was as if he had fashioned the spear and kept it near not as a threat to anyone but to protect himself from Nascimento's dripping false solicitude.

Yes, I understand.

Fortunately, everyone stopped in time, first the doctor, inches from the tip of the spear, then Charlie Pell who had begun to rush back from where he had been talking with Alberto, then Kyle himself, who stood unmoving except for a slight shivering in his arm that caused the spear tip to waver noticeably back and forth.

For a moment all pretext fell away from Doctor Nascimento. His eyes gleamed, sweat glistened on his cheeks with their shading of shaved beard. You could see he wanted nothing more than to shove that feeble stick aside and ram his fist into Kyle's face.

'I have been to your *fazenda,* Doctor,' Kyle said. His voice was quavering but loud. 'You know I have. And I have seen how you treat the people. You are a slave master!'

Nascimento refused to step back. He liked having the spear inches from his throat. He was willing to take a splintery gash in the neck if it justified a response. He forced a slight smile. His eyes, but only his eyes, glanced toward Jolene.

'I am sorry, my dear, but I see now that your husband is crazy,' he said. 'Very crazy. You are very crazy, you know that? Very crazy!'

'I have planted seeds on your *fazenda*, Doctor,' Kyle said.

'What are you talking about? Seeds, what seeds?' Nascimento was grinning.

'Doctor Nascimento, please.' The mayor had stepped away from his car. He placed his hand on Nascimento's shoulder. He looked embarrassed.

'Lots of seeds,' Kyle continued. 'Some day they will sprout. And some day they will bear fruit.'

'What is he talking about?' Nascimento asked, turning toward Almondo. 'He's started a garden on my *fazenda*? He is completely crazy.'

Then Kyle drew back the spear and handed it to me. 'We can go now, Mr. Pell,' he said. 'Now we can go.'

Clint sighs and leans back in his chair. He shrugs his shoulders. So that's it, Connie. You can turn it off, turn it off and leave it off. We all embraced. They got into the plane. The plane taxied down to the end of the pasture and turned around. He chuckles. And so there I was, standing in a cow pasture in Bahia on a hot day in the Brazilian spring of 1965. I was holding a spear and standing between a muttering slave-master and a kind man wearing a gray suit, while Alberto the sky god roared past and disappeared into thin air.

And you never saw them again?

Never saw them. Never heard from them. Not from them or anyone else. Well, Charlie assured me later that your parents had arrived safely in the States and that Kyle would be fine. But then nothing until the call came from you. I rode with the mayor back to town. I had some time before the bus left so I walked back to the house. I dismantled the shrine and locked the place up again. A few days later Vern and I returned with the Jeep. We drove the stove and refrigerator down the road to Ipiaú, where a couple of new Volunteers were just moving in. The snake skins I gave to a boy who said he had worked with Kyle in the garden. I wasn't sure I recognized him, but he wanted them and I gave them to him. The other furniture, the stuff the Hendersons had made or purchased we divided up among their neighbors. When the house was empty, except for the bats, we closed it up and delivered the key to the mayor.

Clinton W. Estergard, Ph.D. finally stops talking. He feels good, content, somewhat amused with himself. After a moment, Connie Scheel leans forward and touches the keyboard of her computer. Up comes the long list of questions she prepared before she came and to which she has been adding and deleting during the last three days. He watches her scroll up and down the list.

Did we get them all?

At first she doesn't answer. She seems somewhat preoccupied. I would like to review them, she says. But, yes, I think so. At least for now. But I believe you did promise to play the violin for me and I have not heard a single note.

Chapter Twenty-eight
THE VIOLIN LESSON

Connie closes her eyes and asks for guidance but receives no answer. Her spiritual modem appears to have crashed. All she gets is a wrenching sensation in the gut.

They're in the lobby of the hotel and Clint is talking about the days she has left in British Columbia. He has found a campus map and marked his building. Now he's pulling brochures off a rack and placing them in her hand.

How about a ferry tour? he suggests. It would be a shame to come all the way to BC and not visit Vancouver Island or get out on the water. You could sail first to Victoria on the southern tip of the island. Then drive up to Comox visiting sites along the way, ferry back to the mainland at Powell River, drive down the Sunshine Coast and take the ferry from Langdale to Horseshoe Bay in time for your flight out. You get a package deal on the ferry tickets and you could spend the nights in B&Bs along the way.

Connie shuffles stupidly through the brochures, not really seeing them. Uh, sure, she says.

It's just a thought.

No, I like it. The Island.

Yes. You'll see some country. Most visitors enjoy the ferries, though we locals love to complain about them. And I can guarantee Victoria will charm you.

All right.

It's settled then. I'll phone to see if a reservation is advisable for your car for a sailing in the late morning tomorrow. And I want you to join me for breakfast at the condo. Say at eight-thirty?

Tomorrow? I would love to, she says, brightening.

Well good. The coffee will be ready, and the violin.

He's working at the low counter when she enters his condominium the next morning. She smells coffee and sauteing onions.

To mix into the waffle batter, he explains. He's in a good mood. He points out the blackberry syrup warming on the stove. Picked ripe by a friend, he says, and still full of sun.

After they have eaten and as she clears the table, he takes out his violin case.

Before I play, you must have a lesson, he says.

I'm not a musician, Clint. I can't stay in tune on Happy Birthday.

For this lesson you don't need to be a musician. All you need is an open mind. Part of our mission at the University is outreach to the community. We reach out to the world community to find students, and we reach out to the province and local community to provide service. Since my retirement I have been putting together a little program I intend to present to high school science classes. It involves the violin and it would be helpful to me if I could try it out on you.

Well, all right. Do you want me to sit down?

I want you to stand right where you are. Clint sets the violin case on the table. In here, he tells her, are two of my favorite objects in the world. He opens the case, removes the violin and hands it to her. When she hesitates, he insists. I want you to hold it, he says. I want you to feel its weight and touch. Hold it up, turn it, look it over carefully. It is, I hope you will agree, a beautiful thing.

Yes, she says. It's gorgeous. So fragile.

It's stronger than you think. Clint removes the better of the two bows and places it on the table.

A violin and its bow are made almost entirely of wood and animal, Connie. The bow hairs are taken from the tails of horses. We don't want to touch them any more than necessary but here, touch the end just to feel it.

Traditionally, and sometimes still today, the strings are made of sheep intestines, though they are often referred to as cat-gut. The strings on my violin, as is normally now the case, are manufactured from metal. Even the glue luthiers use–luthiers are people who make violins and other stringed instruments–the glue luthiers use to hold the violin together is made from animal hides. It's a reversible glue so that the parts can be separated for repair purposes and then rejoined. What I am trying to tell you, is that the beautiful instrument you hold in your hands is the product of wood and flesh. Animal guts, hides, hair and trees, spruce on top normally, maple below.

Okay, Connie says. She holds the violin carefully in both hands, balancing it in front of her chest as if it were a serving tray.

And yet, I am sure you'll agree, Clint continues, that these beautiful, elegant objects are a far cry from a log lying in a forest with a dead animal beside it.

Yes, I can agree with that, she says smiling.

The difference is what we call a qualitative difference and not simply a quantitative one. In other words, the difference is not just a difference of degree such as the difference between say ten degree weather and twelve degree weather. The difference is profound. The violin and bow are something new and very unlike a log and a carcass. Does that make sense to you?

It does.

Very good. So the question comes up. How did we get from one to the other? From the log and carcass to what you hold in your hands? You will agree, I hope, that one time on this earth, there were no violins, no musical instruments of any kind.

Yes, I can accept that.

And we have no evidence that one day a bright Cro-Magnon man was....

Or a woman, Connie injects, feeling braver.

Yes. Or a woman, was walking through the woods and came upon a log and a dead animal and decided to make a violin and bow.

All right, she says, I'll agree that would be unlikely.

The history of stringed instruments is long and our know-ledge uncertain. We can only speculate about the many gaps. We know they've been around a long time. The ancient Greeks had the lyre, for example.

And David the Psalmist played a harp.

That's right. Well, going backwards from the sixteenth century we know that an Italian named Amati made violins. We can't say for sure they were the first, but we know he made them. They were somewhat different in shape from what you hold, but they had four strings and were bowed and were violins in every sense of the word. At least one of them still exists. Before the violin there were other bowed string instruments that Amati would have been aware of such as the rebec and these in turn can be traced back to Mongolia where hundreds of years before Amati's day, horsemen were bowing on two-stringed instruments that used horse-hair both as the bow-hair and as the strings. The idea spread to other places, took new forms and eventually arrived in Italy and the shop of Mr. Amati.

Okay.

But what I have just described represents only the last few minutes of the journey from log and carcass to violin. We had to learn first to make and use tools, to cut and shape wood, to make adhesives to fit and hold the pieces together. Even before that we had to develop, in the first place, the desire to make musical sounds.

All right.

He can tell from the tone of her voice that he is losing her. Okay I'll finish, but I want to simply make two points. One is that what you hold in your hand is more than a violin. It repre-sents in physical form, the insights of thousands of people over thousands of years. It is, in that sense, an assemblage of innova-tions derived from countless experiments and mistakes, of false starts and new beginnings. Second, each of the resulting insights represented but a small or quantitative change from what had existed before. Someone stopped plucking and tried bowing, for example. Maybe with a stick or a bone. Another tried four strings rather than three. On the violin you hold, the neck is longer than the neck on the Amati violin and the strings are metal rather than gut. You see that the bow's curve is convex relative to the hairs whereas on earlier bows the curve was concave. These represent just a few of the small quantitative changes in a lineage that goes from the person who made this violin back to the first creatures who began fashioning tools from wood and even back to those who first made sounds to express themselves and to entertain those around them.

I can see that, Connie says.

Good. And here is the point I will make to the students. What is true of the violin is true of all evolution. We compare an elephant and a single celled animal and we see huge qualitative differences. We ask how one could possibly have evolved from the other. But, as an evolutionist, I am here to tell you that the elephant evolved from a single celled animal through an almost infinite number of tiny quantitative changes over an unimaginable length of time, just as the violin evolved. The two processes are, in that sense, identical.

Connie thinks about that for a moment. Then she says, I'm sorry Professor, but in my mind those two processes are not identical at all. Not the way I understand the theory of evolution.

Clint smiles. I don't apply the word theory to evolution, but that aside, how are they different?

You just said it. The journey from the log and dead thing to the violin is a journey of insights. But under your theory of evolution, or whatever you call it, the journey from the one celled animal to the elephant is just a very long series of accidents, mutations, random changes. In the violin story there is somebody home. There is intent, will, desire, call it what you want. Choices are made, intention is present. In your version of the elephant story there is nobody home. It is an empty mindless string of accidents. She smiles, pleased with herself.

Yes, chance and time, Clint says, agreeing. Those are the variables and in the case of the elephant and the bacterium, a much longer span of time was involved and a much larger chain of small changes, most of which went nowhere. The bacterium didn't intend to become an elephant, but the first guy to hack into a log didn't intend to make a violin either. No, I don't agree that the two are fundamentally different, not as a process. Nor do I agree that there is somebody home in the one example but nobody home in the other. In both cases life is at home. We can argue about where life came from or if it survives the point of death. But in the journey from a one-cell animal to an elephant eating a tree branch, life has always been present. And except in odd and unusual cases, living things want to continue being alive and reproducing themselves. They will act as best they can to fulfil those desires. You lift the rug and the spider you have just exposed runs for cover. You swat at the mosquito and it tries to avoid your hand. Creatures in a changing environment will attempt to adapt to the new conditions. If they see an opportunity they will go for it. The successful reproduce themselves. Those that are not die off.

The violin maker is no different. If he, or she, sees room for improvement, she tries something new. If it works, it survives. If not it ends in the wastebin. Evolution is simply an elegant way of explaining the process.

Life, you say? You're talking about God!

I am not talking about God, Clint says. I'm talking about a blind, random, usually fatal, always bloody, fumbling process.

I can accept the process, Connie admits. Log to violin. Bug to elephant. But the blindness I don't accept. When you talk about life, I think you're talking about God. You call it blind impulse. But you're talking about God. You don't see that because your definition of God is too small.

In my definition God is not necessary.

Then that's your loss, she says.

For a moment the two of them glare at one another, then suddenly they both start laughing.

Now, would you please play something for me? she asks, handing him the violin.

Chapter Twenty-nine
HIGH TEA

Did you ever play the violin for Mom and Kyle, she asks after he has put the violin back into its case.

Certainly not for Kyle. I might have for your mom. It was usually lying around in my room.

Something gypsy like, like that second thing you played for me?

I have no idea what I might have played, Connie, if I did at all. I don't recall that she had any particular interest in hearing me play.

Connie is standing in the doorway of his condo and they are looking at one another. She is in a quandary, it seems to him, ready to say goodbye and yet not wanting to.

I read in one of the brochures about the Empress Hotel.

Yes, in Victoria.

Yes, high tea at the Empress. Have you done it?

Of course. It's a tourist thing, by which I mean no criticism. Nothing wrong with being a tourist. You pay through the nose but the setting is very nice.

I was hoping that maybe...

Ah.

I would like to invite you, Doctor. As my guest. I looked over my list of questions last night and I do have a couple more. I could ask them here, of course, but...

After a moment of uncomfortable silence, Clint says, Well, it does promise to be another decent day. We could have our tea and then I'll return home and you can continue on your own.

Connie seems to relax suddenly. Thank you, she says. Yes, I

would enjoy that very much.

In her rental car she follows his van to the ferry terminal at Tsawwassen. She boards with her car. He parks and boards as a foot-passenger, though as he says to her the term is in his case a slight misnomer. On the deck waiting for departure, they both find themselves in cheerful moods, she having been granted a reprieve, he enjoying the pleasure that comes from suddenly and unexpectedly giving yourself over to an enjoyable but frivolous activity.

But later at the hotel sitting with their tea and stack of treats, the conversation is mundane, desultory, and he realizes that accompanying her to Victoria had been a mistake. They have chosen to delay the inevitable in a sentimental, clumsy way when they could have parted on the high note of a good honestly-stated difference of opinion. Now they are just passing time. After a while, Connie sighs deeply and he can see that she feels the same. But then she makes a comment that surprises him.

I was conceived in Brazil, you know.

He didn't know and so thinks about it. If you're suggesting that Jolene was pregnant when she left Brazil I find that hard to believe. Married Volunteers made a deal with the government to not get pregnant during their tour. Even though Kyle was Catholic I can't believe they were using the rhythm method to avoid pregnancy. I know 1965 may sound like the middle ages to you, Connie, but the revolution had happened. The pill was available and the regimen easy to follow. If your mother was anything, she was not the type to slip up or violate the rules. Of that we can be very sure.

Connie's laugh is sudden and loud enough to cause people at neighboring tables to glance their way.

Well, you're the biologist, Doctor, so you know a lot more about this than I do. But tell me, back in the middle ages, I mean back in the sixties, was the gestation period different than it is now?

Clint does not find this as funny as she does. When were you born?

In 1966.

When in 1966?

In May. May 23rd. Seven pounds twelve ounces. Hardly a premie.

He calculates for a moment. I'll be damned. I thought sure it was October when they left.

It certainly wasn't September. The last entry in the journal is from September 30th.

And since I sent the journal, it had to have been written before...

A rumination on the Lord's Prayer that I found heartbreaking, and some might say blasphemous. But my point is that seven months and twenty-three days before I was born Jolene and Kyle Henderson were still in Brazil.

Clint shrugs. Okay, so Kyle got her pregnant and they would have had to leave anyway. That's ironic, isn't it? Christ, maybe they were using the rhythm method. He holds up a finger. Old joke. What do you call a couple who uses the rhythm method to avoid pregnancy?

Parents, she says.

He frowns. I guess it's not as old as I thought. Anyway, Charlie Pell would've enjoyed this. Clint chuckles. He reaches for the scone again and takes a large bite.

That's not quite correct either, Connie says softly, watching him.

What's not...?

What you said.

He chews very slowly. He takes a sip of tea and then studies her closely. Kennedy's Disease, he says.

Connie nods. My sons can't have the gene because I am not a carrier.

And that's a hundred percent?

For the daughter it is. For a daughter's sons, if she's a carrier, it's fifty percent. But for her it's a hundred.

I see.

Connie finds herself staring at the tendons running the length of Clint's neck. They're bulging out and his neck looks suddenly very thin and drawn to her.

When did you learn this? he asks.

After Mom died. Dad had already started showing symptoms when she was going through her cancer. But at that time we didn't know what it was. A year after she died, we got a definitive diagnosis. So we had blood tests, myself, both of the boys. Dad was very relieved to learn that the boys were clear. I lied to him about myself.

Good for you, Clint says absently. He is looking away, past her shoulder to a distant part of the large room. When he looks back, Connie has placed her hands in her lap. She is staring down at her plate. That errant strand of dark hair has fallen again across her forehead. It touches her eyebrow like an arc of energy.

There is a photograph in the album, she says, not looking up. I wonder if you remember it. It was taken...Wait, I'll get it. She reaches under the table, pulls up the large back bag and sets it in her lap. She withdraws the album, shuffles through the sheets of photographs and hands it to him. The one in the hospital room, she says, pointing.

A color print, the colors tweaked by age. It shows Jolene Henderson lying in a hospital bed holding a newborn with dark hair and a red scrunched up face. Kneeling beside the bed, his arm behind his wife's shoulders, is a glowing Kyle Henderson.

That's me, Connie says.

Yes.

That's been me all my life. Me, my mother and my father. That's who I was. That's who my mom was and my dad was.

Yes, Clint says again.

Only it turns out that's not me.

Not you? Clint looks again at the photograph, then closes

the album and sets it on the table.

No, I was that infant all right. But now the whole picture had changed. I couldn't trust that photograph any more. I studied her expression and his. I became obsessed with that photograph. I went so far as to take my mom's hairbrush to a lab so they could get a sample of her DNA. I felt awful doing that. Connie glances at him with those dark eyes. Sordid. Ugly.

I see.

Turns out I was not adopted. I am my mother's daughter. All right.

The lab had Dad's DNA. I ordered a second test comparing our samples. Not for the disease, but for parentage. Ugly business, Clint. An ugly business. But it was like an obsession. I could not leave it alone. Anyway, the second test confirmed the first. I am not Kyle Henderson's birth daughter.

I see.

No one in the world knows this. No one but you, me and my doctor.

I see.

So, what did I have? I had the happy photographs from their wedding and I had this happy photograph of my birth. And I had their lives, their long marriage, what I thought had been their happy marriage. And I had our lives, the lives of our family, our home. And it all made sense, it was all clear. But between the wedding photographs and the one in the hospital there was a dark and mysterious hole. Something had happened there. What had driven my mother....

I understand.

Connie shakes her head. Her expression suggests disgust. But the whole idea, the idea of searching, it made me sick. I would live with it. I did live with it. I *have* lived with it for more than five years.

Yes.

And then Andre found the journal and after that I found you.

Good detective work, Clint says. He remembers Yvonne Munch speculating at her desk and struggles to keep from smiling.

Those questions on my computer?

Yes, I remember them.

I know you think I am selfish.

No, I...

No, you're right. I am selfish. Making up all those questions. Coming all this way, taking up your time. For what?

No, Clint says again.

To restore my mother, that's what I told myself. To restore my mother. I was not coming here to learn who my father was. I knew who my father was. My father was Kyle Henderson. A wonderful, kind man. A truly wonderful man.

Yes, Clint says.

I was coming to learn my mother's story, that's what I said to myself. To find some explanation. Connie reaches across the table. She grabs Clint's hand and squeezes it. You have no idea how grateful I am for the time you have spent with me, the information you have given me. You have restored my mother to me. You have. And I thank you.

You are quite welcome, Connie. Clint's tone is both formal and casual, as if he were speaking with a student who has just returned a borrowed book. He feels very uncomfortable. He wants to pulls his hand away but Connie continues to squeeze it tightly.

And I promised myself I would never tell you. Whatever I found out, I would never tell you.

I see.

But here I am spilling my guts. I am a selfish, pushy beast, that's obvious. So, the violin lesson, the ferry ride, this tea....

Yes.

And now here we are, the end of the road, and I have to ask you a very personal question.

Clint does pull his hand free now. He places them both safely away in his lap.

Do I understand that this has been one long job interview?

You're tormenting me! she says sharply.

You're right, of course, I am being unfair. But I have to tell you, I am relieved to hear this news, Connie.

Pardon?

From the first day we met you have been trying to hook me up with your mother. All those probing questions. 'Did you say you found her attractive?' 'So, the two of you were alone?' 'So she stayed over at the hospital?' Endless insinuations.

Connie's blush is intense, her dimples pronounced.

I could find no explanation for this probing except that perhaps you were a devoted reader of romance novels, bodice-rippers, I think they are sometimes called. Or maybe your tastes run to more prurient X-rated fare. Hardly what one would expect from a good Christian lady like yourself.

Thanks a lot!

At least now I can see that you had cause for your suspicions.

You are positively cruel!

True. I am. We do make quite a pair don't we? You selfish and me cruel. Clint pauses and to Connie he looks suddenly older and sadder.

I don't believe I have mentioned the country between Jequié and Vitoria da Conquista, the town where Vern was stationed.

No, but...

It was very different from the terrain around Nova or Jacarandá. Not Conquista itself which was high. I mean a stretch of the country between the two cities. Dry, stark country. In Portuguese, it's called *caatinga.,* Geographically it resembles the great arid northeast of Brazil, a harsh landscape of thorny brush that alternates between long periods of drought and a brief rainy season when the stream beds fill and the landscape is green.

I don't....

My most vivid memory of that country was the time I took the bus through it at the end of the vacation trip I told you about.

After my parents left?

Yes, that's the one. Vern and I had ridden together on the bus from Rio up to Conquista. It was touchy between us but we were okay. Then after Conquista I was alone. It was the dry season in the *caatinga*. Everything looked dead. The scrubby trees, still with leaves, all the bushes, even the grass. From one long horizon to the other, there was no color other than a lifeless dusty gray accented by the occasional gray-green of a cactus. But our species endured there. I saw a scattering of colorless clay houses. People wearing colorless clothes, walking through the thick reddish-gray dust. At one point the road followed the course of a dry stream bed, which was really just a path of rounded stones strewn around below and parallel to the highway. The bus passed a bit of water among the stones below the road. A puddle, maybe ten feet across, the green water shot through with fibrous strands of algae. Several women had gathered there, washing their families' clothes...

Why are you telling me this?

I want to tell you what happened and then I will get to your question. Please.

Yes, I'm sorry.

So, the bus roared through that country as it had through all the others, as fast as it could go. We passengers sat passively staring out at the scene as if watching a movie of devastation. Then suddenly, the bus driver slammed on his brakes and pulled off onto the shoulder. As soon as the bus had come to a halt the driver jumped out. He ran back across the road and stopped before an elderly woman squatting there in the dust. The driver gave the woman some money and came running back toward the bus.

'Wait,' a young man yelled from the back of the bus. He too got off. He ran over to the woman and handed her a large slab of cheese. When he came back, other passengers had their windows open. We handed him out cash and fruit and bread which he delivered to the old woman. Then he ran back. The driver closed the door and we drove on to Jequié.

Okay, Connie says.

You could say that bus ride was the highlight of my Peace Corps experience, Connie. I became a man on that bus, if that doesn't sound too pompous. Eduardo was gone. Kyle and Jolene were gone. Smookie was gone and my friendship with Vern altered. I was alone. Looking out at those people, I thought to myself: yes, that's the way we are. We endure. Sometimes we injure. Sometimes we reach out and help. Other times we receive. But deep down, we're alone, each of us in his or her own way. It was as Oscar had instructed me. My responsibility was to get back to Jacarandá, do my job, live my life, be kind to my fellow human beings and take what pleasure I could find along the way.

Clint falls silent for a moment. Then he adds, I guess I needed to remember that. To remember it and express it. I was feeling sorry for myself just now.

So you...

Clint shakes his gray head. No, Connie, I was not your mother's lover and I am not your father. Your mother loved me. But she loved me as a brother. I have promised to tell you the truth, and that is the truth.

He watches tears flood her dark and lovely eyes. Eyes that seem now familiar.

Then who?

There is only one possibility as I see it. Which means I was wrong about him too.

Vern?

Vern? No, of course not. Besides, Kyle and me, there is only one person your mother loved. And yes, I know I am using that dreaded word. You are the granddaughter, I have to assume, of a very rich *fazendeiro*. A man who wanted a lot of grandchildren.

Eduardo! But you said....

I know what I said. Apparently I'm no better sleuth than Oscar was. Now you should drink your tea. It's getting cold. Then, please, if you have the journal in that monstrous bag of yours would you mind reading the last entry? The one about the prayer.

When she has found and placed the journal on the table, Connie hesitates. I'm not comfortable reading it, she says. Or hearing it read.

I see.

But if you want to read it. Silently, to yourself, that is okay.

When Clint has finished reading he hands the notebook back to her. She closes it and carefully places it and the album back in her leather bag.

Thank you, he says.

I am the one who should be saying thanks.

You may not agree with this. In fact, what I am about to say may make you angry. But I would wager that there was no time in your parents' lives when they were as vital, as full of life, as during those last few months in Bahia. When Kyle was trekking through the forest with João the hunter searching for the meaning of life and Jolene was living a double, or should I say, a triple life, in Nova and Jacarandá. Reading that entry was like sitting once more in a room with Kyle Henderson. I could hear his voice as I read the words. You had extraordinary parents, Connie. Forty-three years since I have seen them. Both now dead. And yet today your father has again moved me and once again your mother has proven herself the most mysterious woman I ever met.

Thank you for calling him my father.

It was my pleasure, Clint says.

Connie drives him back to the ferry terminal at Swartz Bay. On the tarmac she kisses his forehead.

I wish it had been you, she says.

I'm flattered, he responds, embarrassed.

She leans down and whispers into his ear: You are wrong

about being alone. You are not alone. You are in my prayers. And with that she says goodbye to him and returns to her car.

On the ferry ride back to Tsawwassen, Clint positions himself outside on the passenger deck on the lee side near the stern. He's lucky. A few minutes after they leave port a gull suddenly appears above the stern of the boat. The bird is astonishingly adept at sensing and utilizing the air currents above and around the rapidly moving ferry. For twenty minutes it moves back and forth above and beside the boat, sometimes it is forward near the bow, other times above the stern and in all that time he never once sees it flap its wings. A free ride, he thinks, a pure glide. Nothing moving but its head as it seems to peer down at him from different angles.

After a while a couple comes out from the cabin and stands nearby, watching the wake.

We're being watched over from above, Clint says to them. The expression on the woman's face when she turns to look at him is apprehensive, suspicious. Perhaps she thinks he's a kook. Then he points to the gull and they all laugh.

ABOUT THE AUTHOR

Doug Ingold divides his time between the Redwood Coast of northern California and the Sunshine Coast of British Columbia. A graduate of Southern Illinois University and the University of Illinois College of Law, Ingold served in the Peace Corps in Brazil from 1964 to 1966. He is married and the father of a daughter and a son. His first novel, *In the Big City*, is also available from Wolfenden.